D1471848

Dani Redd lives in Norwich with her husband. She has an MA in Creative Writing and a PhD in Creative and Critical Writing from the University of East Anglia. Her PhD involved research trips to some of Europe's remotest islands, such as Spitsbergen.

After her PhD, Dani spent two years living in Bangalore, where her mother-in-law valiantly tried to teach her how to cook Indian food. The recipes she was taught are featured in this book.

The

ARCTIC CURRY CLUB

DANI REDD

avon.

HarperCollins*Publishers*
1 London Bridge Street
London SE1 9GF

www.harpercollins.co.uk

HarperCollins*Publishers*
1st Floor, Watermarque Building, Ringsend Road
Dublin 4, Ireland

A Paperback Original 2021
1
First published in Great Britain by HarperCollins*Publishers* 2021

Copyright © Dani Redd 2021

Emojis © Shutterstock.com

Dani Redd asserts the moral right to be identified as the author of this work.

A catalogue copy of this book is available from the British Library.

ISBN: 9780008469115

This novel is entirely a work of fiction. The names, characters and
incidents portrayed in it are either the products of the author's imagination
or used in a fictitious manner. Any resemblance to actual persons,
living or dead, events or localities is entirely coincidental.

Typeset in Minion by Palimpsest Book Production Limited,
Falkirk, Stirlingshire
Printed and Bound in the UK using 100% Renewable
Electricity at CPI Group (UK) Ltd

All rights reserved. No part of this text may be reproduced,
transmitted, down-loaded, decompiled, reverse engineered, or stored in
or introduced into any information storage and retrieval system, in any
form or by any means, whether electronic or mechanical, without
the express written permission of the publishers.

MIX
Paper from
responsible sources
FSC™ C007454

This book is produced from independently certified FSC™ paper
to ensure responsible forest management.

For more information visit: www.harpercollins.co.uk/green

For those who live with anxiety

'No, the Arctic does not yield its secret for the price of a ship's ticket. You must live through the long night, the storms and the destruction of human pride. You must have gazed on the deadness of all things to grasp their livingness.'
– *Christine Ritter,* A Woman in the Polar Night, *1938*

Part One

1

As the plane flew further north, I leaned over Ryan to look out of the window.

'There's nothing to see – it's already dark,' he said apologetically.

I pressed my face against the glass (not too hard, I'd worry about it cracking), and squinted down at the faint outlines of clouds below me.

'I wonder if we'll see the Northern Lights,' I said.

He smiled at me.

'We'll go out on snowmobiles and find them.'

'What if I can't ride a snowmobile?'

Ryan squeezed my hand.

'Of course you'll be able to. It's easy – just like a quad bike.'

I'd never ridden a quad bike before either, but I decided not to say anything. Ryan thinks that I can be quite down on myself, and I wanted to be on my best behaviour for our Big Adventure. He'd worked unbelievably hard to get this fellowship and I wasn't going to ruin it by being negative.

'I'm looking forward to checking out all the restaurants,'

I told him. 'There's one with a greenhouse full of plants in. It serves whale *and* reindeer.'

'Let's go this weekend!'

I was about to reply, but was cut off by the loudspeaker.

'We are now beginning our descent into Longyearbyen. Please return to your seats and make sure your seatbelts are securely fastened.'

The strange plummeting sensation in my stomach didn't just come with the drop in altitude.

I'd laughed when Ryan told me he'd been offered a fellowship monitoring polar bears in the closest settlement to the North Pole. But he hadn't been joking – he showed me the email and told me how cool it would be if I went with him. I'd visualised the two of us huddled in a smoke-filled hut, clubbing seals for breakfast, speaking to nobody but each other until we went mad and started eating our shoes. He reassured me that Longyearbyen was a proper little town, with a supermarket, hotels, pubs and restaurants. Slowly, it had stopped seeming like a crazy idea.

Of course, there are countless examples of the idea of a thing not matching up to the reality. Like dresses you order online, worn by much thinner models. Like attempts to make intricate novelty cakes. Like communism . . .

'Maya? Are you alright?'

Ryan was looking at me, eyes wide with concern.

I forced a smile.

'Yep. Fine. Completely fine.'

'I can tell you're anxious. It's completely understandable. If it makes you feel better, I'm nervous too.'

'You?'

'Sure. I'm dragging my gorgeous girlfriend to the northernmost town on earth, and I don't want her to regret coming. I'm starting a new job and I'm worried I won't be as experienced as everyone else.'

'You'll be amazing. They're lucky to have you,' I reassured him.

'And I'm lucky you agreed to come with me.'

He extended his arm and I nestled into his shoulder. My bum's so big that sitting down we're similar heights, and it actually hurt my neck a little, but I was reassured by his warmth and solidity.

The plane juddered as the wheels hit the asphalt and then taxied to a halt. The seatbelt signs went off and we got up and grabbed our bags. Queuing in front of me was a family with two children, both of whom were already moaning.

'It's going to be fun,' the mum said, in a tired voice.

'Fun' was one of the most misleading phrases in the English language. It had connotations with crazy golf and corporate away days, with parties where you stood in the corner, ears ringing, wondering when it was socially acceptable to leave.

The kids didn't buy it either. They started moaning about Disneyland, of all places.

I followed the family down the aisle towards the front of the plane, trying to remember the images of Longyearbyen I'd seen online. Colourful wooden houses against a backdrop of snow-covered mountains. Towering icebergs with deep blue undersides. The Northern Lights undulating in green and purple ribbons across the sky. Mugs of hot chocolate by a roaring fire. But the picture of the Arctic I had in my mind dissolved the minute I stepped outside the plane.

The cold hit me like a slap in the face and my legs nearly buckled with the shock. It was also completely dark, despite being three o'clock in the afternoon. I froze, both literally and figuratively.

'Babe? We're holding people up.'

I could hear the embarrassment in his voice as the people queuing behind him began to passive-aggressively grumble in several different languages. But there was no way of backing out now, for the choice had been made the moment I stepped onto the plane.

I forced myself down the stairs. The cold penetrated my down jacket in seconds. It lacerated my face. The insides of my nostrils felt like they were being sliced with tiny razors. Every country has a different scent – it's normally the first thing you notice when you get off the plane. England smells like rain and concrete; bitter but fresh. When I went to Dubai last year, the air was swampy with humidity, infused with petrol fumes and moist vegetation. But here, I couldn't smell anything at all.

Once we reached the bottom of the stairs, Ryan put his arm around me.

'Fucking freezing, isn't it? We should have worn our bala-clavas.'

'I couldn't wear that on a plane, I'd be arrested,' I said.

The skin on my face felt stiff, as if it was covered in a layer of frost. I wouldn't have been surprised if it was.

'Quick, let's get inside.'

We crunched through several inches of snow, past men in snowsuits who were unloading the luggage. Others were in vehicles surrounding the plane next to ours, shooting what was presumably de-icing fluid at it.

I glanced past the plane, hoping to see the scenery beyond the airport, but there was only darkness. Instead, I focussed my attention on the illuminated terminal building in front of us. Looking through the glass doors, I saw people (mostly bearded white guys) in puffy outdoor jackets and chunky snow boots gathered around a single luggage carousel.

6

When we stepped through the automatic doors the temperature rose so rapidly I groaned out loud in relief.

'Wow. That was bracing,' Ryan said.

'You're telling me.'

We glanced at each other. His cheeks were bright red and his eyes were streaming with the cold, but he was smiling. I found myself smiling back, and then we both began to laugh. I'm not sure why. The relief of being warm, perhaps . . . or maybe mild hysteria on my part. (Like, what the fuck we were doing here, really?) Still, at least we were in it together.

2

Outside the terminal, the coach was waiting to take people to Longyearbyen. I climbed onboard as soon as I could, leaving Ryan to stow our bags in the luggage compartment. From my window seat I could see him helping two frail, bundled-up figures with theirs, and pausing to chat to them afterwards. He was good at making small talk with everyone he met. It was a quality I envied because I couldn't hold a conversation without thinking whoever I was talking to was: A) trying to work out my ethnicity, B) wanted to be left alone, C) thought I was boring, or D) all of the above.

'Hi, is this seat taken?'

I looked up to see Ryan standing in the aisle.

'It's password-protected.'

'Squidge,' he said.

'All yours.'

Squidge was one of the words from our Gross Couple Lexicon, as Nina called it. Nina's my best friend and has a PhD in Development Studies, hence the vocabulary. Thanks to her, and Ryan, pretty much everyone I've been hanging out with for the past couple of years is a PhD student, which can be quite intimidating when you never went to a 'proper' university.

Ryan finished cramming his bulky jacket into the small overhead locker and sat down.

'I just spoke to a couple who've come all the way from Thailand. They're visiting their daughter. Apparently a lot of Thai people live here.'

'Yup, around two hundred; like, ten per cent of the population,' I said.

'You've been researching?'

I nodded.

'You know how sexy I find it when you do that.'

My mind is full of useless titbits of information. It means I'm great at pub quizzes, though that's not the reason why I seek them out. I like the weight of facts, the satisfaction of recalling something I read years ago. Especially given everything I know I've forgotten.

The loudspeaker crackled and the bus driver stood up. He looked like a heavy metal version of Father Christmas.

'Welcome to Longyearbyen, the world's northernmost city on the island of Spitsbergen. I hope you like darkness and I hope you like the cold, because you will get a lot of both here. And, of course, the polar bears. Remember not to leave the settlement without an armed guide. Now, please put on your seatbelts and keep them on for the duration of the journey.'

The bus rolled its way slowly out of the airport.

'I should ask if you can come to the university's rifle training,' Ryan said.

'That's alright – the thought of shooting a gun terrifies me.'

'Yeah, but you aren't allowed to leave town without a rifle.'

'I'll hardly be going off into the wilderness by myself in the middle of winter,' I pointed out. 'Besides, you can protect me.'

'Course I will. Hey, did I tell you that Dad used to take me hunting when I was a kid?'

'No.'

'Yeah. Deer, ducks, possums . . . Anything we could find. He was in his element out in nature. It was the only time I ever saw him remotely happy.'

'My dad was more a Disney movie and popcorn kind of guy,' I said.

'I can see that.'

Ryan sounded kind of wistful. His dad took off when he was thirteen, leaving him with his mum and brother. Growing up in a one-parent household was one of the things we initially bonded over.

The way we met happened like this: I had a job in a university careers department (which was ironic, considering I'd failed so spectacularly at following my own chosen career path) and Ryan was the cutest face in the small crowd who came to my talk on achieving a good work-life balance while working towards a PhD. I remember thinking that postgrad students must live pretty humourless lives, because they were all cracking up over my jokes and the dorky cartoon illustrations I'd drawn.

A week later, he booked in for a one-to-one career guidance session. After that, I kept seeing him about. On my coffee break. At lunch. Then at the grad bar when Nina and I went for a cheeky G&T. He came to join us and the night ended with an over-enthusiastic, gin-laced kiss.

I admit it's not the most exciting meet-cute ever, especially when you compared it to my parents'. They'd met when Dad was working in India. He was completely bowled over by my mum, and defied his conservative (by which I mean, racist) family to stay over there. And it's not like her family were thrilled to bits either; he had to spend months talking them round. But while my parents' romance sounded like a movie plot, I was happy having a drama-free relationship.

These days, it was bloody hard to find anyone at all, and it seemed like dating apps had only made it harder. Now, guys had the illusion of endless choice and it felt to me they were always looking over their shoulders, waiting for someone better to come along. Dating had never felt like an effort with Ryan, and because he'd moved to the UK from New Zealand so recently, I was the person answering his questions about Britishness (like 'what the hell is toad in the hole?' and 'why are you all so obsessed with where people went to school?'). It was a welcome change from the earnest white guys who wanted to know more about my 'native culture'. Ugh.

'You've gone quiet. Are you alright?' Ryan asked.

'I was thinking about you, actually.'

'That's sweet. Excited to be moving in together?'

'Yeah, course.'

'Sorry it can't be just us. But we'd be silly to turn our noses up at university-subsidised accommodation. I doubt there are many other options.'

'Don't worry. It's not like we're sharing a room with anyone else.'

'Maybe a sauna, though. There's one in the basement.'

'Naked?'

'God knows. I'll send you in first to check it out.'

'That'll give everyone nightmares.'

'Baby. You know I don't like it when you talk down about yourself. You have a gorgeous body.'

'Huh.'

I was five foot three and pear-shaped. Ryan loved my ass but it made buying trousers a nightmare, as they gaped at the back and were too tight around the thighs. He was pretty buff; although he'd been a chubby teenager, he'd lost it all in his early twenties. The only remaining evidence was the stretchmarks on his bum and stomach – he couldn't understand why they were one of my favourite things about his body.

'It is hard to see now, because of the darkness, but that small blue light on the left marks the location of Svalbard Seed Vault,' the bus driver announced over the loudspeaker. 'People from all over the world send their seeds to the vault, keeping them safe from manmade and natural disasters.'

I leaned my forehead against the window and peered outside. I could just about make out a small blue light winking in the distance.

'Sad, isn't it, that we need things like this?' Ryan said.

'Yeah.'

That was another thing we had in common – the fact that we felt as if we were living in a dystopian reality. We talked about doing more, but despite our best intentions, we still ate meat.

We reached the town and I caught sight of buildings illuminated by floodlights. There were no roads connecting them, just expanses of snow striped with ink-black shadows, drifts piled against the walls. It occurred to me that we wouldn't see the town properly until March, when the sun rose above the horizon again, signalling the end of polar winter. Now *that* was really dystopian. Thankfully, it's not as if we'd be living in a draughty cabin, surrounded by ice and darkness. We were sharing a flat with two other researchers. I'd seen pictures, and it looked comfortable, if a little institutional. That could be easily sorted with the colourful bedlinen and the posters I'd brought with me. In the kitchen, I'd line up jars of spices in neat rows and cook until the condensation steamed up the windows. Then it would feel like home, however dark it was outside.

3

I clung tightly to Ryan's hand as we walked through the snow with our new flatmate, Bjorn, who'd invited us to the pub. I wasn't normally so needy, but I really didn't want to go arse over tits and embarrass myself on the first night. It would have been a totally normal amble back in Norwich, but walking anywhere in minus fifteen degrees Celsius made it feel like an epic mission. I'd put a snowsuit on over my outfit, and was even wearing a balaclava. I was sure I'd get frostbite if I took it off, although I noted that Bjorn had rolled his up to talk. Perhaps testosterone made you immune to the cold.

'Here is the high street,' he told us.

It had been swallowed up by several feet of snow and I could only tell it was there by the position of the streetlamps and the parallel rows of darkened shop fronts. Behind one window was a hulking white shape.

'Shit.' I clutched Ryan's arm with my free hand, making him jump.

'Relax. It's stuffed,' Bjorn said.

I looked at the glazed, sightless eyes of the polar bear.

14

'What a way to attract people to a shop; stick an apex predator in the window,' I said.

Ryan chuckled.

We passed a woman walking two huskies, and a couple of lean men in Lycra, skiing down the middle of the street like it was the easiest thing in the world.

'We should definitely get skis,' Ryan said to me.

'My cousin Astrid is selling a couple of pairs of old ones,' Bjorn said. 'You can ask her about it – she'll be at the pub.'

I was terrible at sports, but perhaps skiing would be different. I liked the idea of gliding over the surface of the snow. It seemed a lot more dignified than trying to wade through it.

We reached the pub and followed Bjorn into a small ante-chamber, lined with outdoor shoes, which was ripe with the wet-dog smell of damp clothes. Bjorn pulled a pair of fleece-lined slippers out of his coat pocket.

'There's some plastic ones over there. Nobody wears shoes indoors here.'

I found some crocs my size, then removed my boots and snowsuit. I'd agonised over the right thing to wear to a pub in the Arctic, finally settling on a crimson sweater-dress and chunky gold earrings. As soon as I stepped inside, I realised I'd goofed. The other women were all wearing ski trousers, fleeces, or thick woollen jumpers. If it hadn't been so, well, Arctic outside, I would have hurried home to put on something less dressy.

'Gin and tonic?' Ryan asked me.

'Yeah, please.'

'Don't worry, you look smoking hot.'

Ryan had an uncanny knack of knowing when I was starting to freak out about something. Either that, or I was: A) super predictable, or B) constantly freaking out.

He pushed his way forward to a bar lined with rows of backlit bottles. I glanced around for a place to sit, taking in booths illuminated with low-hanging lamps, and high-contrast black and white murals on the walls. The world's so globalised that most places could be anywhere, and this was no exception. Maybe that's why everyone was wearing their outdoor clothes and the men hadn't shaved – proof that they really were in the wilderness, even as they sipped their triple-distilled whisky and pints of Amstel.

'There's Astrid,' Bjorn said.

I looked in the direction he'd indicated and saw a friendly-looking woman wearing a knitted jumper, her sandy hair scraped back into a messy ponytail. She was talking to a man who'd successfully achieved the grizzled explorer look the younger guys appeared to be going for, and then some. He was sitting with a group at the next table and knitting as he spoke to her. Astrid broke off her conversation to wave us over when she spotted Bjorn.

'These are my new flatmates, Maya and Ryan,' Bjorn told her.

'Hi, guys,' she said, sliding up to make space for us. 'Did you just arrive tonight? Where did you travel from?'

'Yes, we did. And we came from London,' Ryan said.

'But that isn't a British accent. It's . . . Australian?'

'Close. I'm from New Zealand.'

'Oh, sorry.'

Ryan shrugged. 'No biggie.'

'And what about you, Maya? You are originally from New Zealand too?'

'No, I grew up in the UK.'

'She spent the first seven years of her life in India,' Ryan said.

'I don't know much about India. Except that it is very hot, which is why I've never been,' Astrid said.

'To be honest, I don't know much about it either. I can't really remember my life there. I guess I was too young,' I confessed.

'Oh, really? My first memory is of urinating in my snow-suit when I was two years old, because the zipper was stuck,' Bjorn said.

'Thanks for sharing,' Astrid said, punching him lightly on the shoulder.

I shifted uncomfortably under their enquiring gazes. I didn't like being the centre of attention at the best of times. Bjorn and Astrid weren't the first people to find my lack of memory odd, but a psychologist had reassured me it was common for immigrants to forget their past, due to the stress of moving countries. He even had a fancy term for it: 'Dissociative Amnesia'.

'So, Astrid, what do you do here?' Ryan asked, quickly jumping to my rescue.

'I run a dogsledding tours business.'

'She used to work in corporate finance in Oslo,' Bjorn added. 'I always went on at her for being a sell-out, but she was just saving up to do something like this.'

'Wow, that's awesome,' Ryan said.

'If you two are interested, I will take you out on the sleds. It's quiet this time of year.'

'We'd love that, wouldn't we, Maya?'

'Totally,' I said. Dogsledding was one of the things I was desperate to try.

'And what about you guys? What are you doing here?' Astrid asked.

'I'm on the polar bear research project with Bjorn,' Ryan said, and embarked on an enthusiastic explanation.

17

'What about you, Maya?' Astrid asked, when she could finally get a word in.

'I was working in the careers department of a university, but I might struggle to find something like that here.'

'Maya's thinking of applying for cheffing work,' Ryan said.

'Well, maybe.'

'She's a great chef. She went to catering college and she can cook anything – soufflé, bouillabaisse, dim sum.'

'Wow. I don't even know what those things are,' Astrid said, looking impressed.

He'd pronounced it 'booly-bayse', but I didn't correct him. Underneath the table he reached for my hand but I pulled away and stood up.

'Just going out for a cigarette.'

I rushed off to grab my coat. I knew Ryan would be embarrassed at my abruptness, and probably a little hurt. He was always encouraging me to put myself out there more but I had to get away from the conversation. I'd been off the anti-anxiety meds for a year now, and had been relatively stable for months, but the thought of returning to a professional kitchen had triggered immediate stomach cramps.

Outside, the cold had me reeling. Since there was no way in hell I was taking off my gloves, it took an eternity to light up. But I got there in the end and stood in the shelter of the building, watching snowflakes whirl in the glow of a nearby streetlamp. Smoking was the only real excuse I had to go and stand outside by myself at a social gathering. That meant it was one of my safety behaviours – basically, something that decreased my anxiety in the short term by removing me from a socially stressful situation, but over a longer period created a pattern of avoidance that stopped me facing my fears – and a habit I couldn't kick.

I knew what Ryan would say later. That I shouldn't let my anxiety get in the way of what I wanted. That sometimes you had to work hard to get places. On both counts he was right, but he'd also never encountered the toxic environment of some professional kitchens. Whenever I started to feel bad about giving up on my dreams of becoming a chef, I reminded myself why I had stopped.

Reasons why I gave up cheffing:
- *The long hours and always working evenings and weekends.*
- *The fact it made you dislike food. Make a hundred chicken kievs a week and you soon won't be able to stand the sight of them.*
- *My nightmare boss, Craig. What a twat he was. You'd spend an hour making a sauce. He'd taste it and chuck it down the sink because it didn't have enough salt, or was slightly too thin: things that could be easily fixed.*
- *Being the only woman in the kitchen. Constant references to my boobs, my arse, queries over whether I was 'on the rag' every time I stood up for myself.*
- *The racist sous chef, Jack, who repeatedly told us that all lives mattered.*

Unsurprisingly, all this conspired to give me some of the worst bouts of anxiety I've ever had in my life.

After I quit, I'd really spiralled. I moved back to Dad's and spent several months there, mostly in bed, eating tomato soup, Honey Nut Cheerios and pork chow mein. I'd decided to find myself a stable career I didn't care too passionately about, and had hit upon HR. An entry-level vacancy opened up in Norwich at the same time Nina was moving there, so we got a flat together. By the time Ryan and I met, she and I had been there eighteen months and had made some cool friends. Work was over at five p.m., which gave me time to cook elaborate dinners for everyone, thereby conveying the somewhat inaccurate impression that I was the 'Life and Soul of the Party'. Poor Ryan. In the early days, he'd referred to me as 'laidback'. But that's dating for you. Nobody's themselves at the start. You're on your best behaviour, wondering how long you can keep the most fucked-up parts of yourself under lock and key.

The door behind me opened, and the wild-looking man who'd been knitting came out. He pulled a cigarette out of his pocket, lit it, and exhaled in contentment. Then he looked over at me.

'Hi,' I said.

He nodded in response. Then he cleared his throat.

'I heard inside that you are looking for cooking work?'

'Nothing full-time,' I said warily.

'I need a part-time cook.'

'I don't really chef anymore.'

'But you can make soufflé, bouillabaisse *and* dim sum,' he said, his pronunciation impeccable.

Luckily, it was too cold to blush.

'I guess I'm just . . . waiting to settle in. Seeing what's around.'

'I have an outdoor company. We run polar survival courses and day trips. These poor fuckers spend all day in the snow. They need a hot meal after. Just something easy, like a stew or a soup.'

'Oh, so I'd be the only one cooking?'

'Yes.'

'What sort of hours?'

'Maybe three to eight p.m.? You'd be making dinner and a soup we can reheat for lunch the next day.'

It was a very reasonable-sounding timetable, especially given the fact that I'd regularly finished catering shifts at two or three in the morning before.

'I might be interested,' I said cautiously.

'I'm busy this week, and you will want to settle in. But why don't you send me an email soon and we can arrange for you to come up and do a trial shift?'

'Alright.'

'Here's my card.'

It read: 'Mikkel Olafsson: Guide and Survival Expert'. Underneath was a phone number. I slid it into my pocket and watched him walk off down the street. Perhaps this *was* the type of thing I had been looking for. A way of cooking for people without having to suffer the indignities of a professional kitchen. Crazy that he had overheard us and had this opportunity to offer me. Maybe it was a scam. I stubbed out my cigarette and went inside to tell Ryan what had happened.

4

Darkness was still nudging the window panes when Ryan kissed me goodbye. I rolled over and went back to sleep, returning hazily to consciousness hours later, feeling like I'd been drugged. It was already eleven. In my pre-trip research I'd discovered that polar night messes with your circadian rhythms; so far, I'd been averaging about twelve hours of sleep a night, which was no bad thing, in my opinion.

I got out of bed and had a leisurely breakfast followed by an even more leisurely shower. By the time I was done, I had a message from Dad asking if I was free to video chat. He answered the call from the kitchen, which hadn't changed in two decades. The walls were still covered with the paintings I drew as a kid, now faded by the sun and curling up at the corners.

'Hi, darling. You've settled in alright?'

'Yeah. The flat's nice. We're sharing with two other people, although one's currently away on fieldwork.'

'That's good. And how's the weather?'

'It's cold. So, so cold. You can't even imagine.'

'I had to go to St Petersburg for business last year. In winter. It was freezing. Barely left the hotel.'

Around the time I moved to Norwich, Dad had been offered a job that involved a lot of travel. Although I'd missed spending time with him, it had definitely given him a new lease of life.

'So when's the next trip?' I asked him.

'That's actually something I need to talk to you about.'

'Fire away.'

He cleared his throat.

'I'm going to be moving,' he said slowly.

'Moving? Are you finally following through on your dream of a country cottage?'

'No, not exactly. I'm actually heading out to India for a while.'

I felt a strange tugging sensation in my chest, like water being sucked down a plughole.

'Where in India?' I asked, my voice coming out more squeakily than I'd intended.

'Bangalore. About ten minutes from the flat where you grew up, actually.'

Neither Dad nor I had ever been back to Bangalore. I had assumed that the streets and the buildings held too many painful memories for him. But perhaps twenty years was long enough for them to fade.

'You see, I've met someone . . .'

'Dad, that's amazing!'

He'd been single since forever – at least, I'd never been introduced to anyone. He'd once confessed how empty the house felt when I wasn't in it, and I'd always hoped that he would find someone to share it with.

'Is she Indian?' I asked.

He nodded.

'Okay, so spill. How did you meet her? When?'

'This might sound odd to you, but do you remember Uma?'

'The lady who sends birthday cards to me?'

'That's right. She was a good friend of ours. But I never liked her husband Ram much. He died around seven years ago. She went on to set up her own business and contacted me for advice, so we started talking. Slowly, we rebuilt our friendship and it became more . . . romantic.'

He was looking at me in trepidation, worried I was going to throw a stinking hissy fit. Luckily for him, I was no longer a stroppy teenager. But I did have questions.

'How long has it been romantic for?' I demanded.

'We've met a few times. When I travelled to Thailand for work, and to Hong Kong. It was fun. But to really commit to it, we need to be in the same country.'

I was a little miffed that this mysterious woman hadn't been mentioned sooner, but I decided not to mention it. Dad had probably wanted to keep it under wraps until he could see where it was heading.

'I'm really pleased for you,' I said instead. 'I guess it's kind of weird it's Mum's mate but, I mean, it's been twenty years.'

'I would have mentioned it at our goodbye dinner. That was my plan. But then you seemed so anxious about the move that I decided not to overload you. Sorry if it's a shock now.'

'It's fine, don't worry. So, how long are you going over there for?'

'I don't know. I'll be renting the house out while I'm gone, though. It's a twelve-month contract . . . initially.'

He couldn't quite meet my eyes.

24

'But all my stuff is in my room.'

'Don't worry, I've found a decent storage facility nearby. You never know, by the time you get back from the Arctic I might even have stuffed things up, moved home and unpacked it all again.'

'Dad! You've got to go in fighting. So what's this Uma like, then?'

'She's very independent, very creative. She loves to read and to cook. I think she's very attractive. I, how do they say it, have punched far above my weight.'

'I'm sure that's not true.'

'Anyway. Enough about me. Why don't you tell me about the Arctic? I hope you're staying warm.'

Fifteen minutes later, I hung up. Of course I was beyond pleased for Dad, but the information had me reeling. This was the most spontaneous thing I had ever known him do. That house in Croydon was like his second skin, and I couldn't imagine him anywhere else. I wondered if things would work out. He deserved them to, although I wasn't entirely sure how I felt about potentially going out there to visit him. My mind moved up a gear and was quickly filled with various scenarios of possible futures – never seeing Dad again because I was too scared to get on the plane, him dying in a traffic accident over there just like Mum did, me going over there and being shunned by everyone for my British accent. In therapy speak this is called 'catastrophising', and it is considered 'counterproductive'.

Time to go out and get a breath of (very) fresh air. There was a museum just down the road which I hadn't yet visited – that would take my mind off it.

The clothes I put on to leave the house in Svalbard:

- *Undies*
- *Socks (three pairs)*
- *Thermal vest*
- *Long Johns*
- *Merino base layer*
- *Outdoor trousers*
- *Fleece*
- *Ski jacket*
- *Balaclava*
- *Hat*
- *Gloves (two pairs)*
- *Fleece-lined ski boots*

I've always enjoyed making lists. It gives you a sense of purpose, breaks things down into conquerable steps. A way of organising the chaos.

By the time I was dressed I was as bulky as the Michelin man. But once outside, the cold quickly penetrated the layers of clothing. I hurried past the student flats, darkened buildings with only the odd window illuminated. A man hunched over a laptop in his bedroom, face bathed in the blue glow of the screen. A woman standing by a kitchen stove, her body smudged by the steamed-up window, giving her the uncertain outlines of a ghost.

I reached the end of our road. Away from the street-lamps, I could see the darkness wasn't absolute – the sky was deep cobalt and there were faint silhouettes of mountains in the distance. It would be months until I could see my surroundings properly. I looked in the other direction. Here and there were the shapes of buildings, floodlights illuminating foyers and piles of snow. Without any visible roads to connect them, everything seemed isolated and far apart.

As I approached the university building I saw the sign for the Svalbard Museum. I'm a complete museum junkie. I like the badly-taxidermied animals with their weird fake eyes. The tableaus of 'ye olde' people with paint peeling from their faces. Glass cases filled with shards of unrecognisable objects. And, of course, they're crammed full of facts.

The museum door opened into the cloakroom area. My hands were raw and useless; it took several minutes before they'd defrosted enough for me to unlace my boots so I sat for a while, disoriented and dripping. Then came the clumsy dance to remove my layers of clothing.

Over the next hour, I slowly absorbed facts about Svalbard. The archipelago was discovered in 1596 by Willem Barentsz and was far too cold and isolated to be inhabited. By humans, at least – there were plenty of animals. First they came for the whales. Pulled their carcasses onto the shore and carved them up for blubber, extracting oil and baleen for corsets. When the whales were gone they came for the polar bears and foxes, hunting them for their furs. The first woman trapper to travel to Svalbard was Wanny Wolstaad, a taxi driver from Tromsø. She overwintered four or five times so was clearly a total badass. I couldn't imagine spending winter up here in a draughty cabin without electricity or running water.

There was a whole room devoted to Arctic Exploration as dudes searching for the Northwest Passage or the North Pole had to travel across the archipelago. Normally they failed, or got lost, or died. Even when that happened they were hailed as heroes, even though the only thing they'd fought was the elements. Surely the North Pole looked much the same as the thousand miles of icy expanse surrounding it? But white guys want to stick their flags in everything.

I left as a large group of elderly American tourists arrived at the museum. As I watched them stream into the atrium, photographing the stuffed polar bear and seabirds hanging on strings from the ceiling, I wondered if Arctic explorer John Franklin was turning in his grave.

Outside, it was snowing heavily. When it snowed in the UK people would call in to work pretending their street hadn't been gritted or their car wouldn't start. Back in January, Nina and I had taken a snow day and gone sledging with a couple of our friends, then spent hours sitting by the fire in our favourite pub, getting drunk on mulled wine. But this was a different type of snow altogether. The flakes that landed on my exposed face were so cold they burned. I couldn't imagine ever getting used to it . . . and it was only going to get colder and darker.

I thought about the flat I'd lived in with Nina in Norwich, the beautiful rosewood coffee table her parents had gifted us and the mustard armchair from IKEA we always fought over. The courtyard garden with the pots of herbs and the barbecue we'd bought cheap off Gumtree. Long summer evenings spent outside, drinking cheap white wine and chatting shit. But someone else lived there now. And soon someone else would be renting my childhood home, while Dad moved thousands of miles away.

I now lived on a remote island populated by polar bears, where the temperatures plunged into the minus thirties. How long would it take me to feel at home here?

5

Something inside me uncoiled as we drove away from Longyearbyen. This was the furthest I'd travelled from our apartment since we'd arrived.

'Thanks for taking us sledding,' I said to Astrid, who was driving.

'Yeah, thanks,' Ryan echoed from the seat behind.

She was driving us up to her cabins in a minibus alongside an American couple and their teenage children, who had booked a tour. Astrid had been insistent I sit up front with her. It was a sweet gesture but I had been racking my brain for things to say ever since we started out.

'Mikkel was asking about you,' she said.

'Who's Mikkel?' Ryan said.

'That guy I told you about; the one that asked if I was interested in the cooking job.'

'And you haven't emailed him yet?'

'No. I'll get to it, okay?' I said, more sharply than I'd intended. Since moving in with him, I'd noticed that Ryan rather enjoyed giving advice. So far he'd told me how best to wash the dishes, how to cut down on smoking and how to snack more healthily.

'He's nice,' Astrid said. 'Much friendlier than he looks.'

She pulled off the main road and drove towards a cluster of wooden huts, which were illuminated by floodlamps.

'Sorry I snapped,' I whispered to Ryan, once we'd gotten out of the minibus.

'It's chill, Squidge, don't worry. C'mon, Astrid's talking.'

We joined the American tourists.

'Welcome to Spitsbergen Adventure Tours. I hope you're looking forward to dogsledding with us today. All in all, the activity will last two and a half hours, which includes the safety briefing and a hot chocolate by the fire afterwards. First let me find you all something to wear.'

As we followed her across the yard, I looked upwards and saw a huge moon leaking cold light into the sky. Weird that it was there in the middle of the day. I turned to Ryan to ask why, but he had gone on ahead. I hurried to catch up.

Astrid led us into a small hut. On one wall was a rack of snowsuits, while the others were lined with benches and cubbyholes filled with boots. Astrid was wearing a chic black and red snowsuit emblazoned with her company's logo. The rest of us were given khaki green ones. Once dressed, I looked like a cabbage. But if it kept me warm, I didn't care.

Our headtorch beams flickered over hollows in the snow and the silhouetted outbuildings as we headed towards the sleds. I tried not to think about things that hide in the darkness, and felt a sudden sympathy with the explorers from decades and centuries ago who'd had to huddle in draughty cabins, waiting for the light to return. The Ryans of yesteryear, if you will, seeking adventure. Only, they hadn't brought their girlfriends along.

I heard the dogs before I saw them, their ear-splitting, high pitched howling cutting through the darkness. The snowbound hillside before us was lined with kennels, smelly, bright yellow patches of piss staining the snow out front. The dogs were straining against their chains and looked far less cute and fluffy than I'd imagined. I inched closer to Ryan as Astrid led us past them to a row of wooden sleds. He took my hand.

'The sleds will take two people, one driving and one sitting up front. Mine is slightly larger and can accommodate two up front, so if anyone is feeling anxious, they can ride with me.'

I glanced over at Ryan, who shook his head and indicated the American couple. Seconds later, they timidly asked if they could ride with Astrid.

'That's fine. Now, can anyone help me with the dogs?'

'I will,' Ryan said.

'Me, too,' said the teenage girl.

They disappeared back down the hill while the rest of us shivered.

'I hope we don't get lost,' the boy said.

'You watch out for your knee, Donald,' the woman said to her husband.

'I told you already . . .'

As they began bickering, I stepped away from the group and switched off my headtorch. The moonlight reflected onto the snow, giving it an eerie blue tint. In the distance was a flat plain surrounded by purple-shadowed mountains. It was midday – the time when the darkness became a little less dark and uncertain shapes became visible; when the snow lightened and the sky paled at the horizon. Nautical twilight, it was called, alluding to the time when sailors navigated by the stars. Since coming to the Arctic I'd learned there were three different grades of twilight: civil, nautical, and astronomical, each darker than the one before.

Astrid, Ryan, and the teenage girl returned with one of the other guides, each of them holding two large huskies by the collar. Astrid harnessed hers expertly to the sled I was standing next to.

'Maya, meet Blizzard and Kojak. Look after them for me.'

Easier said than done as I watched the two start snapping and barking at each other. Why put two dogs who were obviously enemies so close together? Maybe the competitiveness made them run faster.

'Why don't you try being friends?' I suggested.

Blizzard turned to me and snarled.

'Nervous?' Ryan asked a few minutes later, once the dogs had all been harnessed to the sleds.

'A little,' I confessed.

'Don't worry, I'll drive first. That way you have time to settle into it a bit.'

'Thanks.'

We made our way over to the others.

'Driving is a lot easier than it looks,' Astrid was saying. 'Especially as the dogs know the way. There are several important things you need to know. One, don't let go of the sled or you'll fall off. Two, you stop the sled by pressing on this metal footbrake right here. Three, if you're going up a hill and you're the driver, then you can get off and run to lighten the load.'

'How do you turn left and right?' Ryan asked.

'The dogs respond to commands, which I will say quietly now, but you must shout when you're driving. You say "Hike" to go, and "whoa" to stop. "Haw" is right, and "gee" is left.

32

But you don't really need to remember "haw" or "gee" – I'll go at the front and your teams will just follow mine. Is everyone ready to have a go?'

'Yes!' Ryan said enthusiastically.

I sat down on the sled, while Ryan stood behind me. Astrid made sure the American family were settled, then took up her position.

'Hike,' she shouted, and the dogs began to run.

'Hike,' Ryan yelled, seconds later.

Much to my surprise, the dogs began shitting copiously as they ran. I scrambled backwards to avoid a face full. Luckily the faecal storm began to ease off after a couple of minutes. The dogs' harnesses jangled as we moved – the only noise aside from the wind – and the snow glowed softly in the moonlight. Our sled even cast a suggestion of a shadow as we sped across the plains. It felt like an experience from another time and place, a world away from the usual activities I enjoyed on a regular basis, like drinking wine with Nina, or chilling with Ryan. If it were ten degrees warmer I could have enjoyed it for hours. But before long the cold penetrated my thick clothes. Then a dark cloud slid across the moon, and seconds later it started to snow, the wind whipping stinging flakes into my face. This is a great experience, I told myself firmly.

Finally, Astrid shouted 'whoa', and as Ryan echoed her we came to a stop.

'Everyone alright back there?' Astrid shouted.

'Y-y-yess,' came a wavering voice from behind us.

'How's everyone feeling?'

'Great!' Ryan called.

'Now would be a good time to change drivers,' Astrid said.

'Want to swap?' Ryan asked me.

33

'Sure,' I mumbled.

Maybe it would warm me up.

'Put your foot on the brake here. Then I'll let go,' Ryan said.

'And then?'

'Then you drive. Don't worry, Gorge, it's easy.'

Astrid had swapped places with the guy on her sled.

'Hike,' he shouted.

Our dogs followed suit, before I'd even commanded them. We lurched forward and I heard Ryan swear.

'Sorry, Squidge,' I shouted to him.

At first I clenched my hands tight against the rail, my heart pounding at the thought of something going wrong. But despite my complete inexperience, the dogs continued their smooth trajectory across the snow. It soon became obvious that they knew every detail of the route. Astrid was right. It was way easier than I'd thought. I was driving a dogsled in the fricking Arctic – how cool was that?

But the appeal of driving soon wore off because I was now even more exposed to the Arctic wind. 'Freezing' didn't even begin to cover it. There needed to be another word to describe how you felt after experiencing temperatures lower than minus twenty – perhaps there already was, in a language I didn't know.

The sled in front veered suddenly to the left and my dogs followed, catching me off-balance. My hands slipped off the rail and I had a horrible plummeting sensation before I hit the snowy ground with a jolt.

There was a burst of pain in my side and my eyes streamed with the intensity of it. An iron band tightened round my chest. Where was the sled? Had the dogs carried on without me? I didn't have the energy to lift my head and look.

Instead, my brain chose that moment to remind me that people had died of hypothermia in warmer temperatures than this. I closed my eyes and felt waves breaking over my head. It felt as though translucent jellyfish were drifting past me, sending stinging jolts across every area of exposed skin.

'Maya? Are you alright?'

I opened my eyes. Ryan was standing over me. He reached down and pulled me up into his arms.

'Oh, baby. You're shivering.'

'Maybe you should drive now,' I mumbled.

'That's okay. It's always best to get back on the horse when you fall off.'

'I don't want to get back on.'

'Are you sure? This is such a great opportunity.'

'I'm fine,' I replied, suddenly conscious that everyone else had stopped and was waiting for us.

'Let's head back to camp now,' Astrid called over to us.

We sledded back in a darkness that felt thicker and more oppressive than before. After what felt like an eternity I saw the lights of the camp. By this point I was basically a human icicle. Somehow I managed to stagger down the hill after the others and (helped by Ryan) extricate myself from the snow-suit, which was coated in ice.

By the time I was seated next to the fire with a cup of hot chocolate I was feeling much warmer, although still slightly shell-shocked by the experience. Luckily, Ryan had more than enough enthusiasm for both of us.

'This has been on my bucket list for ages! It was so exhilarating.'

'My grandfather kept dogs, and whenever I visited him we would take them out sledding,' Astrid said. 'In March I'm going to do a long-distance sled race in Alta. Just half the course — 500 kilometres.'

'That sounds so cool. How long will it take?' Ryan asked.

The two of them began talking earnestly about it. Astrid was like a modern day Wanny Wolstaad — perfectly at home in these sub-zero temperatures, whether she was holding a rifle or controlling a team of aggressive dogs. It was easy to see how Ryan, who was naturally sporty (and seemingly already used to the cold), could one day be like that.

On the way back into town, Ryan sat up front with Astrid. I sat behind them, looking out of the window and seeing nothing. I wished Nina was here. She would have lasted about two minutes before demanding we go back to the hut, and she would have brought a hip flask so we could lace the hot chocolate with something stronger.

'You're being very quiet,' Ryan said, when we were finally at home by ourselves again, stripping off our many layers in the cramped bedroom.

'Yeah. Well.'

'What's wrong?'

'Nothing.'

He gently nudged my chin upwards with his finger, so my eyes met his.

'Sure there is. Are you feeling embarrassed about falling off the sled?'

I shook my head, feeling my eyes begin to sting.

'You don't need to be. It could've happened to anyone. If you'd tried again then you wouldn't feel so bad.'

'Everyone here's so sporty. Whenever Astrid and Bjorn talk about skiing or camping out on the ice I don't feel excited, I just feel scared.'

'Oh Gorge, don't worry. It takes time. You just need to have confidence and be patient.'

I wiped my eyes with the back of my hand.

'Hey, come here. Don't cry,' he said, pulling me towards him and wrapping his arms around me. 'You don't have to do anything you don't want to. Why don't you focus more on the things you do like? You haven't really done much cooking since you've arrived.'

'The food here's so expensive, and I'm not earning anything,' I mumbled into his shoulder.

'That doesn't matter. The accommodation's subsidised, and it's not like we're spending money on anything else.'

'I don't deserve you.'

'Don't be silly,' Ryan said, unclasping his arms. 'You're funny, and beautiful, and very talented. You just took a nasty fall and it's shaken you. Now, why don't you warm up in the shower, and I'll go out and get us a takeaway pizza and a huge bar of chocolate.'

'You'd do that?'

'Course I would.'

He put his outdoor clothes back on, then kissed me goodbye. God, I was lucky to have him. I undressed and got into the shower, finding there was a bruise on my hip from falling over onto the snow. It had stung – the impact *and* the embarrassment – but it was over now. I turned up the water temperature and tried my best not to think about it.

6

The kitchen was so warm that the dough had risen quickly. Now the loaf was baking in the oven and the room was suffused with a warm, yeasted aroma.

'Do you want me to cut the onions and garlic?' Ryan asked.

'Please.'

I turned on my cooking playlist, which featured the likes of Otis Redding, Aretha Franklin and a bit of Solange, humming under my breath as I chopped carrots and celery. As Ryan came over to give me the vegetables he'd chopped, he gave my bum an affectionate squeeze.

'What would you like me to do next?'

'Peel and chop a couple of potatoes?'

'Sure.'

I gently sautéed the onions with the fish bones and heads from last night's supper. The hot water sizzled as I poured it into the pan. Next, the seasoning: a sprinkle of salt, a couple of bay leaves and a bouquet garni I'd brought from Norwich, made from herbs I'd grown myself.

'Do you want me to put the potatoes in yet?'

'No, the stock needs to infuse first. Then I'll strain it, add all the vegetables and later some salt cod, prawns and cream.'

'That sounds great,' Ryan said.

The familiar opening chords of Aretha Franklin's 'Say a little Prayer' filled the room and Ryan picked up the soup ladle and held it like a microphone, crooning tunelessly, fluttering his eyelashes, and making me laugh.

He put the ladle down and swept me up in his arms, still singing. We danced clumsily around the room and had just started making out when the kitchen door opened.

'Sorry to disturb you, lovebirds,' said Bjorn.

Astrid was with him. She couldn't quite meet my eyes and I wondered if PDAs embarrassed her.

'No worries,' Ryan said, stepping away from me. 'What are you two up to?'

'Training for the ski marathon,' Bjorn said.

'That sounds rad.'

'Come with us,' Astrid said.

'We don't have skis yet,' Ryan told her.

'I have two pairs I want to sell. You can try them – they're at my apartment.'

'That's alright, we're cooking . . .' I began, but Ryan answered with 'Sure, that would be great . . .' at the exact same time.

We broke off and exchanged looks. Today was supposed to be about the two of us – we'd already spent loads of time with Bjorn and Astrid this week – but I didn't want to come across as a needy girlfriend.

'I'll stay here and look after the food. You go,' I said.

'It's cool, I'm happy to stay in.'

'No, you go. I want to talk to Dad anyway. And it's soup – it won't spoil.'

Ryan kissed me.

'Babe, you're amazing. I won't be long, I promise.'

After they'd gone, I wondered if Astrid and Bjorn thought I was lame for staying in. But the thought of being outside for an extended period was distinctly unappealing, and skiing would require significantly more athletic prowess than dogsledding. They'd been friendly to both of us, but they had far more in common with Ryan than with me. Where were the women in this town who liked cooking elaborate dinners, drinking too much red wine and watching movies?

Feeling slightly despondent, I FaceTimed Dad. He was sitting on the sofa in what looked like Uma's living room. Sunlight flooded in through the windows, highlighting a glass table, an earth-toned rug, and some richly detailed cushion covers. A ceiling fan whirred gently overhead. Dad looked happier than I'd seen him in ages, but his expression soon changed to one of concern.

'Darling? You look upset.'

'I'm fine. Really.'

'Are you sure?'

'I'm finding it harder here than I thought I would. It's so cold that I don't really enjoy going out. Ryan just went skiing with two of our friends in, like, minus twenty,' I said, feeling like a whiny teenager again.

'Are they all mad? I hope he's looking after you.'

Dad wasn't particularly keen on Ryan, which wasn't surprising – he thought most of my boyfriends weren't good enough for me.

'He's being really supportive, honestly.'

'You can call me any time you need anything.'

There was a noise in the background.

'I'm back!' a woman's voice called. 'Such traffic out there today. It took me forty-five minutes just to . . . oh.'

'I'm just talking to Maya. Come and sit down.'

I saw a slender woman with an elegant silver bob and kohl-lined eyes, wearing an ochre tunic. Dad was right – she *was* very pretty.

'Maya? It's Uma. Do you remember me?'

I shook my head, feeling embarrassed.

'I'm sorry, I don't. It's nothing personal, though. Thanks for all the cards.'

'That's quite alright. So, did you tell her yet?'

'Not yet,' Dad replied, looking at me warily.

'Tell me what?'

'Well, last night Uma and I were having dinner—'

'And I proposed to him!' she broke in.

'And I said yes! Obviously.'

The two of them were beaming at each other. My ears were ringing with shock.

'Congratulations,' I said weakly.

Uma leaned forward.

'Maya? Are you alright?'

'Of course. I'm really pleased for you,' I said.

I tried to smile but my head was still buzzing with white noise.

'I want you to know that I would never try and replace your ma.'

'It's not like that,' I said, twisting my hands in my lap.

'Maya gets anxious about sudden changes. She feels out of control,' Dad said.

'But I know this is a good change. Don't worry – I'm totally on board.'

'You'll come to the wedding?' Dad asked.

'Of course I will. When is it?'

'In a month. Just after Christmas.'

'So soon?'

'In India, people don't send wedding invites very far in advance,' Dad explained.

'Yes, because if everyone came you would be in trouble,' Uma added.

'Well, I'll definitely be there.'

'I'll buy your ticket,' Dad promised. 'I know it'll be expensive coming from Svalbard at such short notice and I don't want you to be out of pocket.'

By the time I hung up a few minutes later, my head was throbbing and my fingers felt weird and tingly. Recognising the danger signs, I closed my eyes and took several deep breaths. When I opened them again, I tried to quiet my mind by focussing on the sounds in the kitchen. The whirring of the oven fan. The stock bubbling in the pan. The faint whistle of the wind outside. I took the bread out of the oven and stirred the stock, just to have something to do with my hands. A fish head protruded from the surface and glared at me balefully.

'I am happy for him, you know,' I said to it. 'But it's bloody sudden.'

Unsurprisingly, there was no response. I drained the stock and threw the fish bones in the bin.

Life was about to change. Again. What would it be like to have a stepmother? Uma seemed really sweet, but it had been me and Dad for as long as I could remember. Still, I wasn't a teenager anymore, and he deserved to be happy. The thing that really got me, though, was that visiting Bangalore was now unavoidable. The thought of it made me feel lightheaded and gave me a churning in my gut that no amount of present moment focus exercises would shift. It was a sensation I'd named 'The Schools', because it was how I had felt on my first day at Fairchild Primary.

I remember clinging to Dad's hand as we walked across the concrete playground. It was raining (it seemed like it rained all the time back then, and I was always, always cold) and we had to shuffle around puddle after puddle. The elastic of my socks was tight around my legs and my pinafore itched. Once inside, Dad left me with Miss James, kissing the top of my head before he left. Once he was gone I burst into tears and Miss James tried her best to comfort me, but I was distraught. What if Dad had an accident on the way to work, like Mum did? What if that was the last time I saw him? Eventually, Miss James managed to shut me up with a tube of Smarties and the colossal fib that Dad was walking to work on a special car-free footpath. Then she took me to my classroom. Thirty faces turned curiously to mine when I stepped inside and Miss James told me to introduce myself.

'My name is Maya and I moved here from India,' I said, suddenly aware how different my accent was to hers. But there was ultimately no need to worry – a decade later I sounded just like her.

The vegetables had begun to soften so I added the salt cod and prawns, then measured out two tablespoons of cream. There was nothing more reassuring than following a recipe, measuring out flour by the gram and cream by the spoonful, everything unfolding exactly according to plan. Even when you'd memorised the method, you still knew the recipe was there, providing structure, like bones under skin.

Slowly, my pulse returned to normal.

In a month I would be returning to India for the first time. When I was younger, Dad was worried about it being too traumatic. As a teenager, I was in flight from the Indian part of myself. It was the thing that made me different and all I wanted was to be the same as everyone else. The Indian kids at school didn't want to hang out with me. What did I know about their lives anyway, with my white dad and my white friends? And then I met Nina. She took me out to the best curry houses on Brick Lane, forced me to come and try on saris with her, and took me for my first arm waxing appointment. She'd been nagging me to go on holiday to India with her for years, but I'd found myself making excuse after excuse.

'I just don't understand what you're so afraid of,' she'd said once, in exasperation.

'I have anxiety – I'm afraid of everything.'

'Bullshit. You love going on holiday. What is it?'

'That the food will be too spicy for my western palate . . .'

She'd rolled her eyes.

It had taken me a while (and a fair amount of therapy) to understand my reluctance. Most of the time I felt like an alien that had turned up on a hostile planet. It was a feeling I had come to associate with my Indian heritage. But what if I went to India and my Britishness made me the odd one out?

7

Ryan had left a small pile of krone notes by my side of the bed, and a note asking me to get something tasty for dinner. The implicit message being that he wanted to make sure I left the house today. But my appetite to explore had diminished. I'd visited the two museums, the cafés, the restaurants and even the sports centre alone and each short trip outside left me reeling with the cold. With each passing day the temperature dropped lower and the darkness became more absolute. I was beginning to see why depression was common in high longitudes. At a loss, I rang Nina.

'Hello, Nina Patel, how may I help you?'

'You're at work?'

'That's right, madam.' She lowered her voice to a whisper. 'I'll call you back in five minutes from the bathroom.'

While I waited, the pains in my chest intensified. She'd ask me if I was having fun in the Arctic and she'd see right through my response. What would Nina think if I told her I'd started getting out of bed around midday? Pretty much everyone I knew was working so hard at the moment, and here I was, completely wasting my days.

The phone rang, making me jump.

'Sorry about that. I'm still on probation – need to be on my best behaviour.'

'That's okay. How's it going?' I asked.

Nina launched into an enthusiastic description of her new job – how interesting she found it, but how she constantly worried about fucking up.

'There's a really sexy guy in the campaigns department. I'm tempted to ask him out. What do you think? Should I shit where I eat or will I get a reputation?'

'I don't know,' I said dully.

'What's up? You usually love dissecting this stuff with me.'

'I'm sorry. I just . . . my anxiety's kind of bad today,' I said.

My voice felt as if it were coming from somewhere far away. My vision was blurry around the edges.

'Shit, Maya. I wish I was there with you. Just be easy on yourself, okay? It's hard enough moving countries, especially to the fucking Arctic. I'd be having a complete meltdown. Anyone would.'

'Not Ryan,' I said glumly. 'He's loving it.'

'He's been obsessed with the Arctic for years, whereas you wouldn't have set foot there if it weren't for him. Besides, he's too busy to freak out. Have you spoken to him about it?'

'Yeah. But I don't want to shit on his dreams.'

'Feel free to moan to me anytime. Have you seen the Northern Lights yet?'

'Nope.'

'Oh, babe. You're so brave for going there. Just remember that. Everything will fall into place. Is there anything you can

46

do to meet cool people? A language class or a supper club or some shit?'

'Probably.'

'I'm starting a desi book club via Zoom with a couple of other girls. You should join. We're reading *Erotic Stories for Punjabi Widows* first.'

'That sounds fun.'

'Listen, I have to get back. There's a big staff meeting in like five minutes. But I'll call you after work and we'll talk about this properly. I promise.'

'Sure.'

'Love you! Stay strong.'

After she'd hung up I fought the urge to get back into bed. She was right, of course. I shouldn't beat myself up. I should get out there and make friends. At the very least, I needed to email that Mikkel guy. Every night this week, Ryan had asked me gently if I'd gotten round to it yet. Today, I would answer 'yes'. First, though, I would shower, eat a healthy breakfast and go grocery shopping.

Half a packet of biscuits and a bowl of Coco Pops later, I was fighting my way through the snow to the town's only supermarket. The wind quickly picked up, driving the snow sideways and making it difficult to walk, but I gritted my teeth and continued onwards. Eventually, I caught sight of the artificially lit aisles of neatly packed food, which were visible through the supermarket's glass doors, their familiarity made uncanny by the surrounding darkness and whirling gusts of snow.

I walked through the double doors, past the sign telling people to leave their rifles outside. Ryan and I had come here when we first arrived; he'd piled food into the trolley and I'd been too confused by the exchange rate to fully comprehend the prices. Now, I realised how extortionate everything was – an orange pepper was being sold for seven quid. Half the vegetables weren't even ripe and the range of spices was dismal. Thank god I'd brought my own. I walked slowly up and down the aisles picking up the cheapest things I could find: tinned potatoes, vegetable oil, sausages, and ingredients for homemade pizza.

By the time I was done and had paid for my purchases, the snow was falling thicker and faster. I stood in the shelter of the building, watching as it slanted across the ground in diagonal sheets.

'You should hurry. It will get worse,' said a woman next to me, pulling on thick gloves and a balaclava. Seconds later, she vanished into the storm. Realising I couldn't stay here forever, I followed suit.

The wind drove the snow straight into me, almost knocking me over. I braced my body against the force and shuffled down the steps, clutching the handrail. It was difficult to see anything, but I knew I needed to turn right. I made my way slowly down the street, reassured by occasional glimpses of the lit-up shop fronts. When I reached the end of the road, there was nothing to guide me. I needed to carry on past the Radisson Blu and hang a left. But the Radisson had been swallowed up by the whirling darkness.

I staggered onwards, hoping I was going the right way. It was snowing so hard I quickly lost all sense of where I was. I could barely distinguish up from down, left from right.

The realisation hit me with the force of a hammer-blow.

I was lost.

In the Arctic.

In an actual blizzard.

'Help!'

The wind carried my voice away.

Panic rose in my throat like bile. If I stopped walking I'd freeze to death. Finding shelter was imperative. I knew I should retrace my steps but when I turned around, the high street had vanished. There was nothing but driving snow and darkness.

I reached for my phone. Cupped my hand around it as a shield. The screen quickly went blank; like me, it couldn't deal with the cold. I forced my way onwards, fighting against the wind, eyes streaming and hoping to fuck that I was going in the right direction. After a few minutes, lights appeared out of the blizzard like a mirage. By a small miracle, I'd found the hotel. I practically wept tears of relief. I could go inside and wait it out with a drink. Grab a taxi back to the flat once it eased off. But as I drew closer, something inside me switched.

Everyone would stare if I entered a place like that. What if the drinks were super expensive and I had to nurse one for hours, enduring pointed comments about whether I wanted something else? What if the receptionist was a snooty bitch who wouldn't help me get a taxi? Or the driver didn't speak English? My mouth was dry and my stomach began to cramp, making it even harder to think.

Code Red.

Code Red.

I couldn't face anyone feeling like this. So I chose what now felt like the lesser of two evils: the blizzard.

As I struggled onwards, I thought about how fucking stupid I was. Going into the Radisson had been the safest course of action. But my anxiety had made it feel as dangerous as jumping off a building or following a stranger into an empty house. My mind had betrayed me. Again.

Somehow, I ended up back at the museum, and from there

49

I managed to locate our street. Finally, the lights of our apartment block appeared. I pulled the entry card from my pocket and practically fell through the front door. It then took several minutes to get inside our room because my hands were too numb to grip the key. Finally, the door clicked open. Water dripped from my frozen clothes and hair as I pulled off all my clothes and dived into bed. I concentrated on getting warm, and once the feeling returned to my extremities, the shame hit.

I couldn't manage a trip to the shops without getting lost. I was too much of a freak to step inside a hotel – a place where people were literally paid to be hospitable – and ask for help. I wasn't tough or brave enough for a place like this. I'd have to stay inside and become the human equivalent of a slug; nothing but a waste of space and oxygen. I reached for my phone and sent Ryan a message.

Pls come back. Really freaking out. I was lost in the snow.

The response was almost immediate.

Hang tight will be there asap xxxxxx

I burrowed down under the covers and curled up tightly in a ball.

By the time the door opened five minutes later, I was hyperventilating.

'Squidge? Are you hurt?'

The covers were pulled back. Ryan's eyes were wide with concern. I looked up at him, too breathless to speak, and shook my head.

'What's wrong? You're scaring me.'

This wasn't the response I'd been expecting. I turned over so I was facing the wall.

'Maya? What did I say? I came back here on my lunch hour to check on you.'

50

I couldn't help it; I began to cry. Ryan sat down next to me, and began stroking my back.

'I'm sorry. I didn't mean to upset you.'

'No, I'm the one who's sorry. I'm so fucking stupid, I can't handle the snow.'

'Hey, don't be silly. It's pretty wild out there right now.'

'But *you* handled it just fine.'

'C'mon Squidge.'

I heard the sound of a jacket being unzipped, and then he climbed into bed next to me. I turned over and threw my arm around him. My ear was squashed against his chest and I could hear his heart beating as regularly as a metronome. The sound of it began to calm me down. I was safe inside now, and I wasn't going out again until the snow stopped.

'Feeling better now?' he asked after a couple of minutes had passed.

'Yeah, a little.'

'Do you often get like this?'

I wiped my eyes and sat up. He was looking at me with an expression I couldn't quite decode. Pity? Disgust? I told myself that was just the anxiety talking; that right now I was reading too much into it.

'There've been a few panic attacks since I came off the meds. Usually around my period. Nothing this major.'

'I haven't seen you like this before.'

'It happens sometimes. I shouldn't have messaged.'

'Of course you should. I'd hate to think of you going through this on your own.'

'Thanks for coming.'

'Oh, don't worry about that – it's hardly far. But I actually have to go back now; there's a team meeting at two. Will you be okay?'

I tried to smile.

'Yeah. I'm just going to relax.'

'Sorry this is so hard on you. We'll work out a solution together, I promise.'

He kissed me goodbye, grabbed his coat and left. After he'd gone, I slumped back on the pillows. I admired his optimism but my anxiety wasn't something that could be fixed, like a faulty mechanism in a clock. It was like a large snake coiled up inside me, rearing its ugly head again and again.

8

A few days later, my eyes were stinging and I had a headache from watching two rom-coms back to back: *When Harry Met Sally* and *The DUFF*. It's weird how things that make you laugh when you're in a good mood make you feel worse on a bad day. Would I ever be able to fake an orgasm loudly in a diner, showcasing my confidence and sex appeal? Hold my head up high after a cringe viral video? Declare my feelings for someone in a public place if I was unsure of how they felt? No, no and hell no. At the moment, even getting out of bed was proving difficult.

'Sometimes, you have to be kind to yourself,' my last therapist had said. So, today, I'd allowed myself to relax with a movie or two. Now I felt like a useless sack of shit. As I summoned the energy to get up, the thoughts I had been trying to drown out with escapist movies got a whole lot louder.

You should be getting out and meeting people, exploring, keeping fit. Why are you even here? You shouldn't be here. Ryan's starting to get annoyed that you aren't faring better, that's why he wants to hang out with Bjorn and Astrid all the time . . .

The Etruscan shrew has the fastest heartbeat in the world: an average of 1511 beats per minute. Mine must have been going a similar speed because it was beating so fast and giving me such stabbing pains in my chest that I wondered for the umpteenth time if it was possible to die from freaking out. Recognising the beginnings of a panic attack, I wriggled under the covers and concentrated on Calm Breathing. Once I felt more under control, I reached for my phone. There was a message from Nina.

> You've put a lot of pics on Insta recently. I hope you're feeling better! Or are you doing that thing where you post loads to disguise the fact you're feeling like crap? Talk to meeeee xxxxxxx

I looked at my Instagram feed. A photo of me standing outside the shop with a stuffed polar bear in the window. A video of snow whirling in the glow of the porchlight, taken as I smoked on the steps of our apartment. A photo of a mug of hot chocolate with whipped cream, next to a book about Arctic exploration. My life in pictures was exciting. But Nina was right. I'd shut the door on the snow as soon as I'd finished my cigarette, scooped the cream off the hot chocolate (I'd put on a kilo since I'd been here), returned the book to the shelf, and gone back to bed.

Poor Ryan. He'd been so patient. The evening of my panic attack he'd come home from work earlier than usual, his pockets full of chocolate bars from the university vending machine. We were supposed to be going out with Bjorn and Astrid but he'd told them I wasn't well – instead he made hotdogs and we spent the evening cloistered in our room, watching reruns of *Brooklyn Nine Nine*. Even so, I felt like I was pushing it. How much can one guy take? I didn't want to drag him down. But my limbs felt so heavy, and when I sat up, my head started spinning.

Anxiety was something I'd lived with for a decade and a half or more. Back in the days of early puberty and dial-up internet connections, I was allowed fifteen minutes a night online. It was supposed to be for homework, but instead I'd go straight onto MSN Instant Messenger and talk to strangers. Each conversation began the same way: 'A/S/L' – age, sex, location. One day I ended up talking to flirtyunicorn666 (13/f/Pittsburgh). Unlike the other bottom feeders online, she actually had something to say about books and school and movies. We made a date to talk again. She asked me if I wanted to see a pic. Yes, I said. The photo was so slow in loading that each part was revealed in turn. A face. Brown hair in a ponytail, pale skin, braces. Naked shoulders. Then two adolescent boobs. I cancelled the conversation. Then I began to freak out.

I can never talk to her again. What if she tries to talk to me?
I looked at a stranger's boobs. Am I gay? Am I perverted?
Surely people shouldn't be sending such things on the internet?
Surely there's someone who checks all the files being sent? Surely THEY know and will come and find me?

I began to hyperventilate. My vision started to cloud and I got needle-like pains in my chest. I staggered downstairs.

'I think I'm dying,' I told Dad.

Turned out it was just a panic attack.

Cue CBT. Cue anti-anxiety medication that made me feel like a space cadet. Cue a different type of anti-anxiety medication that gave me the shits and hot flushes. In my

55

mid-twenties, they'd put me on an SSRI (aka: Selective Serotonin Reuptake Inhibitor) called Escitalopram – finally, I'd found the one that worked. And cue the theories. The men I dated had plenty of ideas about my mental health that they helpfully loved to share. Loss Of Mother At An Early Age was the most popular.

'To go from such a place of security to one of loss must have really destabilised you,' one ex had said, with the authority of someone who had spent a couple of hours online. At the time I had hotly argued against this perspective, but maybe there was a grain of truth in it. According to Dad, Mum had been The World's Most Perfect Woman. She had read me bedtime stories and made up elaborate pretend games. She was a total whizz in the kitchen. After her death, I hadn't spoken for a fortnight. Thinking about it now made me feel strangely hollow, even though I couldn't remember a thing about her.

I liked to think about how she would handle certain situations if she were still alive. What would she say if I called her now?

'Stay in bed, darling. Don't get up before you're ready.'

Or maybe she would dole out the tough love.

'A walk would do you good. You have to keep busy.'

Tough Love Mum was right. It was important to occupy yourself before you spiralled too far down. But every time I looked out of the window I thought of being lost in the snow and felt my stomach drop. How quickly I'd fallen apart, without my friends and my daily routine. I'd even started having The Dream again.

It's the same every time. I'm on a beach, toes encrusted with sand. Waves break against the rocks around me. Salt spray soaks my clothes. I shiver. The sun burns red, too large for comfort. It sinks down towards the horizon, giving the waves a hellish glow. This doesn't sound like a dream you'd wake from crying. But it is. It's the way it makes me feel, like I've just seen something awful and incomprehensible, and now the world is darker and stranger than before.

Once I googled what dreaming of big waves meant. It means that you're witness to someone else's uncontrollable and turbulent emotions, apparently. Knowing this didn't make matters any clearer as I'm the most emotionally turbulent person I've ever met. But maybe we all think that. I like to imagine that everyone else is freaking out inside their heads too, but I don't know if it's true. I wonder if being able to read minds would make me feel more or less like everybody else.

The front door of the flat banged open. I heard confident footsteps and scrambled out of bed. When Ryan opened the door I was sitting at the desk in front of my laptop.

'Hey Gorge,' he said, kissing me on the forehead. 'Still in PJs?'

'I went for a walk earlier. I got changed when I came back. Just working on my CV.'

He sat down heavily on the bed. I joined him.

'God, I'm exhausted. Almost too tired for the gym.'

'Want to stay in?' I asked hopefully.

'No, I should go. I haven't been all week. Come with me.'

'It's alright, I'm not really feeling it.'

Ryan took his hands in mine and looked me in the eyes. I wondered what he was seeing. A voluptuous, vulnerable woman? Doubtful.

'C'mon, I want to spend time with you. Honestly, you'll feel so much better if you come with. It's all about small steps.'

57

Small steps my arse. It must be at least two hundred steps through pitch darkness in minus twenty. My hair would freeze and so would my snot. And for what? The indignities of the gym. Flesh spilling over my waistband. Thighs wobbling when I ran. Sweat gushing out of every pore after two minutes. Supposedly there were benefits to exercising, but I rarely reaped them.

'I don't think I'm built to exercise.'

'That makes no sense,' Ryan snapped. 'Everyone needs to keep fit.'

I felt my lip tremble.

He sighed.

'Look, I'm sorry. It's been a long day. I just want to let off some steam.'

I had to snap out of this, for both our sakes. With a massive effort, I swung my feet onto the floor. Fought hard with myself and stood up.

'Alright. I'm coming.'

The smile was back.

'Fantastic.'

He planted a lingering kiss on my lips. Then he turned away and started getting ready. I felt a stab of irritation. He had no idea that I'd just scaled a mental mountain.

As we walked to the gym, he told me about his day. About how smart the other guys at work were, how he'd be going out to radio-track polar bears next week. Ryan had followed his passion and I had followed Ryan. He was happy and I just felt lost. I should have thought things through better. Everything had happened so quickly. Friends, a house of my own, a job – it had all disappeared in a blink.

By the time we arrived, I felt like crap. I have strong feelings about gyms at the best of times. The floor-to-ceiling mirrors might be great for narcissists, but everyone else just sees their physical inadequacies reflected back at them. Running away wasn't an option, so I did the next best thing: taking as long as I could in the changing room.

'Your friend says to hurry up,' said a woman with an eight-pack.

Considering most of Longyearbyen's population were young explorer types, this gym was particularly gun and ab-heavy. Ryan was over by the mats, stretching his hamstrings. I joined him, bending over and failing to touch my toes. A fortnight spent mostly in bed had done little for my flexibility. But five minutes later my muscles had begun to warm up, and I was feeling a bit better. So what if I wasn't going to run for miles or start bench-pressing heavy weights? I was proud of myself for getting here at all.

'I'm heading to the running machine, then the weights,' Ryan told me.

'What shall I do?'

'Why don't you start off on the elliptical? Then the rowing machine?'

I climbed up onto the elliptical. From the corner of my eye, I could see Ryan on the running machine, practically sprinting already. He caught my eye in the mirror and smiled. I might not be as sporty as him, but I'd showed up. As I walked, I felt my thoughts settle into a more regular rhythm. The anxiety attack and Ryan's growing impatience made it apparent I needed to get my shit together. People, unlike animals, couldn't hibernate through the winter. As soon as we got home I was going to email Mikkel about that trial shift.

9

I paced around the kitchen as I listened to Ryan's pep talk.

'Honestly, you'll be fine. How many people will be working up there?'

'I'm the only one cooking.'

'That's great. Nobody to boss you around.'

'But I'll be in trouble if something goes wrong.'

'Astrid says Mikkel's really nice.'

'She would. She's so laidback.'

Ryan raised his eyebrows.

'You say it like it's a bad thing.'

'Yeah, well.'

'I don't get it – why are you so upset?'

It was hard for me, in the heat of the moment, to articulate exactly why I was pissed off. So I moved on to something else that was annoying me.

'Did you look for flights to India yet?'

'Even the cheapest costs several thousand, minimum. And I wouldn't be able to take more than a week off work.'

'So you're not coming?'

'I'm sorry, Squidge. I'd love nothing more than to get some sunshine, have a decent curry and see your dad walk down the aisle. But he didn't exactly give a lot of notice.'

'I'm going alone?'

'I can't hold your hand through everything, you know.'

I surprised us both by bursting into tears. By the time Ryan had mopped me up and assured me that he was sorry, he hadn't meant to be so insensitive, he was late for work. He promised he wasn't pissed off, but the speed with which he left indicated otherwise. I needed to give him a break. It wasn't his fault that the tickets were so expensive. And deep down I knew that Dad would prefer to have me there by myself. But I'd slept really badly last night; tossed and turned my way into a fevered nightmare where I'd burned the food up at the cabins.

'You've ruined my pan,' dream-Mikkel had said.

He'd opened the window and forced me out onto a rickety, splintered plank. I took slow, stumbling steps, caught sight of the dark, churning water underneath and experienced a moment of vertigo. Some people dream they have super-powers or look mega-hot. But my dream self was no more agile or attractive than I was. I had fallen, and woken up as my body made contact with the icy water. In the warm darkness of our room I reached for Ryan, snuggling up against him until I calmed down enough to fall asleep.

The doorbell rang, bringing me back to the present.

Feeling distinctly shaky, I grabbed my hefty outdoor anorak and pulled on my boots. I considered telling Mikkel that I was feeling unwell and asking him if we could reschedule, but when I opened the door I saw he was already back in his Jeep, the engine idling.

'Hello, again,' he said, as I opened the door.

The car light illuminated his features. He was younger than I'd initially thought – the beard and unkempt hair made him look decades older. And he definitely looked a lot kinder than he had in the dream. Maybe I wouldn't duck out. After all, the anticipation of doing something was normally way more anxiety-inducing than the thing itself. And since I'd got through the anticipation stage . . .

'You are letting the cold air in.'

'Argh, sorry.'

I climbed into the passenger seat and shut the door. The light in the cab faded. Mikkel drove slowly down the street, past the blocks of student flats and onto the main road that led away from the town.

'I can smoke?' he asked.

'Only if I can.'

'Of course. Have one of mine. In the glove compartment,' he said, pressing the buttons to lower our windows a couple of inches.

I extracted a dented tobacco tin. Inside were a few neatly rolled cigarettes and a lighter. I lit two, and passed him one.

'How do you find it here?' he asked.

We'd left the settlement by now. I could see nothing but the snowflakes whirling in the glow of the headlights.

'It's really good, yeah.'

'I smell bullshit.'

I tried again.

'It's such a unique place, but the darkness is getting to me a bit.'

'Are you employing the classic British understatement?'

I thought about how much I'd cried over the past fort-night.

'Perhaps a little.'

'My good friend is British. When he says he is in a little pain it means he is at death's door. The darkness can cause depression. But it is also a good time to catch up with friends. Less tourists. And the aurora, it is very clear from my cabins, away from the pollutions of the city.'

'How long have you lived here?' I asked, amused that he'd called Longyearbyen a city.

'Thirteen years.'

'Seriously? Wow, how did you . . .' I began, and then tailed off.

'I grew up in Northern Norway. Near your friend Astrid, in fact. It was not so different – my hometown was still in the Arctic Circle. I used to work on the cargo boat between Longyearbyen and Tromsø. Then I heard a tour company was being set up here. I was one of the first guides. The plan was to stay for one year, but the place got under my skin. Takes my breath away sometimes. Nothing better than taking the snowmobile out into the middle of nowhere, stopping the engine, and just listening.'

'Listening to what?'

'Sometimes you can hear the wind or the call of the terns. Sometimes the ice creaking and cracking. Sometimes nothing. You can finally hear yourself think.'

I could hear myself think all the time. Too loudly. The last thing I wanted in my life was silence. My incessant interior monologue would seem even louder in comparison.

'Sounds amazing.'

I thought I had done a better job of emoting this time, but Mikkel just laughed.

'This place will grow on you.'

We carried on driving for a while longer, passing the airport and then winding up a hill. It was the furthest I'd been from

Longyearbyen so far. The headlights picked out a wooden sign that read: End of the Road Cabins.

'Is this really the end of the road?'

'About twenty metres further up that way.'

As we lurched slowly up a snow-covered track, I felt The Schools return. We were getting further and further from civilisation. Would there be running water and central heating? Electricity? A smoking fire and a cast-iron pot in place of a kitchen? I clenched and unclenched my fists in the darkness.

'It's just up ahead,' Mikkel said.

There were some lights in the distance, and as we drew closer I made out the shapes of buildings. A couple of outhouses and some wooden cabins, the windows illuminated with an amber glow.

We stopped and got out.

'That's the main hut. It's where the kitchen is. But first, I show you around.'

He switched on a large torch and gave me a quick tour of the accommodation – ramshackle log cabins with a few bunk-beds and kit lockers in each – the equipment hut, and a basic shower block.

'We have two long-drop toilets, but there is also one with a flush inside the main cabin.'

Then he took me to the dog yard, which was smaller than Astrid's and consequently less noisy.

'Sometimes we go out on the sleds for a few nights and camp on the ice. We will need an expedition chef with us.'

'Um, well, I think . . .'

Then I noticed his lopsided smile.

'Oh. Ha, ha.'

'Ready to cook?'

'Yup.'

I followed him through the door of the main cabin into a large, wooden-panelled room. A few shabby, comfortable-looking sofas and armchairs were clustered around a blazing fire. It was undeniably messy; there was a mezzanine piled high with god knows what, and a long wooden table covered in a mountain of paperwork. An assortment of walking poles, ski goggles, and torches were scattered around the room. Normally, clutter sets my teeth on edge. But in the middle of nowhere, any signs of human habitation were welcome. In Longyearbyen, most restaurants and hotels tried to copy the style of the old trapping cabins, but their imitations came across as something for the tourists. This felt like the real deal.

'Nice place,' I said.

'Well. Let's see what you think of the kitchen.'

In the corner was a doorway covered with a motheaten patchwork blanket. Mikkel pushed it aside and gestured me through.

'Here.'

I looked around the small room. There was an oven with a gas hob. It was a similar model to the one in my first house-share, which had often gone out halfway through cooking. An ancient microwave and a kettle. Beyond that, very little else. Cold, too. I could see my breath. How would I be able to cook anything halfway decent in here?

Mikkel glanced at me.

'I will bring a heater in.'

'Thanks. What would you like me to make?'

'There are some sausages. You could fry them and cook some potatoes.'

'That's all you want?'

He shrugged. 'Do what you want. Use anything in the fridge.'

Fifteen minutes later, I was standing in the kitchen, a portable heater warming the back of my legs. I'd decided Mikkel's suggestion was nowhere near exciting enough. Instead, I'd found half a bottle of cider and a jar of mustard. Sausage stew with mustard mash was on the menu.

I chopped onions with a knife that kept slanting sideways, resulting in an uneven dice. Hopefully nobody would notice. I sliced apples, minced garlic, and started browning the onions in the dented old pan. My worries about coming up here felt laughable. This was a dish I could make in my sleep. Nobody was forcing me to work faster, or making nasty remarks. Having the kitchen to yourself was just like cooking at home. By the time the stew was simmering on the stove, I was in the best mood I'd been in since arriving in the Arctic. I messaged Ryan.

It's going really well. Sorry I was so emo earlier xxx

The sound of deep male voices filtered into the kitchen. A minute later, Mikkel pushed the blanket over the doorway aside.

'How is the food?'

'It's done.'

'Let's serve it in here. Otherwise they will take too much. They are like wolves. You should eat with us.'

'Are you sure?' I said, uneasy at sharing dinner with a horde of slavering males.

'Yes. There is no need to hide away in the kitchen like Cinderella.'

A few minutes later, I was sitting around the table surrounded by men with brawny forearms and ham-coloured faces. They were the type who normally intimidated me, but since I'd sat down they'd been piling on the compliments thick and fast.

'You've saved us. We had spam and burned smileys yesterday. Sucked worse than school dinners,' a young guy with a posh voice said.

'On Monday, Mikkel tried to make spaghetti carbonara. He just chucked a pot of cream over some overcooked pasta, and then added some processed ham. No seasoning, nothing.'

'I am giving you the Arctic experience of hunger and deprivation,' Mikkel told him.

'Yeah, I'm sure all the trappers used to eat shit carbonara when they overwintered,' Posh Kid said.

Mikkel waved a fork at him.

'Watch it, or you will be on kennel-cleaning duty tomorrow.'

I laughed at the look of alarm on his face.

'I'm Adam, by the way. One of the tour guides,' the guy next to me said suddenly. He'd been eating stolidly in silence, and had already scraped his bowl clean.

I turned to face him and saw a burly, dark-haired guy in his late forties.

'I'm Maya. You're from England?'

'Up Yorkshire way. And you?'

'Croydon.'

'I thought I heard a South London twang. So what brings you to the Arctic?'

'My boyfriend. He's here, so I'm here. You know how it goes.'

'Sure,' he said.

'What about you?'

'It's a long story.'

'I'd like to hear it,' I said, smiling at him.

'When I was younger I used to love climbing. The riskier the route, the better. I had quite a serious accident and when I was recovering, there was nothing to do but read. Someone gave me a book about Shackleton's expedition. Fascinating stuff. I started reading all about the Arctic. When I recovered, I knew I had to come here. There's a guiding course at the university. I did that. Then there was a job going at Mikkel's place. Everyone in my cohort applied, but he gave it to me, god knows why.'

'Maybe he fancied you,' one of the guys suggested.

He and his friends burst out laughing.

'No, it was because he had a background in the marines,' Mikkel snapped.

'Do you live up here?' I asked Adam.

He shook his head.

'I rent a flat in town. But I end up staying here most nights.'

'So, Maya, will you be back to cook for us again?' someone asked.

'That depends on Mikkel.'

'Well, *ja*, obviously. But do you want to?'

'Yes,' I said promptly. Who wouldn't accept a job like this? The stakes were low, the hours good, the clientele grateful. 'The only thing is, I'm going to India over Christmas.'

'Don't worry about that. We have two weeks without groups.'

'Are your parents from India?' Adam asked.

'My mum.'

'Do you know how to cook Indian food? I'd kill for a curry.'

I'd learned how to cook a few basic dishes from Nina – tarka dal, saag paneer, aloo gobi – but not as many as I should

68

(Indian food was too labour intensive to bother with, she said, and made her feel like her mother). Left to my own devices I preferred the clean, crisp flavours of the Mediterranean, or Middle Eastern mezzes.

'Not really,' I said.

'I spent my gap yah in India,' Posh Kid said. 'Can you do us masala dosa?'

I looked around at the circle of expectant faces, hesitant to reveal I had no idea what a masala dosa was.

'Sorry. I don't know how.'

'But you cook so well. If I find you a recipe, surely you can follow it?' Posh Kid said.

Following recipes was something I could do. Some students at my college had been renowned for their creative flavour combinations, their innovative use of technique. Not me. My skill had been to follow instructions down to the word, producing exactly what was required. But it had to be the right recipe. Something hearty, warm and spicy to combat the cold. I was sure Uma would be able to point me in the right direction.

'Alright. I'll have a go,' I said. 'But I'll get hold of a recipe myself.'

10

Recipes from professional kitchens were polished, proficient works of art. They detailed precise cooking temperatures, ingredients measured out by the gram. But Uma's recipe was a sketch, not a finished picture. 'Fry onions' was the first instruction. For how long and on what heat? I squinted more closely at the phone screen, searching for comments pencilled in the margins. She'd sent me a photo of a handwritten page. The writing was barely legible, the page splotched with transparent grease stains. 'Butter Chicken', it read at the top.

'It only requires a few different spices, and it's very easy to make. A real crowd pleaser,' Uma had promised, when I'd rung her and Dad to ask for a recipe.

As promised, the only spices required were garam masala, ground cumin, ground coriander and Kashmiri chilli. By a small miracle, I'd brought Kashmiri chilli from the UK – it dyed sauces a rich red colour, but was relatively mild, and I had used it in kitchens a fair amount. However, the recipe gave no quantities for the spices. I'd have to rely on my intuition.

* * *

Over the next hour, I did my best. I fried onions, garlic, and ginger, then added chopped tomatoes. Pureed and strained the mixture. Added a hefty dollop of butter, and a small splash of cream, then honey, to offset the acidity of tomato. Then I focussed on the spicing. At first, I was conservative, adding just a level teaspoon of each. But after tasting the sauce I knew I had to be more generous. I doubled, then tripled the quantities. Sealed the chicken in another pan, then added it to the simmering sauce. You were supposed to eat butter chicken with rotis, but I knew from living with Nina that making them for two people was labour intensive, let alone twelve. Instead, I made rice.

While I was washing up, the doubts crept in. These guys probably knew way more about Indian food than me. I hoped they wouldn't show off their expertise by telling me how 'inauthentic' my butter chicken was. I was taken aback by how under pressure I felt, like I would be letting the side down if I failed. But at least it would be more palatable than the food polar explorers used to eat. I sketched a mental list in an effort to calm down.

Arctic Explorers' Cuisine:

- *Pemmican (otherwise known as corned beef): Everyone who's read an Enid Blyton or an Arthur Ransome book will have heard of it. We had it for school dinners sometimes. Tasted like shit, and this is from someone who grew up eating Dad's cooking.*
- *Biscuits: I'm not talking digestives here. Large, hard discs of flour, fortified with milk protein to increase calories.*
- *Hoosh: A gruel made with melted snow, scraps of meat or seal blood, sometimes thickened with biscuits.*
- *Rock tripe: A type of moss found on rocks. It was how*

*explorers got their vitamin C. But it was very bitter and
often led to indigestion, or the shits.*

- *Their dogs: Hey, desperate times call for desperate measures.*
- *Tinned food: This is what people think Captain Sir John
  Franklin's men died of. In 1845 canning technology was
  pretty new, and the lead cans contaminated the food the
  explorers ate, resulting in delusions, anxiety and paranoia.*
- *Each other: It was likely lead-poisoning-induced madness
  that led to Franklin's team cannibalising each other (see
  above). Or perhaps they were just really hungry.*

My butter chicken suddenly seemed infinitely more appe-
tising, no matter how it turned out. Besides, I hadn't even
tasted it. I needn't be so quick to condemn it. I dipped a
spoon into the sauce and lifted it to my lips. It was rich
with butter, tangy with tomato. I felt a tickle of chilli on
my tongue, tasted the earthy flavours of cumin and garam
masala.

*I'm sitting at a table, surrounded by people I don't recognise.
There's a blue bowl in the middle and I stretch my small hands
towards it. A rumble of laughter, then more chicken is heaped
into my bowl . . .*

Just like that, it was gone.

I froze, spoon still hovering near my lips.

It had only been a few clouded seconds, and yet I felt
profoundly shaken. I tried another spoonful. This time,
nothing happened. I felt hollow with disappointment. Maybe
Ryan would have an explanation.

'Hey Gorge. I thought you were working?' he said, when
he answered the phone.

'I am.'

'Are you alright?'

72

'The weirdest thing just happened. I made this Indian curry and when I tasted it, I had a memory of Bangalore. Of eating dinner with people.'

No sound came out of the receiver.

'Hello? Are you still there?' I asked.

'Yes.'

'So? What do you think the reason for that is?'

'I have no idea.'

'There must be a scientific explanation.'

With Ryan there always had to be.

He cleared his throat.

'I know how much you want to remember, but . . .'

'But it was just my mind playing tricks on me?'

'I didn't say that.'

'You thought it, though.'

'Well . . . you must admit, it sounds kind of far-fetched. What would you say to me if I told you I'd suddenly recalled something from two decades ago through eating a meal?'

'Yeah, I guess.'

'Sorry, Squidge, I didn't mean to upset you.'

'You didn't,' I said, trying my best to inject some positivity into my voice.

'Good. Now, I'll let you get back to work. I'm heading off to the gym.'

'Have fun.'

'You, too.'

I terminated the call, feeling flat. Ryan wasn't the right person to have spoken to. He called himself a rationalist – someone who doesn't and won't entertain the possibility of miracles, aliens or ghosts. I guess it did sound a little far-fetched spoken out loud. I knew what he'd say if I brought it up again: just because two things had happened

73

simultaneously, it didn't mean they were connected. And yet I couldn't shake the feeling that they were.

I took out my phone and messaged Uma.

Where did this recipe come from?

The curtain across the door twitched, and in walked a woman around my height, with short curly hair and a ring in her nose. She was still wearing her outdoor clothes. Ski goggles with gold rims shaped like cogs were perched on top of her head.

'Finally, another woman working here,' she said with an American accent.

'I'm Maya.'

'Rita.'

'So, you work here too?'

'Yeah – I do ad hoc guiding for Mikkel. I came to see if you needed help serving up.'

'That'd be great, thanks.'

We piled the bowls high with generous servings of chicken and rice, then carried them out to the table.

I sat down next to Rita and watched as everyone tucked into their food. When I tried mine, no memory came back. Perhaps, as Ryan so clearly believed, I'd imagined it.

'Delicious,' Adam said.

'It is better than I thought it would be,' said Mikkel, who was sitting next to him.

'God, it's so nice to taste something with a bit of spice,' Rita said.

'Hey Rita, where are you from?' one of the guys asked.

'I was born in Montana, but then I moved to New York. My mom's Puerto Rican, though – that's what you're getting at, right?'

He nodded, unembarrassed.

'When did you move over here?' I asked her.

'Just over two years ago now. I did the same course as Adam, then stayed on to work.'

'And you went on your mission,' Mikkel added.

'Your mission?'

'Yeah, a couple of us took a boat to the north of Svalbard and then skied all the way back to Longyearbyen. We camped in tents and old trappers' huts when we could find them. It was fucking epic.'

'Sounds it,' I said.

'Have you been out exploring much?' she asked me.

I shook my head. 'I can't use a rifle, and to be honest, I'm finding the darkness a bit overwhelming.'

'We need to teach her to shoot,' Mikkel said to Adam, who nodded.

'You'll get used to it in no time,' Rita said. 'But until you do, there's some decent bars to check out. We should go out for a drink together sometime.'

'Thanks,' I said gratefully. Rita looked like she'd be a laugh to hang out with.

Adam had already finished his food.

'I'll drive you home this evening, Maya,' he said. 'And Rita, you can grab a lift too, if you don't fancy going on the snowmobile.'

'Yeah, that'd be great.'

'I thought you would stay here tonight,' Mikkel said to him.

'I need to do my washing.'

'We have a washing machine up here.'

Rita rolled her eyes.

'Not a dryer, though. Besides, I need a decent night's sleep,' Adam said.

'Well, alright,' Mikkel said, somewhat begrudgingly.

By the time I was done eating and washing up, I was feeling exhausted. I was looking forward to getting home and curling up in my bed with my Kindle – for the first time in ages, it felt deserved. I dried my hands and reached for my phone, noticing that Uma had replied to my earlier message.

It was your ma's.

I felt my breath catch in my throat. Without realising it, I had cooked one of my mum's dishes. I'd known she loved to cook but Dad had never mentioned that she'd written any recipes down. Heart pounding, I typed a reply.

Are there any more?

11

Uma had sent me a second of Mum's recipes – chicken biryani. Standing in the cabin kitchen, I looked down at the photo for the umpteenth time. Mum's handwriting fascinated me. I'd even gone to the extent of trying to analyse it on an internet graphology site. The letters were small, suggesting she was an introvert, and slanted to the right, which meant she was sentimental and valued friends and family. But I could go no further than that because her script was curiously uneven. Some letters were connected and others weren't, the pressure varied, as did the size of the loops in both the upper and lower zone. Telling myself graphology was a load of rubbish didn't stop me from feeling disappointed.

A biryani was made by marinating chicken in spices, cooking it in yoghurt, and layering half-cooked rice on top. Then everything was left to steam and infuse. Although it sounded easy in theory, the recipe was harder to follow than the one for butter chicken; the writing had faded in places, and the instructions were vague. There had also been a couple of issues with the ingredients. Mikkel hadn't been able to find fresh mint at the supermarket, and instead of basmati he'd bought cheap, 'easy cook' rice. The final result was a saucepan full of claggy, watery rice, pieces of anaemic chicken bobbing in it like drowning men. Tasting it transported me nowhere.

'Why do you look so upset?' Mikkel asked me, when we were eating.

'The food went wrong.'

'Tastes okay to me.'

'It's a really unusual risotto,' Adam said. 'I love how you've put some Indian flavours in there.'

'Actually, it's biryani.'

'Oh. Sorry.'

Throughout the meal I tried my best to laugh along with the others, but I couldn't shake the disappointment. I knew I could have done better. It was only when I was alone, doing the washing up, that I realised why I was so upset. By being unable to cook Mum's recipe, I felt like I'd done her and her memory a disservice. Perhaps I could get some tips from Uma when I visited.

My phone buzzed. A message from Ryan.

Hey Gorge, I'm going to find the northern lights with Bjorn and Astrid. Look out for them! Forecast tonight = gr8 xx

Why hadn't he told me about it earlier? Did he *want* to go without me? I pushed the thought from my head. Ryan wouldn't do anything like that – the three of them had just made spontaneous plans together. I wished he'd thought to invite me, though. They could have driven up this way and picked me up as they passed.

Have fun!!!!xxxx I replied.

It wouldn't do to moan about it. He'd heard enough complaints from me over the past few weeks.

I returned to the living room. A couple of the guys were playing cards at the table. Adam and Mikkel were sitting on the sofa; Adam was reading, while Mikkel was knitting a russet scarf with a dark blue trim, half-moon glasses perched on his craggy nose.

'That's a nice-looking scarf,' I said.

'My godmor taught me. I loved knitting when I was a child but then I grew up and was embarrassed. Now I am too old to care. You must have something to do over winter.'

'I think it's pretty cool. It shows you aren't worried about your image.'

'Nobody could accuse him of that,' Adam said.

'So that's why you do it, Mikkel? To get the chicks?' one of the lads said.

'Definitely,' Mikkel told him, exchanging an amused glance with Adam.

The scarf was piled up around them and I noticed that their thighs were touching pretty hardcore underneath it.

Mikkel looked up at me.

'Finished?'

'All done.'

'They're all going into town for drinks. They've hired a minibus taxi that'll be here in twenty minutes. You can get a lift in,' Adam said.

'Great, thanks.'

I suddenly felt like a third wheel.

'I'm just going out for a cigarette,' I said.

Mikkel stood up. 'I will come.'

'Mikkel . . .' Adam said.

'Yes, Adam?' Mikkel replied, in a tone that brooked no argument.

Adam frowned, and returned to his book.

We exhaled clouds of smoke that drifted out of the floodlit porch and into the darkness.

'So, how long have you been together?' I asked.

Mikkel glanced sidelong at me.

'What?'

'You and Adam.'

'How did you know?'

'I just guessed. Is it a secret?'

'No. But don't tell anyone. We try to be professional, that's all. Rita knows.'

His voice had become deeper, rougher. I wondered if he was embarrassed. If you wanted to know something about someone, being pushy didn't help. But if you went quiet they felt compelled to fill the silence. I took a drag of my cigarette. A dog howled. I could hear the buzz of a radio from one of the huts and someone singing tunelessly along.

'It has been about one year.'

'Great you managed to find love all the way up here.'

'Not love,' Mikkel said sharply.

'Oh, sorry.'

'He wants me to quit smoking. Get a shave and a haircut.'

'I'm with him on that one,' I admitted. 'You have a nice face. And smoking is bad for your health. Maybe you could try it out? After all, relationships are about compromise. I mean, look at me. I left my job, my friends, and came out here with my partner, Ryan.'

'But that is not a compromise at all.'

'Oi. Mothers' meeting! Turn out the lights and get over here!' someone yelled.

'Why?' Mikkel bellowed back.

'It's the Northern Lights!'

'I will get Adam.'

He went inside. Seconds later, the lights around the encampment went out. I stepped out of the porch and craned my neck upwards.

'Wow,' I said, to nobody in particular.

The sky was beautifully clear. Above me hung thousands of stars and a bright gibbous moon. As my eyes adjusted, I made out a dim green ribbon of light. It flickered across the sky, becoming rapidly brighter. Soon it was joined by other colours – sinuous threads of purple and blue that rippled across the darkness.

'What a sight,' said a voice behind me.

I turned. Adam and Mikkel were sitting on the bottom steps of the porch, gazing upward. I experienced a sudden longing for Ryan. The Northern Lights would be nice to watch with a partner, like fireworks. We had gone to a show last year; Ryan standing behind me, arms circling my waist. But now he was miles away in the darkness. That was my fault, for wanting to stay in all the time. Once I got back from India I'd try harder. Join the others on their skiing trips. Stop moaning about the weather. Maybe, when it got warmer, we could even take a snowmobile out by ourselves. I knew Ryan would appreciate it if I made an effort.

I took a deep breath and turned my attention back to the aurora, watched the ribbons of light as they danced across the sky. They were so beautiful they seemed impossible, and I realised why years and years ago early humans thought they must have signified the presence of another world right next to this one; a world visible in glimpses, but never accessible. My spirits lifted as the lights intensified. Suddenly, I was hit by a moment of unreality. It had been a difficult month. But I had come through the other side and now I was sitting here, watching this. Maybe the Arctic wasn't so bad after all.

Part Two

Part Two

12

I barely slept on the flight to Bangalore. My mind whirred chaotically as I went over what I knew about India, garnered from conversations with Dad, and Nina, and the Bollywood movies she sometimes forced me to watch. Population: around 1.38 billion. Divided in 1947. Known for its love of cricket, huge variety of spices and the world's highest mountains. Fetishised by white middle class hippies for its religious festivals, temples, ashrams, and full moon parties. These half-formed fragments only made me realise how little I knew and I felt sick with nerves at the thousands of possible mistakes I could make. Would I be able to fit in if I stayed completely quiet and wore the indigo kurta Nina had given me? Or would people know that I didn't belong? If only I hadn't left it so long. If only Dad had ignored my resistance as a teenager and taken me back for a visit. But I guess we'd both had our reasons, ones which had magnified and distorted with every passing year.

Wherever I lived, I kept the same framed photograph of my family on the bedside table.

Dad, gangly in an ill-fitting suit, and Mum wearing an embroidered skirt and a red cropped blouse, revealing a body I wished I'd inherited, with an itty-bitty waist and curvy hips. They looked like they were from different worlds. Or they would have done without me standing between them, my skin darker than Dad's but lighter than Mum's; her same eyes and his same nose on my face. I had run my thumb over her face so many times the glass had smudged and blurred her features.

I wished I could remember something about her. I couldn't even remember the process of forgetting. All I knew about Mum was what Dad told me.

Things Dad told me about Mum:
- *She grew up in Delhi and had been all set to marry her childhood sweetheart, but the groom's family suddenly broke off the engagement. Because he was part of her community, she had to see him at every social gathering, and it was so awkward she went to live with her aunt in Bangalore until shit died down. Big mistake. She got a job as a stenographer at an import-export firm, where she met Dad. He was there on a six-month placement. Little persuasion was required for him to stay.*
- *According to Dad, Mum loved animals. Especially the local street dogs. Every week she went to the market and picked up some bones and other offcuts. She'd cook them with rice to make doggy-ani (biryani for dogs), then she'd take out a huge vat of it and feed all of the twenty-odd dogs in the street.*
- *Mum was posh – before she got practically disowned for marrying Dad, that is – and she'd never cooked until she came to Bangalore. But when she found herself craving her*

86

childhood food, she got her aunt to teach her the Punjabi
classics. She slowly became accustomed to South Indian
food and started picking up recipes from neighbours and
friends. Then Dad started telling her about the stuff he
grew up eating, dishes that he missed, and she would try
and recreate them according to his descriptions. 'They were
never the same, but sometimes they were even better. Once,
my mother came to visit and brought some dried pasta.
Your mum cooked spaghetti Bolognese. It tastes so much
better with a hefty kick of chilli,' he said once, misty-eyed.

Mum died soon before her fortieth birthday. It was a traffic accident. They're really common in Indian cities. She'd gone out to get us kebab rolls for supper, Dad said, and never came back. We've both spent a lot of time wishing we'd opted for a home-cooked meal that night.

These were the memories I armed myself with as the plane began its descent into Bangalore. There was none of the nervous excitement I'd experienced on the journey to Longyearbyen; just a sick, wrenching anxiety.

I often repeat facts in my head to help me calm down (yeah, I know it's probably a safety behaviour, but nobody's perfect) so I began going through my list again.

India is the second most populous country in the world after China.

India is the second most populous country in the world after China.

It's home to the wettest town in the world, Cherrajpunjee.

It's home to the wettest town in the world, Cherradge-pun-gee.

Hell, I didn't even know how to pronounce it.

I fought back the nausea and the fatigue as I shuffled off

the plane. At immigration, I joined the foreigners' queue. As I handed my passport to the official, I got a mild case of The Schools. I'd never used my Overseas Citizenship of India Card before and had a sudden image of being turned away at the border.

'Maya . . . Reed-Kaur?'

'That's right.'

He smirked, scrutinised my passport for far longer than seemed necessary, and finally handed it back.

The first thing I noticed when I stepped outside was the warmth. Five thirty in the morning and I was comfortable in leggings and a thin jumper. The air was smokier than Longyearbyen, sweeter, too; the dusty fragrance of concrete cooling overnight. I scanned the sea of people leaning against the barrier and it wasn't long before I saw Dad, waving frantically. My stomach unclenched a little at the sight of him.

'Dad!'

I threw my arms around him, like a little kid.

'How was your flight, love?' he asked, gently unclasping me.

'I'm glad to get off the plane.'

'You must be desperately tired. Let's get you home. Uma went to get some tea.'

We walked past brightly lit food stands and crossed the road, passing the taxi stand where groups of people were queuing for cars with trolleys heaped high with luggage. I wondered what country they'd visited and where they were going now.

'You'll like Uma's flat,' Dad said. 'The guest bedroom has a fan but no AC – I hope you won't be too hot.'

He was nervous, I realised.

'It'll be absolutely fine,' I said.

More than anything, I wanted to support Dad; I had no intention of flying off the handle like a stroppy teenager.

Uma was standing next to the car, sipping from a small paper cup. She was wearing an oversized woollen hat and a gilet, and looked much smaller than she had on Skype.

'Hi,' I said awkwardly.

'Maya!' she said, hugging me. 'You must be freezing.'

'Not really. It's about minus fifteen in Svalbard at the moment.'

Uma cried out loud as if wounded.

'How do people even survive in that temperature?'

'Beats me why anyone would want to go and live in such inhospitable conditions,' Dad said.

I noted the subtle diss at Ryan, but decided to ignore it.

We got into the car and Uma drove us out of the airport. Dawn was only just beginning to lighten the sky, but the roads were already busy. Vehicles streamed around us, headlights blazing and horns blaring. There were no lanes – everyone was edging forward into any available space as if they were actively seeking death. On either side of the roads, high-rise apartments sprouted upwards like mushrooms. Some were still in the process of being built, forming spectral shapes in the early morning mist. I suddenly felt flat and bone weary. I wasn't sure what I'd expected to find, but it wasn't this.

'I don't recognise anything.'

'None of this was here when you were growing up. There was a different airport then, located on the outskirts of the city. Now, those outskirts are in the middle of the city,' Dad said.

'When you lived here, there were a million people. Now there are twelve million,' Uma said. 'Wait until you see the traffic in the morning.'

'After you get some rest, the three of us can go to lunch,' Dad said. 'There are some fantastic new restaurants here. Every type of food you could think of – Goan, Italian, Japanese.'

'Can't wait,' I replied faintly.

My head was starting to ache. Tiredness had finally eclipsed anxiety and all I cared about was finding a comfortable bed as fast as possible. I closed my eyes and began to drift . . .

'Maya?'

I opened my eyes.

'We're here, sweetheart.'

Uma had pulled up outside an apartment block with a pastel-pink façade. A balcony on the ground floor dripped with plants casting sinuous shadows across the walls. I followed Dad and Uma through a lobby painted a punishing shade of brown, and into a rickety lift. My body sagged in relief when we finally entered the apartment.

'Here's the guest bedroom,' Uma said, indicating the first door.

'Do you mind if I just go to bed?' I mumbled.

'Of course not.'

I found myself in a room with two single beds, white walls and a marble floor. The curtains were sea-green and so were the blankets. On the floor was a rug woven in an abstract pattern of turquoise, blue and white. I caught sight of my travel-rumpled appearance in the mirror.

'Something to eat or drink?' Uma asked from the doorway.

'Just water, please.'

I brushed my teeth and washed my face in a haze. By the time I came back into the bedroom there was a glass on the bedside table and the ceiling fan had been switched on. I collapsed into bed and pulled the covers up to my chin. For a moment I experienced the surreal panic that comes from finally being *here*, in the place you've anticipated arriving at for years. I had pictured narrow gullies, women wearing colourful dresses, clouds of orange dust. Instead, I'd been faced with a darkened highway surrounded by construction sites. Maybe tomorrow I'd see more of the Bangalore I expected to find. For now, though, any hopes of feeling at home had been dashed. I had disembarked in a place that looked and sounded completely foreign to me. But although disappointing, it was not unexpected. Overwhelmed by tiredness, I closed my eyes. The whirring of the fan blades quickly lulled me to sleep.

13

I woke up to a patch of drool on the pillow. Light flooded through the crack in the curtains. Opening them, I looked out at the apartment block opposite. The walls gleamed in the bright sun, a sight which made me curiously emotional. Never again would I take daylight for granted. I opened the window and stuck my hand outside, feeling the warm air caress my skin.

There was a knock on the door and I withdrew my arm.

'Come in.'

Dad stood in the doorway, holding a cup of tea.

'You'll let mosquitos in. Put the netting across.'

I shut the window and took the cup he held out to me. 'Thanks. What time is it?'

'Midday. Uma's just on the phone to a client. We were thinking of going out for lunch afterwards.'

'Sure. I'll just take a shower.'

'You need to wait for the geyser to heat up,' he said, leading me towards the bathroom.

'What's a geyser?'

'An electric water heater. There's no mains hot water. This is the switch. It should take about twenty minutes.'

While I was waiting, Dad gave me a tour of the apartment. It was similar to the room I'd slept in; white walls, dark-wood furniture and pale marble floors. There were books in piles on tables and lining the shelves. The soft furnishings pulsated with colour and texture. There were ornately detailed rugs. Hand-dyed cushions. Shimmering wall hangings. Each room had a different palette – earth tones in the living room, pale blue and indigo in their bedroom.

We returned to the living room – I sat down on the sofa and Dad took the armchair opposite. I sipped my cooling tea, which was sweeter than I was used to but bloody delicious.

'So, what do you think of the apartment?'

'It's gorgeous,' I said. 'But don't you miss having a garden?'

Dad's garden had been his pride and joy. Although it was small, he'd been able to squeeze in a vegetable bed where he grew potatoes, leeks, chard and peas. Next to the fence was a wildflower border of thistles, cornflowers and poppies. There was just enough space on the patio for a small picnic bench where he read the newspaper on summer mornings.

'Sometimes you lose something to gain something else,' he said.

'Or someone,' I said, jerking my head at the closed door of Uma's office. I could hear her talking rapidly in a language I didn't know, or knew once and had forgotten.

'I hope you aren't too uncomfortable with the situation,' Dad said.

'If you're happy, I'm happy.'

'I'm looking forward to you getting to know Uma. She's

such a fascinating woman. When I first met her she was so timid, but since her husband passed she's really blossomed.'

'That says a lot about her first marriage.'

Dad shot me a look which I translated as 'we shall not be discussing this any further' and promptly changed the subject.

'Tell me how you've been finding it in Longyearbyen.'

I paused, wondering how to phrase it without worrying him

'It's been a lot to get used to. Especially the darkness. And the snow. I guess I'd taken my ability to leave the house for granted.'

'I can imagine. It's such an inhospitable environment out there. I don't know what Ryan was . . .' He tailed off. 'How is Ryan, anyway? I hope he's looking after you.'

'Yeah, of course he is,' I said, leaping to his defence. 'But, I mean, I can look after myself. I'm a grown woman.'

'Of course you are darling, I just meant—'

At that moment, the study door opened. Uma stood in the doorway, wearing blue linen trousers and a loose, patterned shirt.

'Hi Maya. Did you sleep well?' she asked me.

'Yes, fine thanks. How's your day going?'

'Good so far – John, I think I've found a new supplier.'

'That's fantastic news.'

'What do you do?' I asked her.

'See if you can guess.'

She gestured me into her study, which overflowed with a cascading mess of fabric samples and lengths of cloth. A cork noticeboard buckled under the weight of the paper pinned onto it.

'Dressmaking?'

'I did a dressmaking course, but now I've expanded into sourcing and exporting textiles. Your pa is helping me with that.'

'But you don't know anything about textiles,' I said to Dad.

'He helps in other ways. He's a specialist in distribution and customs,' Uma said proudly.

'Uma's the creative brains of the outfit, and I'm just the grunt guy.'

'Next year we'll travel to the villages, meeting weavers and dyers. Buy direct, give them fair pay. And, of course, we'll learn a lot about all the different patterns and crafting techniques,' Uma told me, her face alive with enthusiasm.

Dad looked at her like he couldn't quite believe his luck. It was so unusual to see such naked emotion on his face that I felt embarrassed and looked away.

Half an hour later, we stepped outside. The street was stippled with sunlight that filtered down through the oversized trees in the park next door. A pack of lean dogs sunned themselves on the pavement. As we walked, the street became dustier and noisier. New apartments were being built on either side, dwarfing a couple of older bungalows. One of the bungalows looked abandoned; its red paint was blackened with age, and weeds thrust through the cracks in its stonework.

'A developer will buy it up and turn it into a block of flats before long,' Uma said.

'I would love a bungalow to restore,' Dad replied. 'Think of the garden – it would be such an oasis in a city like this.'

'Well, when you sell . . .' Uma began, and then fell silent.

I pretended I hadn't heard.

We turned onto a busier road. Horns blared, music

pumped from bars and restaurants. Neon signs offered cheap beer and buffet lunch deals. A group of teenage girls tottered across the road in heels, narrowly avoiding rickshaws and motorbikes. On the other side of the street, a barefoot woman thrust a bunch of roses at two men passing her, trying to get them to buy one. They gently detached themselves and carried on walking.

'Here we are,' Uma said.

We'd arrived in front of a narrow, white-walled restaurant. Inside was equally plain, with unadorned walls and two rows of wooden tables packed closely together. There were very few customers. I looked dubiously at Dad.

'This is Bangalore's best kept secret,' he said.

The man at the reception counter visibly brightened when we entered. So did the waiter, who hurried over to our table with a menu.

'Don't feel rushed, Maya. You choose what you want,' Dad said.

Menus are a source of fascination to me. This one was particularly interesting, and I got totally caught up in reading it. Friends sometimes got irritated by how long I took choosing what to eat, but Uma and Dad were busy talking floral arrangements and didn't seem to care, so I took my sweet time. Eventually I ordered three kebab starters: peppered lamb, fish tikka and murgh peshwari, which the menu told me was chicken marinated in cashew nut paste, cheese and cream. For mains I selected dal makhani – black lentils cooked with butter and cream, and palak paneer, cubes of cheese simmered in a spinach gravy.

'Let's get some roomali rotis too. They're a speciality here,' Uma said.

'That sounds good to me.'

'Your ma loved dal makhani and palak paneer,' she continued, once the waiter had left.

'I've tried them in the UK.'

'They're Punjabi foods, like butter chicken. How did the recipe turn out, by the way?'

'Pretty good, I think. I had the impression I'd eaten it before. Something close to a flashback, in fact.'

'It was your favourite,' Dad said. 'You ate it so often that I'm unsurprised you remembered the taste.'

'Was it served in a blue bowl?' I asked.

The two of them glanced at each other, and then back at me.

'Your mother had a blue ceramic bowl she used quite a lot,' Dad said. 'Did you remember anything beyond that?'

I shook my head. And then it was my turn to be confused – the expression on Dad's face seemed to indicate he was relieved.

'How did the biryani turn out?' Uma asked.

'Not so well. Very soggy. Can we cook more of Mum's recipes?'

After a quick glance at Dad, Uma agreed.

'What's this new interest in Indian food for, anyway? You never wanted to cook it when you were younger,' Dad asked.

It was true. Despite his best efforts, I hadn't wanted to learn. As a teenager, my experience of Indian food was limited to a friend's mum's scorching curries, Dad's shoddy attempts and the oil-drenched offerings from the local takeaway. But mainly I had been too worried that the smell would get into my clothes and everyone would take the piss. I had heard it happen at school, although of course you didn't need to *actually* smell of anything for someone to start spreading a rumour about you.

'It seems like I'm not the only one whose interest in India has been rekindled,' I said. 'Now you two are getting married, will you stay here or move back to England?'

'Uma doesn't like England very much.'

'So cold. So much rain. The people were so rude. Everything so expensive.'

'When did you visit?'

'Last year, to see your pa.'

That's why he'd been so evasive when I'd asked him how long the relationship had been going on. Why had he waited until he was literally packing up to move before mentioning it? I glared at him, but he was looking down at his napkin like it was the most fascinating thing on the planet.

The arrival of the kebabs prevented a showdown. I hadn't eaten since yesterday and got distracted by the steaming plates piled high with pieces of chargrilled chicken, lamb, and fish, accompanied with thinly sliced raw onion, and small pots of mint chutney. I managed to restrain myself long enough to send a photo to Adam, who wanted to know all about the food I'd be trying. I groaned out loud as I took my first bite of fish tikka.

'I don't remember the last time I tasted fish this tender. And the spicing's so complex.'

'Try the chicken,' Uma urged.

I needed no second bidding. I tucked into pieces of chicken thigh, tenderised by the indulgent, creamy paste they'd been coated in, and peppery lamb, the fat perfectly caramelised. Then the waiter carried in the main course: metal curry dishes containing dal drizzled with cream, generous chunks of paneer in a vibrant green sauce. It easily outstripped the versions I'd tried in England; the dal was rich and buttery, while the soft cheese was perfectly complemented by the smooth, slightly bitter spinach gravy. I copied the way Uma and Dad ate, scooping up mouthfuls with pieces of paper-thin roomali roti. Afterwards, I leaned back in my chair and discreetly undid the top button of my trousers.

'We need dessert,' Uma said.

'I don't think we do,' I replied, rubbing my distended stomach.

'What about a kulfi? There's a stand just down the road.'

Uma was persuasive. Ten minutes later, we were standing at a small kiosk on the side of a very busy road. I was beginning to sweat in the afternoon heat. When I was handed a kulfi, I unwrapped it eagerly. A cold, creamy burst of sweetness on my tongue. Flavours of pistachio and cardamom.

My kulfi's melting on the floor. Ants are beginning to scurry over the surface, but I don't care. I have to pick it up before it melts. I bend down. A hand on my shoulder. I look up to see an older boy, silhouetted against the bright sun. He shakes his head. I begin to cry. Then he squats down next to me, and hands me the kulfi he's been holding.

I almost dropped the kulfi again.

'Are you okay?' Dad asked.

'Yeah . . . it's just, I think I've tried this before. When I was younger. And I dropped it. But some kid gave me his.'

'You've remembered that just now?' Dad asked.

I nodded.

Again, that quick glance between the two of them.

'That's fantastic,' Uma said, sounding slightly strained.

'Who was the boy, do you think?'

'Jobin, perhaps. He was very kind to you,' Dad said.

'The son of our friends, Saji and Theresa,' Uma added.

'How odd. I wonder why I didn't remember Mum?'

'I have no idea,' Dad said.

I glanced at him in surprise. You'd think he'd be more excited about the whole situation.

'Come on, let's walk home,' Uma said.

As we stood by the side of the road, waiting to cross, the kulfi began to melt, dripping down my hand and onto the ground.

14

'I can't believe I'm not with you for the Big Comeback,' Nina moaned.

'Dude, I'm not an ageing pop band. It's not that big a deal,' I said.

'Yeah, it is. So how are you finding it?'

'It's different to how I imagined. A lot busier. Everyone goes on about India being so colourful, but I don't know, it's not?'

She laughed. 'Well, it's not like "Hymn for the Weekend" with Holi every day or anything. I guess "colourful" is more a state of mind. There's so much life there.'

I walked over to the window, phone against my ear. A crow was perching on the balcony opposite, cawing noisily. A woman came outside and scattered some leftover rice across the wall. The crow started eating greedily and I saw her lips move as she spoke to it.

'I think I know what you mean,' I said. 'But I feel self-conscious all the time, like everyone's looking at me.'

'They probably are,' Nina replied.

'Thanks.'

'No, not like that. But India's a contact culture, so standing close to people or looking at someone when you're curious about them isn't considered rude. And Britain's a non-contact culture, which is why it feels jarring.'

'That makes sense.'

'What have you been doing there?'

'Wedding errands, mostly.'

'Well, you'll see colour at your dad's wedding, alright. How's Muscles?'

'You know I hate it when you call Ryan that.'

'Yup,' Nina said unrepentantly.

'But yeah, we're okay. I haven't spoken to him properly since I've been here because of the time difference, but we've scheduled a Skype for later. What about you – did you ask out the guy from work?'

'Amir? Yeah, I did. He's cool. We've been on a couple of dates and no awful personality traits have emerged yet.'

'Oh good; I'm glad.'

'I'm trying not to get overexcited. You know how these things fizzle out.'

I heard the Skype ringtone coming from my computer speakers.

'Listen, Nina. I have to go. Ryan's calling – I think he got the time difference wrong.'

'Oh, misters before sisters, is it?'

'C'mon, it's not like that. I'll call you later?'

'I'll be washing my hair.'

'Bye, Nina.'

I accepted Ryan's call. He was sitting at the desk in our bedroom and the curtains were open, revealing thick slabs of darkness. I repressed a shudder.

'Hey Squidge. It's nice to see your face,' he said.

I leaned forwards. 'I miss you. I feel like we haven't spoken in ages.'

'It's my fault. Work's been busy, and I've been really going for it in the gym. How've you been? What do you think of your new stepmother?'

'She's sweet. And she's making a real effort to get to know me.'

'That's good. I told you it would be fine. So, have you been feeling anxious?'

'Actually, no, not really. I've been enjoying it – we've been eating out lots. The food's amazing!'

'My friend came back from India raving about the street food.'

'I haven't tried much street food yet. Just kulfi – an Indian ice cream. And actually, when I did, it happened again.'

'What did?'

'When I tried the kulfi, I had a memory of eating one in the past, and dropping it on the floor. Some little kid gave me his. I think I knew him.'

'Really?'

'Yeah, and Uma and Dad had the oddest reaction. They didn't seem pleased at all . . .' I trailed off. Ryan wore the same expression he would if someone brought up crystal healing or acupuncture.

'Don't you believe me?' I asked.

'I've never heard of this happening before.'

'You'd have no problem reading about this in a psychology paper, but when I say it you're immediately sceptical.'

He shifted in his seat.

'Aw, come on, Gorge. Fine, I believe you. I just worry . . .'

'Worry about what?'

'I don't want you to read too much into this, and then get disappointed if you can't remember anything more. And the stuff with your dad and Uma – I'm sure that's your anxiety making more of the situation.'

'So you're calling me paranoid?'

He sighed.

'I didn't mean it. I just want you to enjoy your trip.'

'I will,' I snapped.

We both fell silent. My head was beginning to throb. I'd been so excited to hear from him but the conversation I wanted to have had escaped us, swerving out of control until it somehow became the beginnings of a quarrel that neither of us could remember arriving at. I needed to steer things back to safer waters.

'How's the Arctic?' I asked.

'There was an amazing aurora display the other night. And there are reports that a polar bear came into the town. I didn't get a chance to see it, unfortunately.'

'Good. I don't want you getting mauled to death while I'm gone.'

Ryan laughed. 'I'll still be here when you get back. Any plans for Christmas?'

'I don't know. We haven't discussed it.'

'You know it's tomorrow, right? We've been planning it all week.'

'We?'

'Me and Astrid. A traditional Norwegian Christmas dinner, then out on the snowmobiles for a night ride. And a party later.'

He said it with such excitement I felt a twisting sensation in my stomach.

'Bjorn's going too, right?'

'No. He's gone home for Christmas. I think he's back a couple of days after you.'

'So it's just you two?'

'No, there'll be a few other people – some of her mates, a few of the guys at the lab, and god knows who at the party.'

'Oh nice. It sounds fun,' I said.

'Yeah. It should be. Although it would be more fun if you were here.'

He smiled and I suddenly found myself wishing I was there with him too.

'Anyway, listen, I need to get on. Do you mind?'

'No, not at all. But we'll chat soon?'

'Obviously,' he said, blowing me a kiss.

After he'd hung up, I wondered what exactly he'd had to head off for. The gym, perhaps. But when I checked online, I saw it was closed on Christmas Eve. Maybe he was going out for drinks with people. Or, worse, he'd prefer to be chilling out alone in our room than talking to me. There were 4954.193 miles between Bangalore and Longyearbyen, but it suddenly felt like we were further apart than that.

I heard laughter, and padded down the corridor to the living room to investigate. Dad had wrapped himself in a long length of gauzy fabric and both he and Uma were in fits. When they saw me, they stopped what they were doing, looking up at me like guilty children.

'I'm trying on Uma's wedding outfit,' Dad explained, rapidly unwinding the fabric. His sparse hair was standing on end; Uma smoothed it down for him.

'You look very pretty,' I said.

'Darling, are you alright?'

'Yeah, I've been talking to Ryan.'

'Did you argue?' Uma asked.

I shook my head.

'I'm fine. Everything's fine.'

Ryan was probably right. It was just my anxiety getting the better of me – I was reading too much into their reactions, and into his.

15

We'd been stuck in traffic for what felt like hours, on the way home from another wedding-related errand. The air conditioning in Uma's car was faulty so I cranked open the windows and inhaled a lungful of warm, particulate-laced air. At least there was plenty to look at. In front of us, a woman in a burka cut a red light on her bicycle, narrowly avoiding the traffic streaming towards her. The motor scooter next to me wobbled under the weight of a family of four. Men swarmed the pavements outside a tea stall, drinking from paper cups and smoking cigarettes, while school kids queued for chaat sold by a street vendor from a tin pail. I felt ashamed to be looking at a place I had once called home with the eyes of a foreigner, finding differences not similarities. How long before the unfamiliar became familiar again? Or had the connection been severed irreparably?

I had no idea where I would fit in this frantic, sprawling city. It felt like someone's eyes were always on me. Despite what Nina had told me about India being a contact culture, I still felt intensely self-conscious. That was what I missed most about the UK, I realised suddenly – the lack of stares. I could go about my day, buying groceries and catching the bus to work, without drawing attention to myself, simply because I knew how things worked. Most of the time, at least.

Still, the food alone had been worth the trip. The highlight of each day was the snacks we grabbed between our appointments with tailors, florists, and caterers. Today we'd bought coconuts from a street corner vendor. They were large and green, full to the brim with liquid so fresh it zinged. After we'd finished, the vendor chopped the coconut in half so we could scoop out its tender, viscous flesh. For lunch I had masala dosa, a crispy rice and lentil pancake stuffed with a spiced potato mixture, eaten with coconut chutney and sambar. Later, we'd sat in a concrete courtyard shaded by Banyan trees and had dahi papdi chaat – deep-fried rounds of dough liberally covered in raw onions, crunchy sev, yoghurt, tamarind chutney and fresh coriander. I was taken aback by the complexity and depth of flavour. But no new memories had been revealed. Perhaps this was because Mum hadn't often cooked South Indian food.

'Alright back there?' Dad asked.

He was driving. Aside from a dicey moment where we'd got stuck at a gnarly junction for ten minutes, he was coping pretty well with the traffic.

'A bit hot.'

'Maya can stay back tomorrow. Or we can take her to the club for a swim,' Uma said.

'Swimming sounds good.'

Uma suddenly clapped a hand to her forehead.

'We forgot to pick up your suit from the tailor's, John. Shall we do it tomorrow?'

'It's in the opposite direction to everything. I'll drop you two off and get it.'

Neither of us protested.

As the lift doors shut back at the apartment, I realised this was the first time Uma and I had been alone. There was still a veneer of politeness between us. Luckily, she didn't have an awkward bone in her body.

'What would you like to do now?' she asked.

'I'm just going to grab a shower. Then maybe we could cook one of Mum's recipes?'

'Okay, if you're not too tired from all the errands? I don't want you to overdo it, especially still feeling jetlagged.'

'I'll be fine after a cup of tea.'

'Well, alright then.'

I sensed reluctance, but pretended not to notice.

'How about something I could make at the cabins? Filling, and not too spicy.'

'Aloo parathas? Roti stuffed with potato.'

'Sounds good.'

After I'd washed the city from my skin, I went to find Uma. She was in the kitchen, a small, neat room with white cupboards and marble worktops, boiling ginger tea. I waited impatiently as she added sugar and milk, stirred, and strained. Once the tea was ready, she handed me a cup and sipped her own slowly. Finally, she reached into a cupboard and handed me a black, leather-bound notebook.

I opened it with a pounding heart. 'Renu's Recipes', the flyleaf read. Three spiders were scrawled underneath. Looking closer, I realised it was a child's drawings of three people with stick-thin limbs, no bodies and oversized faces. My drawings. Someone – presumably me – had scribbled violently over the

109

face of the medium-sized spider. Had I been annoyed with her that day? I turned the page. The paper felt as soft as fabric between my fingertips, worn smooth from being thumbed through so much. But the recipe was written in the neat, angular script of what must be Punjabi. I suddenly felt the weight of a tradition I didn't fully comprehend bearing down upon me, like an imposter handed a script in a foreign language. Looking at it made my chest ache.

'I can't understand it,' I said, handing the book back.

'Most of the later recipes are written in English. I had never tried Punjabi food until I met your ma. In return, I taught her some of the Kannadiga dishes I knew. She wrote them down in the book too.'

'Is the food so different between states?'

Uma nodded emphatically. 'Yes. Each region has different ingredients to hand, and different colonisers. Goa and Karnataka are next to each other, but Goa was ruled by the Portuguese for hundreds of years, so their food is very different. Of course, these days, thanks to the internet, people cook food from all over.'

'It's so nice to have her cookbook to remember her by,' I said wistfully.

If only Mum had kept it. Surely something like this was supposed to be passed from mother to daughter?

'My husband got offered a job in Madras and the day I found out I was so upset that she gave me her recipe book as a going away present. I've cherished it ever since.'

I felt myself soften towards her.

'She must have really cared about you,' I said.

'Yes, I think she did.'

Uma flicked rapidly through the book, then handed it back.

110

'Here's the recipe for aloo paratha.'

It was written in pencil. I raised it up to see more clearly.

'Make atta (2:1 + more if necc)', the first line read.

'What's atta?'

'Dough. Made with wholewheat flour,' Uma told me. 'Start off with two cups of flour and one cup of warm water. You'll probably need to add extra water, to make it the correct consistency.'

'Which is?'

'Slightly sticky. But elastic.'

As I mixed water and flour, I imagined Mum standing in a kitchen much like this one, her fingertips white with flour. What would she be thinking about as she kneaded? Would her thoughts have strayed to me and Dad? Daydreams of holidays and houses she couldn't afford? Or perhaps her mind would be blank, concentrating only on the texture and consistency of the dough taking shape under her hands.

'I think you need more water. Shall I add some?' Uma asked.

'Please.'

By the time I finished, she was already peeling and chopping potatoes.

'Cook for two whistles,' I read out. 'In the pressure cooker, right?'

'Yes. You know how?'

I nodded.

'I used one at my old job.'

'If you want to make Indian food at the cabins, you'll need one. We use them for everything,' Uma said.

She dropped the potatoes into the pan, sealed it shut and turned on the flame.

'There. Five minutes.'

Her phone rang and as she looked down at the screen, her whole face transformed.

'Hi John. No, we're fine. Making parathas . . . Okay, see you in twenty minutes, bye.'

She hung up, still smiling.

'It must be strange for you, seeing your pa getting married so suddenly.'

'Well, yeah. But he's been single for a long time. I'm really happy for you both.'

'Did you know that he was the person who taught me to write in English?'

'No, I didn't. That's sweet.'

'Yes, your pa is sweet. Funny, too. Before I even met him and your ma, I could hear them laughing together through the wall.'

The pressure cooker went off, disgorging steam into the kitchen.

'You need to chop this,' Uma said, when it was finished.

She placed an onion and a chopping board in front of me. I turned my attention back to the recipe, which called for diced onions, green chillies and fresh coriander. The pressure cooker went off for the second time and Uma took it off the heat. She used a wooden spoon as a lever to raise the gasket and release the pressure, then she drained the water, and mashed the potatoes with a wooden spoon.

'Here.'

I added the onions, chillies and coriander to the mixture.

'Season with salt and amchur,' I read out. 'Amchur?'

'Dried mango powder. Your ma's secret ingredient.'

When I was done, Uma got out the rested dough.

'Roll dough into rounds. Place mixture in middle. Fold. Roll out thin,' I read.

'Watch me. It will be easier.'

She broke off a piece of dough and rolled it into a circle a couple of millimetres thick. After placing a spoonful of potato in the middle she folded over the dough on both sides, top and bottom, and sealed everything together. She was left with a fat square of potato-stuffed dough, which she rolled out again.

'Now your turn.'

Uma had made it look like the easiest thing in the world. But when I tried, I tore the dough and the filling came out. I suddenly felt as though I'd only just started cooking – that all my years of experience had melted away.

'Try again,' Uma said.

My second attempt was much the same, and my third attempt was passable, although still lumpier and thicker than Uma's. She, meanwhile, had made three perfect parathas.

'I've made this recipe at least once a month since your ma showed me how,' she explained.

A few minutes later, we had more than enough parathas for dinner. Uma heated up a tawa. When it was hot, she laid the paratha on it, brushing the top and sides with oil. The dough puffed up in the heat. She flipped it over with her bare hands and turned to the fridge.

'Pickle, curd and ghee,' she said, laying them out on the counter.

I felt oddly nostalgic as I looked at the plastic pot of ghee. Perhaps we'd had one like it when I was a kid. I couldn't remember the taste. Much like butter, presumably. When Uma turned back to the stove, I dug a spoon into the viscous yellow mixture. It was deliciously rich, with a grainy, slightly oily texture that coated the roof of my mouth.

I'm perching on the worktop in a kitchen with red and white

113

*cupboards. The shelves are lined with spices and ceramic plates.
A woman with a red birthmark on her cheek is at the stove.
On the counter next to me is a large jar full of ghee. Quickly,
I shove a heaped spoonful in my mouth. Then another, and
another. The woman turns and sees me, her mouth round with
surprise. The jar is snatched from my hands.*

I was taken aback by the clarity of the memory. Who was
the woman with the birthmark? Mum's face was unblemished
in all the photos I'd seen. Perhaps she'd learned how to hide
it with foundation, or always turned that side of her face
away from the camera.

'Did Mum have a birthmark?' I asked Uma.

She turned to me.

'No. Her maid did.'

'Oh.'

I bit back disappointment. Why hadn't I seen Mum? I
guess memories aren't like buses, dropping you off in the
exact place you want to go.

'What did you remember?' Uma asked.

'I was sitting on a counter top, eating ghee. The maid was
making parathas. I'm surprised – I thought Mum cooked
most of our meals?'

'She did when she could.'

'What do you mean? I thought that she didn't go to work?'

'Yes, that's right.'

So what did she do all day, I wanted to ask. Was looking
after me a full-time job?

The front door opened, making Uma jump. Seconds later,
Dad came into the kitchen.

'Parathas, my favourite!'

'I'll make you up a plate,' Uma said.

She started chatting to Dad, laughing a little too loudly at

114

his lame jokes. It felt like there was no space in the conversation for me to explain what had just happened. Uma's odd reaction had completely wrongfooted me.

'Maya, are you eating?' Dad asked.

'I'm just going to the bathroom first.'

I walked loudly to my room, then turned around and tiptoed quietly back along the hallway, hiding out of sight around the corner from the kitchen.

'It happened again. She remembered the maid this time,' Uma was saying, her voice hushed.

'Why did you let her cook Renu's recipe?'

'I couldn't prevent her from doing that. Besides, she has eaten lots of things here, and the memories have only returned a couple of times.'

'For now.'

'If you feel that way, you should tell her.'

'But she's going through so many life changes at the moment, and I'm really worried about the effect this will have on her.'

'The longer you leave it . . .'

'Let's talk about this later; she'll be back any minute.'

I crept rapidly back to the bathroom and flushed the toilet so they would hear it from the kitchen. Eavesdropping hadn't answered any questions, just given me more. What was Dad trying to protect me from? It was strange to think that the answer was submerged in the inky depths of my subconscious. Close by and unfathomably far, all at once.

16

Saji and Theresa had once lived in the same apartment block as Mum and Dad, and Uma and her husband. Now they occupied a sprawling house with high metal gates and a security guard standing outside. We were ushered into their living room where ornately carved furniture, embroidered cushions, and golden crucifixes vied for attention.

'Drink?' Saji asked me.

'What do you have?'

'Anything you want: whisky, wine, beer, vodka, gin . . .'

'I'll take a gin and tonic, please.'

The gin was so strong it burned, but I didn't mind. It helped me overcome my unease at listening to everyone narrate forgotten parts of my life.

'I had the apartment in the middle,' Uma told me. 'Your parents and these two would come over for drinks and leave you, Jobin, and his big sister sleeping, as we could hear if you woke up.'

'Such good dinner parties we had,' Theresa said.

'Do you remember when Amit came to stay? With the whisky?' Saji asked.

Everyone assured him they did, but Saji embarked on his anecdote anyway – 'for Maya', he said. Theresa rolled her eyes. As it dragged on, I realised her reaction was totally justified. How many hours had she spent listening to her husband talk shit at dinner parties?

'So, Maya, how's the Arctic?' Theresa asked suddenly.

Everyone was looking at me.

'I'm cooking for an adventure company.'

'Do you go on the expeditions?'

'No, thank god. It's about minus twenty degrees outside at the moment. Twenty-four-hour darkness, too.'

'Good show Maya. Stay inside in the warm!' Saji boomed.

But Theresa frowned. 'It sounds awful. Couldn't you be a chef somewhere else? Like here in India?'

'My partner got a research job over there.'

'Partner? You aren't married?' Saji asked.

I shook my head.

'Still time to find you a nice Mallu husband instead!'

I took a large gulp of gin.

'Don't tease the poor girl,' Theresa chided.

'Where's Jobin? Is he coming tonight?' Uma asked.

'He is. Running late as usual. Always working, that boy. He needs a good Indian wife!' Saji said, subtle as a brick to the face.

'Look,' Theresa said, handing me a photograph. 'I thought you might like to see this.'

Saji and Theresa were dominating the photo in a horrendously gaudy his and hers ensemble. Uma, wearing a simple blue sari, was standing next to a mild-looking man with grey hair and glasses. Dad looked as gangly and nervous as ever. And there was Mum, elegantly dressed in a white tunic and turquoise leggings. Her face was turned away from the camera, as if something outside the frame had caught her attention.

'Was that your husband?' I asked Uma, pointing to the grey-haired man.

She nodded.

'What was Mum looking at?'

'Why, I think it was you and Jobin playing together,' Theresa said.

'Sorry I'm late. I got held up at the office.'

A man around my age had walked into the room. He was smaller and skinnier than Ryan, with a big nose and a wide, easy smile.

'Uma Auntie, nice to see you. Hi Uncle. Ma. Pa.'

Then he reached me.

'Maya? Maya! I haven't seen you in years.'

The boy with the kulfi. His eyes were still just as kind.

'Jobin? Nice to meet you.'

'Oh wow, you sound so British now.'

'Well, I am.'

There was a pause.

'Here,' he said, reaching into his jacket pocket and taking out a large seed pod. 'I brought you a present.'

I turned it over in my hands. It was brown and bulbous. Through a crack in the pod I glimpsed the seeds inside, which were coated in a sticky brown residue.

'What are they?'

'Suck one and see,' Jobin said with an impish smile.

I hoped he wasn't flirting. I knew it was something his family would encourage. I turned away from them and cracked open the pod. The seeds were coated in sticky brown pulp.

'Eat the pulp and spit the seed,' Jobin said.

I popped one into my mouth and immediately sucked in my cheeks at the tanginess of it. It was sour like citrus, but sweet too.

'It's tamarind.'

Uma was staring at me like I was about to explode. I ignored her and turned to Jobin.

'I like the taste – it's tangy. So, um. Where do you work?'

'Jobin's a therapist. He makes good money. Everyone these days thinks they are sick in the head,' Saji informed me.

'Pa . . .'

'But all they need to do if they feel anxious is be more prepared. If you are worried about getting to the airport on time, leave earlier. If you are scared of a work presentation, have a practice.'

The air in the room suddenly felt a whole lot thicker.

Don't be so ignorant, I wanted to yell. My jaw ached with the strain of staying quiet.

'Pa, we've discussed this, remember?' Jobin said.

'Mental illness is nothing to do with a lack of discipline,' Saji intoned, sounding utterly unconvinced.

'Want to come and make appams?' Jobin asked me.

I nodded, suddenly desperate to escape.

'Sorry about that,' he said quietly, as we walked through the living room.

I shrugged, unsure of what to say without causing offence.

'Pa has some fixed ideas about mental illness. I've been trying to convince him otherwise for years.'

'Good on you for trying,' I said.

'I used to be angry about it, but the more people I meet,

the more I realise the extent to which people's ideas are shaped by those around them. It's hard to rewrite decades of conditioning, to go against what your relatives and peers believe.'

'That's a very sympathetic perspective,' I said.

He smiled, and led me into the kitchen. I immediately felt more comfortable here. The shelves were lined with brass pots and glass jars full of spices. A small, grey-haired cook was chopping mangoes, watched by a much younger woman. A pot simmered on the stove next to them, its fragrant aroma mingling with the sweet perfume of mango.

'What's cooking?' I asked Jobin.

'Chicken stew. Made with fresh coconut milk. We have it with the appams.'

The younger woman handed Jobin an apron with the outline of a curvy woman in front. She and the cook laughed as he put it on and made a big show of rolling up his sleeves. He picked up a bowl full of thick, white batter.

'It's made with ground rice and fresh coconut milk. In the past they used toddy to ferment it, but now we use yeast. Much quicker.'

He placed a curved tawa on the stove and added a little oil. The two women were watching us. What did they think of me? I couldn't imagine having an army of domestic staff cleaning my house and cooking my meals. But Jobin seemed totally comfortable in their company. He spooned some batter into the pan, tilting it so the mixture spread to the edges, and placed a lid on top.

'So, what food do you eat in Britain?'

'We tend to go out for roast dinner on Sundays. Fish and chips. Toad in the hole is a British dish, although I find it bland.'

'That's in the Harry Potter books. But I don't know what it is.'

'Sausages in batter, baked in the oven so it puffs up.'

Jobin lifted the lid off the pan.

'Appams were your favourites, once. But you went off them suddenly. I don't know why.'

'Hmmm, me neither.'

He picked up a spatula and slid the appam onto a plate in one smooth, practised movement.

'You like cooking?' I asked, trying to change the subject.

'I learned before I went to college in the US. Ma was worried I'd eat burgers every night if she didn't teach me the basics. But you studied it?'

'Yeah. Not Indian food, though. I'm a total novice in that department.'

'Have you learned how to cook any dishes here?'

'We made parathas yesterday. It struck me it would work well up at the cabins where I work – relatively cheap to make.'

'You should go to Food Street. There'll be lots of South Indian snacks. Pure veg.'

'Good idea. Would you like to come with me? Show me around?'

'Totally!' Jobin cleared his throat. 'I mean, cool, maybe.'

His enthusiasm was touching, but I didn't want him to get the wrong idea.

'My boyfriend would never go out to eat vegetarian street food. He's such a carnivore.'

'You have a boyfriend?'

'I do. Ryan. We've been together almost two years. He's actually the reason I moved to the Arctic.' I cleared my throat. 'Can I make the next appam?'

'Go ahead,' he said, passing me the ladle.

I scooped batter onto the tawa, but had trouble tilting it to spread the mixture.

'It's not very crispy,' I said, a minute later.

He shrugged. 'It'll taste the same. Try again.'

'Alright. Second time lucky . . .'

I repeated the action.

'So, my parents said you don't remember your life here.'

Perhaps I should tell him. He was a therapist, after all.

'Actually, since I've been in India, a couple of memories have come back.'

'Oh really? Like what?'

'This time I dropped my kulfi. And you gave me yours.'

'You remembered me? I'm flattered,' he said, looking up at me and mock-fluttering his eyelashes.

'Ha, not *just* you. I remember sitting on the kitchen counter, eating ghee. Butter chicken, too. It seems like the memories are linked to what I'm eating. Does that sound weird?'

'Memories of food are common, as they've imprinted themselves on all five senses. The hippocampus, the part of the brain that remembers, has strong links to the digestive system. Revisiting familiar environments is probably also helping.'

'So, you believe me?'

'Why wouldn't I?'

'I don't know, it all sounds a bit . . . well . . .'

'Did you ever talk to anyone about why you've repressed memories of your childhood?'

I nodded. 'The therapist said it was the trauma of moving countries, and losing Mum.'

'I remember you at the funeral. You didn't speak, didn't even look at me.'

'God, really? I'm sorry. I have no recollection of that – I can't remember Mum's funeral. Were you there on the day of the accident?'

He shook his head. 'We moved out of the flats about a year before your ma died. I'm sorry I wasn't there for you.'

'Hey, don't worry about it. You must have been what, like eleven?'

'Twelve.'

He was looking at me sympathetically. I was surprised at myself for talking about stuff this personal. But Jobin was so easy to confide in. And we had been best friends once. Although I had forgotten our history, I could still feel it, softening the space between us.

'Oh shit, is something burning?' he said.

We looked down at the smoking pan. Jobin flipped a charred appam onto the plate, and the cook said a few short, sharp words that made him laugh.

'She wants us to go so she can finish up. We'd better leave her to it.'

Ten minutes later, we were seated around the dining table. It was laid with a stacked plate of appams, a bowl of chicken stew and a salad of diced tomato, raw mango and onion. The stew was tinted yellow with turmeric, and flecked green with curry leaves. Jobin spooned some onto an appam and began eating it with his fingers. I followed suit. It was cloud-like in the middle and crispy at the edges. The stew was fresh and subtly layered with spice. After the ghee-laced curries and kebabs I'd been eating, it was very welcome.

'You know, Maya's starting to remember things about India,' Jobin told his parents.

'But how fantastic!' Theresa said.

123

'Can you remember me?' Saji asked.

I couldn't meet his eyes. 'Sorry, no.'

'The memories seem to be related to food,' Jobin told the table.

'To kulfi. And ghee,' I elaborated.

'All dairy foods. Next will be a memory of meat,' Saji said.

'Or maybe something South Indian,' Theresa said. 'Your ma had a good rasam recipe.'

'Now, now. Let's not get ahead of ourselves,' Dad interjected.

'Do you want her to be completely in the dark?' Uma whispered, as a sudden hush fell over the table. I glanced at Dad, but he was looking fixedly down at his plate. Saji and Theresa were also studiously avoiding my gaze. Jobin was glancing around at everyone in bewilderment. I took another bite of stew, which had begun to cool down.

I'm sitting at the same table in a much smaller room. Younger versions of Saji, Theresa, Jobin, and Dad are all there. Dad's eating mechanically, looking unhappy. The woman next to him is even more miserable. I watch as she slowly drags a spoon around her untouched bowl of food.

'Ma,' I say.

She doesn't reply.

'Ma, MA!' I repeat.

Dad looks up from his plate.

'Enough now, Maya.'

I exhaled, releasing a breath I didn't know I'd been holding. My chest ached – the pain my younger self had felt at being ignored still lingered. 'Miserable' didn't even begin to describe the way my mum had looked. I wondered what had upset her. Had I been misbehaving before dinner, refusing to do my homework or wash my hands? Maybe – hopefully –

124

it wasn't my fault. She and Dad could have had a bust-up. Or someone close to her could have died. There was no way of knowing, and now was not the time to bring it up. Besides, they might not know the answer.

Around me, conversation was flowing again. Uma and Dad were talking about the upcoming wedding to Saji and Theresa, and appeared to have tacitly made up. I should have been pleased for them. But I felt nothing much at all. Everyone felt very far away, as if I was looking at them through the wrong end of a telescope. Numbly, I forked up another mouthful of appam and stew. It seemed to swell in my mouth, almost choking me. Finally, I managed to swallow it. I put my cutlery down. It was only then that I noticed Jobin watching me.

17

The doorbell rang just after eight. Jobin was wearing a smart shirt and jeans, his hair artfully spiked. When I hugged him I smelt citrus shower gel.

'Ready to go?' he asked.

'Yup.'

'Is that Jobin?' Uma called from the living room.

'Yes, Auntie, it's me.'

'Have fun! Don't keep her out too late.'

There was a sleek black car waiting for us by the gates. As we got into the back, the driver said something in a language I didn't understand. Jobin laughed and responded; I suddenly felt terribly out of place.

'What are you guys speaking?'

'Malayalam.'

'How many languages do you know?'

'Malayalam, because my parents speak it at home, and Hindi, because we learned at school. I'm also fluent in Kannada now, because my patients speak it. Oh, and I'm learning French, because in February I'm going to Paris.'

'Wow. Five languages. You're such a prodigy.'

'Well, you know Hindi and a bit of Kannada.'

'I've forgotten it, alongside everything else,' I said.

'It must be hard, coming back. If you spent more time here you would start to feel at home.'

'Maybe,' I said doubtfully.

'I understand how you feel. When I returned from college in America I saw India with different eyes. It seemed much noisier, more inefficient – naturally, I quickly forgot all the negatives about the US, like how expensive healthcare can be. The crowd I hung out with before college had pretty immature ideas about women, and they hadn't really grown out of them. And having studied what I do, it hurt when Ma and Pa made dismissive comments about mental illness, even when they were joking. I don't mean to sound like I'd become all self-actualised and enlightened by my exposure to the West – I think I just felt dislocated, and pretty lost. It's hard to explain without coming off as a jerk.'

'I remember how strange England felt when I first moved. So cold, and different to everything I knew. But I'm sorry about how you felt. I remember what your dad said about anxiety at dinner the other night. It's the same in the UK with a lot of the older generation. Luckily, things are starting to change.'

'Here, too. But there's still a lot of social stigma attached to mental illness.'

'How do you feel about Bangalore these days?' I asked.

'I've settled back in. It's a lot more cosmopolitan now, and the food scene is great. I have very progressive friends, and a job I love.'

'And you're going on holiday to Paris, which is the height of sophistication.'

'Not a holiday. A six-month placement. There's a psycho-therapist there who specialises in transcultural therapy with refugees. I'm getting training so I can help migrant labourers, dalits and anyone who's struggling to get access to counsel-ling.'

'That's very worthy of you.'

'It's just . . . you've seen my family's house. They – I – have so much more than millions of the people in this city. My life is so different to people I pass every day on the street.'

'Everyone has a couple of things in common. People every-where fall in love and hate each other's guts. Everyone eats and everyone shits and everyone dies,' I said.

Jobin laughed.

'You have such a British sense of humour now, it's kind of crazy.'

'I don't know what you mean by "British".'

'A dry wit.'

'Thanks, I guess.'

'I still can't get used to seeing you again after so long. Your accent, your mannerisms, they've all completely changed.'

'Something about me must be the same, surely?'

'Well, you used to ask a lot of questions when you were a kid, too.'

'Ha, ha,' I said, nudging him with my elbow.

A couple of minutes later, the car stopped in front of a narrow pedestrianised street lined with stalls, the steam rising from vats and saucepans. It was as crowded as a rock concert, and almost as noisy. I had been to four gigs in my life. The result: two bad hangovers from drinking to cope, one panic attack, and one tearful flight from the venue. Maybe I should tell Jobin I wanted to go to a restaurant instead.

'I normally go to the top and eat my way down,' he said.

Of course he did.

He moved so easily through the crowd and I struggled after him, accidentally elbowing people and being elbowed in return. Neon signs blazed like sirens. There were dense thickets of bodies. People yelled at the tops of their voices. I tried to manoeuvre past a large family.

'Excuse me,' I said.

Nobody moved.

'Maya!'

Jobin had doubled back to find me. I grabbed his outstretched hand and he pulled me through the knot of people.

By the time I arrived at the top stall my nerves were jangled. Luckily, the crowd had thinned slightly.

'What do you want to try first?' Jobin asked.

I looked at the menu. The only word I recognised was 'dosa'.

'I don't know what anything is.'

'Choose your favourite word. If you don't like it, we'll buy something else.'

'Um . . . Alright, let's get an obbattu.'

'I'll get us an uthappam too.'

The uthappam was a cross between a dosa and an appam – a thick, spongy pancake with chopped onions, green chilli and fresh coriander sprinkled on top. The obbattu was a yellow roti stuffed with a paste of toor dal and jaggery, liberally smeared with ghee. I took a picture for Adam.

'The guys would love these as a snack after a day in the snow,' I said.

'They take ages to make,' Jobin warned. 'Come, I'll show you something easier.'

At the next stall we tried pav bhaji, which Jobin said was

a snack from Mumbai. It was a rich, spicy mixture of mashed vegetables, served with bread rolls dripping with butter, garnishes of coriander, lemon and diced raw onion. A perfect blend of fat, acidity and spice – great comfort food for the cabins. By the time I finished it, the urge to bolt had all but disappeared.

We ate chillies deep-fried in gram flour, followed by channa batura – a chickpea stew served with a puri, a large flatbread immersed in a vat of boiling oil to make it puff up and turn crispy.

'I'm stuffed,' I said, rubbing my stomach. 'You know, we've spent less on all this food than it costs to buy one pepper in Longyearbyen.'

'That's insane.'

'It is. That's why I have to eat as much as possible here.'

'You have to try one more dish. Something sweet. Jalebis.'

'We eat those on Diwali in the UK.'

'They taste better fresh. There was a jalebi stall near our apartments and you loved watching them being made. You used to call them scribbles.'

'Nice to know I was cute once upon a time.'

'You still are,' Jobin said.

He gave me a shy look that I would've found really flattering if I was single. But I wasn't. Had I been leading him on? He knew I had a boyfriend, but everyone here seemed to think there had to be a ring on it for it to count.

I turned away from Jobin and caught sight of the crowd. There were so many people; a teeming mass of limbs and teeth and eyes.

Just like that, my carefully constructed sense of 'alrightness' collapsed.

The food churned in my stomach. Acid rose into my mouth. My chest was being squeezed by an iron band.

'Come on, let's get jalebis,' Jobin said.

He was quickly absorbed by the crowd. I could see him in front of me, getting further and further away. I jostled, trying to reach him.

Someone grabbed my arm – a skinny girl wearing a tattered party dress. She was holding a bunch of roses in her other hand, and chattering in a shrill voice.

'I'm sorry. I don't understand.'

Her eyes blazed malevolence and she carried on tugging at me. The hairs on my arms stood on end. I shook my arm free. Too hard. She stumbled backwards and dropped the roses. People were turning to look, accusations in their eyes. They were pressing closer and closer, taking up all the air and all the space.

ALARM BELLS. CODE RED. CODE RED.

You're not going to die, you're not going to die, you're not going to die.

The lights and voices merged into an awful, hallucinatory blur.

I ran.

Ran for what felt like an eternity, pushing my way through a crowd that felt like it would never end, alarm bells and sirens screaming through my head, every accidental contact with another person an electric shock. Finally, minutes – or perhaps years – later, I reached the end of the street, rounded the corner, and saw some concrete steps. I collapsed onto them and inched back into the shadowed corner of the building, as far as possible from the crowds, the noise, the lights.

My throat was tight. I couldn't breathe.

131

You can. You can, I told myself.

There was a sharp, needle-like pain in my chest.

It'll pass. It always passes.

But this time I really felt like I was dying.

You always feel like you're dying, and you never do. Now, take deep breaths.

In . . .

Out . . .

In . . .

And out . . .

Slowly but surely, it became easier to breathe and the panic began to recede.

My sense of self slowly returned, accompanied by a deep sense of shame. That poor girl had just wanted me to buy a rose. I'd literally pushed her over. Why couldn't I do something as simple as grabbing a bite to eat? Would there ever be a day without The Schools, a day without chest pains or stomach cramps, when tasks were as simple for me as they appeared to be for everyone else?

My anxiety was considered to be somewhere between 'mild' and 'moderate'. Neither were words I associated with my panic attacks. Well, not until I'd joined an anxiety sufferers support group a few years ago. I'd never seen so many anxious people in one room. Lots of blinking, fidgeting, nobody looking each other in the eye. The scene was rich in comic material. In fact, one guy, TJ, wanted to be a stand-up. Except he hadn't performed yet because each time he tried he had a panic attack beforehand. A couple of times he even passed out. He was one of the funniest people I ever met.

The group took worrying to new and obsessive heights. Annie worried about what to wear for a doctor's appointment.

If she looked too good they might think she was feeling better, and stop prescribing the anxiety meds she popped like Pringles. But if she looked too unwell, they might section her, or take her kid away. She never had a doctor's appointment before four, because it took so long to get ready. A guy named Bill was so worried about sprouting a spontaneous stiffy in public he wore a heavy duffel coat all year round. Then, whenever he met a woman (he was addicted to Tinder, so it was a relatively frequent occurrence), he worried about not being able to get it up. That, of course, was a self-fulfilling prophecy. Jenny worried about the amount she worried. After all, there were billions of people in the world worse off than her – she had a great husband, worked freelance as a designer – so what on earth was she getting so worked up about?

Thinking about the group dispelled the last traces of my panic attack. I wasn't alone. All across the world there were people who struggled to leave the house, to make doctor's appointments, to hold down jobs. People who engaged in daily battles with invisible demons. Christ, it was exhausting. Frustrating, too. However much therapy you had, the anxiety would always be there, dogging your footsteps like a shadow. The only way forward was to find the humour in the weird shit you did. Talking of finding things, I needed to look for Jobin.

It didn't take long. He was at the entrance to the street, holding a couple of paper plates and looking around frantically. His body sagged in relief when he saw me.

'Where did you go? You feel okay?'

'Fine. The crowd was just a little much.'

I led him back to the steps and he handed me a plate. Panic attacks always gave me an appetite for sweet things.

The jalebis – hot, crispy deep-fried squiggles of batter drenched in sugar syrup – didn't disappoint.

'Maya, I'm sorry,' Jobin said suddenly.

'What for?'

'I should have asked. Your ma disliked crowds, too.'

'It's alright, I should have mentioned it. Anyway, Jobin, how old are you?'

'Thirty-three.'

'Four years older than me. So you must remember her.'

'Of course. She was a really sweet woman. Used to feed all the stray—'

'Yeah, yeah. But did she ever, I don't know, get sad?'

Jobin took another jalebi.

'Everyone gets sad.'

'I remembered something when I was at your house. Eating appams. Mum wouldn't look at me. She was so miserable.'

'I don't remember it.'

'There must have been other occasions. Surely you saw something?'

He avoided my eyes.

'I'm sorry. I was young, too – unconcerned with what the grown-ups were doing.'

For the first time since I'd met him, he seemed flustered.

'Please, Jobin.'

'I guess I do remember her being a little up and down,' he said eventually.

'Like how down?'

Jobin shrugged. I fought the urge to shake him.

'Dad gave me the impression she was the happiest person in the world.'

'He's bound to dwell on the high points of his relationship. But . . .'

'But what?'

'Look, why don't you stay on in India for a while? You might remember more.'

'I have a job to go back to. And a boyfriend.'

'Ah yes. So you said.'

The jalebis were finished now, the plate soggy with syrup. Jobin folded it up and threw it into an overflowing bin. We used the water from his bottle to wash our hands. I glanced across at him to see if he had any more to say, but he remained silent.

18

Uma's sister had booked herself a room at Bangalore Club, which we were using to get ready for the reception. In the privacy of the bathroom, I applied some last minute make-up. I was wearing a hot pink sari that Uma had bought for me, and as I looked in the mirror I realised it was actually quite flattering, completely covering my protruding stomach. The phone rang as I was admiring myself.

'Hi, stranger,' I said.

Ryan and I had spoken briefly on Christmas morning, and since then, nothing.

'Hey Maya. I'm sorry I haven't been in touch.'

He sounded truly contrite.

'It's chill,' I told him. 'You've been busy, I've been busy. I'll be back in a few days anyway.'

'Yeah.'

'Well, I can't wait to see you. I've missed you loads.'

'Listen, are you free to talk right now?'

'Not really. Tonight's the wedding. It starts in like five minutes. I think Dad's going to make a speech.'

'Oh, okay.'

'Shall I send you pictures? Do you want to see me in my wedding outfit?'

'Sure.'

'Ryan, you don't seem yourself. Is something up?'

'I'm fine. Just tired. I'll leave you to it.'

'Let's talk s—'

He hung up, cutting me off. Ryan was never normally this abrupt. I did my best to push it from my mind, otherwise I'd only concoct ridiculous, anxiety-generating scenarios with no basis in fact. Tonight was not a night to be upset; it was a time for celebration, and I was going to make sure I enjoyed it.

Back in the bedroom, Uma was looking at herself in the mirror.

'I look so old,' she said.

It worried me when women in their fifties still had insecurities about their appearance, especially when they were as confident as Uma. I hoped to come to terms with myself long before then.

'Don't be silly. You look great,' I replied, and meant it.

Her sari was a shimmering tapestry of sea-green, cobalt and gold. Her skin was clear and there were only the faintest shadows under her eyes – her family had forced us all to get up at the crack of dawn to do puja.

'You need more make-up,' her sister said.

'Maya, can you find your pa? Tell him I'll be along in five minutes.'

'Sure.'

The sun had just set and the evening air was warm against my bare skin. I walked quickly through the club compound, feeling self-conscious in my sari. But Dad looked even more

137

ill at ease than I felt. He was wearing a suit with a sea-green tie, to match Uma's outfit.

'Nervous?' I asked.

'A little,' he admitted.

'Well, it was quite sudden,' I told him.

'Not about marrying Uma. I'm just worried about whether I'll recognise all the guests she invited.'

'Ah, I see.'

There was a pause.

'I know this might seem spontaneous to you. But when you get to our age you know what you want. And those things might slip through your fingers if you're indecisive.'

'Well, I'm proud of you for taking the plunge.'

'And I'm proud of you for coping so well in the Arctic.'

At that moment, an elderly couple approached Dad and he greeted them like old friends.

'Oh Christ,' he muttered after they'd left. 'I have no idea who they were. I hope Uma gets here soon.'

'She said five minutes.'

But quite a few more guests arrived before Uma did. The women all wore colourful dresses and saris, with huge gold earrings dangling in their ears. Most of the men wore suits, although some were dressed in kurtas and a couple of Uma's older relatives were in dhotis. When Uma eventually arrived, she and Dad were quickly sucked into greeting their guests and posing for photographs. I sat at a table with Aunt Emma – my dad's sister – and my cousin Millie, who'd arrived from the UK yesterday morning.

'Do you know what's for dinner?' Aunt Emma asked.

'A buffet.'

'Indian food?'

I nodded.

'Oh dear. I hope it won't be too spicy for me.'

'My stomach feels very sensitive. I think I'm becoming lactose intolerant,' Millie said.

'Maybe it's stress.'

'You're right. I have been busy, sorting out the windows and the life-coaching exam . . .'

I felt like I'd scream if I heard any more. But it would be worse to stand alone in a corner, neck prickling as I imagined what people were thinking when they saw me.

As Millie and Aunt Emma started talking hand sanitiser brands and low FODMAP diets, I zoned out of the conversation completely. The lawn looked dreamy. Fairy lights dripped from every tree. Beautifully dressed women sat gossiping at tables covered in crisp white cloths. Waiters were busy manning the bar and ferrying food to white-canopied stalls. At the front of the lawn was a stage garlanded with marigolds. Uma and Dad were standing near it, greeting the guests as they arrived. A group of middle-aged men descended on Dad just then, clapping him warmly on the back. One handed him a glass of whisky, and Dad said something that made the others laugh. I'd never seen him hang out with a group of guys his age before. When I was growing up he stayed at home every night, looking after me. I guess the habit remained ingrained, because nothing changed when I moved out. It was as if he had spent the last couple of decades in stasis, waiting for his life to begin again. Maybe it was that he had been waiting to return to India, which seemed to offer him so much more than it offered me.

Jobin was making his way towards me, wearing a well-cut navy suit.

'Wow, you're looking sharp,' I said.

'You too. Pink looks good on you.'

'Thanks. I feel a little weird though, wearing it. Like I'm being culturally appropriative.'

'You may be British but you're also Indian. Your mum liked wearing pink.'

'Really?'

He nodded, and I wondered if he were telling the truth or trying to make me feel better.

Someone coughed into the microphone and I saw Dad and Uma were now onstage.

'Um. Hi. Hello. Can you all hear me? Well, okay. Um, great. I'd like to thank you all for coming, especially my friends and family from the UK. This isn't the traditional type of wedding, as you may have guessed. But we will have a ceremony for you called a mangalsutra,' he said, glancing across at Uma to make sure he'd pronounced it right. 'This will be followed by the giving of the vows – a very British custom. Then food and dancing.'

He stepped back, visibly relieved not to be talking anymore. Unfortunately for him, it wasn't over yet as he had to endure a ritual, which Uma had told me symbolised the bride being given to the groom by her father. In the absence of both father and brother, Uma's sister was supposed to be giving her away. Uma's sister glared at Dad as he tried to tie a necklace around Uma's neck, his fingers fumbling with the knots. I think he was supposed to be saying a hymn or something while he did it, but it looked like he was muttering drunkenly under his breath.

Afterwards, Dad and Uma exchanged rings, and looked at each other like teenagers as they said their vows. I tried to imagine myself standing up there with Ryan. He'd never mentioned marriage, but sometimes guys needed a little longer. Once I got back and we settled into a rhythm, perhaps I should find out his thoughts on the matter.

There was a sniffing sound next to me and I turned to see that tears were rolling down Jobin's face.

'I always cry at weddings,' he said, wiping his eyes. 'So sweet that they found each other in later life. Makes me think there's still hope for me.'

'There's obviously still hope. You're a guy. You get distinguished, not old. You can even be a dad in your sixties.'

'A woman in India gave birth at the age of seventy. Uma and your pa are only in their fifties – maybe they still have a chance.'

'Don't be disgusting. Anyway, come on. Let's get smashed.'

'Really?'

'Of course. I'm half-British, remember. We get absolutely trolleyed at weddings.'

'I mustn't get in the way of cultural expression.'

He extended his arm, and together we walked into the crowd.

Any previous anxieties I'd had about feeling out of place quickly vanished. My good friend, Ms Gin, was instrumental in this, but the atmosphere was friendly too. In England, people would have clumped together in little groups until they got drunk enough to hit on each other or pick a fight. Here, people were happily introducing themselves. Jobin knew quite a few of the guests, and entertained me with gossipy titbits.

'I need to eat something. I feel very giddy,' he said, eventually.

'I'll come with you.'

We walked over to the buffet area. The first thing I saw was a station where a chef in a white hat was grilling chicken tikka stained orange with spices. After filling my plate, I followed Jobin to an empty table. I started off with a piece

141

of chicken. It was spicy, lightly charcoaled and tender – a far cry from the cardboard-tasting tikka I'd tried in the UK.

Everyone is here. Uma and her husband. Saji and Theresa. Dad. And opposite me, Mum. I can hear the clink of cutlery and the buzz of conversation. The air smells of grilled meat and cigarette smoke. Yet we're cut off from all the warmth and the laughter. The whole table is watching Mum. Her hair is greasy and the top buttons of her shirt are undone, revealing the deep hollows of her collarbones. She picks up a piece of chicken tikka, and begins slowly ripping it to shreds. Rubs her hands across her face, leaving smears of grease behind.

'Bits and pieces, bits and pieces . . .' she mutters, over and over.

I burst into tears.

The half-eaten piece of chicken tikka that was dangling between my thumb and forefinger dropped onto the plate and I stood abruptly.

'What's wrong?'

'Nothing . . . just . . . just . . . bathroom . . .'

I shut myself in a cubicle and collapsed onto the toilet. My hands were shaking and the walls of the cubicle wavered in and out of focus. That was Mum? I thought of how she'd looked in the photos Dad had showed me. Radiant in flowing dresses. Smiling down at the baby in her arms. The woman I had glimpsed in my memories didn't bear any resemblance to her. Were they all just poses? It didn't seem like she could look after herself, let alone me. There was a huge, palpitating ball of tension in my chest. I reached for the toilet roll, leaving orange grease stains on the paper.

Remarkably, nobody was in the bathroom when I emerged from the cubicle. I washed my hands and face, stood in front of the mirror and forced myself to smile. I watched a TED

Talk recently on the power of smiling. It activates neuropeptides that reduce stress and release endorphins. But my body could obviously tell I was faking it because I didn't feel any better. A cigarette would be more helpful.

Jobin was standing outside the bathroom, waiting for me.

'Hey Maya. Are you alright?'

'I'm fine. Just going for a cigarette,' I said, pushing past him.

'Can I have one?' he asked, following behind me.

'I didn't realise you smoked.'

'I do sometimes.'

'Fine,' I snapped.

We went outside. In front of the lobby was a walkway covered by a trellis of twisting vines. In the middle was an ornamental fountain with no water in it. I sat on the stone rim and lit up. Jobin took a cigarette from me, inhaled and coughed.

'What happened at the table?' he asked.

'I just got really bad stomach cramps.'

'You're a very bad liar.'

I waited for him to press me further, but he said nothing. I listened to the sound of the cigarette paper burning as I inhaled, watched the tip glowing in the darkness. Once I'd calmed down a bit I realised there wasn't any harm in telling him. He had, after all, been there at the time. And perhaps he could cast more light on the memory.

'I had another flashback. We were eating dinner. You, me, our parents, Uma. Mum was there. She looked awful. She was tearing up the chicken, and . . .' I broke off, not trusting myself to speak.

'I remember,' Jobin said quietly.

'Why was she doing it?'

'Look, I was a kid, like you. She didn't regularly rip her meal to shreds.'

'Don't joke about this. Just tell me what happened before and after.'

'I'm not sure if it's my place.'

'But I've already seen the worst. I hope. I just want some context.'

'I can't really remember how it started, but your ma was quieter than usual. Afterwards, your family left pretty quickly. I asked what had happened to Auntie. Pa said it was a practical joke. But Uma took me for a walk. She told me that sometimes grown-ups get very sad and it makes them do funny things. And I said that when I got sad I never did anything like that. "You know the radio in your kitchen," she said. "Imagine if your sadness is like the volume turned down low. Auntie's sadness is the volume turned up to maximum, so loud you have to put your hands over your ears, and you can't think of anything else."'

'So . . . depression?' I asked.

Jobin nodded. 'I think so.'

'Why didn't you tell me earlier?'

He didn't reply immediately. I smoked the cigarette down to the butt and ground it under my shoe.

'Come on, spit it out.'

'I . . . Listen, Maya. Maybe you should talk to your pa.'

'Did he put you up to this?'

'He called my parents before that dinner and asked us not to mention Renu's "down days". He said he wanted to tell you about it.'

'So everyone's in cahoots,' I said angrily.

'Mental health disorders weren't spoken about openly twenty years ago in India. Even today, it's something to hide.'

'But Dad's British!'

'I don't want to make any excuses for him, but I can see why he did it. An opportunity for him to focus on the good parts. Rewrite the past, excluding everything he wanted to forget.'

'I want to go home.'

'I'll tell them you feel sick. I'll call my driver, get him to take us.'

'You don't have to come.'

'It's fine – I want to.'

After he'd gone, I stepped out from under the trellis and looked upwards. The sky was a luminous purple colour. Large bats swooped in circles above my head. My body felt leaden. I thought about what Uma had said to Jobin about sadness as a noise, something that could be turned up or down. My own volume was turned up pretty high right now – I felt nauseous and cold, despite the warmth of the evening. Dad had invented Mum from a carefully curated set of memories and photographs. In twenty years, he'd never mentioned her depression. It was hard to believe he was capable of such long-term deception.

'Maya? Are you ready?'

'Yes.'

I sat rigidly in the back of the car, numb to the traffic that screeched around us, until we pulled up at the apartments.

'Want me to come up?'

I nodded. Jobin followed me to the apartment. As soon as we were inside, I burst into tears. I felt like I'd lost her all over again; swapped the World's Best Mum for a woman who couldn't look her daughter in the eye.

'Come here.'

Jobin put his arms around me. I collapsed against his chest and bawled my eyes out.

'Sorry,' I gasped.

'Please don't be.'

I extricated myself. My eyes felt puffy and my nose was running.

'I must look like shit,' I muttered.

'Who cares? I'll get you some water.'

I stumbled into my room and lay down on the bed. My head was spinning. A minute later, I heard the clink of a glass being set on the nightstand.

'Here you are. Would you like some tissues?'

'Yes, please.'

'Here you are,' he said a minute later, handing me a roll of toilet paper.

I wiped my eyes and blew my nose noisily.

'Thanks. And sorry again. About all of this.'

Jobin was hovering in the doorway. I wondered if he wanted to get back to the wedding. He'd barely had a chance to eat.

'Do you want me to go? Or I can wait in the living room?' he asked.

'I want you to stay here.'

He sat awkwardly on the other bed.

'Will you lie with me?'

'Are you sure?' he asked.

'Yeah.'

I wanted to feel the solidity of another body. Something comforting. Something real. I turned over onto my side. The mattress sagged as Jobin climbed onto the bed next to me. He lay on top of the covers with his arm loosely round my waist. I didn't fully register his presence. My mind was whirling in chaotic circles. Why was Dad being so secretive? Mental health issues held no stigma to me, of all people. Had Dad also told Uma not to say anything? Perhaps that's what she'd been about to mention when we were making parathas.

I closed my eyes and tried to calm myself. Eventually, my thoughts started to settle and I became aware of the warmth and weight of Jobin's body against mine, the evenness of his breathing. Comforted by his presence, I felt myself begin to drift.

. . . *I'm standing on the beach. The sky glows with a sick red light, gilding the tops of the waves with fire. I'm shivering so much but I can't go home. Not now, after what I've seen. I crouch down among the rocks, seeking shelter amongst their jagged surfaces. The world slowly darkens. Shadows stretch across the beach. I wonder if anyone will find me here, or if I'll get carried away by the tide . . .*

That dream again. I felt the rolling emptiness of grief, although what I had lost was unclear. My head was thumping and my chest felt hollow, like something had been scooped out of it. Jobin had gone, leaving my bedroom light on. I was still in my sari but he'd removed my sandals. It was a relief to be spared the embarrassment of his presence. I turned off the light and listened to the ceiling fan whir above my head. It was a long time before I slept.

19

There were a couple of hours until I had to leave for the airport. Alone in my bedroom, I finished packing. I hadn't had a chance to talk to Dad properly since the wedding. Friends and relatives had stuck around, blistering their skin by the hotel pool, demanding endless shopping trips to buy glitzy statues and harem pants and 'real chai tea'. Some of them had treated Dad and Uma like travel agents, expecting tickets printed and taxis booked. Even going out to eat was a chore. Millie couldn't stop going on about her supposed allergies, Uncle George wanted a decent steak, and Dad's mate, Joe, was desperate to visit what he referred to as 'authentic places'. By the evening, I felt too tired to talk. I tried my best to be civil in front of everyone, but Dad and Uma must have known something was up; they kept asking me if I was okay.

Keeping the stuff about Mum to myself had taken its toll. Normally, I would have blown off steam by ranting to Ryan. But he always seemed to be at the library, or work, or the gym, and it was obvious something was eating at him. I remembered he'd been a bit down in the dumps last Christmas, too, being so far from his mum and brother. In the end, I figured it was better to just wait until I got back. Meanwhile, Jobin was only too keen to talk. Every time a message from him flashed up on my phone screen, I felt a jolt of embarrassment. Needless to say, I hadn't replied.

There was a tentative knock on the door.

'Come in.'

Uma stepped into the room, holding something behind her back.

'How's the packing going?'

'Nearly finished.'

'I have something extra for you.'

My suitcase was already crammed with her gifts: Dal, spices, blocks of tamarind, a huge rock of jaggery. Even a pressure cooker. Any more and I'd need to pay an overweight baggage fee.

'You've already given me so much.'

'I know you'll want this.'

She handed me a black, leather-bound notebook. I felt my breath catch in my chest and put it down quickly on the bed.

'But Mum gave it to you.'

'If she knew how much you enjoyed cooking, she would have wanted you to have it.'

'I doubt it.'

She looked at me sympathetically.

'Listen. Jobin just told me what happened at the wedding.'

I felt a hot burst of anger. I hadn't asked him to keep it secret, but I'd assumed he would.

'He shouldn't have said anything,' I muttered.

'Don't blame Jobin. He was worried. Said you haven't been replying to his messages.'

149

'All this could have been avoided if people just told the truth,' I said, more angrily than I'd intended.

She bit her lip, and looked down at the floor.

'I wanted to, but . . .'

'But Dad's your husband; you have to look out for him, not me.'

'I want to look out for you both.'

'Does he know that I know?'

She shook her head.

'You should talk to him,' she said.

'When? I'm leaving in, like, half an hour.'

'We'll get him to drive you to the airport, and I'll stay back.'

She spoke gently to me, despite my sharpness. I felt myself softening towards her – after all, none of this was her fault.

'Sorry for snapping. I just don't know what to think. Nothing seems real.'

'This,' she said, gesturing at the notebook. 'This is real. Look for her mutton curry recipe. Everyone loved it.'

Once she'd left, I hid the book at the bottom of the suitcase, and all too soon it was time to go.

'I'll stay behind,' Uma said.

'Are you sure?' Dad asked.

'I'm exhausted after the wedding. Besides, it will give you the chance to say your goodbyes.'

I hugged Uma, and followed Dad out the flat.

At first we drove in silence. I looked out the window at the roads of boxy houses, at the crush of traffic, the illuminated shops and stalls. I knew nothing more about Bangalore than I had two weeks ago. The only thing that had been revealed was the depth of my ignorance.

'Looking forward to seeing Ryan?' Dad asked.

'Yeah.'

'Do you have any plans for New Year's?'

'Nope.'

'When does work start up again?'

I shrugged.

'What's wrong?'

I paused. It was difficult to know where to begin. Hadn't he told Jobin's parents that he would talk to me? But somehow the responsibility to start the conversation was mine.

'Maya?'

'Nothing. Nothing's wrong.'

'These past couple of days you've been awfully quiet. Are you worried about returning to the Arctic?'

'It's not that.'

'Well, what is it then?'

'It's just . . .' I paused. My mouth felt dry. I cleared my throat. 'You didn't tell me.'

'Tell you what?'

'Mum. Her depression.'

I noticed his hands grip the steering wheel a little tighter.

'What on earth do you mean?'

'I remember, Dad. I saw her playing with her food at Saji and Theresa's, not paying attention to me. And ripping bits of chicken to shreds like a fucking psycho.'

'Don't use that language to talk about your mother.'

'Well, what should I say about her?'

I was dangerously close to tears. Again.

'I'm sorry that you remembered those moments. And I hope you don't think she was that way all the time. She usually had a very sunny disposition.'

'Did she feed stray dogs?'

'Yes, of course.'

'Did she really like cooking?'

'Yes. Why are you asking this? She just felt down from time to time, that's all.'

'Seems like it was a lot more than that. Jobin said he thought she suffered from clinical depression.'

Dad sighed heavily.

'I didn't want to upset you. Especially not now, when so much is changing for you.'

'It's far more upsetting to realise you've been keeping this from me. This is the twenty-first century. One out of three people in the UK suffer some form of mental distress, including your own daughter, so, you know, she was hardly unique.'

'Sorry.'

Is that all you fucking have to say? I wanted to ask. But I remained silent. I had, after all, learned from the best.

The city slid by under a night sky stained with the light from malls and restaurants and office blocks. I experienced a sharp longing for something familiar. For the house in Croydon, my bedroom with the posters of my teen crushes still plastered over the walls. For the flat I'd shared with Nina, the galley kitchen overflowing with appliances and spices and recipe books. For Ryan.

'I don't know if she had depression,' Dad said eventually. 'Some days it felt like her energy was boundless. She spent hours cooking and writing poetry . . .'

'She wrote poetry? Why haven't I seen any?'

'Because she burned it all. She said she didn't want her words around to embarrass her. Not that I could read it anyway. It was in Punjabi.'

'Oh.'

I glanced over at him but he had his gaze fixed on the road ahead.

'She had dark days. That's what she called them. When she would stay in bed, without eating or washing.'

Dad's voice had thickened. My chest ached. If only I had known. Maybe I would have felt less isolated when I had my own dark days. Perhaps, if she was still alive, she would have helped me through them. But then I remembered the way she'd turned her face away from mine, ignored me when I called her name, and thought, maybe not.

The city blurred into a mass of lights.

'You should have said something,' I said, wiping my eyes with the back of my hand.

'I was just trying to protect you. You had so much to deal with: moving countries, starting a new school . . .'

'Dad, all that was twenty years ago. I'm not a little girl anymore.'

'I was worried if I told you about her lowest moments, that's all she would become to you. Besides, when you couldn't remember, I . . . I wondered if it had happened for a reason. There were times when I wanted to forget.'

'I wish we could've swapped. All I want is to remember.'

'No. You don't.'

'How do you know?'

'Darling. I'm sorry. This isn't the way I wanted you to find out.'

'Well that could have been easily solved.'

We reached the toll booths a few miles from the airport. Dad stopped to pay and then drove onwards. It felt as if we'd crossed a threshold. The ache in my chest intensified. I wondered if he was right. Perhaps I should stay. But I wasn't sure I could face any more revelations.

The airport materialised out of the darkness.

'This was the wrong time to be having this conversation,' Dad said, as we drove towards the terminal.

153

'You're telling me,' I said.

He pulled over outside Departures.

'I don't want you to leave like this. Not knowing when you'll be back, if you've forgiven me,' he said.

'We've had years to talk about it,' I said, determined to continue giving him the cold shoulder.

'Oh darling, it's just . . .'

'Just what?'

'Nothing. It doesn't matter.'

'Alright. Well. Goodbye, Dad.'

'Goo–'

I slammed the door, grabbed my suitcase from the boot, and walked away.

I only turned around once. He was hunched over the wheel, head in his hands. As though he was the one who had been broken. But he had lied to me for years, rewriting my childhood to suit himself. No wonder he hadn't taken me back to India sooner.

The policeman guarding the entrance looked at me curiously when he checked my ticket and passport. I stared back until he dropped his gaze and nodded me through the automatic doors. Away from this city with its tides of people, its traffic-choked roads like clogged arteries. Away from memories of a mother who turned away from me. Away from Dad, who seemed to think I was still seven years old. The city and I had unfinished business, but I needed to walk away and get some headspace. I wasn't sure what I had expected to find in India, but this definitely wasn't it.

Part Three

20

The feeling of sunshine on my skin was a memory I clung to as I shivered outside the airport, waiting for the bus into town. Time spent in India had only made the darkness more oppressive and the cold more of a shock. My head ached and I was trembling with exhaustion. I had replayed the conversation with Dad over and over on the flight home. He still saw me as his little girl, needing to be protected. But that was no excuse. If anything, knowing Mum had suffered from a mental illness would have made me feel less alone.

The bus pulled up and people crowded onto it. I wondered why it was so busy, then remembered that it was New Year's Eve. I'd chosen this date to travel because it was slightly cheaper; naively, I'd imagined that after a nap I would be ready to go out for drinks. But there was no chance of that happening now. I wanted nothing more than a warm bed, Ryan's arms around me, and to sink into what would be my first untroubled sleep in days.

Once again, the bus driver pointed out the seed vault for the benefit of the new arrivals. The blue light winking in the distance looked lonelier than before. It was fucked up that we needed to hide seeds in the permafrost for safekeeping, like we were all waiting for the places where we lived to catch fire or be swept away.

As I walked from the bus stop to the flat, open curtains revealed glimpses of people's living rooms. Somewhere, someone had blown something up. Identical images of mushroom clouds of smoke and fire beamed out from multiple television screens, spilling red light onto the snow. Why didn't more people suffer from anxiety? We were all teetering on the brink. I sped up, desperate to get back to Ryan.

By the time I arrived at the flat, my hair and eyelashes were frozen. Even my clothes were stiff with ice. It took several minutes before I thawed out enough to remove my boots. Ryan's were lined up by the front door, a woman's pair next to them. Perhaps the absentee flatmate had finally returned from doing fieldwork. I padded down the corridor, unlocked our bedroom door and pushed it open.

For a moment, I felt as though I had strayed into a parallel universe. One even more messed up than this one.

Ryan was there.

So was Astrid.

Ryan and Astrid were on our bed and they were fucking with such intensity that they hadn't even noticed me, their eyes locked onto each other. Astrid was on top and Ryan's hands traced her body like he couldn't believe what he was touching.

Astrid turned then, and saw me. She yelped in surprise and quickly dismounted. I caught a glimpse of Ryan's cock, hard and slick with . . . Bareback? Really? He quickly pulled the covers over himself as Astrid grabbed her clothes, ran to the bathroom, and shut the door.

'I didn't think you were back until the new year,' Ryan said.

'New Year's Eve. Sorry I've arrived at such an inconvenient time,' I replied, in a voice that didn't feel like my own.

Finally, my mind registered what I'd seen. Everything sped up and I was suddenly hot with anger. I grabbed the nearest book and lobbed it at Ryan. It hit him on the shoulder with a gratifying thwack.

'Jesus, that was a hardback.'

'Fuck off, Ryan.'

'I'm sorry. Really, really sorry.'

I collapsed onto the desk chair and put my head in my hands. The blood was roaring in my ears and I felt faint with shock. I could hear Ryan fumbling for his clothes. The bathroom door opened.

'I'm going to go,' I heard Astrid whisper.

I didn't look up at Ryan until she'd gone.

'Are you going to tell me it wasn't how it looked?'

He shook his head.

'Of course not. It's completely, utterly awful that you saw that.'

'I thought you were one of the good ones.'

He looked down at his hands, and then back at me, almost hopefully, as if in that split second things might have changed.

'How many times have you fucked her?'

'It wasn't something I'd intended. Or even thought about. Honestly, that's—'

'Just answer the question.'

'Once over Christmas. I guess we'd had too much to drink. And today we didn't intend . . . We were supposed to be planning a snowmobile trip . . .'

'And you fancy each other so much you couldn't keep your hands off each other?'

'It's not like that. It isn't. But we have so much in common. And you and I, well, you must have noticed it isn't going so well.'

'I was struggling with the move. But I thought things had gotten better. You never said anything.'

Ryan's hands were suddenly fascinating to him again. His shoulders were slumped, as if he were the one who deserved to be upset. When he spoke, his voice was little more than a whisper.

'Oh, Maya, how could I? You've been so fragile these past couple of months. I didn't realise how much, how difficult . . . Look, I'm sorry.'

'But I came all the way out here, just for you.'

'Maybe that was part of the problem,' he said.

'You wanted me to come.'

'I know, I know. But you're just sticking around here for me. You should put yourself out there more. Pursue *your* goals, not mine.'

'Just like Astrid, right? And that's why you fucked her – because she's goal oriented?'

I burst into tears.

Ryan, acting on instinct, got up and put his arms around me. But the gesture felt awkward. Of course it did – right now, he wished his arms were around someone else. I pushed him away.

'You'll thank me eventually, I promise. Besides, you hate the Arctic. Now, you can leave. And follow your dreams.'

'What if my dream is to be with you?'

Ryan shook his head. 'We aren't right for each other. I just realised sooner than you.'

The guillotine fell.

Us, severed.

I was dizzy with the suddenness of it. Relationships are all about compromise but break-ups are totally one-sided. More than anything I wanted to be held and reassured. But the person who normally did that was reaching for his coat, desperate to leave.

'I'll get out of your hair. Stay somewhere else for the night. I'll come back and pick up my clothes tomorrow.'

'And then?'

'Listen, I know the room comes as part of my employment package. But you can stay here as long as you need. Until you book a flight home.'

'Home?' I echoed hollowly.

I needed to be somewhere familiar. Norwich? But someone was living in my house and someone had taken my job. And every street corner, every pub and coffee shop would remind me of him. The Schools took root inside me with a vengeance.

'I feel completely lost,' I said.

'You could go back to India. Stay with your dad for a while.'

I thought of Dad, begging me to stay. Of the memories that had flooded back, each taking me further from what I thought I knew about Mum. Of Bangalore, a city where I had to brace myself against the noise, the traffic, the stares; where each street felt unfamiliar. I shook my head.

'You can do anything you want. There's someone out there who'll make you happy. Someone who's far more suited to you than I am,' Ryan said.

'You said you liked how different we were.'

He smiled sadly. 'That's what I thought.'

Surely this was all a mistake? A temporary madness we'd laugh over in a month's time. Of course I'd make him grovel. But we'd get back together. I looked at him hopefully but he was already leaving.

There was something so final about the noise of a door slamming.

The sound of everything falling apart.

Bits and pieces.

The room expanded and contracted before my eyes.

A Code Red of epic proportions. It felt like a heart attack.

You're not going to die, you're not going to die . . .

Things degenerated quickly from there.

21

I was dragged out of oblivion by the phone ringing. Nina.

'Hello,' I mumbled.

'Were you asleep? It's, like, midday.'

'Ungh.'

I struggled into a seated position. My head ached. Last night, after I'd finally stopped hyperventilating, I had unwisely downed all the alcohol in our kitchen cupboard.

'Muscles messaged. He said you were going through something and I should call.'

I clutched the phone.

'I walked in on him shagging someone else.'

'You're fucking kidding me?'

'Nope.'

An audible intake of breath.

'Jee-sus. What a sleaze. I never liked him,' Nina said.

'You did. He's been so supportive about my anxiety.'

'Maya, he just left you alone in the middle of the fucking Arctic.'

The thought of it made the edges of my vision tremble.

'I followed him here like a sheep.'

'Is that what he told you? Fuck, he's such a gas-lighter. He begged you to go.'

'Oh god, Nina. What am I going to do now?'

'Maybe it's a blessing in disguise. You hate it over there. Come to London. I'm looking for a new flatmate.'

For the next few minutes, Nina tried to convince me. We'd be living together again. We could cook great meals, go out for cocktails. I could find a job and catch up with my friends from catering college. But something was on my mind.

'Ryan said I never pursue anything. Is that true?'

'No. Not at all,' Nina replied, a little too quickly.

'You're my best mate. I can tell when you're lying.'

'You're totally vulnerable right now. This is no time for truth bombs.'

'So it *is* true?'

'You're not lazy. But you have low self-esteem. It can get in the way of doing what you want. And keeps you in situations that aren't right for you. If you had more self-confidence you would have walked out of that awful cheffing job on day one, and found something better.'

I inhaled; a long, shuddering sigh. Nina had been right – I wasn't ready for a truth bomb.

'I don't know what to do,' I said again.

'You need to be with people who love you right now. Come and stay with me.'

I hung up fifteen minutes later, feeling marginally better. At least there was someone who wanted to be around me. And Nina was right. The Arctic was Ryan's dream, not mine. It had only made me miserable. And that misery had cracked the image of the perfect girlfriend I'd been trying to project.

164

Throughout our relationship I'd tried my hardest to be the person Ryan wanted to come home to. I had listened to him practise his conference papers. Made him packed lunches and cooked him dinner. Laughed at his jokes. But it hadn't been good enough – as soon as I'd showed my vulnerability, he'd run away. He wasn't the first one to have done so, by any means.

Heartbreaks I have survived in the past:

- *When I was sixteen, I was obsessed with Paul Yates, one of the most popular boys in school. I was always hanging around outside his house, and even made him an anonymous mix-tape. One glorious day I was invited up to his room, where we ended up snogging like fish in our death throes. Then he grabbed my hand and placed it on his crotch. He had a happy ending but we didn't. The next day he told everyone we'd had sex and that it had been like doing it with a sack of spuds. I was devastated.*
- *At a party in my early twenties, I met Akhil. Like me, he was half-Indian and half-British. He'd grown up only a few streets away, but we'd gone to different schools. We both referred to ourselves as 'allergic to exercise', loved pub quizzes and were obsessed with food. My crush on him raged like a wildfire. Despite how well we got on, nothing ever happened. Eventually I confronted him. 'We're just too similar,' he said. Then he met Tilly, the star of my catering college; an elfin woman with a pixie cut who could just look at a fish and it would fall into perfect sashimi slices. Now she and Akhil were married, and lived in Devon. She had her own farm to table restaurant and he helped with the marketing. I stalked them obsessively on Instagram.*
- *And then there was Leo. We dated for about a month when*

I first arrived in Norwich. We had great sex, loads of fun,
and stayed up talking for hours. I was convinced that I'd
found a good one. And then he went totally AWOL. My
calls, texts, and emails went unanswered. I knocked on his
door and got no reply. I even called a couple of the local
hospitals to see if he'd died. A year later, I saw him
shopping in Tesco Metro. He was with a woman and a kid
who looked like him, chirruping loudly about strawberry
milk.

Each time it happened I'd stayed in bed for entire weekends mourning these shitty men. Months later, the intensity of my sorrow felt laughable. Maybe one day I'd feel the same about Ryan. But right now, that was hard to believe.

I was beginning to feel uncomfortably warm. Last night's alcohol felt as though it was seeping out of my pores, and I suddenly had a flashback to the previous evening, of drunkenly jabbing at the keys of his laptop, watching as gibberish scrolled across the screen. I reached for the laptop and checked 'recent documents'. It soon became apparent I had sabotaged a paper entitled 'A study on factors determining perfluoroalkyl concentration in female polar bears on Spitsbergen'. This riveting read had been improved by additions such as 'hate you Ryan' and '!!!!!!!! Q*()Q #%)^ QQO)_$% &^&^&%&.' As I erased the traces of my presence, I wondered if I'd deleted any important sentences. I couldn't make enough sense of the paper to tell.

Then I noticed that Ryan had left his Facebook open. So what if I was invading his privacy by reading his messages? He deserved it for invading Astrid's vagina. I scrolled back to the beginning. He'd sent the first one, asking her the best place in town for outdoor gear. Before long they were swapping links to drippy Scandinavian music and *National Geographic* photographs of polar bears tearing seals to pieces. After the sled ride, things got more intimate.

It's been so difficult trying to cheer up Maya today. I wish I could come out with you and the dogs instead of sitting about at home doing nothing.

Be patient with her, Astrid had advised. And you are welcome any time.

The messages became more frequent when I was in India. Ryan peppered his with irritating and uncharacteristic emoticons. Can't wait to spend Christmas with you 😊, he'd written. Then, the day after:

Last night was a dream 😍. You're beautiful, but I can't, for Maya's sake. It would destroy her. She really needs me right now.

I slammed the computer screen shut. My hands were shaking. It was difficult to breathe. He liked her. Properly, really liked her. I was just someone he felt obligated to be with. His albatross. His ailing Victorian wife. Well, fuck him. I wasn't going to be a burden any longer.

After a shower and an abortive attempt to repair my puffy face, I caught an extortionately priced taxi up to the cabins. It was only once I arrived that I realised I should have called ahead. No way I wanted to see another couple at it like rabbits. I felt acutely self-conscious as I knocked on the front door.

'Come in!'

Adam was curled up with a handsome, square-jawed guy, watching something on the laptop. Then I noticed the prosthetic leg leaning against the armchair.

'What the . . .'

'It's me. I got a haircut and shaved,' the stranger said.

'Mikkel!' I said, relieved. I couldn't cope with another dramatic relationship shift.

'I have been alone with him for over a week. He is very good at wearing people down,' Mikkel said, but he was smiling.

'I'm dating a hunk,' Adam said proudly, kissing Mikkel's newly exposed cheek.

It was time to resolve the second mystery.

'Um, there's a leg there,' I said, pointing to the limb.

'That belongs to me,' Adam said.

'So that means . . .?'

'Remember I told you I had a climbing accident? That was the unfortunate result,' Adam said.

I waited for him to elaborate. But he just picked up the leg, and refastened it with a sigh. Mikkel was looking puzzled.

'Did I tell you the wrong dates? Work isn't until Monday,' he said.

'Didn't you only get back yesterday?' Adam added. 'I thought you'd be in bed with that sexy boyfriend of yours.'

That did it. My face crumpled.

'Come here. Sit down,' Adam said.

Mikkel thrust a handkerchief that smelled of diesel at me. 'Do you want whisky?'

'Chocolate's a better bet,' Adam told him.

I sat between them, and fortified by the sugar, explained what had happened.

'What a way to begin the year,' Adam said sympathetically.

'Out with the old, in with the new,' Mikkel commented.

'I don't want to intrude. I just came to hand in my notice. I'll be leaving soon.'

'Leaving?' Adam said.

'I'm sorry to let you down. But there's no point me staying here now.'

'You have this job,' Mikkel said.

'What about all the photos you sent me over Christmas? And the dishes you were learning? Don't you have a suitcase full of spices? Why let that go to waste?' Adam said.

I swallowed. I hadn't banked on them trying to persuade me to stay. It was touching that they cared.

'I'm going back to London. Moving in with my friend, Nina.'

'What will you do there?' Adam asked.

'Get a job, catch up with people.'

'The city is not going anywhere,' Mikkel said.

'I'm not built for the Arctic.'

'You have two legs,' Adam pointed out.

I was temporarily roused from my self-pity.

'It must be hard. Does it hurt more in the cold?'

'Yes,' Adam said simply. 'It's difficult. But I can put up with it to be here.'

Mikkel squeezed his shoulder, eyes radiating pride.

Then they both looked at me expectantly.

'I'd love to carry on working for you. But I have to be realistic. I can't stay in Ryan's room and the apartments in town are so expensive.'

'Stay up here. There's a woman's dorm. It is barely used,' Mikkel said.

'That's so kind. But I couldn't. I don't want to intrude.'

'You wouldn't be intruding,' Adam said.

'What about your place in town? Do you need a flatmate?' I asked him.

'I don't have one now. Seemed stupid to pay rent when I was never there.'

169

I was beginning to crumble under the pressure. I also kind of liked feeling needed. But I wasn't Astrid – I couldn't deal with the darkness and the bone-aching cold.

'I can't.'

Mikkel leant forward. 'Can't? Or don't want to?'

I paused. Since I'd arrived in Longyearbyen, I'd been desperate to leave. The Arctic hadn't been kind to me. I had been scared to step outside, spent interminable days waiting for Ryan to come home. But things had started looking up when I came to End of the Road Cabins. I enjoyed cooking for the guys, sharing meals like one big, very macho family. But living at the cabins? Literally at the end of the road?

'Hello? Maya?'

'I don't want to overstay my welcome.'

'She means she doesn't want to commit to working here for long,' Mikkel told Adam.

'No, it's not that,' I protested.

'At least stay until the light returns. This place is so beautiful in March,' Adam said.

Three more months in the Arctic. Enough time for Ryan to realise I wasn't a wet blanket and come crawling back. Enough time for Dad to see that I could stand on my own two feet. And enough time for me to start applying for jobs in London, get something lined up for when I returned.

'March is when it starts to get busy,' Mikkel grumbled.

Adam gave him a look.

'Fine. Stay until March. And then we talk again. The summer months are when I most need a cook.'

'Alright. I'll stay *at least* until March,' I said, feeling guilty.

'Excellent,' Adam said. 'This calls for a toast. Shall we have some port?'

I nodded.

'I'm going out for a cigarette first. Mikkel?'

'I have made a New Year's resolution to give up smoking.'
Adam was looking triumphant.

'How did you convince him?' I asked.

'A war of attrition. But I don't mind if you smoke one last cigarette with Maya.'

Mikkel grinned, blew a kiss at Adam, and came outside with me. He sucked tenderly on his cigarette.

'I will be a monster in a couple of days.'

'Can't wait.'

'I will try to be a bastard only to Adam. This is his fault.'

'It's admirable he finally persuaded you.'

Mikkel blew out a cloud of smoke. 'He is staying here for me. So I have an epiphany. I should stop being a dick.'

'Well, I don't know. He loves the Arctic.'

'This is not the best place for an amputee. Uneven terrain, cold temperatures. Doing this job is hard on him.'

'He's a braver person than I am,' I said.

'He is braver than most people I know. But you are not a coward either. You just agreed to spend your winter in a cabin in the Arctic with us. I guarantee that in three months we will have made an explorer out of you.'

'I doubt it.'

If I could get through the three months without having a spectacularly embarrassing meltdown, or dying of hypothermia, it would be a huge achievement.

'I still remember that I must teach you how to shoot. And ride a snowmobile.'

'Yay,' I said weakly.

I was beginning to wonder if I had made the right choice. Would there be central heating in the women's cabin? If I

171

needed a piss in the middle of the night would I – god forbid – have to use the compost toilets? I felt The Schools squirming in my gut. But Ryan's words were still at the forefront of my mind.

You give up as soon as it gets hard.

Not this time.

22

I struggled after Adam, dragging my suitcase across the snow. His torch flickered ahead of me, the only point of light in the darkness. Outside of the beam I could see nothing, not even my hand when I waved it in front of my face. What if there was no electricity in the hut? Nothing to keep away this impenetrable night?

'Here we are,' Adam said.

His torch picked out a small wooden cabin. A shed, if you were being uncharitable. He opened the door and reached inside. I heard the click of a light switch and my knees went weak with relief. A solitary bulb illuminated a small room containing a table and chair, two bunk-beds and a chest of drawers with a weird blue-green glow. It looked like a set from a horror movie. I searched for something positive to say.

'Oh great, there's electricity in here.'

'Yep. It's powered by a big battery, which is in an insulated box outside. Me and Mikkel recharge ours about once a week in the main hut, to make sure we don't get sudden blackouts.'

I shuddered at the thought.

'Is there WI-FI?' I asked hopefully.

'I'm not sure, to be honest. The router's in the cabin. We don't get it in ours but you might be lucky, given that you're closer. And there's no central heating, obviously, but the log burner works amazingly well. I just lit the fire – it'll be toasty in about ten minutes.'

'Thanks, Ad, I really appreciate it.'

'Sorry I didn't have time to tidy. I've put some cleaning stuff there,' he said, indicating some spray, a cloth and a broom in the corner. 'Do you want me to help you with it now?'

'Oh, no, don't worry about it.'

I had no intention of becoming any more of an imposition.

'Well, is there anything else I can help with?'

'How do I get the fire to last all night?'

'I'll show you.'

Adam indicated a narrow vent at the top of the wood burning stove.

'This controls the airflow. The more oxygen a fire has, the faster it burns. Shut the vent almost all the way and it'll burn slowly. But make sure you put enough fuel on it first.'

'Fuel? Like petrol?'

Adam looked at me.

'Logs, Maya.'

'Oh right, yeah. Obviously.'

'Anyway. I'll leave you to unpack.'

And go tell Mikkel how inept I am. But it wasn't my fault. Outdoorsy guys like Ryan always colonised the fire on camping trips and nobody else got a look-in. I would have to learn quickly, or I'd freeze.

I shut the door. So this was where I would be sleeping for the next few months. If I made it through the night, that was. The bulb wasn't very bright, so the corners of the room remained in shadow. The chair looked like it would collapse if I sat on it and the place smelled of wood smoke and rising damp. I couldn't even tell myself that it would look better in the morning, since it was still two months before the sun rose. A log shifted in the fire, making me jump. At this very moment I could have been sitting in a cocktail bar, with Nina. Not for the first time, I found myself wondering why I'd decided to pursue this option instead. And then I found myself cataloguing decisions I'd made and immediately regretted.

My biggest regrets:

- *Not giving Sally Coulter-Potts the last piece of cake in Year Five. She called me Fatty-Fatty-Bum-Bum and the name stuck for the rest of Junior School.*
- *Losing my virginity at a party before I was ready. I can't even remember the guy's name. I can remember that his breath smelled of beer and pickled onion Monster Munch. After the first tearing, painful thrust, it only lasted a few seconds. There's something so inescapably violent about the first time. It was years before I had sex again.*
- *Not visiting India sooner. If I had gone when I was twenty there would have been a decade less of lies. Jobin might have flattered me into dating him. Perhaps he would have made me amazingly happy. Then I might never have met Ryan. Never moved to the Arctic, never had my heart broken into itty-bitty pieces, and never gotten stranded in this creepy-ass hut.*

I paused.

It had been my decision to stay.

I was sick of feeling useless. Sick of being defeated by the smallest tasks. Even Nina had said I didn't have the self-confidence to pursue what I wanted. But did I really, truly want this? At least it would prove I could stick at something.

When I felt stressed, it helped to clean. Impose order onto chaos; make a visible difference to something. I put on my tidying up playlist and Queen's 'Another One Bites the Dust' blared from my phone speaker as I swept the floor, dusted the furniture, and beat the rug until a faded blue and red pattern emerged. Tomorrow I'd see if there was a spare oil lamp. Maybe I could even stitch a pair of curtains for the window. It occurred to me that Ryan would be jealous – he had always wanted to spend a season living in an old trapper's hut, experiencing the 'True Arctic'. I wondered if he was thinking of me right now. Probably not.

I folded my clothes into drawers, lined up my shoes on the doormat and my books on the table. Soon the only things left in my suitcase were the spices, the pressure cooker, and Mum's cookbook. It was a shock to see them. The break-up had dominated my mind over the past couple of days, but as I looked down at the pile of different coloured powders I was reminded that not all heartbreaks are of the romantic kind. I remembered Mum's hands, stained with orange grease. Her head bent over her plate, refusing to acknowledge me. Perhaps I should throw them all away and be done with it.

I grabbed a handful of packets. Ochre-tinted turmeric. Vibrant red Kashmiri chilli. Black mustard seeds. Moong dal and urad dal, which would be impossible to find here. The golden lump of jaggery and a packet of tamarind pulp. Finally, I extracted a Ziploc bag full of Uma's homemade garam masala. I opened the bag and inhaled the spicy fragrance of cloves, the sweetness of cinnamon, and the sharp warmth of star anise. A comforting scent, and surprisingly complex. My mind wasn't assaulted by memories I would rather forget. In fact, I was reminded of Christmas; of eating spiced biscuits with a glass of mulled wine. A sprinkle of garam masala would transform basic dishes like vegetable soup or apple cake. So, fine, I'd keep it. And the mustard seeds; they added a nice crunchiness to dishes. In fact, maybe I'd keep all the spices.

Then there was the pressure cooker. I remembered being in the kitchen with Uma, watching as she made dal. A chorus of whistles had filtered in through the window. In the apartment block opposite, other women were also cooking lunch. Mum had once been one of those housewives and in another world, perhaps I would have been too.

My hand made contact with her cookbook and I fought the urge to recoil. It was a book, not a sentient creature actively seeking to harm me.

All her recipes, thousands of painstaking hours of labour. Had they been undertaken willingly, or had she fumed as she chopped onions and pounded spices?

I opened the book at random. 'Saaru', the title read. It was, according to the recipe, a lentil and tomato-based soup dish flavoured with curry leaves, asafoetida and dried red chillies. I was curious to try it. But the thought of being exposed to any more of Mum's dark days gave me a strange feeling in the pit of my stomach, like I'd just reached the top of a rollercoaster and was suspended in that horrible pause before the plummet downwards. The Arctic was a long way from India. Surely dishes I cooked here wouldn't evoke memories as powerful as those experienced in Bangalore?

I placed the spices and the cookbook back into the suitcase, and zipped it up. Mum's book belonged with me. But that didn't mean I was ready to cook from it yet.

It was then I was faced with one of the joys of cabin-living in the Arctic: no indoor bathroom. I cleaned my teeth and spat the foamy water out of the front door. There was no way I was going to use that long-drop toilet, or venture back to the bathroom in the main cabin. Hopefully, I would fall asleep before I got too desperate.

I turned out the light and got into bed. This was Black Hole Dark. Darkness Before The Big Bang Dark. But there was nothing inert about it – the night was swirling with sound. Outside was a symphony of rattles, scrapes, and a long, low howling.

I told myself it was just the wind around the walls of the hut.

But then my brain unhelpfully reminded me that there are more polar bears than people living in Svalbard.

I heard a scratching sound, like claws skittering across the wooden floor.

You're imagining it.

A sudden thudding sound made me dive under the blankets.

It's just a log shifting in the fire.

The night howled and creaked and thudded. I had to wedge balled-up tissue into my ears and pull a pillow over my head to block it out. But even then I couldn't sleep. My need to pee became increasingly urgent. Soon it was all I could think about. There was no way in hell I was going to step outside though.

In the end, I went in the only receptacle I could find – the pressure cooker. Even after emptying my bladder, it felt like I stayed awake for hours.

When I eventually nodded off, I had the dream.

The waves are a dark purple colour, their crests tinted sallow yellow. They break violently on the rocks where I'm standing, scattering spume into the air. Soon my dress is drenched, and my legs are numb.

'*Ma,*' *I call, scrambling backwards across the rocks. '*Ma!*'*

My body was stiff with cold and for a moment I thought I was still trapped on the rocks. I pulled the blankets down an inch and was confronted with an icy blast of air. Shit. The fire must have gone out. I had no idea how to relight it. Last time I went camping, Ryan had told me to gather lots of little twigs. Kindling will help the bigger logs catch, he'd said. But where would I find twigs here, where nothing grew? I wouldn't last the night without a fire.

'I told her she should have just gone back to England,' I imagined Ryan telling my friends and family.

I groped for my phone. It was so dark I thought it must be the middle of the night. To my surprise, it was seven in the morning. Somehow, I'd made it through.

23

I could connect to the WI-FI if I jammed the phone right into the front corner of the hut. When I logged onto Instagram, I saw that Ryan's feed was already filled with photos of him and Astrid. Someone had taken a photo of them in the pub, holding pints. 'Nursing our NY hangovers', the caption read, suggesting it must've taken Ryan mere minutes to get over our relationship ending. The most recent picture was a selfie taken with one of Astrid's huskies in between them. She'd caught herself at an unflattering angle so her chin looked much larger than usual, but her smile was radiant. I hoped that all the sex they were having gave her a UTI and him a friction burn.

If only he'd talked to me about his feelings for Astrid, instead of confronting me with it in a moment I kept replaying; his body against hers, the animal intensity of their expressions. I'd wasted so much time and energy on a relationship that had gone nowhere. Now every time I looked on social media, there'd be endless photos of cute couples and kitsch marriage ceremonies and new babies, reminding me of what I'd missed out on. Furiously, I threw open the door, bent down and picked up a handful of snow.

'Fuck you, Ryan!' I yelled, chucking it into the whirling darkness.

It hit something – presumably the shed wall opposite – with a satisfying thwack. If only the wall was Ryan and the snow was a grenade. Well, I could pretend. I chucked another snowball, then another.

'You stupid arsehole!' I shouted.

'What the hell?'

A torchlight flicked on and I saw Adam. The side of his head was covered in snow.

'Oh god, I'm so sorry.'

'First Mikkel and now you. What have I done to piss everyone off?' Adam grumbled, brushing off the snow.

'Not you – Ryan.'

'What happened?'

'He's posted loads of pictures of him and Astrid on Instagram.'

'Show me.'

I held out my phone. Adam took it from me and slid it into his pocket.

'And your laptop.'

'No way.'

'Just for a week. So you don't check social media. Trust me – it'll really help.'

I handed over the laptop and immediately regretted it. No more Netflix. No more googling useless facts. No more Skype sessions with Nina.

'But what will I *do* now?'

'You need a project. Something to keep you occupied. I'm

sure you'll work it out. Do you want to come up and have a coffee?'

'That'd be great.'

Maybe I could snatch the phone and laptop back when Adam wasn't looking. But when we arrived at the cabins, he quickly padlocked them into a metal box.

Mikkel was nursing a mug of coffee, looking as haggard as I felt.

'How're you feeling?' I asked.

'Like shit.'

'C'mon, Mikkel, no need to be an arse,' Adam said.

'This is your fault for making me quit.'

'You'll thank me in the long run. Maya's not feeling much better. I caught her having a yelling fit about Ryan.'

'Want me to shoot him? It would improve my mood,' Mikkel said.

'Can you shoot Astrid while you're at it?'

'Ya, okay. She might be nice but she is business competition.'

'You know, it's not a bad idea,' Adam mused.

We looked at him in confusion.

'Not shooting *people*. But we should take Maya to the range and teach her how to use a rifle. It'd be good for getting out some of your pent-up aggression too, Mikki.'

'That is not the worst idea you've ever had.'

'And that's the nicest thing you've said to me in the past couple of days.'

Mikkel had the grace to look ashamed. 'I have been smoking since age thirteen. That is a lot of nicotine.'

'I know. And you're doing so well, you really are,' Adam said, putting his hand on Mikkel's shoulder. Then he turned to me.

'So, up for the range?'

'I was going to make some meal plans.'

'This'll just be a short trip. It would do you good to get out – I'll invite Rita, too,' Adam said, sounding firmer than before. I sensed that it would take a lot to dislodge the idea. The only way was to convince him of my ineptitude, a technique I had employed successfully on many occasions with Ryan.

'I've never held a gun before. I'm not sure if I can.'

'It's easy, honestly. It'll be so useful if you can learn to shoot properly. It means you can go off by yourself on a snowmobile.'

'I can't drive a snowmobile either,' I said miserably.

'We'll teach you that, too.'

Half an hour later, we set off in the Jeep. Mikkel had cheered up and he'd put on a tape of seventies punk rock songs, which he was now singing tunelessly along to.

'Ever fall in love with someone, ever fallen in love, in love with someone you shouldn't have fallen in love with . . .'

I was sitting in the back with the rifles and trying to panic as unobtrusively as possible. I fumbled for my phone to find out how many people accidentally shot themselves – or someone else – each year, and then remembered that Adam had it. Feeling curiously bereft, I shifted as far away from the rifles as possible.

We drove to the outskirts and stopped outside a large, open-fronted hut. In the distance were the targets, square boards illuminated by a floodlight. Hitting them would be impossible. I wanted a cigarette to steady my nerves, but it wasn't fair on Mikkel. As we walked towards the hut I realised someone was already there – a short, very curvy someone wearing a balaclava and steampunk ski goggles.

'Hey guys,' Rita said. 'Hey Maya, how's it going?'

'Good, thanks.'

'Maya moved up to the cabins,' Mikkel said.

'Oh hey, that's cool. I thought you were more of a city girl,' she said to me.

'She had no choice. Her boyfriend ran off with Astrid,' Mikkel replied, with his characteristic bluntness. Adam gave him a reproachful look.

'What? It's the truth.'

'It is,' I confirmed. If I said any more about it I would ugly-cry in front of them.

'That's a rubbish start to the year,' Rita said. 'I guess he's revealed his true colours.'

'It's not like that,' I replied, jumping in to defend him out of habit. I'd made him sound like a fuckboy and that wasn't entirely the case. 'He just couldn't cope with my anxiety.'

'A convenient excuse,' Rita muttered.

Adam and Mikkel didn't reply. What do you say to that, anyway?

'Um, shall we crack on, then?' Adam asked.

'Okay,' I said, grateful for the change in topic.

I stood next to Rita, watching as Adam checked over the guns.

'I'm going to load it for you this time,' he said, removing a square metallic thing from the bottom of the gun. 'This is the clip. You put the bullets in here, between these two bits of metal, see?'

I nodded, watching as he deftly loaded the bullets.

'Then, I insert the clip back into the gun. Turn off the safety, and it's ready to fire.'

Adam handed me the rifle. It was heavier than expected and I wasn't sure if I'd be able to hold it up, let alone load it. I struggled to open a champagne bottle – a gun was way beyond my capabilities. And I was very aware of Rita and Mikkel's eyes on me.

'If you shoot lying down you don't have to support the weight,' Rita said.

'Let me show you,' Mikkel said.

I handed him the rifle. He lay down on a rubber mat, and aimed it at the target.

'Push the butt of the gun against your shoulder. It will recoil, so if you do not keep it wedged you might get the butt in the face.'

'Which isn't the worst thing in the world,' Adam murmured behind me.

I was too wound up to laugh.

'Now, this is the sight. You look into it and line up the target. Then you pull the trigger.'

'Before Mikkel shoots we should put on ear protectors,' Adam said.

He handed a pair to me and placed some over Mikkel's ears. Rita had her own pair.

I watched as Mikkel fired off a round of bullets with practised ease. The sound made me jump. Luckily, it was over in seconds.

'How did I do?' Mikkel asked, lowering the rifle.

Adam walked over to the target to investigate.

'Six out of seven hit the board,' he yelled over to us.

'Any bullseyes?'

A slight pause.

'Four.'

'Liar!' Rita yelled.

'Wait until you see him shoot. Seven out of seven on the board, and most bullseyes on a good day,' Mikkel said.

'Well he is an ex-marine,' I said. 'Although you wouldn't know it.'

'He used to be a brute. I think the accident made him nicer,' Mikkel said, almost regretfully.

Adam returned and vaulted back onto the platform, wincing as he landed.

'What are you lot chatting about?'

'We are saying that you are too out of practice to hit the targets,' Mikkel said.

'Oh yeah?'

Adam put on his ear protectors and picked up the rifle. He loaded it and fired off seven shots in quick succession.

'Show-off,' Rita murmured.

'I can totally see you're ex-special forces,' I said.

'Thanks,' Adam said, sounding gratified. And he was even happier when he came back and told us he'd hit five bulls-eyes.

After that, Rita wanted a go. She loaded and fired the gun.

'You made that look effortless,' I said.

'My dad taught me,' she replied.

I thought of my own dad, who wouldn't even let me slice vegetables until I was thirteen years old because he was so worried I would cut myself. If he knew what I was doing now he'd be having sleepless nights.

'Now it's your turn,' Mikkel said.

'Do I have to?'

'You have to,' the three of them chorused.

As I lay down on the ground I felt my teeth chattering.

'Here.'

Adam handed me the rifle and I took it with shaking hands.

'Press the butt against your shoulder, remember, to absorb

186

the recoil. A little higher. Okay, great. Remember to take the catch off.'

I fumbled with the catch. It was stiff, but by some miracle I managed it.

'Now, squeeze the trigger,' Adam said.

There was a loud bang and the gun jerked backwards, smacking me so hard in the shoulder that I yelped in pain.

'Guys, I don't think this is going to work. I suck.'

'You only had one go. Nobody can do it the first time,' Rita said.

'When you aimed you moved the gun away from your body. You have to keep it braced against you. Try again,' Adam said.

Once, on holiday with Ryan, I'd plucked up the courage to jump off a cliff into the river below. The only thing that happened was I got water up my nose. But even so, I couldn't do it a second time. What if something went seriously wrong? I'd got lucky once, what if I didn't again? Courage, like luck, was finite. I explained my theory. Nobody agreed.

'It's hardly a leap of faith. Just squeeze the trigger. This instant!' Adam roared.

Chastened, I picked up the rifle, took aim, and fired. This time I was anticipating the recoil and it didn't come as such a shock.

'There, that was better, wasn't it?' I said.

'Well . . . you had your eyes shut. Do it again, and try and relax this time,' Adam said.

It was hard to relax when you were lying on the ground, holding a gun in sub-zero temperatures. I decided not to complain. Instead, I fired off some shots into the darkness. Rita went off to look, and cheerfully reported back that none of them had hit the target.

'The next lesson can be about aiming. But let's go back now. I'm bloody freezing,' Adam said.

I'd thought they were impervious to the cold. I felt less of a wimp realising it wasn't the case.

'We should have put more clothes on,' Mikkel said.

He coughed. A horrible, painful, gasping cough.

'That sounds nasty. Maybe you should go to the doctor's,' Adam commented.

'It is from giving up smoking.'

'Worth checking out, though.'

'I hate the doctors. I always worry that they will find an incurable disease I never knew I had,' Mikkel said, as we walked back to the car.

'Better to know than not to know,' Adam said.

'I am scared of dying slowly. If I get sick, or when I get old, I will start walking and keep going until the North takes me.'

'Until the North takes you? Why are you talking like fucking Franklin, you madman? Shut up and get it checked out. No point walking around with a chest infection for the next fortnight,' Adam said angrily.

'Like an old married couple,' Rita said to me.

She and I had hung back, allowing the two of them to walk on ahead together.

'I feel like they got closer over Christmas,' I said. 'I wonder if Mikkel will be more public about it now.'

'He just doesn't like the clients to know. Makes him feel like they'll see him differently.'

'Are you dating anyone?'

'There was this girl, Ivy, back in New York. But now, no. Sorry about Ryan.'

'I still can't quite believe it. And I know it's pathetic but I keep hoping he'll see sense and come back.'

'You're better off without him. Look what you're doing now. You get to live amongst all this,' she said, gesturing at the darkness.

I snorted in amusement before I could stop myself.

'You'll appreciate it, when the light starts to return.'

'Everyone says that.'

'It's true. Anyway, at least you got some sunshine in India. How was the trip?'

'Pretty good.'

'You don't sound very enthusiastic.'

'I had an argument with my dad. About . . . well, he kept some stuff from me.'

'As far as parents go, that doesn't sound too bad. Mine have inflicted much worse.'

'He said he was just trying to look after me.'

'Maybe it's worth giving the guy a break if his intentions were pure. I mean, now Ryan's out of the picture, you need someone in your corner.'

'Yeah, but . . .'

We'd reached Rita's snowmobile by now. She opened up the seat, extracted a helmet and put it on.

'Well, it's your decision,' she said, her voice muffled. 'Anyway, I should head.'

'See you soon.'

'See ya.'

She straddled her snowmobile and rode off into the darkness like a heroine from a dystopian movie. I thought about what she'd said. Should I forgive Dad? There were so many 'buts'. The duration of the lie, for a start. His refusal to treat me like an adult. Thinking about it made me angry all over again. But deep down I knew Rita was right.

24

The arrival of the next residential group coincided with an Arctic blizzard of such intensity I worried my hut would get blown away. I cracked open the door of the cabin and watched as the snow whirled in relentless, chaotic rhythms. The wind swelled to a howling crescendo. Overnight the storm grew teeth and claws, became frenzied in its intent on destruction. I was sure I could hear noises inside as well. When I finally slept I dreamed of being lost in the Arctic, staggering like a sleepwalker across the ice in search of something familiar. Finally, I saw a light in the distance. As I drew closer I realised it was an igloo, the interior illuminated. Dad and Uma were huddled on the sofa, a large furry blanket tugged across their laps.

'Make a curry from it, won't you? There are so many recipes to choose from,' Uma said, holding something up.

It was the carcass of a polar bear, teeth still bared in a snarl.

I woke up with a start. Since I'd moved up here, I'd been having the strangest dreams. But this one was easier to decode than most.

There are so many recipes to choose from.

Mum's recipe book was still in the suitcase. I extracted it and I experienced that strange plummeting sensation again. But it was less intense this time, and mixed in with something else. Curiosity. Perhaps even excitement. Slowly, I turned the pages. Most were dishes I hadn't heard of before. Bisebele bath. Poriyal. Payasam. Karela fry. Sometimes the handwriting was neat, measured. Other times it was so illegible I couldn't tell what language was being used. One recipe had been scribbled over so violently that holes had been gouged into the paper. Feeling unsettled, I flipped to the next page. It was a complete contrast, the writing neat and evenly spaced. She'd even doodled some flowers in the margin. Khichdi, the title read. The name was familiar – I was sure I'd heard Nina mention it before.

A high-pitched noise made me drop the recipe book onto the bed. It sounded like a demonic baby. *It's just the wind*, I told myself. The sooner I was back in human company, the better.

There it was again; a shrill wail that made my scalp prickle.

Something, or someone, was in the room.

I jumped out of bed and threw my body against the door. It didn't budge. I looked out of the window and saw the glass was covered with snow. It was like the whole hut was completely submerged. My pulse skyrocketed. I hammered on the door as loudly as I could.

'Help! I'm snowed in!'

Why had Adam confiscated my phone? Now I'd just have to sit here and wait for help. Perhaps whatever was in here would devour me before I got rescued. I redoubled my hammering on the door.

'Maya,' said a muffled voice from outside. 'It's Adam.'

'Get me out of here!'

'I need to get a shovel.'

'There's something in here. Something that shrieked.'

'It might be an Arctic Fox.'

'Oh shit. Is it dangerous? What do I do?'

'No, it's just seeking shelter. Hold tight, I'll send someone to dig you out.'

'Adam? Adam!'

I closed my eyes and tried my best to pretend I was somewhere else, somewhere where there were no epic storms and no wild animals hiding in my room. But the blizzard hurled itself against the walls and the high-pitched yips started up again, both refusing to be ignored. I opened my eyes.

'Fine, you little bastard. Where are you?'

There were a lot of dark corners in here. But there was nothing under the desk, nothing curled up against the stove.

I peered under the adjacent bunk-bed. There was a small, huddled shape in the corner. A shape that shifted and moved before my eyes. I jumped back, as far away from it as possible. This wasn't what I'd had in mind when I said I wanted company. How the fuck had it gotten in anyway? It was like the Houdini of foxes.

Outside, there was a scraping sound.

'Hey guys!' I yelled.

No response, save for a lot of grunting and shouting.

'Is it still snowing?' I bawled.

'Like a bitch.'

I quickly grabbed everything I might need for the day – notebook, slippers, my Kindle – and shoved them in a rucksack. After a moment's hesitation, I put Mum's recipe book into the bag too. After all, I couldn't leave it in here with a wild animal.

192

The scraping had gotten louder.

'Try opening it now,' one of them shouted.

This time, the door yielded and icy air rushed into the room. Gritting my teeth, I forced myself through the gap. My rescuers had already left to dig out someone else and snow assaulted me from all directions. The whole world had disappeared. The only things left were ferocious winds and howling snow, two elements bent on extinguishing all traces of human existence. This was definitely a Code Red situation; screams and sirens and flashing lights.

'Hello?'

Nobody replied.

I was alone at the very edge of the world. If only Ryan was here. But standing here moping wouldn't get him back – it would just give me frostbite.

I switched on my headtorch and stepped off the porch. I knew the main hut was only about twenty metres to the right, but within seconds I was completely lost. It wasn't just that left and right, and up and down were confused; it was that they had ceased to exist. I had already been half-rubbed out, my mind invaded by gusts of wind and snow. I barely knew who I was, only that I had to keep upright, keep breathing, putting one foot in front of the other.

The blizzard intensified. It knocked me to my knees. I tried and failed to get up. There was nothing for it. I'd have to crawl. My heart and lungs were bursting with the effort of the struggle. I began counting, hoping I'd be safe and warm by the time I'd reached twenty.

One, two, three . . . four . . . five . . . six . . . seven . . .

Twenty came and went. The exposed skin of my face was burning with the cold. My ears rang with the noise of the storm. I struggled to my feet and was almost blown over again. Somehow, even though every limb in my body was frozen, I continued forwards.

Weirdly, my panic began to abate. All my energy was concentrated on remaining upright. I was nothing but a body, nothing but blood pulsing through veins, heart pumping, lungs inflating and deflating, muscles contracting, slowly moving forwards . . .

A smudge of light appeared. The main cabin. I almost cried in relief.

As I pushed open the door, I realised that most of the group were already inside. I headed straight for an armchair by the fire. People were talking, but I couldn't understand what they were saying. My nerves felt jangled and my heart was beating as fast as the Etruscan shrew's. My frozen balaclava had started to melt in the heat, and icy water was dripping down my face. I pulled it off, then my boots and thick, sodden outer layer. My hands were so numb it took forever. By the time I was done, I was shaking.

'Here.'

One of the lads handed me a thick woollen blanket.

'Thanks,' I said gratefully.

I moved to a drier chair, and finally began to warm up.

Out there, all thoughts and sense of self had been driven away. Maybe that was one of the reasons people felt compelled by the Arctic. Because face to face with it, you disappeared. Total self-annihilation. All your worries gone, replaced by the innate, primitive need to survive. Walking in the blizzard, I hadn't thought of Ryan once. And sure, I'd freaked out, but nowhere near as badly as the first time I'd gotten lost in the snow, when I'd got into bed and got Ryan to run home from work and comfort me. In fact, this wouldn't even make it onto my list of scary life moments.

Some of the scariest moments of my life:

- *The first time Dad was late to pick me up from school. It happened during our first few months in the UK, which had been spent navigating unfamiliar rules, and accents, and conversations about toys and TV shows I hadn't seen. When he didn't show up, I went to pieces. Despite the teacher's protestations, I was completely and utterly convinced he'd been killed in a car accident, just like Mum. Later, Dad told me he was only fifteen minutes late, but in my memory it feels like years and years passed while I waited.*

- *When I was in my early twenties, I went to our local shopping centre to pick up a birthday present for a friend. While flicking through some CDs I looked up and locked eyes with an unremarkable guy about a decade older than me. The intensity of his gaze made me feel horribly uncomfortable. I quickly moved on to another shop. The fucker followed, staring at me like he could see through my clothes. The sensible thing would have been to call security. But I was too young and scared to be sensible. I hightailed it out of the mall as quickly as possible. He came down the escalator after me, tracked me across the concourse. Luckily, I managed to lose him at a crowd near one of the exits. Even thinking about it now makes me feel cold.*

- *After the breakdown I had in my mid-twenties I suffered several instances of sleep paralysis. The most vivid occurrence was, quite frankly, terrifying. Picture a tall, faceless figure walking slowly towards you. Picture being unable to move, unable to scream, however hard you tried . . .*

But I'd survived them all, just like I'd survived out there in the snow today. The thought made me feel oddly euphoric and I bit back the urge to break into hysterical laughter. Maybe that was one of the after-effects of the blizzard. I glanced around the room to see if anyone else was experiencing anything similar.

Mikkel was standing in the doorway, surveying the room. 'Where's Adam?' he asked.

'He's gone to check on the dogs,' someone said.

Mikkel looked alarmed.

'Alone?'

'Yeah.'

'Stupid bastard,' Mikkel muttered, making for the door.

'I'll come with you,' offered a stocky, tough-looking guy.

'And me,' said someone else.

The three of them disappeared back outside again. A couple of the younger guys seemed relieved not to be joining them.

I opened my bag and pulled out Mum's recipe book. Again, I found myself looking at the khichdi recipe. The neat handwriting and the cutesy doodles were reassuring. Thanks to Uma, I had everything I needed aside from ghee, which could be made from butter.

The kitchen was cold and draughty, but soon the portable radiator and the heat from the stove began to warm it up. The rattling of the window panes was obscured by the sound of butter bubbling in the pan, and a rich, milky smell infused the kitchen. The windows steamed up with condensation, obscuring the darkness. Once I'd strained the melted butter to make ghee, I added a couple of spoonfuls to my cooking pot and tossed in some whole spices. There was something comforting and oddly familiar about the spicy-sweet combination of cardamom, pepper, cloves and ginger. I added cumin seeds, then moong dal and rice, sautéing until the grains smelled nutty. Finally, I added chopped cauliflower, sliced carrot, turmeric and water. Now the khichdi would simmer until it was ready. The recipe recommended serving it with fried potato slices and a raita made with yoghurt, tomatoes and diced onions. I got on with these while the khichdi was cooking.

As I inhaled the fragrant steam, I felt my resistance towards the recipe book dissolve. The memories that had resurfaced in India felt a world away from this cramped kitchen in the middle of the Arctic. Back then I had been Ryan's girlfriend. Now my heart felt rubbed raw, as painful as a newly-opened wound.

The handwriting blurred. I wiped my eyes, and tried to focus my attention on the recipe.

Add 3 spoonfuls of ghee. Take upstairs to Maya, the final instruction read.

I reread the sentence several times. For me. She'd made this recipe for me.

I did as the recipe said, and sprinkled ghee liberally over the khichdi. Then I took a slice of potato, dipped it into the mixture, and bit into it.

I'm lying in bed. The sheets feel scratchy against my skin. My head hurts and my body feels hot and cold in turn. I start to cry. Then the door opens. Mum comes into the room, holding a steaming bowl. She sits next to me, places a cool hand on my forehead.

'Oh my poor baby. Come on now.'

She helps me sit up. Spoons the khichdi in my mouth. The rich, buttery mixture soothes the soreness in my throat and eases the pain in my stomach. But more comforting than

197

anything is her presence beside me, her hand stroking my hair.

Even now, surrounded by dirty pots and pans, darkness and snow pressing against the windows, I can still feel the warmth of that moment.

So Dad had been right. There had been dark days, but she had cared for me too. Cared for me so much I could still feel it, decades after her death and thousands of miles from India. I picked up the notebook and hugged it to my chest. I was touching something she had once touched. Uma was right. It was more intimate, more real, than any photograph. And it was mine.

25

Adam finished tying the last of a complicated-looking set of knots, and straightened up.

'And that's how you build a stretcher made of rope. Is anyone even listening to me?'

A couple of the politer guys wiped the bored look off their faces and nodded. But others were talking amongst themselves and one or two looked like they'd fallen asleep.

'Get into threes and try it yourselves. Remember, at least one of you will have to try the stretcher out,' Mikkel said. He was sitting in one of the armchairs, knitting an intricate-looking jumper.

The guys wearily got into groups. From my position on the sofa, I could hear them grumbling.

'. . . Thought we'd actually get to go outside . . .'

'. . . Fucking blizzard . . .'

'. . . Stinks in here . . .'

It had snowed for the past two days. The guys had to dig their huts out of the snow to go to bed, and climb out of the window in the morning. To avoid doing the same, I'd spent both nights sleeping on the sofa in the main cabin. The walls were much thicker than in my hut, and blocked out the noise of the blizzard. I also got first dibs on the shower in the morning. The only downside was that Mikkel had allowed his favourite dog, Frostie Williams, to come inside. He was an old, squint-eyed huskie with a tendency to let rip sulphurous farts that had everyone scrambling backwards in disgust.

Adam sat down heavily next to me.

'Tough crowd,' he said.

'People are going stir crazy from the blizzard, that's all,' I reassured him.

'Thanks for all your help,' Adam said to Mikkel.

'But you are doing such a great job,' he replied, without looking up from his knitting.

There was a loud thump followed by voluble swearing. Someone had fallen through their rope stretcher. Adam sighed and heaved himself up from the sofa.

'This has more holes in than a Swiss cheese,' he said, holding it up.

Seconds later, another dog fart suffused the air.

'Jesus . . .'

'That's so thick I could cut it with a knife.'

A couple of guys made for the door.

'Hey, it's not snowing nearly as much,' one of them yelled back.

'Does that mean we can go out later?'

Mikkel coughed. There were dark circles etched under his eyes.

'Perhaps. Let's see how it goes.'

Over the next hour, the wind dropped and the snow eased off, but the noise in the room reached fever pitch. When

200

Mikkel finally told everyone to get ready for a dogsledding trip, the news was greeted with ear-splitting cheers. As they tramped out of the hut, he turned to me.

'Will you make something for dinner? Not lentils this time.'

Yesterday I'd tried out a dal recipe from Mum's cookbook. Somehow the gasket in the pressure cooker had gotten blocked and starchy lentil water had shot out from under the lid, spattering all over the kitchen and making me scream. I flushed with embarrassment at the memory.

'I'll just make hotdogs,' I promised him.

'Enjoy the quiet,' said Adam.

'Ad, can I have my phone back? It's been a week.'

I wish I could say I'd learned a valuable moral lesson about the evils of digital communication, but I got a massive serotonin rush from watching ten days of messages and emails load at once. Some were from friends who must have seen Ryan's Instagram, and who were: A) sympathetic, or B) nosily trying to pump me for information. There were also some increasingly frantic messages from Nina.

ARE YOU DEAD????? the last one read.

I had my phone confiscated so I couldn't obsess over Ryan. We can Skype after you're done at work? I typed back.

Jobin had also messaged.

Happy Belated New Year! Hope you're ok? Your dad and Uma came over for dinner and he said you hadn't replied to his email.

Feeling panic squeeze my chest, I checked my emails. There were two from Dad. The first had been sent just hours after Adam had taken my phone.

Maya,

I've been going over and over our conversation. What I did was wrong, and the last thing I wanted to do was upset you. The longer I left off telling you, the harder it became. I want you to know that your mother loved you very much, despite her illness, and so do I.

Miss you, Dad x

I'd seen Dad try and compose emails before, agonising over how to phrase simple requests or ask questions. I pictured him bent over the laptop, writing and then deleting sentences. My sympathy towards him increased as I read the second email.

Hi love,

I hope you're not still upset with me? I saw Jobin earlier and he said he thinks you and Ryan have broken up? Something he saw on Instagram, apparently. Please get in touch asap; I have no idea where you are and if you're alright.

Miss you, Dad x

I called Dad. He answered after a couple of rings, like he'd been waiting by the phone.

'Maya! Where on earth are you? Are you alright?'

'I'm fine. Someone at work took my phone for a week.'

'Why did they do that? What are you supposed to do in an emergency? I've been worried sick.'

'Breathe, Dad. I'm safe.'

But Dad wasn't ready to dial it down. Over the next five minutes he proceeded to outline the various scenarios that had gone through his head when he hadn't heard from me, such as: A) I'd flown back to the UK to see Nina and been involved in a horrific accident, B) I was so upset about the break-up I'd drunk myself into oblivion and was still in hospital, or C) I had been blown away in a blizzard. I decided not to mention how close I'd come to option C. At times like this it was obvious where I'd acquired my anxious temperament.

'Didn't it occur to you I might be too angry at you to reply?' I asked, once I could get a word in edgeways.

'Oh. Are you?' he asked, tentatively.

So much had happened since our quarrel. I'd broken up with Ryan. Moved to a remote cabin in the middle of nowhere. And, most importantly, I'd begun to realise how much Mum cared about me. But when he asked the question, I felt my body tense and my pulse quicken – I wasn't quite ready to forgive him.

'Well, yeah,' I said.

'But you haven't hung up on me yet,' he pointed out.

That was something I had done all too often in my teenage years.

'This is going to take me a while to process.'

He sighed into the receiver. 'I want nothing more than to turn back the clock and do it differently. But I can't.'

'You can change how you treat me in the future, though. Can you promise not to lie to me like that again?'

There was a pause. Perhaps he hadn't heard.

'Dad? Connection's okay?'

He cleared his throat.

'I promise.'

'You have to stop treating me like your little girl. I'm going to be thirty soon.'

'Gosh. Time does fly. It feels like just yesterday I was walking you to school and you were crying when I left—'

203

'Mikkel and Adam are teaching me how to shoot,' I interrupted.

'Shooting? Be careful, darling. There are so many accidents . . .'

'Dad. I'm not a kid, remember?'

'Sorry.'

'It's fine. Anyway, how's Uma?'

'She's well. We're planning a honeymoon in Bhutan . . .'

I listened to him talk about potential dates and itineraries, before moving on to describe a meal he'd eaten at a new seafood restaurant. I made enthusiastic noises but my mind was elsewhere.

'You're being very quiet,' he said eventually.

'I'm just trying to understand.'

'How they cooked the prawns? Me, too.'

'No, Dad. Why you did it. Why you kept so much from me all this time.'

'You were so traumatised after your mother's death. And then we made the move. It took several years for you to return to your old self. When it became apparent that you'd forgotten India, I thought maybe that's what your mind needed to do to move on. I didn't want to undo your recovery . . .'

'You're supposed to process trauma, not repress it. Any therapist will tell you that.'

'But you saw therapists.'

'I did. They encouraged me to talk about Mum, and her death, and how I felt. But I had nothing to say. Until recently it was all a complete blank,' I told him.

'Have you . . . remembered anything more?' he asked.

'Yeah, in fact I have.'

I told him about the khichdi recipe I'd made. About Mum smiling down at me as she gently lifted the spoon to my lips.

'Whenever you were ill she'd make you khichdi. She loved looking after you,' Dad said, his voice warm.

We talked for a short while longer. But I didn't bring up Mum again. I was happy to end on a good note, remembering her together. Even so, after I'd hung up, I couldn't shake an odd sense of disquiet. I grabbed a cigarette and went to smoke it on the porch, which was covered in several inches of freshly fallen snow. I looked out into the darkness and could see nothing at all. The huts and the mountains had been entirely swallowed up. I could have been staring into a void.

26

The group had gone, leaving an eerie calm in their wake. I took advantage of the quiet to browse through the recipe book. Halfway through, I found a page titled simply 'Mutton Curry', covered in splatters of rich red sauce – Uma had mentioned this was Mum's speciality.

'*Make masala with 5 cloves, 3 cardamoms, 2 star anise, 1 cinnamon*', the first step read. In Bangalore, Uma had explained that masala was the base for a lot of Indian dishes – a paste made with onions, ginger, garlic, chilli, and tomatoes. Different combinations of spices, butter or coconut milk could be added to create variations suitable for different dishes. In other words, cracking it was vital.

As the onions were frying with the whole spices, my phone vibrated. Jobin. We'd been messaging pretty much nonstop since I'd got my phone back. He'd sent me a video of a bush baby seeing a strawberry for the first time. I wondered what his motives were. Did he assume I needed cheering up after the break-up? Or was he trying to remind me of his presence without being too intrusive?

Either way, it was a cute video and I watched it several times.

Something was burning. The onions had caught. I took out the blackest among them and carried on, adding ginger and garlic. A sharp smell suffused the air. To obscure it, I added turmeric, red chilli, and ground coriander. When the spices began to stick to the bottom of the pan, I added more oil. Now the kitchen smelt like grease and burned powder. As I added chopped tomatoes, I noted how unripe and insipid they looked.

Several minutes later, I had produced a lumpy mess. The subtle flavour of the whole spices had been obscured by the burned onions, and I couldn't even taste the tomatoes. I tipped the whole thing into the bin and collapsed onto the sofa. So much for childhood memories. The masala was barely palatable, let alone evocative. I could make puff pastry from scratch, produce a crystal-clear consommé and delicate ravioli filled with egg yolk and truffle mousseline, but I had been defeated by a masala; something millions of women made each day, as easily as blinking.

The front door opened.

'That fox is here again,' Adam said. 'It's sitting outside your hut. Hungry, I expect.'

'Stupid thing. I hope it doesn't find a way back inside.'

'It's doing no harm,' Adam protested.

'That's easy for you to say. It didn't shit under your bed.'

Adam's mouth twitched.

'You should tame it. Feed it. Give it a name.'

'Ha, ha. Very funny.'

Adam wrinkled his nose.

'Are you cooking? I think I can smell something burning.'

I sighed. 'Yeah, you probably can. I was trying to cook one

of Mum's dishes and it went tits up. I burned the onions and for some reason I still used them in the masala. It was so gross I had to chuck it.'

'Ah. Maybe you need a break. Do you want to come for a snowmobile ride?'

Getting out of the hut was appealing. But getting out of the hut into the freezing cold Arctic wilderness was not.

'I don't know how,' I told him.

'Don't worry, it's really easy – I'll teach you.'

'Why don't you go with Mikkel instead? Where is he anyway?'

'Oh, he's still in bed. He was coughing and wheezing all night. I wish he'd go to the doctor.'

His worried expression indicated he needed a diversion even more than I did.

'Come on. Let's go out,' I said.

Fifteen minutes later, I was regretting my decision. It was twenty below, the type of weather where your eyelashes freeze and any exposed skin feels like it's being sliced to ribbons. Just a regular January day in Longyearbyen.

'Want to borrow an extra layer?' Adam asked.

'Please.'

I followed him out of the bone-aching cold and into the kit locker. He handed me a fleecy onesie and a snowsuit. After I'd put them on, alongside a pair of gloves and a snowmobile helmet, I felt slightly warmer. Never again would I moan about winters in England.

In my absence, Adam had gotten out two snowmobiles. I sat astride one of them.

'You start it by turning the key. Then pull the cord.'

After several attempts, my machine juddered into life.

'That's the throttle. This is the brake. It's like driving a scooter. There isn't a reverse, so you have to walk it backwards. Stay a safe distance behind the snowmobile in front. Here's a couple of signs you need to know. When I wave my arm like this, it means "pay attention". When I hold it up, it means "stop". Alright, you got all that?'

'I think so.'

'Grand. Well let's go on a little ride. Ready?'

'Ready.'

He accelerated away. I gingerly squeezed the throttle and lurched clumsily forward, following Adam's tracks. After the jolty start, I slowly began to recover confidence. My headlight illuminated the snow-covered ground and the spray of the runners as the darkness sped by. I felt far more in control than I had with the dogsled, and even relaxed enough to look around. At first, there was nothing much to see. But as my eyes adjusted to the light, I noticed the faint silhouettes of mountains in the darkness. Mostly obscured by ink-blue clouds, the moon was illuminated by silvered cracks of light. I had been happy enough indoors, but I couldn't deny the sense of exhilaration I felt as we skimmed across the snow.

A few minutes later, Adam held his hand up in the 'stop' position. I braked and he turned around and pulled up alongside me.

'See if you can do a U-turn. Doesn't matter if you take a wider loop than me.'

I accelerated forward. Once I had some speed I turned to the right, leaning out as I'd seen Adam do. Miraculously, I didn't fall over.

'Excellent. You're a natural,' he told me.

'Thanks.'

'Want to go back to the cabins? Or turn round and go

209

into town? It takes twenty minutes. We could grab a hot chocolate.'

'Let's do that.'

We carried on, and I became more confident with every minute that passed. What a relief it was to find something here I could actually do. If I learned to shoot I could even go out exploring. There was an old radio station, which had been converted to a luxury hotel, somewhere out there. And a Soviet ghost town. In Svalbard there was a rule that you weren't allowed to demolish anything. Abandoned trappers' huts, explorers' camps, defunct mines – they were all still here, slowly degrading in the wind and being covered over by snow and ice. An archipelago of ghosts.

We reached Longyearbyen, gliding past a snow-covered playground where a few kids bundled up in winter clothes were playing. They'd be tough as nails before they hit double digits. I parked next to Adam and we walked up the high street, passing shop fronts where clean white mannequins wearing soft fleecy sweaters and beautifully embroidered boots were on display. The street was busier than I'd ever seen it. It was easy to tell who lived here and who was just visiting. The tourists wore garish ski clothes that looked like the tags had just been removed. They sauntered slowly, peering through shop windows and taking photographs of each other. The residents were more purposeful, walking dogs and running errands, their clothes far more suited to the weather. Some of them swaggered about with rifles slung across their backs, basking in the glances they attracted from tourists.

We stepped inside the warm interior of the café; a cosy place with a few wooden tables and a glass-fronted display of cakes and pastries. After being up in the cabins, it was absolute heaven. Adam went up to order drinks and I picked a table, suddenly feeling acutely self-conscious about my appearance. A look at my phone confirmed that yes, my hair was standing on end, and my cheeks were as round and red as Babybels. The smell of wood smoke rose from my clothes as I clumsily removed my snowsuit. There was no tumble dryer up at the cabins so I hung my wet clothes next to the fire instead. Up there, I hadn't smelt a thing.

Adam returned with two hot chocolates heaped with whipped cream. He put them down and stepped neatly out of his snowsuit.

'How did you do that so easily? I had such a struggle.'

'Just gotta practise; like anything, really.'

'Sometimes I wish I was one of those people who could just do things without trying.'

'Those people don't exist,' Adam said, slurping his hot chocolate. 'Talking of trying, I need to start going to the gym again. I get so lazy during the winter.'

'Screw the gym,' I said, taking a huge sip of hot chocolate, which left me with a fetching cream moustache.

It was unfortunate that Ryan and Astrid chose that moment to enter the café. They resembled Olympic skiers in their matching red and blue Lycra. I couldn't remember the last time I'd seen Ryan look so happy. By the tone of his voice, I could tell he was teasing Astrid about something, and she was laughing in response. But it was short-lived. His smile disappeared when he caught sight of me. He nudged Astrid, who looked over at us, waved awkwardly at Adam and immediately headed towards the counter. Ryan, faced with no choice but to acknowledge me, made his way over. I wiped my face with a napkin, my stomach churning.

'Hey Maya? How's it going?'

'Good, thanks. We rode over here on the snowmobiles,' I said.

His eyes widened.

'Really? Where from?'

'From the cabins,' I said, as calmly as possible, even as my internal mechanisms went completely haywire.

'You're still there? I thought you would have flown home by now.'

'The cabins are her home now,' Adam said.

Ryan laughed. 'Very funny.'

'There's nothing funny about it, mate. She's learned to shoot, too. Great markswoman, complete natural,' Adam said.

I kicked him under the table. He was laying it on way too thick.

'Oh. Well, that's great,' Ryan said, sounding uncertain.

'Yeah,' I said. 'I'm actually having fun up there.'

'Listen, Maya, can I talk to you? Excuse me, mate, if you'll give us some space?'

'Go ahead,' said Adam.

He didn't move.

Ryan glared. Adam sipped his hot chocolate and looked back at him mildly.

'Come on,' I said to Ryan, leading him over to an empty table in the corner.

I sat down, but he remained standing.

'You don't have to do this,' he said.

'Do what?'

'Pretend, Maya. This isn't your bag, we both know that.'

'You said I gave up too easily,' I said, stung.

'This is my dream, not yours.'

'You don't have a monopoly on the Arctic.'

Ryan sighed. 'You're twisting my words. Look, I want you

212

to be happy. I don't want you to stay out here just to prove a point to me, when it's obvious that you aren't comfortable.'

'That's not why I'm here,' I protested.

At that moment, Astrid joined us, holding a brown paper bag.

'Hi,' she said, not quite able to meet my eye.

'Hello, Astrid.'

'I got our brownies to go,' she said to Ryan.

'Thanks Gorge,' he said, placing his hand on the small of her back. It was a gesture intended to reassure, and one I recognised well. But 'Gorge' was *my* nickname.

'Bye, Maya. Nice to catch up,' Ryan said, stiffly.

I returned to join Adam feeling mildly concussed, and gulped some hot chocolate to revive myself. I looked down at the table, trying to get control of myself. Ryan never wanted to go out for brownies with me. He'd always tell me just to get one slice of cake and that he might have a bite; something that would occasionally guilt trip me into eating less. Maybe he didn't think Astrid needed to calorie count in the same way I did.

'Alright?' Adam asked.

I blinked back tears.

'He seemed so happy with her.'

'Well, they've been together less than a month. And once a cheater, always a cheater.'

'When did Ryan become such an arsehole?'

'Maybe he always was one, and you just didn't notice,' Adam said.

'He's normally charming.'

'Never trust a man like that. Who knows what they'll get up to behind your back? That's one of the good things about Mikkel. He's so rude I can't imagine him charming anyone.'

213

'Apart from you.'

'He orchestrated a camping trip that was so bloody cold I *had* to get into his sleeping bag for warmth. Somehow we ended up face to face. I hadn't even realised he was gay,' Adam said, smiling at the memory.

'Ryan just kept on turning up in the places where I was hanging out.'

He was the one who'd pursued me. The one who'd kissed me first and who'd often dictated when we met, as he was so busy with his PhD. Everything had been on his terms.

'Forget about him. Focus on your cooking,' Adam said.

I thought back to the dish I had messed up earlier. When Uma had made masala in India, I'd had a shower and drunk a coffee in the time she was frying onions. They'd caramelised to a rich golden brown, and become infused with the taste of cloves and cardamom. And she hadn't chopped the tomatoes – she'd pureed them, then simmered the mixture slowly until it was a smooth, red-brown paste. If treated correctly, ingredients tended to do what was required. They worked together, helped produce something brilliant. Not like men. Adam was right – it was obvious what I should be focussing on.

'I'm going to try and cook the mutton curry again,' I told him.

'Great,' he replied, with less enthusiasm than I would have liked.

27

Mikkel extracted a large, lumpy plastic bag from the freezer and dropped it onto the counter with a thump, making me jump.

'Can you cook this for the group tonight? Two of my friends are coming up for dinner, so you might need to do a bit extra.'

'What is it?'

'Fish. Arctic char. I caught it myself,' he said proudly.

'Oh, nice.'

'Nothing too spicy,' he said.

'I'll cook something mild,' I promised.

I'd finally mastered Mum's mutton curry recipe, but I hadn't reckoned on Mikkel's complete lack of spice tolerance. 'I've spent my entire life in the Arctic Circle. We flavour our food with dill, not *chilli*,' he'd said, eyes watering. Rita, meanwhile, had had three helpings and professed it to be the best meal she'd had in months.

I put the fish in a water bath to defrost and Skyped Jobin. Yesterday, he'd suggested a 'face to face' meeting. Normally, video calls with people I didn't know too well made me horribly nervous, but there was something reassuring about seeing Jobin's face on the screen. His hair was sticking up at all angles and his nose looked larger than usual as he peered forward, trying to see the cabin behind me.

'Why don't you give me a virtual tour?'

I slowly moved the laptop so he could see the ratty sheepskin rug, the fire, and the sofas covered with knitted blankets.

'It looks very cosy up there. What about outside?'

'There's not much to see.'

But I levered myself up off the sofa and pointed the laptop out the door at the snowdrifts on the floodlit porch and the darkness beyond.

'Wow – I can just about see that huge pile of snow. If I were you, I'd never set foot outside.'

'I used to be like that. But now I'm living up here it's unavoidable. I have to go out to feed the dogs, and help clean the snowmobiles and kit.'

It seemed that, with every passing day, an extra chore was introduced. I didn't mind – I wanted to pull my weight. But it made me feel embarrassed for the first week I'd lived here, when I'd been too heartbroken to realise how much Mikkel and Adam had to do on a daily basis.

'It's really impressive, what you're doing,' Jobin said.

'I wish everyone else thought so. Ryan seems to think I'm sticking around to try and win him back.'

'Are you sure you're not?'

I felt myself flush.

'God, that makes me sound so desperate. I don't know. I wasn't thinking clearly when I committed to staying here. And I guess I thought I'd miss him way more than I actually do. I've been really busy.'

'Good for you.'

'What about you?' I asked.

'I've been preparing for France. Cramming in as many French lessons as possible. My accent is terrible.'

'I'm sure people will appreciate the effort when you go there.'

'I saw your dad yesterday, by the way. He seemed much happier. You made up, right?'

I nodded. 'You can't stay mad at family for long.'

'Still, it's very strong of you to forgive him. Some people can be stubborn that way.'

I hung up half an hour later feeling better than I had done in a while. Jobin was ridiculously easy to talk to, and he was so complimentary. I'd felt like I was completely disappointing Ryan with my inability to cope with the cold and the darkness, but Jobin seemed to think I was brave for even trying. He'd been equally encouraging of my culinary experiments.

'Especially if it brings you closer to your culture,' he'd said.

I hadn't even thought of that. But it was all tied in together: Mum, my childhood, and India itself, a country that felt no more home-like than the icy terrain of the Arctic.

I flicked through the recipe book, searching for a recipe with 'fish' in the title. It wasn't long before I came upon 'Mangalore fish curry (Hotel Konkani)', a recipe I could pull together with the ingredients at hand. Theoretically, at least.

First, I made Managalore masala. I combined roasted fenugreek, mustard seeds, dried chilli, and coriander seeds, and pounded them in the pestle and mortar, which released a nutty, fragrant aroma with a syrupy undertone.

Next, I fried garlic in coconut oil, then added the masala, along with turmeric, salt, and a pinch of mild Kashmiri chilli.

The final step was to add coconut milk and tamarind paste.

It was an easy recipe to follow and it smelt amazing – fragrant and sweet and tangy all at once.

I didn't add the fish until the group returned as it would only take a few minutes to cook through. When I picked out a morsel to taste I realised how tender it was, flaking easily with a fork. And the sauce was delicious, the creamy coconut milk complemented by astringent tamarind, and floral undertones of coriander seed.

Dad, Mum, me, Auntie Uma and Uncle Ram are sitting outside under a canopy. We're by the sea and there's a mist at the horizon, making it hard to see where water and sky meet. A light breeze gusts in off the ocean. Men in pressed trousers and crisp white shirts glide around us, laying food in copper dishes gently on the table. Mum takes my plate and puts a little bit of everything on it. Uncle smiles at me across the table.

'Which is your favourite?' he asks me.

I try the rice and the sabzi. Crunch down on Bombay duck rawa fry. Then I have a spoonful of fish curry.

'This is the best,' I say, pointing to my plate. 'Ma, you try it.'

'It's delicious. I will cook it for you at home.'

Five minutes later, a chef in a tall white hat is telling Mum the recipe. She looks up at him, smiling, stopping to write things down. The sun has started to set, tinting the mist a pale red. My mum glows like an angel. Dad looks up and smiles at her. Then I notice Uncle. He's staring at her like she was a sweet jalebi he wished he could eat. When he catches me looking at him, he smiles and winks.

Raised voices from the room next door brought me back to my senses. The walls of the kitchen suddenly felt as fragile as an eggshell. I was sure I could hear the regular rhythms of waves in the wind that blew around the house.

It had been the most fully-formed memory of India I'd ever experienced, and one of the most gratifying. Mum had looked so happy . . . and completely oblivious to Uma's husband's obvious stares. Again, I found myself wondering: why this moment? But I knew by now that memory wasn't a country you could visit whenever you wanted. It was a series of broken fragments, stubbornly resistant to order.

I ran my finger across the recipe. For the first time I noticed a faint pencil drawing. I held the page up to the only light in the room. A spectral figure was being swallowed up by a large mouth. I wondered what it meant, if anything.

'Hey Maya.'

I turned around blearily. Rita was standing in the kitchen doorway.

'Whoa. Are you alright? You look spooked.'

'I just tasted the curry. It triggered a memory. Of eating it on holiday somewhere. And one of my mum's friends eyeing her up. It was really weird.'

Rita frowned.

'I thought you couldn't remember anything.'

'I couldn't, until I started cooking Mum's food. When I was in India I had a couple of flashbacks, for want of a better word.'

'What sort of flashbacks?' Rita asked.

I glanced at her warily.

'Sometimes they're nice. Like, I remembered Mum feeding me khichdi when I was sick. Others, less nice. I found out Mum was mentally ill – like, maybe manic depressive, or bipolar.'

'Oh, so that's what your dad was keeping from you? Now I see why you fought.'

'We made up.'

Her brow was still furrowed.

'It all sounds pretty fucked up to me. Are you sure it was just moving countries that made you forget this stuff?'

I shrugged.

'My dad promised not to keep anything more from me.'

'Ah.'

I could tell she wasn't convinced. But I trusted Dad. He wouldn't risk upsetting me again, would he?

'Do you want help carrying the food out?' Rita asked, which was basically code for 'stop staring into space and get your arse in gear'.

'Sure, that'd be great.'

We carried out large serving bowls of the fish curry and steamed rice. Everyone helped themselves to generous portions, including Mikkel's guests, a burly Norwegian who introduced himself as Gunnar and his wife, Gudrun.

'Delicious,' Gudrun said.

'We love food from around the world. But they closed the sushi place and the Thai restaurant last year. The rest is just burgers and pizza,' Gunnar said, shovelling up the curry.

Mikkel was the only one not yet eating. He looked like death warmed up.

'Sorry. I am not feeling my best,' he said to me.

'Try just a little bit,' Adam said gently.

I noticed a couple of the guys trying not to stare as Adam tenderly lifted a spoon of curry to Mikkel's lips. As he swallowed, he looked a little less pained.

'That is very good. The best you have cooked up here,' he said.

'You should put on a night like this for the public,' Gunnar said.

Mikkel said something in Norwegian. I didn't have to

220

understand to guess what he was saying – likely something along the lines of not wanting to have lots of strangers up at the cabins, the hassle of buying lots of extra food . . .

'But you could charge a lot of money,' Gudrun said. 'People would pay three hundred kroner or more if you added in some extras.'

I'd always liked the idea of running a supper club. Holding one in the Arctic felt truly original. I imagined a group of guests sitting around the table, brought together by my mum's food. Of course, I needed more practice. Still, the Arctic char curry had been a success. It was good, comforting soul food. Pain might be scribbled in the margins of Mum's recipe book, giving rise to memories that hurt my chest, but it created moments like these, too – moments that helped keep all the rest of it at bay.

28

I lay on my stomach, head and shoulders sticking out of the doorway of my hut. This was my new smoking spot – it meant I wasn't tempting Mikkel, and three quarters of me was warm. Even though I was wearing my balaclava, my face was still lacerated by the cold. Needless to say, I was smoking much less these days.

There was a scuffling sound nearby. I shone my torch in its direction, ready to catch out anyone hiding in the shadows, trying to scare me, and the beam revealed two glowing eyes. I almost dropped the torch in fright. Then a shape detached itself, barely distinguishable against the snow. It was that fox again. He stopped a couple of metres away, staring at me with baleful yellow eyes.

'Piss off.'

He came a little closer.

'What do you want?'

Of course he couldn't reply. Food, Adam had said. And to resume his spot under my bunk-bed, no doubt. I wondered if his thoughts ran deeper than that. But there was no way of knowing and besides, I didn't want to start treating a wild animal like a pet.

'Jog on. I don't have any food here – it's all up in the kitchen.'

Finally, he beat it, his pale body quickly swallowed by the darkness.

The silence around me roared.

I'd been alone up here for several hours now. The latest group had left and Adam had driven Mikkel to the doctor's. His cough had worsened and he'd admitted that he was finding it difficult to breathe. I was doing my best not to imagine the worst. This was not something I was very good at.

Real Life Events vs. My Interpretation:

- **R.L.:** *My friends say: It's Maya's twenty-first. Let's organise her a surprise party.*
- **M.I.:** *Why are my friends always talking behind my back these days? I can see them smirking behind their hands. And nobody's free on my birthday to hang out. That's what they say, anyway. I guess they just have better things to do. They must hate me.*

- **R.L.:** *Maya gets onto a bus. A man looks up at her, and then looks quickly away.*
- **M.I.:** *What the hell? Why is he staring at me like that? Not because I'm hot. Nobody thinks I'm hot. Is it because I'm brown? Is he one of those Union Jack waving fascists that thinks British means white? Or is it because I'm a woman and I look like an easy target? What if he follows me off the bus and tries to grab me? If only it wasn't so dark outside. Oh god, oh god, oh god . . .*

- **R.L.:** *Maya and her friends are involved in a car crash. The car ends up being written off. Someone in the passenger seat breaks an arm, another grazes their forehead.*
- **M.I.:** *(Calls 999, calls insurance company, puts on hazard warning lights, comforts friends.) This is fucking amazing. We aren't dead. When I imagine car accidents they're always so much worse than this.*

I was distracted from my list by the sound of an incoming Skype call on my computer.

Dad and Uma were sitting in their living room, which was so full of light I wanted to bottle some and keep it. We'd gone back to talking regularly again, which was a relief. I needed to regularly dial into the outside world, because my own had shrunk down to four rickety wooden walls, to the weather forecast, to endless cleaning, and wood-chopping, and meal preparations. I was all eyes whenever I called Nina, Dad, or Jobin, drinking in the sight of their apartments, where sunlight gleamed on walls or overhead lighting diffused an even glow throughout the room. Yesterday, Nina had ordered in a Thai takeaway and I had stared with such envy at the neat plastic boxes that she'd put a Post-it note over the camera until she finished eating.

'Dad. Uma. How's everything going?'

'Hello, darling. We've just finished work,' Dad said.

'What's the plan now?'

'We're about to see a play with some friends,' Uma said.

'Sounds fun. You guys look great.'

Uma was wearing a dove grey, gossamer-thin dress, and Dad sported a blue, short-sleeved linen shirt with a loose, rust-coloured waistcoat. The outfit suited him – I recognised Uma's influence.

'And what about you, Maya?'

'Hanging out with a woman called Rita. She works up here.'

'Glad you're making friends,' Dad said.

'I hear you've been talking to Jobin,' Uma said, slyly.

'Now he's a nice lad. Incredibly smart, very sensitive,' Dad added.

'Da-ad. We live in completely different countries.'

'But you will come back to India again soon?'

'I'm committed here until March, at least.'

'You're so talented in the kitchen. Take after your mum there.'

'I've been messing up Mum's recipes left, right, and centre. But I also made a delicious fish curry from the Hotel Konkani,' I said.

Dad smiled.

'We went to that hotel every year. Uma and her husband came with us a few times. It was wonderful there, wasn't it?'

Uma nodded. But her body language had completely changed. Her arms were crossed tightly, her shoulders clenched. She'd closed in on herself like an oyster clamped around a pearl. I felt the urge to prise open the shell and get inside.

'Do you remember the trip when we first tried that fish curry?' I persisted.

'I think it was the last time. Or maybe the time before,' Dad mused. 'She wrote down two recipes, I seem to remember. What was the other one?'

He turned to Uma. She stood up abruptly, her face pale.

'Excuse me. I have to go to the bathroom.'

She hurried off.

'Strange. She felt fine just now,' Dad said, looking puzzled.

Then his face cleared. 'Oh – she did have a lot of Keralan beef fry last night. It is somewhat heavy on the stomach.'

'So tell me about the hotel,' I pressed.

'Well, there's not much to tell. It was on a beach north of Mangalore. Our last holiday there was one of the highlights of the year. Your mum was radiant. I took a lot of pictures. I'll dig some out and send them to you.'

A few minutes later, Uma still hadn't come back so Dad rang off to check on her, convinced that the beef had caused a stomach upset.

I relocated to the main hut, and began looking through Mum's recipe book in search of the second recipe from the Hotel Konkani. The search was proving fruitless when I heard the sound of a snowmobile.

'Hey,' said Rita, when she appeared at the doorway several minutes later.

I watched as she stood her rifle in the corner, then removed her rucksack and snowsuit.

'Thanks for driving all the way up here in the cold,' I said.

She shrugged.

'Dad always said there was no such thing as weather, only bad clothes for the weather.'

'Yeah, that's smart.'

'It's about the only smart thing he ever said,' Rita replied.

The vehemence of her tone surprised me.

'Sorry. I know I told you to give your dad a break. Seems like I can't follow my own advice,' Rita said.

'Do you want to talk about it?' I asked.

'I'd prefer to drink this.'

She pulled a bottle of red from the rucksack and brandished it. I tried not to show how wrongfooted I was by the change of subject. She shouldn't feel obligated to talk about personal stuff if she didn't want to, although I couldn't help but feel she knew much more about me than I did about her.

Rita poured us generous portions of wine, and we clinked glasses.

'Cheers.'

'So tell me, what's been happening up at the cabins?'

'Adam took Mikkel to the doctor's hours ago. They still aren't back.'

'They've probably gone to a bar or something.'

'I hope they don't feel like I'm cramping their style. I've been making efforts to stay out their way.'

'They're straight-up guys. I'm sure they'd tell you. Besides, they have their own hut.'

'Where do you live?'

'An apartment in town. It's pretty nice, but the landlord is going to put the rent up soon, and it's already extortionate.'

'I'm sorry.'

Rita took a large gulp of wine.

'Things are always tight over winter. I'm going to look for full-time work in the summer, hopefully with accommodation included. I'll ask these guys, too. If they say yes, we'll be bunkmates.'

'Maybe,' I said, suddenly feeling guilty. 'But I might only be staying until March. I'm supposed to be moving to London.'

'Say what? It's the end of January already.'

'I know.'

'You should stay longer. Otherwise you've literally only been here for the hardest part of the year. Besides, I thought you wanted to do a supper club?'

Now it was my turn to take a large gulp of wine. Since I'd made the Arctic char curry, my mind had been on it.

'Locals would love it. There's no Indian restaurant here and I'm sure there's some tour operators that could incorporate it into a holiday package,' Rita continued.

'You think?'

She nodded emphatically.

'The best thing to do would be to try it out once or twice on a small scale. Gauge interest,' I said, feeling more energised by the prospect.

'I know at least six people who'd be up for it,' Rita said. 'In addition to Gunnar and Gudrun.'

'I'll ask Adam and Mikkel if I can do a trial night.'

'What would you call it?' she asked.

'I haven't even thought about it. End of the Road Supper Club?'

'Total last meal vibes,' Rita pronounced. 'You need a name that tells people what food you're serving. Curry at the Cabins?'

It wasn't quite right. I wanted a name that conveyed the warmth of spice and the cold of the Arctic.

'What about "The Arctic Curry Club"?'

'That's it,' Rita said.

I felt a rush of pride. Naming things brought them to life. But once something was alive you needed to care for it. I would have to plan a menu, order the ingredients and practise cooking the dishes, and advertise on social media so people actually came. And I'd need to tidy. Right now, the room barely looked habitable, let alone restaurant-worthy. I felt the beginning of a stress headache nudge at my temples.

'You really think it would be possible?' I said to Rita.

She leaned forward and topped up my glass of wine.

228

'Sure. You cook for like twelve people pretty much every night. What's the worst that could happen?'

'I could cook something so unpalatable they demand their money back. Or they could make a mess, which would piss Mikkel off.'

Right on cue, I heard the sound of a motor.

'Speak of the devil,' Rita said.

But a few minutes later, it was only Adam who came inside.

'Hey, do you mind if Maya puts on a supper club this weekend?' Rita said immediately.

'Go ahead,' Adam said distractedly.

He collapsed into the armchair. His face was chalk-white, his eyes wild.

'Are you alright?' Rita asked.

'Mikkel's been taken to hospital on the mainland,' Adam said, and then his face crumpled.

My stomach lurched. Rita got up and put her arms around him.

'I'm probably getting snot in your hair,' Adam mumbled, as tears slid down his face.

'That's alright. I haven't showered yet today.'

Adam made a sound that was halfway between a sob and a laugh. Then he disentangled himself from Rita and wiped his eyes.

'Sorry.'

'No need to apologise,' I said.

'There's no shame in crying,' Rita said. 'Tell us what happened.'

'Mikkel has something called a pneumothorax. That's a collapsed lung. The lining tore because it's so degraded, the stupid—'

He paused, composed himself and carried on.

'They're going to fly him to Tromsø for an operation.'

'I'm sure he's in good hands,' I said.

'He said he didn't want me with him . . .'

Tears slid down his cheeks.

'He was just playing the tough guy. Of course he'll want you there when he wakes up,' Rita said.

'You think?'

She nodded.

'It was really scary, seeing him like that. His lips were turning this horrible blue colour.'

'You should go to him. Whatever he said, he'll need your support,' I told him.

Adam sat up straighter and wiped his eyes again.

'I'll see if there's any spaces on the evening flight.'

'That's the spirit,' Rita said.

An hour later, Adam was ready to leave. Rita had offered to drive him to the airport in their Jeep. He hesitated in the doorway.

'Are you sure you'll be alright alone up here?' he asked me.

'Yeah, totally,' I lied.

'Don't worry. I'll stay with her tonight,' Rita said. 'And I'll show her what to do with the dogs in the morning.'

'You're amazing, both of you.'

He hugged me hastily, and hurried over to the Jeep.

I watched the Jeep bump down the track and the lights disappear from view. Only then did I realise the full implication of Adam's words. I had no idea how serious a collapsed lung was; if it was something that you could recover from in a week, or much more serious than that. Adam was right to go to Mikkel, but the thought of being without them both was overwhelming.

Outside, the air was sharp as a knife blade. I walked past the huts, beyond the floodlights, and looked out at the darkened plains below. Soon, my eyes adjusted and I could make out the shapes of stacked clouds above me, and below, the vague contours of the land. Inches of snow covering ancient folds of rock. Metres of frozen earth. Sometimes, it felt as if I were standing on the back of a huge beast, one subject to towering rages and dizzying sorrows. Why had anyone chosen to live here in the first place? It was too vast, too empty, too wild. And now I was suddenly, wrenchingly alone. How would I fill the days until Adam and Mikkel returned?

I'd technically been given permission to do the supper club. I imagined the table laid with a white cloth, shining cutlery and flickering candles. A couple of bottles of wine being passed around. Copper dishes gleaming in the candlelight, filled with piquant, aromatic dishes. That would keep me busy. Maybe I should give it a chance.

29

To keep the anxiety of organising the supper club at bay, I'd created a list of chores I had to complete every day upon waking up.

Daily chores in an Arctic cabin:
- **Light the stoves:** *I wake up shivering and stoke up the fire in my hut. Then I head over to the main hut and repeat.*
- **Defrost the pipe:** *The kitchen gets so cold that sometimes the water pipe freezes solid. I have to stick the portable heater underneath it to warm it through. And only then can I have my coffee!*
- **Feed the dogs:** *It's so cold outside that their food would freeze solid unless heated up first, so I boil up a heinous mess of blood, bones and offal, and carry it out to the kennels.*
- **Shovel shit:** *Next step is to make sure that the snow outside the dog kennels is all clean. Nights when it snows it gets covered over, but if it hasn't I have to get out the shovel and play hunt the poop. I also need to make sure their bed straw is clean.*

- **Chop wood:** *All the firewood here is imported; at the moment we've been using a big stack of pallets that Mikkel picked up from the port. I have to saw each one up so it fits into the burner – a great way to keep warm in sub-zero temperatures.*
- **Dig out the sleeping huts:** *I have to make sure any unused huts don't get submerged by snow. The easiest thing to do is just clean out the porches every day.*

On the day of the supper club, I woke up extra early to complete everything. But even so, by the time I finished it was almost midday. As I returned to the main cabin, I saw Foxy waiting patiently. He turned up at the same time each day and wouldn't budge until he was fed.

'I'm not sure if you'll like today's menu,' I told him.

But Foxy scarfed down the remains of last night's egg fried rice with gusto.

'What do you think, Foxy? Is it going to go well today?'

He didn't have an opinion on the matter.

'Well, you'll have to tell me what you think of the food. I'm sure there'll be leftovers.'

Foxy was more interested in that. He lifted his head and regarded me keenly. I wished he would come closer so I could thread my hands through his fluffy white fur. But he turned around and loped away. Telling myself I had just avoided getting fleas didn't help.

Now I'd finally stopped, I could feel the nerves creeping in again. What if everyone hated my food? Or it wasn't ready on time and they were waiting for hours?

'It's only dal, butter chicken, baingan barta and roti,' I said out loud.

For ten people, though. Why hadn't I gotten started earlier? In the kitchen, I double-checked the schedule I'd made on my phone. Both Nina and Jobin had sent me good luck messages. Dad had also emailed.

Hi darling,

Just wanted to wish you well for today. I'm sure everything will go smoothly, and all the guests will love your food. As promised, I dug up these photographs from the Hotel Konkani. Such a shame you can't remember the holiday; we all had a lovely time.

Dad

There was an image of Mum and Uma standing on the beach, both in saris, a rare, flattering photograph of me, Mum, and Dad all smiling, and the final image was a group portrait, taken on the front steps of the hotel. Judging by the sunburn that blotched Dad's cheeks and the suitcases lined up behind us, it was the end of the trip. Dad stood in the middle. I was in front of him, sulking, and Uncle Ram hovered behind, half-hidden. Mum and Uma were on either side of us, both unsmiling. Mum looked especially unhappy. Her expression was haunted, as if she was thinking about something other than posing for a photo. Maybe I'd been a little shit at breakfast. There was no way of knowing, unless I asked Dad and Uma.

But there was no time for that now. Lentils needed to be boiled, chicken marinated, dough made for rotis . . .

'Wow. You've trashed this place.'

I looked up.

Rita was still in her outdoor gear, cheeks flushed with the cold. She was right. The kitchen counters were covered in onion skins, dirty plates and packets of spice.

'Shit, you're right.'

'Want me to make us both a grilled cheese and do some tidying up?'

'Where would I be without you?'

'I take it that's a yes?'

I nodded.

'But seriously – you've been a total lifesaver this week.'

She shrugged.

'It's chill.'

'Let me at least take you out for drinks?' I persisted.

'I won't say no to that.'

'Have you heard from Adam?' I asked.

'Yeah, he messaged about an hour ago. Mikkel just woke up from the surgery. He's woozy, but there weren't any complications. He said good luck for tonight, by the way.'

'I wonder when they'll be back.'

'Another week at least. They'll have to cancel the next group,' Rita said.

'Did you ask if you'd still get paid?'

I knew Rita would struggle without her wages. She shook her head and gestured at the pot on the stove.

'What's that? Smells good.'

'Dal makhani,' I said, sensing she wanted to change the subject.

'What's in it?'

'Kidney beans and this black dal Uma gave me. Spices, onions, garlic. And tomatoes – I had to roast them so you could actually taste them. But there's not really enough space on the stove to cook them.'

'Stick them over the fire,' Rita said.

'That'll work?'

'Sure. There's a tripod and a cast-iron pot somewhere. We use it to make soup sometimes. I'll go dig it out.'

God, Rita had been amazing this week – I wouldn't have managed alone. She'd exercised the dogs, driven me to the supermarket for a shop, and helped me find my first customers. It was difficult to know what to do in return. I was getting the sense that Rita was not a person who liked asking for anything. I'd already offered to pay her for this evening.

'If you pay me there won't be anything left for you. Or Adam and Mikkel. Save it for them,' she'd said.

At least she'd allowed me to put her down as a non-paying guest, so she could eat with her friends. I sincerely hoped that would be a reward, not a punishment.

The afternoon passed in a blur. I charred aubergines on the gas flame until their skins were black, then scooped out the tender flesh to make baingan barta. I made the silky smooth sauce for the butter chicken. Stewed carrots in milk, ghee, and sugar to make gajar ka halwa for dessert. Then it was time to roll out the dough into rotis.

All too soon, I heard the hum of unfamiliar voices in the main room. A minute later, Rita came in, carrying the dal.

'The first guests are here. I'll lay the table and light the lamps.'

'Thanks.'

'All going to plan?'

I nodded.

'Well it smells amazing in here. Hanna and Ari mentioned that as soon as they came in.'

Despite Rita's assurances, I suddenly tasted the battery-acid tang of fear. What if the chicken was undercooked or the rotis burned? What if some of them had actually travelled to the Punjab and knew how inauthentic my food was? I

236

fought the urge to take off my apron and hide in my cabin. Instead, I concentrated on the present moment focus exercises I'd learned in my CBT sessions – listening to the sounds around me to stop myself from internalising.

The snow lightly striking the kitchen window. The low hum of the oven, keeping the rotis warm. The hiss of the gas stove. The buzz of chatter from the lounge. Someone laughing, followed by the sound of a cork popping. Friendly sounds; a symphony of celebration.

I took a deep breath.

Nothing had gone wrong yet. I just needed to stay calm and complete the finishing touches.

I added the final ingredients to the dal – a huge slab of butter and a generous glug of cream – and carried on cooking the rotis. Several of them got scorched in places, but I told myself it was all part of the rustic charm.

Rita stuck her head around the door.

'Everyone's here. Shall we start serving?'

When I stepped into the cabin, holding serving bowls of butter chicken, I was pleasantly surprised by Rita's handiwork. She'd tidied away the survival manuals and gun parts, thrown a faded chintz tablecloth over the table and lit the oil lamps – the warm, flickering glow hid a multitude of sins.

Everyone looked up expectantly as I put the final dishes down on the table, and I realised they were waiting for me to speak. But I was suddenly lost for words. Thankfully, Rita stood up.

'Hey guys, this is Maya. She's cooked some amazing food she'll tell you about.'

Gunnar smiled at me encouragingly. I cleared my throat.

'The food this evening is from the Punjab region. This is butter chicken, one of India's most popular dishes. I'm serving it with rotis, baingan bharta – a smoked aubergine dish – and dal makhani. There's also dessert. Carrot halwa. Right. Well, I'll just go and make some more rotis.'

I hurried back to the kitchen, cheeks burning, and buried my embarrassment in frantically rolling more dough.

'Don't worry; they love it,' Rita told me, ten minutes later, when she came in to get more rotis.

Once the main course was finished, I collected the plates and served everyone a small bowl of halwa. I was proud of the way the grated carrot had caramelised after slowly being boiled in milk and sugar for ages.

'Your food's amazing,' one of them told me.

'I loved that dal. It was so smoky and creamy. A really unique flavour.'

'Yeah, it was my favourite. I never liked lentils before.'

'I had three helpings,' someone else said proudly.

'Thanks, thanks,' I said over and over.

'Sit down and join us for a glass of wine,' Rita said, pouring me a generous glass.

By the time everyone had left and I'd tidied the kitchen, it was past midnight. I grabbed a plateful of leftovers and collapsed on the sofa. My eyes were heavy and my feet were aching, but the exhaustion was worth it for the sense of achievement I felt. Several of Rita's friends had been really encouraging, and told me I should make it into a regular event. I had half a mind to. At the very least, I'd put on another couple of nights before Adam and Mikkel returned, so there was some money coming into the business while they were away.

Whenever I cooked, I lost my appetite. But now it had

returned with a vengeance. I dug into the butter chicken. It was better than previous attempts, but it still wasn't a patch on Uma's. The baingan bharta was a little too smoky for my taste; I'd have to try and source some fresh coriander to balance it out. Then I moved on to the dal. As my guests had said, it was the undisputed star of the show: rich, sweet, subtly smoky – though anything tastes great when it's been cooked for hours on an open fire.

I took another mouthful, savouring the efforts of my hard work. I'd done it – the Arctic Curry Club was in business.

Part Four

30

Slowly, light began to return to the world. It began with the awareness that the darkness was no longer absolute. Then I began to notice short periods of twilight in the middle of the day, when the sky turned a bruised purple-blue colour, with a band of paler cobalt at the horizon. These twilight hours grew longer and lighter, bathing the snow in an eerie half-light. This liminal period in between polar night and the return of the sun was known as the blue season, and whenever I walked across the encampment I felt like I was moving through one of those vivid, surreal dreams that occur shortly before waking, and are slowly infiltrated by the sounds of the world outside.

Mikkel and Adam still hadn't returned from Tromsø. While recovering, Mikkel had developed pneumonia, and still couldn't be moved. Each time I called Adam, he sounded more and more tired. I knew he was worried about money, and wished I could do more to help.

I missed them both. It was strange being up here alone.

Sometimes it was so quiet that I felt like the loudest human in the world; the snow crunching under my boots, my heart thudding loudly against my ribs. I jumped at the slightest noise, at the sight of shadows. Luckily, Rita was a frequent guest, as she'd started to sub-let her room on Airbnb in the hopes of raising some cash. She'd often persuade me down to the shooting range, or out on a sledding trip to keep the dogs exercised. Both of us had more energy now. Rita had, after a little too much wine, referred to the blue season as a 'rebirth' after long months of darkness, which meant one thing to me: therapy.

Therapists I have had in the past:

- *My first therapist was called Jenny. Her skin was so pale that you could see the blue veins in her wrists and temples. I was seven years old and nowhere near ready to talk to anyone about anything, so I spent most of the time looking at those veins, worried they would break through the surface of her skin.*

- *Just after I had my first anxiety attack, I went to see a therapist called Dave. He had pretty unconventional methods. Every time I used negative language about myself, he pulled out a plastic bow and shot me with an arrow. It was actually one of the more effective treatments I've experienced.*

- *After I stopped working in kitchens, I ended up going to see Salma, a cushiony woman who always wore bright red lipstick. There was always a large jug of water and a glass on her desk. Dry-mouthed with nervousness, I often drank the entire thing (about seven glasses), establishing a safety behaviour that took months to shake.*

I had recently found a new therapist online. I wasn't sure if it would be more or less nerve-wracking than meeting him in the flesh. On one hand, he wouldn't be able to see me sweat. But on the other, anything could be happening outside the screen. Edo, he was called. In my mind's eye I had a picture of a sexy, skinny man with jet black hair and a face full of piercings. Needless to say, this was not the man who appeared on screen. He was balding and wore thick-lensed glasses – much more approachable than the therapist in my mind's eye.

'Maya. I'm Edo. Nice to meet you. Your message said you suffer from anxiety. Is there any other reason why you've reached out, or would you just like to discuss managing it?'

'I had a break-up recently. And I recently found out some stuff. About my childhood.'

My tongue felt too big and too dry. I reached for my bottle. Let the compulsive water drinking begin.

Edo looked at me steadily.

'Okay. You're in the Arctic, you said?'

I nodded, slightly bewildered by the change of topic. We were circling round that hole in the middle of me, getting closer and closer until we were sucked in, like water down a drain.

'What are you doing there?'

'I'm cooking. At this place called End of the Road Cabins.'

'And how is that?'

'Well, it can get tiring. Most days I have to feed the dogs before work, or chop wood for the stoves. But I've started a supper club up here, which is really enjoyable.'

'What sort of food are you cooking?'

'I'm cooking a Punjabi menu. Dal, butter chicken . . . Stuff like that.'

'Your email mentioned a recent trip to India stirred up some memories.'

'Uh huh.'

The email had taken hours to draft and unleashed a maelstrom of emotions. Although Dad and I were very much on speaking terms, it seemed like there was still a lot of residual anger to process.

'Why don't you tell me a little more about the trip?'

I told Edo about the memories that had returned. About the wedding, and the conversation with Dad. Halfway through, I started crying. I was glad of the distance offered by the screen, glad that I didn't have to be awkwardly patted on the shoulder or handed a tissue from the box that most therapists keep on their coffee tables or in a desk drawer. I wiped my eyes and glanced up at Edo. He was silent for so long that I tapped the screen.

'Has this frozen?'

'No. I'm still here. It seems to me that you're looking for an answer.'

'Well, yeah.'

'But perhaps you first need to be clear in your mind about the question you want to ask.'

I paused. There were so many.

'I want to know why Dad didn't tell me about Mum's mental illness. Why eating Indian food made me remember things I'd forgotten for twenty years. Why I forgot them in the first place. And the other day my stepmother was acting weird when we mentioned a family holiday together, and it made me think that maybe something happened there . . .'

God, it all sounded so stupid.

'What do you think will happen if you find the answers?'

I drained the glass of water and poured another.

'Um. I don't know. I guess I might feel better.'

'It's logical to seek patterns to help us through our grief. And you're grieving on three accounts: the loss of a mother, the loss of a childhood, and the recent loss of a lover.'

'Okay . . .'

'Let's imagine a scenario. Let us say that a man's wife is murdered. He becomes obsessed with who did it and why – devoting all of his energy to trying to discover who the murderer was. Yet, when the murderer is brought to light, he doesn't find the satisfaction he was looking for.'

'Why?'

'Because he dealt with his grief by displacing it onto this obsessive quest. And then, when there's no longer a quest, he is left once again with his grief, which has only grown larger and more painful with neglect.'

'So what you're saying is that I shouldn't be searching so hard for answers.'

'Not necessarily. But you need to make sure you have strategies to deal with what you might find. You grew up in Britain?'

I nodded.

'Me and Dad moved there when I was seven. After Mum's death.'

'The search for identity can be difficult when you have to navigate two different cultural contexts. And sometimes there's a danger of assuming that the side you know less well might hold the answers.'

'And it doesn't?'

'Well you can't switch off one side of your identity. In fact, you could say that navigating between two cultures *is* your identity.'

* * *

247

I hung up thirty minutes later, feeling like a wrung-out dishcloth. Rather than talking about the memories I'd had of Mum, Edo had wanted me to focus on my reactions to them. The difficulty sleeping. The feelings of disassociation and isolation. The hand tremors I'd experienced in the toilet cubicle at Bangalore Club at Dad's wedding. We'd discussed making sure I stayed as rested as possible, and taking some time out of every day for relaxing. Edo had also suggested that I write down all the memories that had returned, as a way of reprocessing the experiences. I liked the idea, but as soon as I picked up the pen a wave of exhaustion broke over me.

It was too soon. I put the pen down. Somehow, I'd forgotten how tired therapy made me, even though my last course of CBT had been a little over a year ago, just after coming off Escitalopram. After a particularly tiring session, Ryan had come round to see me with a Thai takeaway and we'd snuggled up in bed and watched *Clueless* together. If only I had someone to do that with now.

Single. Childless. These were not things I had ever intended to be when pushing thirty. It occurred to me that alongside grieving for the past, I was in mourning for a future that would never happen. I felt a flutter of panic. Therapy was weird like that. In tackling one worry, you sometimes ended up obsessing about something else instead.

I stepped outside. The sky was the colour of the ocean at twilight, the snow a few shades lighter. It felt like I would get washed away if I stood still long enough. I lit a cigarette in the hopes of re-centring myself and started walking, hoping the regular rhythm of my footsteps would calm me down. As I passed my hut, I noticed that it was painted dark green. I had assumed it was black, even though that was a pretty bleak colour for a place like this. And the men's sleeping huts were brick red. I hadn't realised how sharply the ground sloped away beyond them. I slowed my pace, taking in these newly revealed colours and contours, and wondering what else would be revealed with the return of the light.

31

As I walked from my sleeping hut to the main cabin, I saw that the sky was streaked with pastel pink, tinted pale yellow at the horizon, like the sun was trying to rise. Just a couple of weeks now. The world was holding its breath. Or maybe that was just me. Back in Norwich I had often felt like I was waiting for my life to begin. In the darkness of winter I had forgotten that keen, yet unfocussed, sense of anticipation. Now, it was returning along with the light. Other things were returning too. Over winter, after Ryan, my body had gone to sleep. Now I often lay awake at night, wondering how long it would be until I felt the warmth and weight of another body against mine. Last night I had dreamed I was making out with Jobin. But when I undid his shirt, I encountered a pelt of thick dark hair. I broke off and saw his face had begun to elongate, his lashless eyes turning yellow. The more time I spent alone up here, the more vivid my dreams became.

I made a coffee and listened to the fire crackle in the grate as I started planning the menu for March's supper clubs. I'd been serving my Punjabi menu for the past few weeks and had run out of urad dal. It was time to change it up.

What shall I cook at the cabins? Something cheap and easy, I messaged Jobin.

Chilli cheese toasts? Pav bhaji? he replied.

'Lunch: pav bhaji', I wrote, remembering our evening at Food Street. Then, after a pause, I added 'coronation chicken?'. That was something I'd made before, and I knew was inspired by Indian flavours. I flicked through Mum's recipe book in search of inspiration for dinner. Maybe I should remake the Arctic char curry? Or have another crack at Mum's mutton? I turned to the very last page. 'Paneer Croquettes', it read. I wondered if this was a recipe for Dad, who loved croquette potatoes.

Twenty minutes later, I had a piece of paper filled with doodles and random words. At a loss, I video-called Dad. He answered, mopping his brow. I heard the whir of the fan in the background. It was hard to imagine a place so hot you needed artificial means to cool it down.

'Hey Dad, how's it going?'

'Bloody boiling,' he complained. 'There's a heatwave here. Thirty-five degrees in February. I can hardly think.'

'It sounds dreamy,' I said enviously.

Dad picked up a cold glass of water and pressed it against his forehead.

'I called because I need some help planning my next menu.'

'Uma! Maya needs you,' Dad called.

A couple of moments later, Uma appeared on the screen. 'Hi, Maya?'

She looked wary. As well she might; she hadn't answered

my messages asking about the second recipe from the Hotel Konkani, and probing for more details about the holiday.

'I'm trying to plan March's menu,' I said.

Uma's expression cleared.

'What do you have so far?' she asked.

'Nothing. I need to plan lunch and dinner. For lunch I was thinking about pav bhaji and coronation chicken sandwiches. They're Indian, aren't they?'

'They are very different. Pav bhaji is street food from Mumbai, and coronation chicken is Anglo-Indian food.'

'What's Anglo-Indian food?' I asked, puzzled.

'Well, it came about during the time of the Raj . . .' Uma told me.

'What's the Raj?'

'Maya! That's when the British occupied India,' Dad said, genuinely shocked.

'Oh. Right,' I replied, momentarily embarrassed.

'During the Raj, the British hired Indian cooks. But they still had British tastes – couldn't take too much spice, wanted their traditional foods cooked,' Uma continued.

'Sounds like you, Dad.'

'Let Uma finish, darling.'

'So the Indian cooks toned down their regional recipes. And they cooked their own version of British foods, using local ingredients. That's how Anglo-Indian cuisine was born.'

'Does it taste good?' I asked.

'I haven't tried much of it. But I know there are some funny names. Like country captain chicken,' Uma said.

'Mulligatawny soup too,' Dad put in. 'Your ma had a recipe for that.'

'What about paneer croquettes? They must be Anglo-Indian, right?'

'That's it! That's the other recipe from the Hotel Konkani your mum wrote down,' Dad broke in excitedly. 'When you woke up from your afternoon nap you'd always have a plate of paneer croquettes and a glass of mosambi juice.'

'Oh no, I wouldn't make those,' Uma said.

Her arms were folded across her chest and her smile had disappeared.

'Why not? Don't they taste nice?' I asked.

'No, no, they were delicious,' Dad reassured me.

'It's just that . . . well . . . they don't really go with the rest of the food,' Uma said.

'But darling, I'm sure croquettes are Anglo-Indian,' Dad said.

Uma gave him A Look.

'I'm only trying to help,' he said, puzzled.

'So is there anything else you'd recommend to cook?' I asked Uma.

I jotted down her suggestions, my mind only half on what she was saying.

'Thanks so much for helping me out. But listen, I have to go.'

'So soon? Can't you spare a couple more minutes for your old Dad?'

'I'm sorry – we have a group coming in any minute,' I lied.

He looked disappointed. 'Enjoy yourself, darling. And do call us back anytime.'

'I will do. Promise.'

I hung up, feeling jittery with excitement.

'Paneer Croquettes'. Here it was, the recipe I'd been looking for. But as I looked down the ingredients list, I hit the first obstacle – no paneer. Luckily, the Internet Gods informed me it could be made at home; a simple but time-consuming process requiring only milk and yoghurt.

In the kitchen, I put on a track by one of my favourite artists, M.I.A., howling along tunelessly as she sang and rapped about living fast and dying young as the milk boiled.

I added yoghurt, which made the milk separate, and the curds, when I gathered them up in a cheese-cloth, felt uncomfortably soft and squishy. I hung the cloth bundle from a peg in the kitchen, watching liquid gush, then drip, into a bowl below. Once the mixture had drained, I pressed it under a weighted board and killed thirty minutes plucking my eyebrows, researching other types of cheeses that could be made at home, and painting my toenails an acidic green. I tried not to think about what might happen when I ate the croquettes, telling myself that it was highly unlikely I'd remember anything. It was lucky that cheese wasn't sentient, or the paneer would have collapsed under the weight of my expectations.

Finally, the paneer was ready. I grated it into a bowl alongside yesterday's potatoes, and mashed them together. Added minced garlic, cumin powder, chopped coriander, and diced raw onion. Rolled the mixture into small cylinders, which I dipped into a mixture of flour, beaten egg, and bread crumbs, and then fried. Familiar processes I'd used many times before. Minutes later, I had a plate of crispy, golden croquettes. I looked down at them proudly as I impatiently waited for them to cool. Finally, I picked one up and bit through the crispy coating to the soft cheesy filling.

I wake up from my nap to a knock on the door. A man in neatly pressed uniform has my snack ready. Paneer croquettes and sweet, sharp mosambi juice. I normally eat and then go find the adults on the terrace. But today I can hear noises from

Mum and Dad's room. If it's Mum, she'll want to try a croquette. Holding my plate, I pad out of the room and across the landing. As I reach the door, I hear a strange, high-pitched whimper. I push the door open.

The air smells sharp. Mum's in the very corner of the room – Uncle is pushing her back against the wall. One of his hands is pressed against her mouth. The other is pulling at her skirt. Her blouse is already undone and her eyes are wild.

I have to save her.

Uncle could squash me like a mosquito. But mosquitos can bite.

I dart forward and sink my teeth into his leg.

He yells. I stumble backwards and drop my plate.

'Don't hurt her,' Mum says.

Uncle turns to me. He looks different to usual, his face red and twisted. Normally, when he holds his hand out, there's a sweet inside. But the hand that reaches out to grab me now is empty. As he leans forward, I realise the sharp smell in the room is coming from his mouth. His hand closes around my dress. I break free and run down the stairs, across the terrace and onto the beach. The sand is almost gone so I scramble across the rocks, the sharp edges biting into my feet, until I find a hollow to crouch down in.

From my hiding place among the rocks, I listen to Uncle calling my name. He sounds like he's worried about me, but I know that's not true. The sun is red like blood. Monstrous purple waves break on the shore and suck at the sand like they're trying to swallow the beach. I wriggle further down out of sight. And I stay there for what feels like hours, until I see a figure walking towards me across the beach. My breath catches in my chest. But it's not Uncle. It's Uma.

My mouth was full of a cold, half-chewed mixture of

255

cheese and potato. I spat it into the bin and swilled my mouth out with water. The sink was speckled with flecks of onion and coriander. I washed them away. If only the memory itself could be erased so easily. It had been so vivid. The tears in her eyes. The taste of iron in my mouth as I punctured the flesh of his leg with my teeth. The vein throbbing in his temple, twisted as a rope. If only it had broken out of his skin and strangled him. That's what men like him deserved. Mild-mannered men who were civil to everyone they met until the veneer cracked and you saw them for who they really were. It happened over and over again, and each time you never saw it coming.

I tipped the plate of croquettes into the bin. The kitchen felt claustrophobic and so did the living room. I pushed open the front door, hoping that the shock of the cold would drive the image from my mind. But it was lodged there, as firmly as a splinter under the skin.

I walked without thinking. All too soon, I reached the camp limits. The crisp silhouettes of mountains lay beyond and below me I could see a vast expanse of ice, as cold and blue as the surface of the moon. Unlike the moon, this was unmarked by a single footprint. The wind picked up, tugging at my hair and clothes. I felt the coldness penetrate my jacket, and then go deeper.

So this was why Uma hadn't wanted me to cook the croquettes. But Dad must be totally in the dark – he'd hardly be describing it as one of his best holidays if he knew what had happened. It was strange that neither I, nor Mum, nor Uma, had ever mentioned it to him. How had they managed to persuade a seven-year-old girl to keep her mouth shut?

I stood shivering, watching as the mountains became

dark, jagged silhouettes, like broken teeth. Longyearbyen was a smudge of light on the horizon. The distance between myself and everyone else suddenly felt vast and white and totally impassable. So this was what remembering felt like. This was the place I had been warned over and over not to enter.

32

There's this weird and highly irritating coincidence that whenever you're feeling at your loneliest, the people you call never pick up their phones. Jobin had gone to his gran's birthday party in Kerala. Nina was shacked up with her new boyfriend, Amir. Fuck knows what had happened to Dad and Uma. Unless he was feeling particularly worried about me, Dad had a tendency to put his phone somewhere and forget about it. But Uma was glued to hers, always looking up art exhibitions and book reviews, participating in endless chat groups about everything from political satire to building maintenance. The fact that I had sent her seven WhatsApp messages, three emails, called twice, and still had received no response was very out of character. I guess she wasn't ready to answer the questions I would be asking about that night. I find digital communication anxiety-inducing at the best of times. It's hard enough to talk to someone when they're right in front of you, let alone when you can't see them, don't know where they are, or if they're even listening.

What I imagine when people don't reply to my messages:
- *Maybe they saw this and they're waiting for an appropriate time to respond, so they look cool.*
- *Maybe they were just pretending they wanted to hang out.*
- *Maybe they hate me.*
- *Maybe they dropped their phone in the toilet and now it's drying out in a bowl of rice.*
- *Maybe they left their phone on a bus.*
- *Maybe they had an accident and now they're in hospital, where you aren't allowed to use phones.*
- *Maybe they're being held hostage, and can't answer calls unless they promise to stay calm and pretend that everything's alright. When I call they'll try and convey the problem using a cryptic phrase or a word that will instil in me an odd sense of disquiet.*
- *Maybe they're dead.*

I tried Dad one last time.

Where's Uma? I can't get through to her and I really need to talk to her.

After that, I put my phone aside and tried to focus on making a food order. Buying everything from the super-market was expensive, so I was ordering in bulk from a UK-based company. Crates of tomatoes, cauliflower, and potatoes. Kilos of ginger and garlic. A huge box of coriander, which would have to be made into a paste and frozen. Even with the shipping fees, I'd be saving money. And a hunter friend of Gunnar's had promised me all the venison I needed for the Anglo-Indian reindeer stew I was planning.

Just when I'd finally managed to apply myself to the task in hand, I got a message back from Dad.

259

She's gone to an ashram. They aren't allowed to use phones or computers there.

When will she be back? I asked.

. . .

. . .

I don't know, darling.

What do you mean?

I waited. No response.

Want to talk about it? I can call.

I'm busy right now. Maybe later? What's the name of the ashram?

Whispering Hills. It's in Ooty.

Finally, something concrete.

I looked up the number for Whispering Hills and dialled before I had a chance to overthink it. The woman who answered spoke in a language I didn't understand, her words distorted by the white noise of a bad connection.

'Can . . . I speak to . . . Uma Krishnamurthy?' I yelled into the receiver, my chest tightening at the thought of being misunderstood and judged.

'Yes? Say it again?'

'Uma. She's one of your . . . "customers"?'

'She cannot speak. This is silent meditation hour.'

'It's a family emergency.'

'Fine,' said the voice, irritably. 'Please hold, madam.'

I paced the room as I waited. Something vaguely approximating daylight filtered weakly in through the windows, as it was now just a little over a week until the sun rose above the horizon. Soon, colours would declare themselves properly, and the outlines of shadows would solidify on the snow. It felt somehow momentous.

'Hello? Uma speaking.'

I almost dropped the receiver.

'It's Maya.'

'What's happened? Is your pa alright?'

'Yeah. I think so.'

'I thought there was a family emergency?'

'No. Not exactly. I just needed to speak to you. Sorry.'

'Next time . . . Oh, never mind.'

'I've been trying to get in touch,' I told her.

'I'm sorry. I haven't had access to the internet here.'

'But you got my first messages. You should have replied.'

'I know.'

The receiver crackled.

I took a deep breath, trying to lessen the pressure squeezing my chest.

'Your first husband, at the hotel . . . on that trip. He, well, he tried . . .' I trailed off.

I could hear her breathing through the static, but she didn't respond.

'Did I tell you?' I asked. 'When you found me?'

Uma cleared her throat.

'Your pa had gone off on a birdwatching expedition, your ma and Ram were in the bar, and I had gone for a long walk along the beach. On the way back, I found you sitting on the rocks. The sun had nearly set. Your dress was wet. At first, I thought you were just shivering from the cold.'

'So what happened next?'

I began to pace up and down the room, unable to keep still.

'I took you back to the hotel. Calmed you down. Sat with you until you fell asleep.'

'Did you talk to Dad?'

'It was not my place to tell him. Not then.'

261

'And Mum? What happened? Did she get help?'

'We argued, I am ashamed to say.'

'About what?'

Uma cleared her throat.

'You have to understand. I spoke to Ram first. He told me it was your mother's fault, that she had drunk too much, been suggestive. Deep down, I knew it wasn't true. But Ram, well, he had a way of—'

'Mum was the victim, not the perpetrator. What happened at the hotel must have done a complete number on her,' I snapped.

'It must,' Uma agreed dully. 'But I wasn't around to see. The week after, we moved to Madras. Ram had a new job there – the holiday was our send-off.'

'What, you stayed with him?'

'You have to understand. He would never have allowed a divorce and my family would have disowned me.'

'Even if they knew about Mum?'

Uma fell silent.

'I should have been there for you and your dad. It is one of my biggest regrets, how I handled the situation,' she said eventually.

'Does Dad know now?'

'He does.'

Now I understood why Uma was at an ashram in the middle of nowhere. Why Dad said he was too busy to talk. Despite my anger, I felt stirrings of sympathy for both of them.

'I shouldn't have gone digging around,' I said.

'No, please. It is not a good idea to start a marriage with secrets. Although now there might not be a marriage at all.'

'I'm sorry.'

The receiver began to hiss.

'What was that?'

Her voice crackled and her words began to blur together.

'Hello?'

She was barely audible.

'I can't hear you!'

Again she said something.

'Still can't hear you.'

'Maya?'

It was impossible. We were thousands of miles apart, shouting into an abyss of static; trying but not quite able to hear each other.

The call dropped.

My hand holding the phone fell to my side as blood roared in my ears. Even though I was standing in a room I'd spent hours – days – in, everything suddenly felt unfamiliar. The fire crackling in the grate no longer sounded comforting. The table was splintered and dark. The sky through the window was the startling turquoise of an old bruise.

I collapsed onto the sofa and concentrated on trying to block out the thoughts whirling through my head. Mum, cornered. Eyes wild in the darkness. A sour smell in the room. Bodies close, minds moving far away. Unable to smile for the camera. Misunderstandings. Denials. Outside the window, the sky darkened to twilight. Shadows moved across the room like fish deep in the ocean.

Now I knew why I always dreamed of waves.

I shut the curtains and lit the lamps. My legs felt weak, as if I'd just recovered from a long illness. I helped myself to a glass of wine and sat back down on the sofa. In the dim light, the liquid was dark as blood in an old black and white movie.

Uma had given me the confirmation I'd been looking for.

But there was no triumph in this discovery. Had I needed to ask? Deep down, hadn't I always known? How many nights had I spent reliving that afternoon on the beach, staring at those churning waves, trying to make sense of it? Now Dad knew too. He had barely started his new life before being dragged into the murky depths of the past. If only I'd left things the way they were. But maybe that was impossible. Secrets, traumas – you can't hide from any of it, because it's all lodged inside of you, threaded deep in your memory, knitted into the tissue of your body.

I called Dad again, even though he'd said not to. Is there a lonelier sound than a phone that rings on and on? I thought of him by himself in the flat, wearing a crumpled shirt and unwashed trousers, looking out of his window at the building under construction next door. In the evenings, you could see the labourers lying side by side on the floor of one of the half-finished rooms, showing each other videos on their phones. I thought of Uma in her ashram, surrounded by mountains. And I was here, at the end of the road – nothing for miles but snow and ice – slowly being swallowed by the darkness.

33

I watched idly as the marshmallow I was toasting caught fire.

'You're not actually gonna eat that, are you?' Rita said, as I blew on the charred skin to cool it.

'Yeah, it tastes best like this.'

I pulled off the blackened exterior, revealing the gloopy pink mass beneath, and popped both parts into my mouth. The fire crackled encouragingly and the flames gleamed off my glass of red wine. It was an evening meant for relaxing, but I couldn't. I'd had a sleepless night after talking to Uma, and I still hadn't managed to get in touch with Dad.

'Penny for them?' Rita asked.

I tore my eyes away from the fire.

'The other day, I remembered something else from my childhood.'

'What was it?' she asked, offering me the wine bottle.

I poured myself a generous glass.

'My mum was assaulted when we were on holiday. By Uma's first husband.'

Rita sucked in her breath.

'Jeez. Does your dad know?'

'Uma just told him. They had a big level bust-up about it.'

'Better now than a few years in,' Rita observed.

'That's true. But I still feel bad for them.'

'Feel bad for your mom. She's the victim in all this.'

I glanced at her, surprised by the sharpness in her voice, but she was looking at the fire, not me, her shoulders hunched.

'I'm sorry. I feel like I'm always moaning to you about my problems and you never get a look-in,' I said.

'Oh pur-lease. The last thing I want to do is talk about my problems. Then we'd be here all night.'

'Really? You seem pretty sorted.'

Rita tipped the last of the bottle into her glass.

'You should see my bank account.'

'The Airbnb thing was a smart move. It helped, right?'

'Yeah. Although my flatmate's not too keen on it.'

She took a big gulp of wine, her body still radiating tension. It was the first time I'd seen her like this; a mood that had seemingly descended from nowhere. Rita was normally so laidback. Then again, people often describe me as 'laidback' when they first meet me.

'Is anything else the matter?'

Rita sighed. 'Nah.'

'Come on, you can tell me. It'll make me feel better for always unloading on you.'

She picked up another marshmallow and skewered it.

'My ex, Ivy, just moved to Portland. We went there for a weekend away once, and it was amazing. We talked about moving there together, getting away from everything in New York. Never happened. And now she's, like . . . doing it without me.'

The marshmallow was on fire but Rita didn't seem to have noticed. I didn't say anything, not wanting to spook her into clamming up. This was the most she'd ever confided in me. Maybe the alcohol had loosened her tongue.

'How long were you together?' I asked.

'Seven years.'

'That's a long time. Do you know why it ended?'

'The white powder I was addicted to didn't help.'

I was caught unawares. Aside from the occasional bottle of wine, Rita was pretty disciplined with her body. She liked her eight hours of sleep, ate healthily, and exercised far more regularly than me.

'I didn't realise. You're so healthy, I'd never be able to guess,' I said.

'That's one of my favourite things about being out here. You're away from temptation, so it's way harder to fuck up.'

'Do you still speak to Ivy?' I asked.

'Now and then. But I mainly just stalk her on social media.'

'I do that with Ryan.'

'How are you feeling about him?' Rita asked, jumping at the chance to steer the conversation away from herself. I let her have it.

'I'm so busy I think about him a lot less now,' I said, which was true, except at night, when the hours stretched out in the darkness.

'And you're talking to this new guy, right?'

'Oh, Jobin? He's just a friend.'

'A cute friend, though,' Rita said, smirking.

She'd walked in on our video chat earlier. Apparently, I'd been 'flirting', which was totally untrue.

'I don't think he's my type,' I told her.

'What, because he's not a lying cheating asshole?'

'Ha, ha,' I said, lightly punching her arm.

'Seriously, though. Nice guys get short shrift with you cis women. You should invite him to stay.'

'It's too soon. And India's way too far away.'

'I thought he was coming to Europe?'

'Yeah, Paris.'

'So get him to come up for the weekend. As a friend, of course.'

Maybe it was the wine giving me Dutch courage, or simply that I wanted to see him, but after a little more encouragement, I found myself sending an invite to Jobin.

'After all, you deserve some fun,' Rita said.

'Yeah, I do.'

'Want to come into town? I'm going to meet some friends.'

I shook my head and was just formulating an excuse when the phone rang.

'Dang, that's keen,' Rita said.

I looked at the screen.

'It's my dad.'

I was suddenly half-afraid to answer it.

'Go on,' Rita said. 'I'll get out of your way.'

'You've had half a bottle of wine.'

'The cold air will wake me up. Besides, this is Longyearbyen – I'm not gonna get pulled over and breathalysed.'

I opened my mouth to argue, and thought better of it.

The phone was still ringing.

'Answer it,' Rita said, pulling on her snowsuit.

'Dad?'

'Hello, darling.'

'I've been trying to get in touch for ages.'

'Sorry. I just couldn't . . .'

268

His voice was thick, like he'd just been crying.

'Dad? I just spoke to Uma. Are you okay?'

In the silence that ensued, I heard Rita put on her boots and close the door softly behind her.

'I've been better,' he said quietly.

'It must have come as a shock,' I said as gently as I could.

I couldn't even imagine the impact it would have had on him, and I knew he wouldn't tell me if I didn't ask.

'Perhaps it shouldn't have. There was always something about Ram I didn't like. But I never expected that of a family friend. Maybe that's why . . .' he tailed off, and then I heard the sound of him blowing his nose. If only I could be there with him, to help him through it.

'Is Uma back yet?' I asked.

'No.'

'Oh, Dad. I'm sorry. Have you thought about forgiving her? You could do a rom-com-style dash to the ashram and declare your undying love.'

'I have forgiven her,' he said dully.

'I don't understand. So what's the problem?'

'Didn't you speak to her?' he asked.

'Yeah, I called her yesterday.'

'You're being so calm about it. Thank you for that. Thank you for understanding why I didn't tell either of you sooner,' he replied.

'What? But didn't Uma tell *you* about the assault?' I said, confused.

'Oh. Yes, she did.'

My head reeled with confusion. I walked over to the window and pulled the curtains open, catching a glimpse of sky pockmarked with thousands of pinprick stars as I tried to make sense of the conversation. Dad might not have known about the assault. But he knew about something else that had happened to Mum. Something he'd also kept from Uma; something bad enough to send her running.

'What are you talking about, Dad?'

'I shouldn't.'

'Come on. Please, for once, talk to me.'

I heard him swallowing into the receiver. Then he cleared his throat.

'It's about your mother,' he said. 'About the accident.'

My heart pounded sickly. The cold brightness of the stars seemed to intensify, like they were flashing warning signals to me in Morse code.

'What do you mean?'

'There wasn't a car accident. It was just what her family wanted me to tell people.'

I gripped the phone receiver tighter.

'Maya, I don't know quite how to say this. And I wish we could be having this conversation in person. But you need to know.'

'Know what?' I echoed.

He was silent for so long I thought he'd hung up. Then I heard him clear his throat.

'Your mum . . . your mum committed suicide.'

The world swung on its moorings.

'After she got back from the hotel . . .' I whispered.

'A couple of weeks after. I wondered why the holiday had triggered a depressive episode,' Dad said. 'I thought it might be because life felt even more stressful in comparison.'

'And you didn't think to ask?'

My voice sounded as if it were coming from somewhere very far away. That it didn't belong to me. That my thoughts didn't belong to me either. I was drifting away from them,

270

drifting away from myself, watching everything from a distance, barely registering it.

'She wasn't responsive. Lay in bed for weeks. Then, one day, she got up. She had a shower, put on her favourite dress. I needed to head out for a meeting and she told me she would be able to look after you. But when I got back . . .'

In the distance, a dog howled.

'. . . she was already gone. And you were sitting next to her, trying to wake her up.'

I sat down heavily on the floor. I could feel the roughness of the wooden wall through my jumper. That was the only certain thing right now.

'Maya? Say something.'

'I . . . I . . .'

'Are you alright?'

'I don't know.'

'I should never have left the two of you alone together.'

'No. You shouldn't have,' I said.

And then I hung up.

For a moment I hung there, suspended in the numb space created by shock. As frozen as the world outside. Then my hands began to tingle. My heart began to jackhammer. And as if to compensate for those moments of stillness, everything suddenly sped up. I got to my feet, stumbled to the bathroom, and threw up so violently that it brought tears to my eyes.

34

The night was a dark kaleidoscope of fractured images. Waves smashing against the shore. A hand gripping my arm too tight. A white door that wouldn't open. Being bounced up and down on someone's knee, until delight became nausea and then a sickening fear. I woke with a gasp, as if I'd been drowning and finally managed to break the surface. My head swam with confused images, and I wasn't sure what was real and what was imagined. Then they disappeared and I was left in the darkness, listening to the wind howl outside.

She hadn't been taken from us at all – she had decided to leave us. There had been no car crash, no visits to the hospital to say our final farewells. And Dad had kept it from me, even after he'd promised to be completely honest. I lay in bed, my thoughts unspooling like tape from a broken cassette, unable to get back to sleep. Eventually, I got up and dressed.

The hills were shadowed purple and the moon was a small, imperfect sphere suspended in a pale pink sky. I took a snowmobile and rode out into the dawn. There was only so far you could travel before the way became impassable, pockmarked with jagged rocks and ridges, mountains rising sharply on either side. I stopped and turned off the engine. Listened to the wind skating over the contours of the land, the strange high cries of birds, and the ragged sounds of my breathing. The sounds of the living.

I could still feel the shock of her silence. The rapid rewriting of my own history reverberating through everything. My whole life had been shaped by her death. That hollow feeling I got in my chest, like something that had been scooped out of me, that was because of her. And I'd missed out on all the things mothers teach their daughters. Like the fact that any man who doesn't want you for you isn't worth having. It had taken me thirty years to work that one out by myself.

Hadn't I been worth staying alive for?

After I'd quit cheffing and moved back to Dad's, I had lain in bed and coolly evaluated the different ways I could kill myself. A blade to the wrists. An overdose of pills. Gassing myself to death in the car. Jumping off something very high. But I didn't.

Reasons why I didn't:

- *Since I had failed at everything else, there was a chance I would fail at this too. And then I'd still be alive and my friends and family would spend the next few years treating me like I was made of glass, and hiding sharp objects from me.*
- *I'm scared of pain. Like really, really scared. It's why I never had my nose pierced or got a tattoo. On my darkest days, I fantasised about stepping into the path of a moving car. It was only the thought of how much it would hurt that had stopped me.*

273

- *But the main reason was that I didn't want to upset anyone. I felt like I'd spent most of my life disappointing people, and vanishing suddenly from their lives was like the biggest fuck you of all.*

I guess for Mum, the pain of being alive was more powerful than the fear of dying. She hadn't acted rationally – in that state of mind, you probably couldn't – and I mustn't blame her for leaving me. I mustn't blame her for being ill. She had fought it for as long as she could. It was Ram who'd tipped her over the edge. Ram who'd tried to take what wasn't his and, like so many men do, had escaped the consequences.

Above me, a tern screamed. I looked up and saw a pale body gliding above me, wingtips rosy in the light of dawn. It was likely flying home after a summer in the Antarctic. Perpetually chasing the light. Weren't we all? It's what my mind had tried to give to me by repressing my memories. And Dad, too. Shrouding his little girl in cotton wool, making sure the cold and the darkness didn't get in. But despite his best efforts, it had. I took a deep gulp of frigid air and screamed as long and loudly as I could. The wind bore the sound away, into the dawn.

35

I felt like the floor was about to crumble underneath me, sending me plummeting down through empty space. My body performed the actions of chopping onions and peeling potatoes while my mind was somewhere else entirely. The fact that I was still cooking to schedule was nothing short of a miracle, and I needed to calm down or I'd make a stupid mistake.

I took a deep breath. Inhaled steam infused with the rich aroma of red meat, tomatoes, and cumin. The curry had been simmering for hours. I looked in the oven and was glad to see that, by some miracle, it hadn't gone out midway through cooking, and the dinner rolls had risen into golden brown domes. I removed them, the comforting scent of oven-baked bread rising into the air.

The kitchen blanket door twitched and Rita came in.

'Wow, it smells great in here. I'm super excited about the new menu.'

'Thanks,' I said dully.

'What's with you? Did Jobin say he didn't want to see you?'

'No, the opposite. He has a long weekend coming up and says he'll book a ticket.'

'That's great. Dirty weekend!'

'Sex is the last thing on my mind right now.'

'What's up? Are you alright?'

I'd confided in Rita too much. I didn't want her to think I was nothing more than a problem on legs.

'Maybe we can talk about it another time?' I said.

She laid a hand on my shoulder and smiled at me sympathetically. Even that small gesture made me want to cry.

'Hello! Anyone here?' yelled a voice in the living room.

'Guests – I better go check on them,' Rita said.

Ten minutes later, I joined her in the main cabin. She was with Gudrun and Gunnar, knocking back the whisky.

'Maya! Have this,' Gunnar said, handing me a glass.

I was only too happy for something to take the edge off.

A middle-aged couple arrived next. They stood in the doorway wearing matching down jackets the same fluorescent yellow as tennis balls.

'Hello. Sorry we're late,' the man said.

I forced myself to smile.

'Don't worry, you're one of the first groups to arrive. Come in.'

'You take off your shoes in Svalbard, don't you?' the woman said.

'That's right. You can pick up some slippers from the box over there.'

'Then come – you must try a whisky,' Gunnar said.

At first, they perched awkwardly on the edge of the sofa. But a couple of shots down, they relaxed.

'You're the chef, aren't you? Maya?' the man said.

I nodded.

'I'm a food writer. I messaged about doing an article on your pop-up.'

'Is this for your blog?' Rita asked.

'It's for *National Geographic Traveller*.'

My stomach lurched.

'Oh, right,' I said, helping myself to another shot of whisky.

'The receptionist at our hotel told us about this event,' the food writer told us.

'We love Maya's food. We are so bored of Minke whale and seal steak and burgers and pizza. Maya is saving us from mediocrity. Her food is delicious. Truly it is,' Gunnar told him, extra enthusiastic after five shots of whisky.

'Mind if I write that down?'

Gunnar was thrilled by the suggestion, and began slowly spelling out his surname as more people began to arrive. As the noise in the room swelled, I felt something inside me shrink. Leaving Rita with the guests, I hurried back to the kitchen. Standing alone amongst the pots and pans, I tried to regain some equilibrium as a wave of exhaustion washed over me. I was back there on the rocks by the seashore, watching the relentless writhing of the tides, my eyes stinging with salt.

I rubbed my eyes furiously. There wasn't time for this now. I couldn't let these thoughts derail the evening, especially if there was a food critic here. Music, that would help. Gloria Gaynor, singing 'I will survive' loudly into my ears, the repetitive chorus drowning out my even more repetitive thoughts . . .

Someone tapped me on the shoulder and I yelped and wheeled round.

Ryan. The last person I had expected or wanted to see. He was leaning against the doorframe, smiling in that cute lopsided way of his. I removed my headphones.

'You scared me.'

'Sorry. I didn't mean to.'

How was he on the guest list without my knowing? Then I remembered that a party of four from the university had signed up without giving their names.

'Is Astrid here?'

'Yeah, she's in the living room.'

Great. I'd have to watch *that* all evening. It was inevitable that we'd bump into each other at some point, given the size of Longyearbyen, but why did it have to be here, tonight?

His gaze held mine.

'You look great, by the way. Have you lost weight?'

I felt washed out and singularly unattractive. Why had he chosen tonight of all nights to come? I took a deep breath and squared my shoulders.

'I have no idea. Why don't you go in with the others? I'm about to start serving.'

Thankfully, Ryan left me to it. I turned back to the stove and looked down at the food I had cooked, trying to centre myself. I just wanted to feed everyone as quickly as possible, then send them packing so I could go to bed.

'Two people still haven't arrived,' Rita said, joining me.

'Let's start without them. They're twenty minutes late.'

I dished up the reindeer curry into the new copper serving dishes, and sprinkled coriander on top. The side dishes were served in black ceramic bowls. Rita and I carried everything out to the guests.

'Tonight I've prepared an Anglo-Indian menu,' I told them. 'It's a fusion cuisine originally developed when the British

278

occupied India, as their cooks had to adapt their recipes to suit British tastes, such as incorporating a soup course, toning down the spice, and doing their best to reconstruct British dishes with the ingredients they had. I'll be serving coconut rice, cauliflower foogath, and railway reindeer curry . . .'

I paused, having noticed that the food writer was scribbling furiously, and suddenly feeling like a total fraud. I'd only learned about Anglo-Indian cuisine a week ago. Maybe he was chronicling my incompetence in that leather-bound notebook.

The sound of someone clearing their throat distracted me.

'*Go on,*' Rita mouthed.

'Sorry. Right, yes. It's an Arctic twist on the Anglo-Indian dish, railway mutton curry, which was first served in the early 1900s on the long-distance train between Bombay and Calcutta. Only in the first-class cabin, though. It was served with buttered dinner rolls, which were considered the height of sophistication. This is a more rustic version, made with locally-sourced reindeer. I hope you enjoy.'

After making sure everyone had been served, I took the only spare seat. It was in between the food writer and Rita. Unfortunately, Astrid and Ryan were opposite me.

'Hi, Maya. This looks very nice,' Astrid said, helping herself to the world's smallest portion of curry.

'Babe, come on. That's not enough food. You need to eat more or you'll starve. Right, Maya?' Ryan said.

Astrid looked mortified. Ryan was giving me the type of encouraging smile he used to bestow on pretty waitresses.

'Um, well . . .' I began.

Ryan dug a ladle into the reindeer and tipped it onto Astrid's plate. A faint flush spread across her cheeks.

'Stop trying to control her portions,' Rita snapped.

'I really think . . .' Ryan began.

I glared at him.

Miraculously, he subsided.

'This is delicious,' the writer said. 'Very inventive to serve it with reindeer.'

I turned to him. This was what I should be focussing on, not Ryan.

'Thanks. I try and incorporate local ingredients into the dishes as much as I can.'

'She's serving bread and butter pudding for dessert,' Rita said.

'It's my mother's recipe,' I told him.

'How fantastic. Was your mother Anglo-Indian?'

'She was Indian – from Delhi – but she spent much of her life in Bangalore.'

'I went to Delhi last year. And wow, the food . . .'

He trailed off, lost in thought. Eventually he lifted another spoonful of curry to his lips.

'What did you put in the reindeer? It's delicious.'

'Coriander, cumin, chilli, and cinnamon bark. Oh, and vinegar and coconut milk,' I told him.

'The acidity of the vinegar really complements the dish.'

'Thanks, that's really generous.'

Reassured, I finally took my first mouthful. I had balanced the spices far better than in my two practice attempts. The dinner rolls were soft and fluffy but that was no surprise as I'd been baking bread for years. The rice was slightly sticky and the cauliflower was unremarkable, but looking around the table, nobody seemed to have an issue.

'Anyone want seconds of reindeer?' I asked.

There were quite a few emphatic nods.

I gathered up the serving dishes and took them into the kitchen. When I turned around, I noticed Ryan had followed.

'The meal was great. It's really taking off up here.'

'Thanks.'

He had a fleck of something dark between his teeth.

'I've missed your food. Astrid's not that keen on cooking.'

I realised it was a piece of peppercorn.

'Well, she has other hobbies,' I said, busying myself chopping fresh coriander.

'She used to have an eating disorder, you know . . .'

'Ryan!'

'What?'

He looked genuinely confused.

'That's not cool. You can't discuss her issues without her consent. Especially not with an ex.'

'Oh, right.'

But the puzzled expression was still there. I remembered the messages he'd sent to Astrid about me, and realised that he genuinely didn't get it.

My phone rang. 'Sorry, I need to take this,' I told him, grateful for an excuse to turn away from Ryan.

'Hi, this is Maya.'

'It is me, Hilda. One of the guests.'

'Oh, hi, Hilda. Are you still coming to the event? We've almost finished the main course.'

'No, we are not. Our hotel said that a polar bear was spotted near your cabins. My husband has a weak heart, so we decided not to come.'

'That's understandable. And thanks so much for letting me know.'

This was the last thing I needed. I sincerely hoped that Hilda was just being alarmist.

281

'Are you alright?' Ryan asked.

'Um. Yeah. Apparently there's a polar bear on the loose up here.'

He raised an eyebrow.

'Says who?'

'One of the guests who was supposed to come.'

Ryan shook his head.

'She's wrong. We spotted one near town yesterday. But we took the Jeep and chased it away.'

'Are you sure you didn't chase it in this direction?'

'It's nowhere near here, I promise.'

He was so confident that I believed him.

'Well, if you're sure. Can you carry this out?'

I handed him a serving bowl of curry.

By the time the guests had finished their second helping, I was feeling better. Neither man nor apex predator had interrupted the meal, and to his credit, Ryan hadn't mentioned the polar bear. I served everyone bread pudding, watching the food writer as he appreciatively inhaled the sugary, cardamom-laced steam.

'Delicious,' he said, a few seconds later.

'Thanks. I'm so pleased you enjoyed it.'

'This is the first time I've had bread and butter pudding,' Rita told me. 'It kinda reminds me of waffle berry pie, but without the berries.'

'What's that?' I asked.

But I never found out the answer, because at that moment the dogs started howling.

The hair stood up on my arms.

They only did that when they were hungry or someone approached their enclosure. Rita had fed them a few hours ago. Something must have spooked them. The food writer's wife looked at me for reassurance.

'Do they normally bark like that?'

'I'm sure it's nothing,' I said.

'They sound scared,' she persisted.

'More like a warning bark,' Rita told everyone.

'That'll be the marauding polar bear,' Gunnar told the group.

I looked daggers at him.

'Wh-what do you mean?' said the food writer's wife.

'Just joking,' Gunnar said hastily. 'Although there was one around town yesterday.'

'We were monitoring the bears yesterday. They aren't near here,' Ryan said, sounding far less certain than he had in the kitchen.

'But did you monitor them today?' I asked.

'I will call Bjorn. He can check the radar,' Astrid suggested.

'Say, Ryan, you're the expert. Why don't you go outside and take a look?' Rita said.

'Don't be ridiculous. These are apex predators you're talking about. There's no need to be rash,' Ryan snapped.

'Let's keep eating, before it gets cold,' I said.

'But what about the bear?' said the food writer's wife.

'The dogs are quiet now. It was probably nothing.'

The guests returned to the bread and butter pudding but I sensed they weren't enjoying it as much as before. It was so quiet I could hear the writer's pen scratching.

'So, what spices did you put in here?' he asked me, lifting his head from the notebook.

'Cardamom, cloves . . .'

A dull thud came from the kitchen. Someone's spoon clattered onto the table. We heard the noise again. It sounded like something heavy throwing its weight against the side of the cabin. The dogs resumed howling.

'Oh god. That's the polar bear,' one of the tourists said.

'It could be anything. Something falling over in the wind. A reindeer,' Rita said.

There was a sudden loud shattering sound and several people screamed. I looked at the circle of pale, stricken faces.

'We have to stay calm,' I said, although I felt anything but.

'What are we going to do?' Ryan said, looking wild-eyed at me.

I stared at him. He was supposed to be the expert and I was supposed to be the wreck breathing into a paper bag in the corner. But oddly enough, I wasn't. Sure, my pulse was racing and my chest was tight, but it looked like everyone else was just as freaked out. I spent so much time imagining the worst that when bad things happened, I couldn't help feeling oddly triumphant. Besides, a polar bear was a tangible threat. It could, theoretically, be removed.

'Someone needs to go in there and check,' I said.

Astrid looked pointedly at Ryan.

'It is your area of expertise.'

But Ryan shook his head. Apparently apex predators were only of interest when you were miles away from them or protected behind bullet-proof glass.

'I'll go,' Rita said.

'Are you sure?'

She nodded grimly, and picked her rifle up from the corner of the room.

I could hear fifteen people trying to modulate their breathing as Rita crept across the cabin. I clenched and unclenched my fists under the table as she tweaked the kitchen

284

curtain aside with her rifle butt. She dropped it again almost immediately, stepped back and beckoned to me.

'Don't go,' Ryan hissed. 'It might be dangerous.'

I figured it was safer to be standing near Rita, who was armed and highly competent, than anyone else in the room. I hurried over.

'Is there a bear in there?'

She nodded.

An intake of breath behind me.

'Listen. It's desperate for that damn reindeer curry,' Rita whispered. 'It's trying to push its arm through the window to get it. We need to shoot at it.'

'No way – you can't kill a polar bear. You'll get investigated for murder!'

'I'm not gonna shoot to kill. Just scare it off.'

'There's a gas stove in there,' I squeaked.

'Trust me, it's the best thing to do.'

'Can't we just . . . yell at it, or something?'

'Be my guest. You walk in there and tell it to go away. See what happens,' Rita hissed.

The movements on the other side of the curtain were getting louder, more frenzied. There was a splintering sound. The reverberation of a pan clattering to the floor.

'Alright. Fine,' I said.

Rita raised her gun.

'Hang on,' said a voice.

The food writer was next to us, holding a large Nikon.

'You have got to be kidding me,' Rita said.

'Derek, get back here,' his wife hissed.

'Don't you want a photo of it in the *National Geographic*?' he asked us.

'I couldn't give a shit,' Rita said impatiently.

'It could get onto the front cover.'

'I don't have time to argue about this,' Rita said.

The sounds from the kitchen were still getting louder. I realised it would take longer to resolve the argument than fire off a few photos.

'Go on then,' I said.

Rita rolled her eyes, but stepped aside. The food writer took a few pictures of us (Rita all the while gripping her gun, looking pissed off), and then we crept behind him to the kitchen. As he parted the curtain I caught sight of the bear, half in and half out of a splintered hole where the window had once been. I clutched Rita. It was far larger than I'd expected. Huge paws. The sharp glint of claws. Pointed teeth. Matted, yellowish fur. A stained muzzle. My stomach flipped. Luckily, the polar bear hadn't spotted us, being fully occupied with the panful of curry, now lying on its side on the floor. It was trying to stick its snout inside to gobble up the contents, but the pan kept on rolling from side to side, scraping horribly against the floor.

I heard the click of a Nikon and steeled myself, hoping the bear hadn't heard. But the sound of the pan must have drowned out the noise.

'Terrible light,' the food writer muttered.

'Don't . . .' Rita warned.

But it was too late. A sudden flash illuminated the kitchen, bouncing off the metal surfaces. The polar bear looked up at us and snarled.

'Idiot,' Rita hissed.

She elbowed him out of the way, lifted her gun and took aim.

The crack of a shot filled the room. I clapped my hands over my ears but it was too late – they were already ringing.

Through my tinnitus, I could hear people yelling. Unfortunately, the polar bear seemed to be the least scared out of everybody. It bared his teeth and I heard the splintering of wood as it forced its way further forwards.

'Shit,' Rita muttered.

Before I could stop her, she stepped inside the kitchen and fired two shots in quick succession. This time, I was just as unprepared and the blood roared in my ears. I stumbled backwards in shock, pulling the food writer with me. I could hear a terrible clattering sound from the kitchen. Then, suddenly, silence.

I looked over at Rita, who was breathing heavily, her rifle still raised.

'Is it gone?'

She nodded.

The relief made me feel lightheaded. My legs were like overcooked noodles as I staggered back to my chair and collapsed into it.

'You're my hero,' I told her.

From above me came a smattering of applause, and I saw that most of the guests had climbed up onto the mezzanine. Several shocked faces peered down at me. I was surprised to see that one of them was Ryan's. But Astrid wasn't with him. She and Gunnar were standing near the door, holding their rifles.

'I'd better go see if it's still outside,' Rita said.

'I'll come with you,' Astrid told her.

'And me,' Gunnar said.

The three of them left the cabin and seconds later, I heard the roar of their snowmobiles. Then the crack of a rifle shot. One of the guests flinched. The food writer's wife burst into tears.

'Come here darling,' he said gently.

Together, we helped her down off the mezzanine. She fell into her husband's arms, shoulders shaking. Everyone else, including Ryan, remained where they were.

'You can come down now,' I told them.

The food writer's wife was beginning to hyperventilate. His eyes met mine.

'Have you got anything sweet?' he asked me.

'What about some tea with sugar?'

'Tea would be lovely,' she managed faintly.

But back in the kitchen, I was diverted by the damage. There was a jagged hole where the window had been, surrounded by buckled, broken timbers. The remains of the curry had been smeared across the floor (although the saucepan had been licked dry), and there was a bullet hole in the wall, and another through the top panel of the stove. The third shot had hit my spice rack. Fragments of broken glass and coloured spice powders were everywhere.

'Lady in there needs her tea.'

Rita was leaning against the doorway, still in her outdoor gear.

When I didn't respond, she crossed the room and put the kettle on.

'What the hell am I going to do? Mikkel's back in a few days. He's going to kill me!'

She laid a hand on my arm.

'I'll help you clear up this mess. We'll just have to board up the window for now. There must be some planks somewhere.'

'The stove looks fucked.'

'It was real old anyway.'

The kettle had boiled so she made a cup of tea, adding generous amounts of sugar. I watched her in admiration.

'You're so good in a crisis.'

'Well you aren't so bad yourself. But Ryan . . . Fucking hell.'

'Yeah. I know.'

'Shame I didn't know you two years ago. Could've saved you the bother.'

Back in the living room, the food writer's wife had stopped hyperventilating, but her eyes were still round with shock. She gulped the tea gratefully while her husband flicked through the photos he'd taken, his camera screen inclined carefully away from her. Everyone else seemed to have recovered and the Norwegians were getting stuck into the whisky. Meanwhile, the table groaned with the leftover plates of bread and butter pudding. I was suddenly overwhelmed with tiredness. As if reading my mood, Rita slung an arm around my shoulders.

'Come and stay at mine tonight. We'll deal with all this in the morning.'

'But what about the washing up?'

'We'll soak it.'

'And the hole in the kitchen?'

'Bin bags?'

Gunnar came over and handed me a shot of whisky. I knocked it back straight away.

'Hey Maya, your food is so good even the polar bears can't stay away.'

The writer smiled, and made a note on his pad.

Pull it together, I thought.

I turned to the group.

'Hi, everyone. I'm so sorry that this evening took such an unexpected turn. But the main thing is that nobody got hurt, and we should drink to that. Wine?'

Pretty much everyone nodded their assent. I grabbed a few bottles from Mikkel's stash and within minutes of handing out glasses, colour had begun to return to people's faces. The food writer's wife wiped her eyes, and then began to laugh (albeit mildly hysterically). The mood of the room had definitely improved so I seized the opportunity to sneak outside for a cigarette. Seconds later – much to my dismay – Ryan joined me.

'Can I have one?'

'Uh, okay.'

He inhaled sharply, and coughed.

'Alright?' I asked him.

'Yeah. I'm not used to the smoke.'

'I meant about the polar bear. You looked scared.'

'No, I was totally fine,' Ryan blustered.

What was it about machismo that made feelings so terrifying to men? I was about to make a comment, but how Ryan behaved was no longer any of my business. Weird that only three or four months ago we were squeezing each other's pimples and now we were practically strangers. He didn't even know about Mum. And I wasn't going to tell him.

'Oh, who am I kidding?' he continued. 'Astrid's going to think I'm a soft touch.'

'I'm sure she'll understand.'

'She's so used to the environment here. The cold's nothing to her – she and Bjorn roll in the snow after the sauna. And she's genuinely going to enter that long-distance sled race.'

'But I thought that's what you liked about her.'

'It's tough, though. Feeling like you're lagging behind your partner.'

I looked at him. 'I know *that* feeling.'

I let the silence stretch between us until the penny dropped.

'Shit. I'm sorry,' Ryan said.

'It's okay. Really. It happened and, well, I'm kind of over it.'

'That's great,' he replied, sounding uncertain.

He inhaled, and coughed again.

'Astrid told me she wants kids. Like, soon – she's thirty-four – and that I need to decide whether I do, too, as there's no point in carrying on otherwise.'

'Oh,' I said, impressed at Astrid's forthrightness. I'd never had the guts to bring it up, being worried it might send Ryan running for the hills – an instinct that appeared to have been correct.

'That's soon, right? What should I do?'

I turned to him.

'Ryan, I'm sorry, but I can't be your support system anymore. You waived the right to that when you cheated on me. It's something to talk to Astrid about.'

'But don't you think—'

I raised my hand to cut him off.

'Listen, only you can decide if you want kids. It's nothing to do with me anymore.'

'Yeah, okay. Well, thanks.'

He flicked his cigarette into the snow and disappeared back indoors. Back to Astrid, and the life he had chosen for himself. A month ago, maybe even a week ago, I would have been thrilled to know that there were problems beginning to emerge in his relationship. But now, all I could think about was the tone of mild surprise he'd had when he'd told me about Astrid's eating disorder, and her desire for children. Had he really thought she was completely without desires or flaws? People weren't products – there was no statutory requirement for them to display a list of ingredients or a safety warning. You couldn't take anyone at face value; you had to deal with what lay underneath the surface. That, I realised suddenly, was something Ryan really struggled with. And that was why I was better off without him.

36

There was a lot to talk about at my next appointment with Edo.

'How did you feel about your mother's suicide?' he asked me, once I'd filled him in.

'At first I was numb with the shock of it. Now I'm pissed off at Dad. He promised that he wouldn't keep anything else from me.'

'But he told you eventually.'

'Only because he was caught out.'

Edo said nothing.

'Do you think it's shitty of me to be angry at him?'

'I'm not here to judge your emotions. Anger is an understandable response given the circumstances. But it shouldn't be something you use to shield yourself from processing more complex emotions, or talking to your father.'

'I don't know what to say to him.'

'Give it time. You'll find the words.'

'Now I've opened the door and seen what's inside, I just want to shut it again.'

Edo smiled gently. 'Unfortunately, it doesn't work like that.'

'Do you think I forgot so much because I was traumatised by Mum's suicide?'

'It's possible.'

'Are there therapists who specialise in recovering repressed memories?'

Edo cleared his throat.

'Not exactly. There was a lot of debate about the therapeutic methods used to recover repressed memories in the nineties – some patients were even convinced by therapists that they'd had an abusive past, when it wasn't the case – but of course there are therapists who help people deal with the aftershocks of trauma.'

'So I might never know what happened that day?'

Edo nodded. 'I know that's not what you want to hear.'

A wave of exhaustion crashed over me.

'I just want to feel like a whole person,' I said.

'What do you mean by that?'

'Like I know exactly who I am. And all the parts of my life fit together.'

Edo paused before speaking.

'That's what everyone wants. But in reality, I don't think I've ever met anyone like that. Have you?'

I had to believe that somewhere in the future was a better version of me. Someone who was more confident, whose anxiety issues had diminished. Someone who'd been luckier in life and in love. Without that, what was the point?

'I'm not saying things can't improve. I saw this show which had a psychoanalyst in called Adam Philips, and he said something along the lines of "Life's not about being happy, it's about being happy enough",' Edo said.

'How do I become happy enough?' I asked.

'Everyone has their own ways of doing that.'

'What's yours? How do you stop yourself from going mad with it all?'

Edo paused again.

'Playing with my kids. Walking in the park in my lunch hour. And I've learned to say no. That was the most helpful of all.'

'Say no to what?'

'It's like a tide, sometimes. Invitations, thick and fast. Commitments at university. Extra patients, extra pupils. A necessity to publish. And sometimes you can't do it all—' Edo broke off, looked like he regretted saying too much. But it was a fraction of what I'd told him about myself every week as I cried myself hoarse.

'I'm the opposite. I should say "yes" more. I always let stuff pass me by.'

'That's not true. You said "yes" to cooking at the cabins.'

'You're right, I did.'

'Do you know what "rose, bud, thorn" is?'

I shook my head.

'It's a talking game. Your thorn is something that's been bothering you. Rose is something you're really enjoying, and the bud is something you're looking forward to.'

'And . . .?'

'So tell me. What's yours?'

'Alright. My thorn . . . that's everything I've found out about Mum, and how I've left things with Dad. My rose is the cooking; I'm getting better, working hard at it. And my bud . . . a friend's coming to visit soon. I'm looking forward to that.'

Edo looked at me steadily. The exercise had proven his point, so there was no need for him to say anything.

Everything that I was upset about had already happened. And what came next was completely up to me.

After the call, I returned to the kitchen. Rita and I had nailed some planks across the hole made by the polar bear and I'd swept and mopped up the mess, but there was nothing that could be done about the bullet holes in the stove. By some miracle, it still worked. This was lucky, because since The Incident – as I've started referring to it – I'd received more booking enquiries than ever. The Instagram post I'd made of the damage, captioned 'our food is so tasty even the polar bears can't resist' had received hundreds of likes. I was hoping to use the fifteen minutes of fame to advertise a special feast night for Solfestuka, a festival week celebrating the return of the sun. I had no shortage of interested customers, but I still needed to plan the menu.

As I opened Mum's recipe book for the umpteenth time, a heaviness descended over me. There was so much history contained within these pages. I no longer saw recipes – instead, I saw memories. Every time the handwriting changed I found myself wondering what her emotional state was. My conversation with Edo had revealed the importance of coming to terms with the past and moving on. Maybe it was time to come up with my own recipes. A menu that drew upon the techniques and flavours of India, but interpreted them in new ways. A menu that relied on Arctic ingredients . . .

My thoughts were curtailed by the phone ringing. Dad. He'd called yesterday and I'd ignored him. But I had to face him sometime. Despite my anger, I hated the thought of him being isolated in India with nobody to talk to.

'Hi,' I said.

'Maya. Thank you for picking up. I'm so glad that at least one of you is.'

'You still haven't heard from Uma?'

'No, I haven't.'

'Well, people get angry when you keep stuff from them,' I said.

I seemed to have told him this many times over the past few weeks. I was tired of saying it, tired of the feelings that came with it.

'You were eight years old, Maya. You'd just moved countries and had a lot to cope with. How could I have added an extra burden like that?'

'Fine, but when I was older you could have talked to me about it,' I said.

'Yes, but then there was the anxiety diagnosis, and then you left home, and after that there was all the trouble at work. It felt like there was never a right time.'

'You thought I was too fragile to take it,' I said.

'I didn't.'

'You did. I'm not Mum, you know. She suffered in ways I never have.'

'I realise that now,' he said, his voice thick. 'I'm so proud of you, darling, and what you're doing out there all on your own.'

Just like that, my defences crumbled. Sometimes, all you need is to be seen.

'You should get Uma back,' I told him. 'Go to the ashram. I'm sure she'll forgive you.'

'Do you really think so?'

'Well, I have.'

As I said it, I felt some of the weight that pressed down on me lessen a little.

'I am so, so glad,' he said. 'Perhaps I will go to her.'

'You should.'

'I will. I'll do it right now. Thank you.'

After he'd hung up, I thought about what he'd said. I was glad he was beginning to realise I wasn't a little kid anymore. But he'd got one thing wrong. I wasn't alone. Rita was becoming a good friend, Adam and Mikkel had helped me out so much, and Jobin and Nina were just a phone call away.

My life had been knocked off course by Mum's suicide. If it hadn't happened, we would have stayed in Bangalore. I would have made Indian friends and retained my knowledge of Hindi and Kannada. I wondered if I would have truly felt Indian. In England, I stuck out, but perhaps I would over there too. One thing was certain: if I'd grown up in India, I'd never have ended up in the Arctic. Even in my wildest daydreams I wouldn't have imagined fighting off a polar bear, learning how to shoot in pitch darkness, or going snowmobiling across the ice alone. I took a deep, shuddering breath. For my whole life I had been looking for home. Perhaps I had to keep moving forward in order to find it.

37

I don't know whether it was the call with Dad or the session with Edo, but that night I slept more soundly than I had in weeks. And when I sat down to plan my Indian-Arctic fusion feast for Solfestuka, inspiration finally struck – I needed to think about the food eaten in the coldest parts of India; the mountainous areas in the north, pushing up against the borders of China, Nepal, Pakistan. The Third Pole, I discovered it was called, and it spanned more than 4.2 million kilometres across ten countries, including India (running through the states of Jammu, Kashmir, and Himachal Pradesh). It was called that because its glaciers held the most freshwater outside the polar regions. I liked the idea of the Third Pole. It disrupted the opposition between north and south. A space connected, but distinctly apart.

After that, everything fell into place. Theoretically, at least. I had great fun selecting dishes from a Kashmiri wazwan – a huge celebration feast of up to thirty-six courses – and working out how to give them a Nordic twist. Why shouldn't rogan josh be made with reindeer? And surely people would be interested in tasting twice-cooked seal ribs?

When I finally ran out of steam and went in search of sustenance, I saw a couple of messages from Jobin asking me what he should bring, how cold it was, and whether he needed to book a taxi. Of course, his visit was only a week away. It had slipped to the back of my mind in the face of everything else that had been going on. Feeling guilty, I gave him a call.

'I'm sorry, I've been so busy this week. But I'm looking forward to seeing you.'

'I thought you'd gotten cold feet.'

'No, not at all. But you will, if you don't bring your warmest socks,' I said, lamely.

'I hope you're looking forward to hanging out with a human icicle.'

'Definitely. And don't worry, there's always spare kit lying around up here. Snowsuits, snow boots, things like that,' I reassured him.

'Great.'

'So how are you enjoying Paris?'

There was a pause.

'Yeah, it's nice.'

'But?'

'It's been a long time since I've visited a place where I know absolutely nobody. And I'm trying my best to understand the language, but most of the time I feel like a kid trying to work out what the adults are saying.'

I felt a stab of guilt for being out of touch.

'When you get here you can speak English and feel like a grown-up again.'

'I'm looking forward to it.'

I could hear the smile in his voice.

'You'll have to have a think about the places you want to visit,' I told him.

'Oh, Maya, there's a *spreadsheet* . . .'

I laughed at his earnestness.

'Listen, I might have to head soon. Rita's gone to pick up Adam and Mikkel from the airport, and I need to make sure everything's ready for them.'

'Are you sure they won't mind me staying?'

'I asked and they said it was fine. They've cancelled their upcoming residential groups so there'll be fewer people than usual.'

'Should I bring them a present?'

'It can't hurt. I'm sure they'd appreciate some French wine.'

After I'd said goodbye to Jobin, I ventured inside Mikkel and Adam's hut for the first time. It was larger than mine, with two single beds pushed together, a shabby armchair and piles of books everywhere. Upon lighting the fire, I noticed a copper pipe had been threaded through the top of the wood burner. It ran up the wall and through a hole into what appeared to be another room. Further investigation revealed a surprisingly plush ensuite bathroom with a toilet and a large freestanding bath, supplied with hot water thanks to the copper pipe in the wood burner. Venturing through another door I discovered a small, wood-powered sauna. No wonder they were never in a hurry to join the shower queue.

Fire lit and snooping completed, I headed back up to the main hut, where I put some beers in the fridge and tidied up. I'd just finished when I heard the sound of a car motor, and bounded outside so I was waiting on the porch as they drove up. Adam got out of the passenger seat.

'Hi, Maya!'

I ran over and hugged him.

'Welcome back.'

'Did you miss us, then?'

'Hell no, we were partying every night,' Rita quipped from behind me.

'How's Mikkel?' I asked.

'Tired. He wants to go straight to bed, although I'm sure he'll pretend otherwise.'

I sucked in my breath as Adam helped Mikkel out from the back and he clung to Adam for support. The clothes which had fitted when he left were now too large and he shivered convulsively in the cold.

'Mikkel!'

Now I was standing closer, I noticed the sores around his mouth.

'From the ventilator,' he rasped, catching me looking.

'Glad to be home?' I asked.

'Fuck, yes.'

'It's all he's been talking about,' Adam said.

Mikkel swayed and Adam tightened his grip on his arm.

'We need to get you to bed. Maya, Rita, can you take the cases?'

'Sure.'

We followed behind them and I was shocked by how quickly Mikkel got out of breath, and how heavily he was leaning on Adam. By the time we reached their cabin, his legs were buckling. I opened the door for them.

'See you back in the living room,' Adam said, struggling inside with Mikkel.

'Pour me a whisky – I'll be there in five minutes,' Mikkel croaked.

Back in the main hut, we decided to pour ourselves one.

'Jeez, he's not looking great, is he?' Rita said. 'I thought pneumonia was more like a really bad cold.'

'Maybe the pneumothorax made it worse. Either way, he doesn't look like he'll be leading any expeditions for a while.'

Rita poured us both another whisky.

'Just before the high season starts, too. It couldn't have come at a worse time for them,' she said, necking the whisky and pouring herself a third measure.

'Everything alright? I asked her, suddenly aware that I hadn't checked in with her in a while – I'd been so preoccupied with my own stuff.

She sighed.

'Unfortunately, I made a new acquaintance.'

'And that's a bad thing?'

'Let's just say, they have good connections.'

'Huh?'

Rita placed a finger against her nostril and inhaled sharply.

'Ohhhhhh . . .'

'Right,' Rita said.

'I guess you just have to try and stay busy. And avoid them.'

'I'm doing my best. But now I know the temptation's there, I keep thinking about it.'

'Maybe you can ask to move up here? There aren't any drugs for miles. I'll bake you brownies instead.'

Rita smiled wanly. 'That actually sounds quite good. Cigarette?'

'Sure.'

We were smoking on the porch when a shadow detached itself from the dusk and made its way towards us.

303

'Didn't you learn your lesson from Mikkel?' Adam said testily.

'Sorry,' I said, quickly stubbing mine out.

Rita defiantly kept smoking.

'That was the cause, then?'

'Of the pneumothorax, yeah. The lung tissue was so weakened that it tore, and that's what depressurised it. And the pneumonia probably occurred because the lungs are so traumatised. Mikkel's now at a great risk of other lung-related illnesses, like cancer. He'll have to get tested—'

'Message received,' Rita said, hastily extinguishing her cigarette in a pile of snow.

We followed Adam back into the living room, where he collapsed into his favourite armchair with a sigh.

'God, it's good to be home.'

There were deep shadows under his eyes. He'd lost weight, too, although not as dramatically as Mikkel.

'You must be tired,' I said.

He nodded.

'And hungry?'

'I'll grab some toast.'

'There's loads of leftovers. I'll make you something.'

There was no way I wanted Adam to see the state of the kitchen.

I heated some railway reindeer curry and rice, sprinkled it with coriander and carried it out to Adam on a tray, accompanied by a glass of cold beer.

'Here.'

'Thanks, this is, this is . . .'

To my surprise, his eyes filled with tears. He wiped them away furiously.

'Sorry, it's been such a difficult month.'

304

'I bet. It can't have been easy,' I said.

'Want a whisky to take the edge off?' Rita asked, pouring herself a fourth glass.

'I'm fine, thanks, the beer will hit the spot,' Adam said. 'So, tell me everything. What's been going on up here since we left?'

Rita and I exchanged glances.

'The curry club's getting pretty popular,' I said. 'You're eating the leftovers.'

'What is it?' Adam asked, his mouth full.

'Railway reindeer curry.'

'Weird name, but great taste. All I've eaten this past month is open face sandwiches and hospital food.'

'Well, I'm cooking more of it tomorrow night.'

'I didn't know you were doing food nights on Thursdays.'

'Yeah. We're running four nights a week now. It's gotten pretty popular since . . .' I tailed off.

'Go on, what were you going to say?' Adam asked.

'Oh, nothing.'

Adam frowned.

'You can tell me. The buildings are all still standing . . . right? And the dogs are all still alive and kicking . . . Oh god. Is one of the dogs dead? Is it Frostie?'

'Stop being such a drama queen,' Rita said affectionately. 'To cut a long story short: a polar bear broke into the kitchen. I shot at it; chaos ensued.'

'I'm sorry,' I added. 'I think it could smell the curry.'

'Trust me, it's the least of my worries,' Adam told us.

'Most people paid in cash for the curry club,' I told him, assuming he was talking about money. 'It's in the safe. I used a bit to buy food, and pay myself, but there's still money left for you guys.'

305

'Thanks, Maya, I really appreciate it. We'll sort all that out tomorrow. I know we owe you money, Rita.'

Rita shrugged. 'It's chill. Whenever you're ready. Sure you don't want a whisky?'

'Oh, go on then. You've twisted my arm,' Adam said.

'Maya? Do you want another?'

I shook my head. 'No, ta. I don't want to be hungover tomorrow. I've got some planning to do.'

'Planning what?' Adam asked.

'I'm going to be doing a special feast night during the Sun Festival. The regulars have told me to sign them up for anything I do, so I have eight places filled already. It's this really interesting concept, a fusion between . . .' I trailed off. In my excitement at planning the menu I'd completely forgotten to ask permission to use the cabins.

'God, I'm so sorry. I should have . . .'

Adam held up his hand to stop me.

'It sounds great. And I'm sure Mikkel will love catching up with people over a decent meal. But after that we might need to scale it down a bit. He still has a long way to go before he recovers.'

'Of course,' I said, trying not to show my disappointment. I'd wanted to do more with the supper club, not less. Maybe there was a bar or restaurant in town that would be up for hosting me.

'What about the groups?' Rita asked.

'We've cancelled all upcoming residentials. There'll be some day trips here and there, but we just want to focus on Mikkel's convalescence. We might even go somewhere warm for a while, if we can afford it.'

'Don't worry about work now – you should get some rest,'

I said, shooting a warning glance at Rita, who looked like she had another question.

'You're right. Christ, I feel as old as the hills.' Adam stood up, holding his plate.

'I can wash it up for you,' I said.

'It's fine. I want to see the damage in the kitchen.'

I hovered anxiously behind him as he cast his eye over the stove and the hastily mended wall.

'Very Wild West,' he commented.

'I know,' I said guiltily. 'I'll pay to get it repaired properly.'

'I'm sure our insurance covers animal damage. Or we'll get Gunnar to do it.'

'Rita was such a hero. Tell him about the polar bear,' I said, turning back to Rita.

But Rita was already gone. And so, too, was the bottle of whisky.

38

I saw Jobin before he saw me, emerging through the airport doors with the passengers from the latest flight. He was wearing a luminous orange jacket and a green bobble hat, and looked far skinnier than I remembered. Seeing him here, so obviously out of his element, was a shock. I suddenly wished I'd prepared more. What on earth were we going to do for four days? Jobin was glancing around, a worried expression on his face. He stepped forward, slipped on the ice, and very nearly fell. I waited for him to recover his balance, then crossed the car park towards him.

'Jobin! Over here!'

His expression immediately brightened.

'Maya,' he said, giving me a hug. 'I didn't recognise you. Looking good – very rugged.'

'Thanks. I think.'

'I just meant you're wearing the right stuff for the environment. I, clearly, am not.'

'Well, at least you won't get lost in a blizzard.'

His eyes widened.

'Has a blizzard been forecast?'

I laughed at his earnestness. 'No, I don't think so. Come on, the Jeep's over here.'

As we walked back to the car, I racked my brains trying to think of what to do first. Would he want to go on one of those overpriced tours, or would everything be too expensive? I still had a lot to prepare for the feast night – what would he do while I was in the kitchen? It took me a few seconds to realise Jobin was talking.

'Immigration hardly took any time,' he was saying. 'Quite amazing, don't you think?'

'Yeah, I guess.'

'And the open borders, that's amazing. I can't believe they let anyone live here. I'm surprised it's not overrun with people.'

I shrugged.

'I guess it's too cold. And it's bloody expensive.'

'Well, I'm excited to look around.'

I opened the back and Jobin stuck his rucksack inside. Once we were both sitting in the car, my pulse skyrocketed. What would we talk about? And what if he hit on me? God, that would be awkward. We hadn't spent more than a few hours in each other's company in decades. I glanced sidelong at him.

'Are you tired? Want to go to the cabins and rest?'

'I'm fine. Why don't you show me around town?'

'Alright.'

I started the Jeep, and immediately stalled it.

'Fuck,' I muttered.

'What's wrong?'

'Nothing.'

'Yes there is. Why are you freaking out?'

'It's just . . . what if we run out of things to say?'

Jobin threw back his head and laughed.

'We won't talk nonstop for the entire weekend. And if you need time to yourself just say. I won't be offended.'

I exhaled shakily. Trust me to make having a guest into such an emotionally charged experience.

'Alright, let's go and explore,' I said.

I started the car again – successfully, this time – and we drove towards the town in a silence that felt far more comfortable than before. Glancing sideways, I noticed that Jobin was looking out of the window at the purpling sky and lilac-tinted mountains.

'What's that?' he asked.

I glanced in the direction he'd pointed at and saw a modern building, all sharp white angles and large windows reflecting the clouds.

'A new hotel.'

'It looks expensive.'

'It is. Apparently it's going to cost hundreds a night.'

'Google maps said there was a river nearby. Is that right?' Jobin asked.

'I think the road runs alongside a fjord.'

'Can we get down to the water's edge and take a look?'

'Yeah, sure.'

We'd reached the outskirts of Longyearbyen by that point. On one side of the road were shipping containers and a power plant; on the other were the skeletons of old mining apparatus, stark and angular in the twilight. I parked and we headed down past a couple of boat sheds to the fjord. The water was still mostly frozen in geometric slabs of ice, but in between them, we caught the occasional flash of inky blue. Looking out into the distance, I could just about make out the shapes of larger ice floes, ghostly in the fading light. This was the first time I'd gone down to the water's edge, the first time I had seen where the fjord began and ended. In just a few days the light would return and the nights would get shorter and shorter until they weren't there at all. I wondered if I would miss the darkness. Where could you hide without it?

'It's freezing,' Jobin said.

This was nothing compared to winter – in fact, today was mild by Svalbard's standards. But he was already shaking with cold.

'Want to go and see the world's northernmost church?' I asked.

'Yes, please,' he said enthusiastically.

The church was a simple structure of red wooden planks, with a high pointed roof, perched on top of a small hill. Jobin took a few photos of it from the warmth of the car.

'I'll send these to Ma. She loves pictures of churches.'

I suddenly remembered the religious art I'd seen in his house – serene saints with golden halos, a carved wooden crucifix. Was Jobin religious? I had a whole host of other questions, but I left them unasked.

Jobin opened the car door.

'Where are you going?' I asked.

'I'm going to see if I can look inside,' Jobin said, grinning. 'Coming?'

The front door of the church was open so we took off our shoes in the cloakroom and headed upstairs to a café area, where we found a stuffed polar bear. The services were held in the room next door, where a few wooden pews faced an altar decorated with red, turquoise, and gold friezes. Directly behind it, a painting depicting scenes from Christ's life stretched from floor to ceiling. To the left was a simple drift-wood cross. I wondered if Jobin felt any emotional connection with these artefacts. Having religious belief must be quite reassuring. Feeling like you weren't alone when you screamed or wept or yelled into the darkness. That everything happened for a reason, even the bad stuff.

'Let's go and grab some coffee from next door,' he suggested.

'But there's nobody there.'

'It's free. I read about it on TripAdvisor.'

Sure enough, there were some mugs and a coffee pot in the seating area.

'It gets dark so early,' Jobin commented, looking out of the window.

I followed his gaze to the pale silhouettes of the mountains against the darkening sky, the lights beginning to come on in the town below.

'I'm just grateful there's any light at all,' I said.

'I can't imagine spending four months without seeing the sun. I guess that's why you need a church.'

'What, to spread the light of Christ?' I said, before I could stop myself.

Jobin glanced at me.

'The wildest parts of the world seem to have the biggest need of a refuge,' he said calmly.

'So you really believe in god and Jesus and all that stuff?' I asked.

'Well, not in a man in the sky. And I don't agree everything written in the bible. But I guess I do believe in some sort of animating matter. That the world isn't pure chaos.'

'It sounds pretty rational when you put it like that.'

'There can't be nothing – there has to be something there, holding it all together.'

We sipped our coffee. I wondered what he thought that something was. Love, maybe. I was glad he hadn't said it, because then I would have felt socially obligated to take the piss. British people can't hear heartfelt declarations without making a sarcastic comment.

'How's your family?' he asked.

'It's been pretty up and down. Uma and Dad had a big bust-up. I persuaded him to go and get her back, but I haven't heard from him since.'

'Why all the drama?'

'Yet another family secret . . .' I began.

By the time I had finished talking, we were holding hands over the table. I wasn't sure if I had reached out to him or if it had been the other way around.

'That's a lot to deal with,' he commented.

'I can't help feeling guilty. And I don't know why.'

'It's probably for surviving, when your mother didn't. Or for not being able to save her. But you shouldn't feel guilty for either. You were just a kid. None of it was in your control.'

The logical part of my brain knew that he was telling the truth. And yet, I still felt the guilt in my body, reverberating like the echoes of a musical note. I knew it was a feeling that couldn't be undone in a few short days. That it was something I needed to work on, to recover from.

'She suffered and I forgot. It's her trauma, and I'm making it about me.'

'That's not true. You're remembering her, discovering what she went through. Finding out that someone you love suffered is bound to cause you pain,' Jobin said.

'Perhaps you're right. At the moment, all my thoughts feel

knotted up. I wish I could extract them from my head and untangle them,' I said.

'Give it time and I'm sure you will.'

'Did you know about it?' I asked him.

Jobin shook his head.

'Pa got his promotion that year and we moved to Hong Kong. We came back for the funeral and you wouldn't even look at me. I remember I was offended, which was obviously a ridiculous reaction. You were grieving.'

'I'm sorry I can't remember being friends with you,' I said.

'Maybe it's for the best. I once cut all your hair off, and another time I persuaded you to stick the head of a Lego man up your nose.'

'But you did give me your kulfi,' I told him, relieved at the change in his tone.

'I did.'

I looked at his kind, angular face, suddenly aware of the curve of his lip, the line of his jaw. I noticed how long and curly his eyelashes were; the type of eyelashes rich Londoners paid hundreds of pounds for. It was as if I were suddenly seeing him in much sharper focus.

'I'm glad we've met each other again,' I told him.

'Yeah. Me, too.'

We were still holding hands.

39

Jobin watched Mikkel knock back a shot, his eyes wide.

'But it's only breakfast time,' he said.

'This is fish oil. Great for your health. You want to try?'

'Sure.'

'It tastes disgusting,' Adam told him.

'Now I'm curious,' Jobin said.

Mikkel poured him a small measure.

'Get that down you, as the British say.'

Jobin swallowed the liquid and immediately retched, much to Mikkel's amusement.

'Told you,' Adam said. 'Eat something to take the taste away.'

Eyes watering, Jobin reached for his coffee mug.

I'd been worried about introducing Jobin to Mikkel and Adam, especially as Mikkel could be spectacularly abrasive when he didn't like someone. But it had gone far better than expected. For a start, Jobin had come with presents – a nice bottle of wine, some amazing smoked duck, French mustard, and even a box of macarons he'd picked up at the airport.

Then he'd taught everyone a card game called teen patti, which Mikkel, already bored with convalescence, had immediately taken to.

'Shall we play cards?' he said hopefully.

I shook my head.

'Sorry, Mikkel, we're going with Adam to the ice cave.'

'How many others?'

'Five. Not including these two,' Adam said.

'And how many dogsledding with Rita?'

'A family of four.'

'I thought it was six people?' Mikkel said.

'There was another couple, but they cancelled this morning,' Adam told him.

Mikkel frowned.

'It's barely worth running them. We should have done more pro—'

He broke off, coughing.

'Mikki, just relax. Don't worry about it,' Adam said, handing him a glass of water.

'Where's Rita, anyway? She's late,' Mikkel said, when he recovered.

It was another ten minutes until Rita arrived, and I noticed the way her hands shook as she poured herself a cup of coffee. There were violet shadows under her eyes and she looked as if she were the one who needed to convalesce.

'Hungover, are we?' Mikkel asked.

'You guessed it,' Rita said glumly.

'Going dogsledding will blow the cobwebs away,' Adam told her.

'It'll do more than that,' said Jobin. 'I practically froze to death walking up here from the sleeping hut.'

'Don't worry, we've got a snowsuit you can borrow,' Adam said.

Rita's eyes swivelled to Jobin, as if noticing him for the first time.

'Hey.'

'Hi. I'm Jobin. And you're Rita, right?'

'That's right.'

'So what's your trick to dealing with the cold?'

'I'm used to it, I grew up in Montana.'

Rita may have been hungover, but Jobin had spent years honing his skills in getting people to open up, and ten minutes later they were still talking, now about the pets they'd had as kids. Jobin's family had adopted a stray, cross-eyed cat called Winston, while Rita had grown up with a border collie called Lucy.

'I remember she got stuck on the roof once,' she said. 'Fuck, we were looking for her for hours. I think she'd been chasing a squirrel.'

'That's amazing,' Jobin said.

Mikkel's phone rang.

'Ja, hello.'

There was a pause, and he responded in Norwegian, his tone and expression serious. Rita and Jobin stopped talking as Mikkel got up from the table and wandered into the kitchen. I looked quizzically at Adam.

'What's up?'

He shrugged.

'No idea. But Mikkel's aunt has been ill for a while.'

'Just what he needs,' I said.

'It wouldn't come as much of a shock. She must be at least ninety. And if you think Mikkel's sharp-tongued . . .'

'You've met her?'

'Mikkel Skypes her every week.'

Five minutes later, Mikkel returned.

'Was that about Hilda?' Adam asked.

Mikkel nodded, his blue eyes swimming with tears. Adam reached for his hand.

'She went peacefully, they said.'

'I'm so sorry, Mikki,' Adam said.

'She was ninety-three. Good innings.'

'Definitely,' I said.

'Sorry, Mikkel,' Rita added.

Mikkel's lip trembled. Knowing that he wouldn't want to break down in front of us, I got to my feet.

'I'll get Jobin kitted out,' I said.

Mikkel looked up at me gratefully as I led Jobin and Rita from the room.

By the time I'd got Jobin as bundled up as it was possible to be and still walk properly, the guests had arrived.

While they were getting dressed in their outdoor gear, I took Adam aside.

'Mikkel's okay?'

'He's upset, understandably. But I left him having an argument with his sister – that'll cheer him up.'

'What about?'

'The will. Hilda left Mikki her house by the fjords. Said that he deserved it because he was the only one who bothered to stay in touch.'

'I guess that's a small consolation.'

'First thing the family did was dig up the will. They haven't even had the funeral yet,' Adam said, shaking his head. 'Anyway, we'd better get on.'

We set out on snowmobiles in the early morning cold, blue-grey clouds obscuring the subtle dawn sky. I was driving and Jobin was sitting behind, arms around my waist. I could feel him shivering and felt thankful for the heated grips of the snowmobile. As we drove, the wind picked up, whipping the snow across the plain in stinging drifts. Visibility decreased as dark grey mist swirled around us, swallowing up the snowmobiles in front. It was the sort of weather that would have scared me months ago. But I was getting used to not being able to see where I was going. There was no clarity in the Arctic. It was a place of sudden changes, of storms and silences. A place unlike anywhere else that I'd ever visited – a landscape that had once been so unfamiliar it was almost alien. Strange then, that it was here, on the edge of everything, where I had learned more about myself and my family than anywhere else.

I let the cold swirl through my mind. Looked at the snow spray arcing against the runners; at the dark, uncertain mist we were heading towards. I wondered whether Uma had forgiven Dad yet. My anger towards him had all but disappeared. But there was still a lot for us to work through together. Once Jobin left, I would check in with him.

We carried on across the ice for what seemed like hours. I felt my thoughts slow, then stop altogether, until all I could think about was how cold I was. By the time we stopped, Jobin's teeth were chattering. The tourists didn't look much better off.

'Come on – we'll warm up in the cave,' Adam told us, pointing at a small depression, barely visible in the darkening landscape. We followed him over to it, the beams of our headtorches dancing across the snow. He bent down and removed a wooden board from the entrance, revealing a small, dark hole.

'Down there?' Jobin asked.

'Yup. There's a rope you can use to lower yourself in. I'll go first. Then I'll be able to guide everyone down. Maya will help from the top.'

We all watched as he lifted a rope from the snow-covered entrance, then lowered himself into the hole and out of sight.

'Well, then,' said Jobin.

'Ready! Do you want to send the first person down?' Adam called up.

The tourists glanced nervously at each other. Eventually, one of them stepped forward.

'I'll go next.'

'Someone's coming,' I called.

The tourist disappeared into the hole without incident.

'Don't worry, it's easy,' he yelled up to us, a few minutes later.

Soon just Jobin and I were left. He looked dubiously at the small opening.

'It'll be warmer in there,' I told him.

'An ice cave is going to be warm, is it? I'm fucking freezing. Why are you smiling?'

'Because it's the first time I've heard you say anything negative. I was beginning to think you were totally saintly.'

'Not *totally*, no.'

'Are you coming?' a muffled voice bellowed up from the hole.

Jobin grabbed hold of the rope. I laughed at his agonised face as he disappeared. Then it was my turn. As I looked down at the dark opening, I felt my body begin to Hamster Wheel. I'd never much liked small spaces. And like most anxiety sufferers, I was intolerant of anything with an uncertain

320

outcome. What did it look like at the bottom? Would there be a chasm to cross? A dark, claustrophobic tunnel? If it hadn't been so cold I might have stayed on the surface. But everyone else had done it, and I hadn't heard any complaints or warnings. I took a deep breath and went for it.

It wasn't a sheer drop like I was expecting. Instead, I found myself in a tunnel that twisted downwards. I descended past different strata of ice, each layer illustrating a different age, like rings on a tree. Before long I reached a small ledge. Leaning against it was a metal ladder, which took me even further underground. Just when I was beginning to feel claustrophobic, the tunnel widened out into a small cave, with curved, icy walls that glistened different shades of blue, white and grey in the light of the headtorches. I let go of the ladder and made my way over to Jobin.

'Kind of amazing in here, huh?'

'Yeah. I want to take a photo, but I'm worried I'll get frostbite.'

'I'll do it.'

I took off my thick outer gloves and photographed the sculpted, glistening walls of ice.

'Oof, my hands are freezing now.'

'Coffee?' Adam asked me.

'Yes please,' I said gratefully.

Taking off his backpack, he extracted a flask and handed us each a plastic cup of steaming coffee. I clasped my numb hands around the cup.

'Drink it – you'll soon warm up,' I said to Jobin.

'Warm up? Here?' he said through clenched teeth.

I wrapped my arms around him. At first he was rigid and shivering, but soon he relaxed a little and hugged me back.

'Well, maybe there are some benefits to being down here with you,' he murmured.

I felt a warm, fluttery feeling in my stomach. I just needed to turn my head a couple of inches, and . . .

'Oi! Lovebirds. Time to go,' Adam said.

I ducked my head, desperate not to meet anyone's eyes.

By the time we emerged from the caves, snow was howling across the landscape. We rolled down our balaclavas and quickly got back onto the snowmobiles. The sky was dark and clouded, the snow like a rain of bullets. I couldn't see shit. I turned on my headtorch and hoped to god that I was going in the right direction. Soon, my mood began to dip. Humans weren't supposed to be this cold. And if I was feeling like this, Jobin would be faring worse. I hoped he didn't get frostbite or die of exposure – his parents would never forgive me.

Thankfully, Jobin was still alive when we got back to the cabins, although he did resemble an icicle.

'G-g-got . . . to . . . g-get . . . w-w-warm . . .' he said, visibly shivering.

'I have to heat up the food for the guests. But you can go back to the cabin,' I told him.

'I'll do the food,' Adam said. 'Go and defrost Jobin.'

'Thanks. There's soup on the stove, which just needs to be heated up, there's coronation chicken filling for sandwiches in the fridge, and I made a coffee cake for dessert.'

Jobin could barely move but I grabbed his hand and we stumbled to my cabin. I pulled him inside and slammed the door behind us. He moaned out loud at the change in temperature and stood dripping on the mat while I struggled to stoke up the fire, the feeling returning to my fingers in hot bursts of pain.

'Take your snowsuit off and get into my bed,' I told him.

I blew on the fire, urging the logs to catch so that I could take my damp clothes off too. By the time I turned around, Jobin's outer layers were in a damp puddle on the floor, and he was lying in bed with a blanket pulled up to his nose.

'Fuck. This is the coldest I've ever been.'

'Not for long.'

I hastily removed my snowsuit and boots, then climbed into bed next to him.

'Argh. Your feet are like blocks of ice,' he howled.

'This is the best way to keep warm. All the explorers do it.'

Even under the blanket and his layers of clothes, he still felt cold, but slowly I felt his shivering subside. Warmth began to creep into my body, then heat . . . and something else. I was suddenly aware of how close we were, bodies pressed up against each other, lips just centimetres apart.

'Well. Thanks. I'm definitely warmer now,' he said.

I could hear the embarrassment in his voice.

'Me, too,' I whispered.

And then I kissed him.

He kissed me back. Softly at first, then more deeply. I marvelled at how easily we fell into a rhythm. Then, as the kiss became more intense, I stopped thinking about anything much at all.

Several minutes later, Jobin broke away from me. I could feel his erection through the many layers of clothing between us.

'Okay, now I'm boiling,' he said.

'Me, too.'

'Mind if I take something off?' he asked, smiling at me.

'It's a good idea. To, you know, regulate your temperature,' I quipped.

There was a scramble as we removed our fleeces, and then Jobin paused, as if waiting for me to take the lead. I removed my base layers, so I was down to my underwear. Then I helped him pull off the various tops he was wearing. If anyone had been watching they would have had a right laugh at our clumsiness. But it wasn't funny to me. There was too much urgency. Finally, I felt the warmth and smoothness of his chest against mine. He ran his fingers up my back, giving me tingles down my spine. I pressed myself against him as we kissed, feeling jolts of desire between my thighs. I cupped my hand over his crotch. He groaned into my mouth. I fumbled with his belt buckle, and for the first time since we'd started kissing, I felt him hesitate.

'What's up?'

'It's just, well, I haven't been with anyone in a few years.'

'I thought you had a girlfriend recently?'

'She didn't believe in sex before marriage.'

'Do you want to take it slow?'

'I'm just worried it'll be over too quickly, if we . . . you know . . . And I didn't think we were going to . . . I didn't even bring any . . .' He tailed off, and buried his head in my shoulder in embarrassment.

'Hey, don't worry. I have an IUD. We can do whatever we want. But no pressure.'

'So if we . . . you wouldn't mind not using condoms?'

'I had an STD test last year. It was clear.'

'I've only had sex with three women. One made me wear two condoms,' Jobin mumbled.

I tilted his chin upwards, and kissed him lightly on the lips.

324

He paused, and then kissed me back.

Minutes later, the awkwardness had disappeared, replaced by a need I hadn't experienced in years. He fumbled with my bra. I struggled with his zipper. We clumsily pulled off each other's clothes. After that, everything became a bit of a blur. I was nothing but a body, blindly following my own desires. Jobin was on top of me and then he was inside me, his eyes open wide in shock. We moved together in desperation, seeking release.

It was over in under a minute and he collapsed with a shudder on top of me.

'Sorry. It's been so long.'

'Don't worry about it. I had fun,' I said.

'Did you cum, though?'

'Not yet.'

'Well, that's a situation we need to change.'

He rolled off me and drew me towards him.

Twenty minutes later, we went in for round two. We were less fevered this time, and so I had time to notice details. The slope of his shoulders. The softness of his lips. What his neck smelled like. There was a sense of inevitability about it all. Like this was what our bodies were supposed to have been doing all along.

'Show me what you like,' he whispered in my ear, and I did.

Afterwards, I lay facing him while he traced the contours of my back and my hips.

'The last woman I slept with wouldn't let me have sex with the lights on. In six months, I never saw her naked.'

'Wasn't that exciting?'

He shook his head.

'No, it was awful. I had no idea what she was thinking or feeling. And it's hard to be aroused when you can't see anything.'

'Couldn't you have asked to have it on, just once?'

'I did. She said no. And it wouldn't have been fair to push it any further.'

'I slept with a guy who was trying to bang people from as many different countries as possible. It wasn't 'til afterwards that I found out. Then I felt pretty ashamed,' I said. 'And another time, I had a fling with a guy who got turned on by the idea of choking me. Needless to say, it didn't last long.'

Jobin kissed me.

'I'm sorry that happened to you.'

'It doesn't matter anymore.'

And it didn't. Not really. My relationship with Ryan hadn't been perfect, but the sex had been kind, erasing a lot of the shit that had gone before. And now, being here with Jobin, the incident with Astrid and Ryan felt like it had happened to someone else. I wondered if everyone found consensual sex as cleansing as I did. Or maybe I just had a talent for forgetting.

But it wasn't long before reality reasserted itself. The day after tomorrow was the return of the sun, and the feast night. Most of tomorrow would be spent preparing, but there were still tasks I wanted to get done today, and recipes I wanted to fine-tune. I had been excited by the prospect, but now I groaned out loud at the thought of getting out of bed.

'What's wrong?'

'Oh, just thinking of the feast night.'

'And everything you have to do to prepare?'

I nodded.

326

'Come on, then. I'll help,' he said, kissing me. 'And then, maybe later, round three?'

That evening, we were treated to one of the best displays of the Northern Lights I'd seen since I arrived. I borrowed a mat and two huge thermal sleeping bags, and we sat on the steps outside my hut to watch. I craned my head upwards, eyes fixed on the weird, undulating dance of the aurora. My body felt loose-limbed from all the sex, like I could easily become untethered from myself and rise upward into the night. I wondered if this was what 'happy enough' felt like. It occurred to me that I hadn't thought about Mum, or Dad, or Uma all afternoon. How easily I had been diverted.

'What are you thinking about?' Jobin asked.

His head was still craned upwards, watching the lights.

'Mum. Dad.'

'Will you come back to India to see him?'

'I have been wondering about it. I don't know how much work there'll be here for me over the next few months. Mikkel and Adam want me to scale down the Arctic Curry Club.'

'If you do, can we . . .?' He trailed off.

'What?'

'Nothing.'

I didn't press him, but instead shimmied along the step towards him in my sleeping bag. He kissed my cheek with warm lips, and turned back towards the lights.

'My neck's starting to hurt. But it feels rude to look away, like I should be appreciating it for as long as it's there. Do you know what I mean?' he asked.

'Yeah,' I said, glad he hadn't pursued the direction he'd been headed in. I wasn't sure it was a conversation I was ready to have.

We sat in silence for a couple of minutes, watching the sky flicker above the small encampment, the mountains, and the town that lay like a circuit board just below us. In the streets there were probably other people much like us, their past and presents as knotted together as a tangle of string, also craning their heads up to the sky.

40

Come morning, we found ourselves looking at the sky again. There wasn't much to see so far though, just a wide, grey expanse with a few purple clouds. I wondered if Jobin was bored. Watching the sun rise was probably a lot more exciting when you hadn't seen it for months.

So much had changed over this long, dark winter. Who I was with. What I was doing. Even my body had become more muscular from all the hard work at camp – chopping wood, carrying food pails to the dogs, lugging brimming saucepans and crates of vegetables around. I still had a huge bum and big thighs, but hey, you can't have everything.

'I don't need any help!' Mikkel shouted, making his slow way towards us, wrapped up in blankets. Adam was beside him, trying to support him over the snow, while also gathering up the fabric that trailed like a bridal train. I raced to grab Mikkel's other arm.

'I told you, I'm fine by myself,' Mikkel said, but he was rasping heavily.

'You shouldn't even be out of bed, let alone outside,' Adam

said. 'Or even in the Arctic at all. We should go to your aunt's place so you can convalesce properly.'

'It is not so cold. Not the way you've wrapped me up.'

'S'freezing,' Jobin muttered.

'Jobin, take one of my blankets,' Mikkel said.

'I'll go and get one from our hut,' I told him.

Our. He'd be leaving in under an hour, and then it would go back to being just mine.

'You stay here. I'll go,' Jobin said.

Adam and I helped Mikkel over to a snowmobile and made him sit on it. His face was completely drained of colour and I looked away while he tried his best not to show how completely out of breath he was.

'So how are preparations going for the feast tonight?' Adam asked, his hands on Mikkel's shoulders.

'There's still loads of work to do. I'm going to take Jobin to the airport after breakfast, then pick up Rita. She's coming to help.'

'We will have to lock up the whisky,' Mikkel commented.

'I think she's going through a lot,' Jobin said. 'She's lonely.'

He'd returned wearing more clothes, with a big blanket wrapped around him.

'Everyone's going through a lot. I had pneumonia. But I am not being a dick,' Mikkel argued.

'That's debatable,' Adam said.

When I'd first met Mikkel, he would have hurled an insult right back. Now, he reached for Adam and drew him closer. I remembered sharing a cigarette with Mikkel on one of my first days up here. He'd been adamant that it wasn't love. Surely he'd changed his mind. 'It's nearly here,' Jobin said.

I looked at the horizon. Saw a pale thread of gold. Watched

330

as it thickened and brightened. Then the first rays of golden light appeared over the blue-shadowed mountains, gilding the snowy peaks. I sucked in my breath as it slowly emerged – a glimpse, and then a semicircle, and then, finally, a shimmering, golden globe of light.

'I told you it wouldn't be too cloudy,' Mikkel said.

'You win,' Adam told him.

He straddled the snowmobile and put his arms around Mikkel, who relaxed back against him. I slid my hand into Jobin's. The four of us watched as the sun rose further, casting soft purple shadows across the snow as the sky slowly lightened from grey to blue. The shapes around us swam sharply into focus and I began to pick out details I hadn't seen before. The grain of the wood on the cabin steps. The paint peeling from the End of the Road Cabins sign. The faint green embroidery around the border of Mikkel's blanket. The sores around his mouth, now beginning to scab over. In this clear light, his skin looked as fragile as parchment. But when he looked over at me, aware he was being watched, I saw his eyes were the luminous blue of the sky at twilight.

'Why are you staring at me?'

'This is the first time I've seen you in the light.'

'If only you'd picked a better day,' Mikkel rasped.

Barely a minute later, clouds had gathered above the mountains. They rolled towards us, grey swathes of mist that obscured the mountains and blocked out the sun. The wind picked up and I gathered my coat more tightly around myself.

'Think it'll be back?' I asked.

'Snow's forecast for this morning. But tomorrow should be clear. Don't worry. Soon you'll have more light than you could want,' Adam said.

Mikkel coughed painfully.

'Come on. It's time to rest,' Adam told him.

'I'll be leaving soon,' Jobin said.

Adam pulled him into a bear hug.

'It was great to meet you. And you're welcome back any time.'

'Thanks for teaching me teen patti,' Mikkel said.

I watched their slow progress across the snow. This time, Mikkel allowed himself to be supported. I suppose he'd finally realised that some things are too difficult to tackle on your own.

'I guess I had better finish packing,' Jobin said, once they'd disappeared from sight.

I looked at my watch.

'Yeah – we'll need to leave in fifteen minutes.'

'I thought we had longer,' he said, his eyes meeting mine.

'We could make it twenty,' I conceded.

Then I took his hand and pulled him into my hut for the last time.

Half an hour later, we were on our way. Jobin's clothes had been hastily shoved into his case as neither of us had wanted to get up, after. There was nothing more comforting than nestling against someone in bed. It made everything else feel like a chore.

'Thanks for driving me.'

'You couldn't exactly have walked; you'd have gotten hypothermia.'

'I could have taken a taxi.'

'It would have cost you a bomb, though. You have everything with you, right?'

'I hope so. Well, everything except you.'

'Jobin, that's so *cheesy*.'

He didn't reply. I hoped I hadn't offended him but I couldn't glance sideways to see his expression. The roads demanded my full attention. They might have been cleared, but I was always anticipating that I might skid, slide, fall . . .

'What is this?' he said.

I looked out of the window. A wide bank of cloud was advancing towards us. So much for the return of the sun.

'What's what?'

'Between us.'

I stopped myself from sarcastically telling Jobin all about the birds and the bees. After all, he was putting himself out there. It was a conversation I'd anticipated we would have, but now it had arrived, I had no idea what I wanted to say.

'I'll come and spend a weekend with you in Paris,' I offered, hoping that would be enough.

'And after?'

I turned his question over in my mind, searching for an answer. The first time I'd slept with Ryan I'd lain awake next to him afterwards, planning everything I would cook at the first brunch we'd have in the house we'd buy together. But I couldn't quite stomach the thought of falling so hard like that again. Not so soon.

'I'm sorry. I don't even know how long I'll be here.'

'I'll be in Paris for the next few months, so we can see each other. Have you thought about coming back to India for a bit? You could learn about all the different foods there.'

'Yeah, I have.'

'You have an OCI, right? So you could live there if you liked it. If you and I . . .' I let myself imagine what he was imagining. Morning coffee in Uma's lounge, enjoying the quiet before the drilling started. An internship in a posh hotel kitchen. Sultry evenings with Jobin in air-conditioned restaurants, meeting his friends, going to concerts, sex on tap. It didn't sound too bad at all. But I had already followed one guy around the world. Look how that had turned out.

'Maya? You're kind of leaving me hanging here.'

'Sometimes my whole life feels like it's been dictated by other people. I moved to England because Dad brought me there. I studied at catering college in London so I could be near him. Got a job in Norwich because my best friend Nina was doing an MA there. And then I came all the way out here because Ryan got a fellowship. I just . . . I think it's time I made a decision for myself. I've loved this weekend with you, I really have, but I can't see myself moving to India right now. I don't *want* to move to India. And I guess that means we're probably better off as friends.'

The words came out in a rush and I suddenly realised that this was the first time I had spoken these thoughts out loud to someone else.

'I shouldn't push. You should never rush into anything before you're ready.'

The disappointment in his voice was palpable.

I laid my hand on his knee and he placed his hand on top of mine, but the gesture felt stilted. It occurred to me that while Jobin was only too happy to suggest I move to India, not once had he brought up the possibility of living here. Was there something unyielding in even the nicest of men?

We reached the airport and I was reminded of my trip to India, of Dad begging me not to leave. It seemed like my life was made up of a series of arrivals and departures.

I parked the car and turned to Jobin. As I looked at his angular features I felt a strange jolting sensation.

334

'Do you want me to come inside with you?' I asked.

'No. It's alright. I'm pretty late. I'll just go straight to the gate.'

'Okay.'

'So, well . . . Thank you.'

'Jobin, I didn't mean to upset you. I had no idea we'd get so . . . close. And the last thing I want to do is hurt you, but I need to be honest.'

'It's okay. Just wasn't what I wanted to hear, that's all.'

'I'm sorry.'

'I should go. I'm running late.'

There was a pause.

The car suddenly felt too small and I wasn't sure what to do with my body, whether I should hug him or kiss him or even, god forbid, shake his hand. Jobin leaned forward, looking similarly tentative. Our lips met clumsily and suddenly we were kissing with the desperation of two people who realise they might be doing so for the last time.

Finally, we broke apart.

'Well. Bye, Maya.'

Still feeling breathless, I watched him cross the car park and head through the doors into the airport. Part of me wanted to run after him, promise to follow him wherever he went. But I knew it was the wrong thing to do.

I had never liked ambiguity, but you couldn't run from it. Every situation had hundreds of possible outcomes. I wasn't sure how Jobin and I would end, or even if we had ended already. Relationships were about timing, as much as anything.

My phone beeped. I checked it, expecting a message from Jobin, but it was from my dad. I opened it up. No words, just a photo of him and Uma standing next to each other.

Behind them was a backdrop of mountains. The sun was sinking down behind it, shining weak golden light on their faces. Both of them were smiling.

We made it to Bhutan. It's supposed to be the happiest country in the world, his message read.

My spirits lifted.

Somehow, they had found the best outcome out of hundreds of possibilities.

41

It was mid-morning by the time Rita and I arrived back at the cabins, and I was woefully behind.

'Why didn't I do more when Jobin was here?' I said, looking down at my list of tasks, which spanned two pages.

'Because you were getting laid, that's why,' Rita said. 'Good choice, by the way. He's a nice guy.'

'I told him I just wanted to be friends. And he didn't take it well,' I said gloomily.

'It's not the best thing to hear directly after a sexy weekend,' Rita said.

'You have a point. I could have timed it better, but it had to be said. He was talking about me moving to India, and us being together there, and it suddenly felt like way too much all at once.'

'You did the right thing. It's not nice to string someone along. But try not to dwell on it. We've got a lot on, right?'

I nodded. 'Part of me thinks we won't get it all done. That I didn't practise enough.'

Rita looked at me levelly.

'You got this.'

But panic was beginning to take hold. I felt the familiar tightness in my chest.

'Do I?'

'You didn't check your emails yet today, did you?'

I shook my head, bewildered by the change in topic. She handed me her phone.

'Check this out.'

It was an article.

'The Arctic Curry Club,' I read out. 'Despite sub-zero temperatures and marauding polar bears, Maya Reed-Kaur has overcome the odds to set up the world's northernmost Indian supper club.'

Below it was a photo of the guests sitting around the table, talking and laughing as they enjoyed my food. I felt my anxiety begin to dissipate as I looked at it – the cabin looked really high-end, the food inviting. Thank god for Photoshop.

'Isn't that so fucking cool?' Rita said. 'Scroll down and you'll see the polar bear.'

There it was, eyes glinting dangerously as if pissed off at being disturbed. And there we were, Rita sternly gripping her gun and me standing next to her, looking wary.

'We'll have to print it out and frame it,' I said. With reluctance, I handed the phone back to Rita. 'I'll read the rest of it later. Right now, we have a lot to do.'

'That's the spirit.'

I handed Rita a menu.

An Arctic Feast Menu
Spice cured salmon, lefse, and hung curd
Arctic char tikka
Reindeer croquettes and tomato chutney

Twice-cooked seal ribs
Red reindeer and lingonberry pulao

*

Mint and basil sorbet
Himalayan style tilslørte bondepiker

*

900 ISK

She frowned down at the page.

'I've never heard of any of this shit.'

'It's an Indian-Arctic fusion menu,' I said.

'What's red reindeer?'

'It's rogan josh – which means "red lamb" – but made with reindeer.'

'And what the fuck is tils . . . tilslørte bondepiker?'

'It's a Norwegian dish. Stewed apple, whipped cream and a crunchy topping. But the cream's infused with cardamom and saffron, and the topping is made with crushed pistachios.'

'That sounds delicious. Twice-cooked seal ribs, on the other hand . . .'

'If they taste like crap there'll be lots of leftovers for Foxy.'

'What have you made so far?'

'I've cured the salmon, made the hung curd, and boiled up some reindeer meat for the croquettes. That's literally it.'

I felt another stab of panic, and did my best to distance myself from the thought. It was okay to be anxious, but I wasn't going to let it paralyse me. Having charged Rita with peeling and boiling potatoes for the croquettes and lefse, I moved on to making the red reindeer. The first step was to marinate the meat in ginger garlic paste, yoghurt, and Kashmiri chilli. Next up were the seal ribs, which I simmered in milk infused with spices: pale green, aniseed-smelling fennel powder, a cinnamon stick, aromatic cardamom, and bitter, ochre-coloured turmeric. I even dropped in a few thin threads of saffron, watching as the orange colour bled into the milk. I loved the complexity of Indian cuisine; the long list of spices added to every dish, each contributing a different nuance. There was a skill to spicing that I hadn't yet perfected, but as I stirred the ribs slowly in the pan, and the sharpness of ginger mingled with the sweetness of the cinnamon and the richness of the milk and meat, I dared to hope that one day I might get there.

The next couple of hours flew by. I marinated fillets of Arctic char in a paste of fragrant spices and yoghurt. Layered saffron-infused rice with browned onions, aromatic coriander, toasted cashews, and dried lingonberries. Blended mint, basil, and apple juice for the sorbet, and stewed the apple for dessert. Meanwhile, Rita made the croquettes and chutney, and went outside to light the barbecue for the seal ribs. The kitchen was full of a complex symphony of scents – boiling milk, the sharpness of garlic, the sweetness of apples and cardamom.

By some miracle, we had just about finished everything when the first guests arrived.

I heard Adam, who was acting as our maître d' for the night, greeting Gunnar, and I felt a sudden lurch of apprehension. What if I'd been too overambitious? Would anyone really want to eat seal ribs stewed in milk and saffron? Maybe I should have stuck to curry and rice. Heat broke out across my neck and cheeks. My chest felt tight.

'I'm starting to freak out.' My voice sounded distant to me. The tightness in my chest had become a stabbing pain.

'Go stand outside for a bit. Take some deep breaths,' Rita told me.

I opened the kitchen door and stepped out. Even now, after months in the Arctic, the shock of the cold rendered me mute and gasping. I put my hood up and stepped over to the barbecue. The coals glowed red in the darkness, giving off an even heat that warmed my numb face and hands. I was grateful to Rita for standing out here in the freezing cold to barbecue things for me. And I was glad Adam was here to help out front, because being two places at once would be nigh on impossible.

I wasn't in this alone.

There were people here to help.

I took another deep, shuddering breath.

This was the biggest event the Arctic Curry Club had ever done. And I was damned if I was going to let my anxiety ruin it.

Fifteen minutes later, Rita and I carried out the first course: a neatly rolled lefse, accompanied by dill-flecked hung curd and a couple of slices of my cured salmon. It had been arranged neatly on plates hired for the night from a local hotel.

'It looks amazing,' said Gunnar.

I was gratified when a few other people agreed with him. It was definitely more upmarket than my usual fare. The cabin also looked better than usual. We'd shifted the sofa into Mikkel's hut and put a second table in its place. Both tables had been covered with crisp white tablecloths and laid with gleaming crockery.

I cleared my throat.

'Before you start tucking in, I'd like to tell you about the menu,' I found myself saying. 'When I was planning it, I wanted to find a way of connecting the Arctic with India, where my mother's from. Then I found out about an icy region covering the Himalayas and the Tibetan Plateau known as the Third Pole, as its ice fields store the largest freshwater reserves outside the Arctic. To me, the idea of a third pole suggests that things aren't just black and white, right and wrong; that there are actually lots of ways of looking at things. And that's how I approached the menu. It's a little bit Indian and a little bit Nordic. Some of the dishes derive inspiration from Kashmiri feasts, known as wazwans, while others are Norwegian classics with an Indian twist. I hope you enjoy it.'

Gunnar and Rita clapped loudly. Seeing this, the rest of the guests followed.

Back in the kitchen, I handed Rita a plate of fish tikka for the barbecue.

'Please be careful with them,' I said.

'Don't worry, I'll cook them to perfection.'

And she was as good as her word.

There was so much work to do, I barely stopped. The kitchen was even more chaotic than usual, piled high with dirty dishes, the stove crowded with pans, the bins rapidly filling up. Yet, despite the chaos, each dish came together more or less how I wanted it to. The croquettes were crispy and golden, the chutney just the right level of tartness. The red reindeer was rich and succulent, the sorbet the perfect palate cleanser after so many meat courses. The only dud note was the seal ribs, which just tasted strange. Most people tried a couple of bites and left the rest. But at least they added a novelty value to the meal.

By the time service was finished, I was euphoric.

'They loved it,' Rita said, coming into the kitchen with a load of dirty plates.

'Great. I saved us some of the reindeer curry, a couple of croquettes and the salmon.'

'Dessert?' she asked hopefully.

'If I scrape the bowls.'

'Cool.'

'Do you want to stay over? The guests all left their booze here – maybe we should have a couple of drinks?' I asked.

'I'll go check with Adam. I'll also see if I can kick out the last of the stragglers.'

She pushed aside the blanket that doubled as a doorway, passing one of the guests on her way out, a slight, dark-haired woman, wearing glasses with thick red rims. She'd come alone and I'd noticed her eating each dish slowly, lost in thought.

'Hi. I hope you enjoyed the meal,' I said tentatively.

'I found your food very unusual. But utterly delicious. It's a unique idea . . .' she said, and fell silent.

I waited. The adrenaline was starting to ebb away, and all I could think about was how much I had to wash up.

'Was it hard to cook such an elaborate meal up here?' she asked, eventually.

'It wasn't easy. There isn't that much space,' I admitted.

'Well, if you're looking for a larger kitchen, I have an opportunity. You've heard about the new hotel just outside Longyearbyen?'

I nodded. Only yesterday, Mikkel and Adam had been arguing over how much it had cost to build. Apparently there was going to be an ice bar and a heated outdoor pool, and rooms with private hot tubs.

'My father owns it.' She handed me a business card. Her name, Hiro Li, was embossed on the thick textured paper in a calligraphic script. I could tell it had cost a bomb. 'I will be managing it and staffing it. Some chefs are currently flying over from the mainland for an interview and practical cooking test. I would like you to come, too, and interview for the position of head chef.'

'Head chef?' I squeaked.

Hiro nodded.

'But . . . but I don't have the experience.'

'Did you do this all by yourself?'

'Rita helped out on the barbecue.'

'If you were a head chef, you'd have people to help you chop the vegetables, cook the meat, plate individual dishes . . .'

'I already have a job.'

'You might change your mind once you see the restaurant.'

My heart was racing, but I forced myself to pull it together. After all, it was only an interview, not an offer. My situation here was hardly secure. And if nothing else, I'd get a chance to see the hotel.

'I'll come. When's the interview?'

'Tomorrow.'

'Oh, right.'

'I can send a taxi for you. It will be here at three in the afternoon. What's your number?'

I told her.

'There'll be a skills test. And we'll also get our chefs to cook a dish from some ingredients we have available. Why don't you bring some of your spices in for that?'

'Okay.'

'See you tomorrow,' Hiro said.

I was left with a stress headache nudging my temples. Coming up with a spectacular dish at hardly any notice? And a skills test? Against professional chefs? It had been years since I'd had to make a hollandaise or dice anything properly.

And what would I cook to impress them? Everything I made up here was simmered for hours. I wandered out into the living room, where Rita was just ushering out the last of the guests and Adam was wiping the table.

'Thanks for helping out,' I said.

Adam looked up at me and smiled, but I could tell he was exhausted.

'What did that woman want?' Rita asked, shutting the door.

'To offer me a job. Or an interview, rather. At that posh new hotel.'

'Maya, that's awesome!'

'It's just an interview for now, and even if I got the job it wouldn't start immediately. I'd never leave you guys in the lurch,' I said hastily to Adam.

'Oh, don't worry about that. I was feeling guilty about asking you to scale back your curry nights. And now Mikkel's been left that house, well, it changes things . . .' he trailed off, glancing at Rita.

'What, you might sell up?' she said.

'We haven't discussed it properly,' Adam said. 'But with Mikkel being so unwell, it's definitely an option. Neither of us are getting any younger. And my leg—'

'I'm going out for a cigarette,' Rita said abruptly.

Adam gave me an anguished glance.

'I better go talk to her,' he said.

Leaving him to it, I returned to the kitchen to tackle the mess. Adam's announcement hadn't come as much of a surprise. After all, to live in Svalbard you had to be able to look after yourself – there was no welfare system here. I wondered how Mikkel would cope, away from the island that he loved.

Doing well at the cooking interview had suddenly become even more important. Not that I had a chance in hell. I'd be up against guys that would have been running their own kitchens for years. But then again, I'd been working hard up here. A few months ago, I hadn't even been able to make dal, and now look at me. This thought was followed by a feeling so unfamiliar that at first I didn't recognise it.

Pride.

What should I cook tomorrow? I wandered over to the spice rack, and my eye caught sight of a small jar of Mangalore masala: a powder of dried chilli, fenugreek, mustard, and coriander seeds. It was what I'd used to make my Arctic char curry. Now *that* was a dish I could put together in under half an hour. But was it too easy? How could I elevate it to haute cuisine? Distractedly, I slid the jar into my pocket. Perhaps tomorrow I'd wake up with the answer.

42

I was standing in a long tunnel made of mirrors, my worried expression reflected to infinity. Which way was I supposed to go? As I began to run, I could see thousands of my selves running in different directions and soon lost sense of which one of them I was. Then I heard a child screaming in pain so loudly that the mirrors began to crack. I wheeled around in circles looking for it, but there was nobody there, just dislocated fragments of my body and bright shards of broken glass. The sound grew louder and more urgent.

My eyes snapped open.

For a moment I was still half-lost in the dream, the frantic high-pitched cries still ringing in my ears. But seconds later I felt fully awake and I could still hear it.

'Rita? Are you awake?' I hissed.

No response. The cries increased in volume. They were accompanied by a new sound, like something was trying to claw its way into the hut. There was frenzied scratching at the door. Not nails, claws. Claws against wood. I suddenly knew exactly who was out there.

I grabbed my torch and opened the door. A pale shape darted away into the snow.

'Foxy, this isn't a game of Knock, Knock, Ginger—'

My words died on my lips.

The main hut was on fire.

I froze, staring at the flames as they licked their way up the sides of the building. A cloud of black, acrid smoke billowed upwards.

'Rita!' I coughed. 'Wake up.'

She didn't stir.

'Rita, for fuck's sake!'

Nothing.

I shone the torch on her bunk. It was empty, the covers pushed back. Her coat and boots weren't here either. Where had she gone? To warn Mikkel and Adam? I grabbed my boots and rushed outside.

There was a sharp cracking sound and the porch of the main hut collapsed. The dogs began to howl.

'Fire!' I yelled, hurrying towards Adam and Mikkel's hut.

The flames cast a faint orange glow across the snow, made shadows twist and elongate. I was running in the opposite direction, but it seemed to me that the noise of the fire was getting louder. I could hear loud splitting sounds, and forced myself not to look back.

'Get up! Get up!' I yelled.

I banged on the door and heard a grumbling sound from inside. Adam opened the door, topless and squinting, pulling earplugs out of his ears.

'What's the fuss?'

'Fire! Fire!' I bellowed.

He looked past me and his eyes widened.

'Shit. Call the fire brigade. I'll get Mikkel.'

348

'They have a fire brigade here?'

'Emergency services. Number's 112.'

I fumbled for my phone. Jammed the buttons. It was hard to think. Everything felt like it was happening to someone else.

'Hei,' said a voice on the phone.

'It's on fire. The hut's on fire,' I gabbled into the receiver.

'Slow down. Where are you?'

'Up at the cabins.'

'Which cabins?'

'End of the Road Cabins. End of the Road Cabins.'

'Ah. Mikkel's place. What started it?'

'I have no idea. But surely the important thing is to put it out!' I yelled.

'Okay. Okay. Stay calm. Is anyone inside?'

'I don't know. One person is unaccounted for,' I said, feeling a horrible drop in the pit of my stomach.

'Make sure everyone else stays clear. On no account should you enter the building. We will send someone as soon as we can.'

I hung up. My eyes were drawn to the flames. The amount of smoke coming off the hut had increased, rising probably fifty metres high. The walls were alight, the timber rapidly charring. It would be ashes within minutes.

'Maya? Glad you're okay.'

Mikkel was behind me, supported by Adam.

'I was dreaming of barbecues,' he continued hoarsely.

'We need to get in the Jeep. Drive as far as we can from it,' Adam said.

'But the dogs. Ad, we can't leave them,' Mikkel protested.

'Mikki, we can't think of them now. The kennels are pretty far away from the flames, and the fire brigade's coming soon.'

'I will not leave without Frostie.'

'We don't have time.'

'I must unchain them, at least. Then they can run if the flames come.'

But Adam was looking at me.

'Where's Rita?' he asked.

'I don't know. She wasn't in the room when I woke up,' I said.

'You're sure she stayed here last night?'

'I know she did. We tidied up, had some wine. Then I told her I was off to bed – she said she'd join me once she finished her glass.'

'Please don't tell me she slept in the main hut.'

I felt as if I were going to be sick.

'We need to go and check,' I said.

At that moment, with a splintering sound, the roof fell in.

'It's not safe,' Adam said.

I ignored him and ran towards the fire. Through the gaping holes in the walls I could see inside was completely ablaze. It couldn't be long until the hut collapsed in on itself entirely. I tried to ignore the unpleasant taste in my mouth, the tight knot in my stomach.

'Rita! Rita!' I yelled until I was hoarse.

Frantically, I ran around the side of the house, getting so close I could feel the heat against my face as I searched for a way inside. But there was none.

Hands grasped my shoulders; someone pulled me away.

'No! No!' I yelled, trying to break free of Adam's grip. But he was much stronger than me.

'We need to wait for the fire brigade,' he yelled.

Still I struggled.

'The kitchen. Perhaps we can get in that way!'

350

'Maya, no.'

I glanced imploringly towards the kitchen door, willing him to agree with me.

It was then that I saw it – the barbecue, lying on its side. Next to it, a shadowy form was crumpled on the snow.

'She's there.'

Adam let go of me and looked in the direction I was pointing. Together, we hurried over. She was lying on the ground, eyes closed.

'Rita! Wake up,' Adam said.

But she was unresponsive.

'Rita!'

He shook her shoulders but she didn't stir. Gently, Adam pulled back her eyelid. In the hellish orange light of the flames we could see that her eyes had rolled back into her head.

'Shit. Help me,' he said, hooking his arms under her shoulders and gathering her up. I lifted up her legs and we stumbled away from the fire, trying our best to keep her upright.

'Let me help.'

'Mikki, stay back!' Adam said.

But Mikkel didn't listen, and suddenly it became a little easier to carry her.

Finally, we reached the Jeep. Mikkel opened the back door and we unceremoniously dumped Rita on the back seat. I took off my glove and placed my hand centimetres from her lips. At first, I felt nothing. Then, a faint, transitory warmth against my palm. She was still breathing. Just.

'What happened to her?' I asked.

'Can't you smell the booze?' Adam said.

I bent closer to her. He was right; under the smoke was the sour scent of alcohol.

'She must have got drunk and started it by accident,' Mikkel rasped.

Looking around, I could see that the fire had started to spread to the surrounding outbuildings.

I'm not sure how long we stood there, watching our world burn. But finally – years, or minutes, or seconds later – I heard the scream of sirens and saw blue lights spilling onto the snow. Water soon arced from hoses onto the blaze, all of it unfolding like a bad dream.

And then there were people around us. Voices in Norwegian. Torches flickering in our eyes, over our bodies. Strong hands guiding us to the ambulance. I sat in between Mikkel and Adam, the three of us wrapped in foil blankets, while Rita was strapped to a gurney.

'Frostie Williams is in the Jeep,' Mikkel was saying in a small voice.

The paramedics didn't reply. They shut the door and, seconds later, we were being driven away. I looked through the rearview mirror and watched the smoking remains shrink down to nothingness. I wondered how much of it, if anything, they would save. Would my sleeping hut remain unscathed? My passport was in there. A couple of fleeces I'd recently invested in. An extra pair of boots. Nothing that meant much—

With a sickening lurch in my stomach, I realised Mum's cookbook had been in the kitchen. The recipe for khichdi, written in careful, curled handwriting. For her mutton curry, the pages splattered with decades' old food stains. I had never mastered it, and now I never would. For the paneer croquettes, which had transported me back to the bedroom in the Hotel Konkani. One of the most painful memories I had ever experienced, but one I was ultimately glad I had. The recipes written in Hindi. The recipes written in Punjabi. The recipes I had yet to try. If only I'd taken photographs, or kept the book in my bedroom. Now, the only thing that connected us had turned to ash. There was a bitter taste in my mouth. For the first time since the fire had started, hot tears slid down my face.

I had lost her, all over again.

43

By the time we reached the hospital, I was exhausted. Rita was unloaded first and wheeled away as I was led slowly inside by one of the paramedics.

'Will she be okay?' I mumbled.

'We will look after her.'

A nurse took me to a small private room, helped me remove my wet clothes and gave me a regulation hospital gown. I was put into bed and swaddled in thick blankets. Something metallic was put in my mouth. I barely registered what was going on. Mum's book was gone. The feeling of loss was unimaginable. I began to shake.

'You will feel better after a rest,' the nurse said.

'But the book,' I mumbled.

'The important thing is that you and your friends are here. Now, lie down.'

Meekly, I did as she said. The nurse pulled the blankets over me. After so long in the cold, they felt delightfully warm. It wasn't long before my eyes became heavy. I struggled to open them, to sit up and ask about the others. But it was futile, and I felt myself spiral down into deep, dark oblivion . . .

'Mikki. We should get you back into bed. The doctor said to rest.'

'How can I rest with so many tests? Besides, I want to see if Maya's alright.'

'The doctor said she was fine. Just exhausted. Let her sleep.'

I opened my eyes. Light flooded my retinas, making me blink.

'It's alright. I'm awake.'

They were standing by my bedside, both wearing hospital gowns. The angles of Mikkel's jaw and collarbones protruded sharply and the sores around his mouth hadn't yet disappeared. But his gaze was steady, challenging me to feel sorry for him.

'You got a touch of frostbite. The doctors had to amputate a couple of toes while you were asleep,' he said.

'Jesus.'

I scrambled into a seating position and pushed back the covers. All of my toes were intact, if a little red.

'Very funny,' I said.

'Mikki, don't be a dick,' Adam said.

'What time is it?' I asked.

'About eleven thirty,' Adam said.

'I've been asleep for hours. Have you seen Rita?'

He shook his head, looking grim.

'We weren't allowed earlier.'

Tears filled my eyes. 'Is she going to be alright?'

'There was so much alcohol in her blood she could have been a thermometer,' Mikkel said. 'Ecstasy, too. Me and Adam think she must have become very high and knocked over the barbecue. She also got hypothermia because she was face-flowered in the snow for so long.'

'Face-planted,' Adam murmured. Normally he enjoyed gently ribbing Mikkel for his pronunciation mistakes, but now irritation laced his voice. Irritation that wasn't directed at Mikkel or at me.

'Are you angry with her?'

'Maya, she burned down our house,' Mikkel said.

'But it was an accident! Surely you won't press charges?'

Too late, I realised I was giving them ideas.

'Of course not,' Adam said.

'But she will end up having to leave the island,' Mikkel added. 'There was a tourist who graffitied some huts a few years ago and he was banned for life.'

'I'm going to try and see her,' I said.

'We're coming too,' Mikkel said.

'Please don't get too angry with her,' I pleaded. 'She's going to feel terrible.'

Neither of them responded.

Together, the three of us padded down the small corridor. A nurse called out to us as we passed, and Mikkel replied in Norwegian.

'She said Rita just woke up. But we can only stay for five minutes.'

Rita was in a private room at the end of the corridor, her body entirely covered by blankets and her eyes closed. When we stepped inside I noticed she was linked up to a drip and her face was ashen. The room smelt sharp and sour.

Rita croaked a greeting as we entered the room, but her eyes were still closed.

'Heavy night last night, was it?' Adam quipped.

356

'Had a bit too much to drink, did we?' Mikkel added.

'Guys . . .' I remonstrated.

'I'm so, so sorry. It was an accident,' Rita whispered, her eyes still closed. A tear trickled down her cheek.

I reached for her hand. It felt bony and cold.

'Why don't you tell us what happened?' Mikkel said.

'I made a mistake,' Rita said, opening her eyes and looking up at him. 'I bought that stuff weeks ago. Kept it in my pocket. Like I was showing myself how strong I could be. But I wasn't.'

'You were asking for trouble, doing that. You should have thrown it away,' Adam said.

'I fished it out the bin, like, three times,' Rita said, her voice hoarse. 'Is there any water?'

'I will get you some,' Mikkel said. 'And I will ask about breakfast. Is everyone hungry?'

My stomach rumbled as I nodded. Rita shook her head. Once he'd gone, she closed her eyes again.

'Will I go to prison?'

'No. But you should go to rehab,' Adam said.

'How? I haven't even got enough money to get off the island.'

'I'm sure you'll think of something,' Adam snapped.

I could tell he was losing patience.

'Maybe you should go and find Mikkel?' I suggested.

He stalked away without a word, shoulders rigid with tension.

'They're pissed,' Rita said, her voice practically a whisper.

'Yes,' I said simply. 'But they're kind-hearted guys. They'll forgive you eventually.'

'I doubt it. If someone burned down my house I'd be mad for years. I don't deserve to be forgiven,' she said.

'You do. It was an accident. At least they have somewhere else to go. They were talking about leaving anyway.'

'I don't know what to do,' Rita said.

'Now's not the best time to think about it. Get some rest and I'll help you work it out,' I said, squeezing her hand.

'Nobody cares.'

'I do.' I placed my other hand on top of hers.

'I should have died in the snow.'

A cold chill ran down my back. The hairs on my arms stood up on end.

'Don't say that.'

'Why? I'm a worthless junkie.'

'You're more than your addiction,' I said. 'It was just one little lapse.'

'More than one.'

'Either way,' I persisted. 'I don't think you're weak, or worthless. You stood up to a polar bear. You've helped me out so much in the past couple of months.'

'And then I burned it all down,' Rita said.

At that moment, the door opened. Mikkel had returned, carrying a bottle of water.

'There's sandwiches out there,' he said to me.

'I should stay . . .'

'It's okay. I want to talk to Rita.'

'I'll be back,' I promised her. She didn't reply.

After I'd closed the door behind me, I couldn't help looking through the window. I watched Mikkel help Rita into a seated position, and lift the water bottle to her lips. Then he helped her settle back down in bed, and tucked the covers in around her.

It's not easy to know when someone needs help. People try and keep their pain to themselves. You have to listen hard, read the signs. I wished I'd paid more attention to her increased drinking, the worries about money; the mention of renewed temptation. I'd thought she was way too strong to need my help. But everyone, everywhere, needs someone at some point.

There was still a chance to make sure that I was there for her.

Not like with Mum.

I'd been too young to know what to do or how to fix it, but that didn't stop me wondering now whether there was something I could have said or done that would have stopped her. But I'd never know. And it was something I'd have to, eventually, let go of.

44

In the early afternoon, Gunnar swung by with some spare clothes and drove us back to the cabins to grab a few important belongings and pick up the Jeep. Because of his weakened lungs, Mikkel had been given strict orders to go straight to the Jeep and stay there. But nobody said anything when he immediately headed to his hut to inspect the damage instead. The fire had been extinguished but the wind whipped up the ash so it swirled through the air like grey snow, alighting on our hair and clothes.

I picked my way around the charred remains of the main hut, where pieces of burned wood jutted upwards like the spars of wrecked ships. I examined what was left of the kitchen. The stove was a twisted husk of metal and all that was left of the spice rack were a few fragments of blackened glass. I knew I should feel lucky to have escaped with my life, but as I looked at the wreckage, I could only see what I'd lost.

Some things we lost in the fire:
- *Mikkel's carefully curated whisky collection.*
- *Adam's well-thumbed SAS Arctic Survival Manual.*
- *The jumper Mikkel had been knitting.*
- *Adam's Nikon camera.*
- *My Kindle.*
- *Every piece of furniture in the main hut.*
- *Every packet or jar of spice in the kitchen.*
- *Mum's recipe book.*

Mum's recipe book was irreplaceable. The way I had connected with her was by cooking her dishes. The memories that I had of her were bound up in its pages. And now that journey of discovery was over.

I turned away from the kitchen and walked back through the camp. The little shed where we kept the firewood was gone. So was the kit room, the snowmobile shed, and the compost toilet. Thankfully, the firemen had managed to save the buildings furthest from the main cabin – all of the sleeping huts and the kennels.

'Where are the dogs?' I asked Adam, who was gazing glumly around him.

'Gunnar picked them up. He'll look after them for now.'

'That's good.'

But Adam's expression was bleak.

'At least we're still here,' I said.

He gestured at the wreckage.

'This place was home. This is where Mikkel and I met. It's what we did together every day. I don't know what we'll do without it.'

'I do.'

Mikkel was standing behind us, holding something in his hand.

'Mikki, you know you're supposed to be in the Jeep. We said two minutes.'

Mikkel ignored him. He took several slow steps towards Adam.

'We will go to live in the house that my aunt gave us. She has a boat that we can fix up. We can take Frostie Williams for walks. Go fishing. Swimming, when the weather is warm. And also, you can be stuck with me forever if you would like.'

He uncurled his fist. Inside was a small black box. Mikkel opened it up and held it out. There was a glint of metal inside. Adam's mouth gaped in surprise, but then he held out his arms. Mikkel stumbled towards him and then they were clinging to each other like they were the one thing preventing the other from drowning, and Adam was crying and saying, 'yes, yes.'

I turned away, a lump in my throat.

They'd found a happy ending.

I wondered what I was going to do next. There was no ring for me, but perhaps there was another journey on the cards. I could go to India, check in with Dad and Uma. Perhaps they would accompany me to Mum's birthplace in Delhi. She'd have liked to see the three of us together; to know our lives didn't end when hers did.

Thinking of Dad and Uma made me remember my phone. I wondered if the fire had made the news – if so, they'd be worried about me. Time to call them and let them know I was alright.

The phone was still in the charger in my hut and there were no new messages. I'd tell them later, once I'd got some sleep – I didn't have the energy to relive the experience. I packed a rucksack with clothes, my wallet, and my passport. As I picked up my toiletries from the bedside table, my eye alighted on a small glass jar. The Mangalore masala. Christ, the job interview! I'd forgotten all about it. I picked up the business card and dialled Hiro's number to cancel, but the phone rang on and on.

Stuffing the masala into my rucksack, I headed back outside. Adam was leading Mikkel back to the Jeep. The sun had come out in my absence, and cast a pallid light over the remains of the camp. Something moved through light and shadows towards me.

'Foxy!' I said.

He stopped a few metres away from me.

'I'm sorry. I have no food to give you now. But everyone's alright, thanks to you.'

Foxy didn't reply, of course. But as he looked up at me, I was sure I saw a flash of understanding in his eyes. Then he turned around and loped away. I remembered how scared of him I'd been when he'd first sought shelter in my cabin. It was lucky he'd kept coming back, or I might not be standing here now.

I headed back to the Jeep.

'Congratulations, guys,' I said, climbing into the back seat.

'I tried to put him off. But he kept coming back. Like that Australian thing, you know . . .'

'A boomerang,' Adam said. He reached for Mikkel's hand.

'Yes. Can we go back to the hotel now? I am feeling quite tired.'

Coming from Mikkel, this meant he was completely exhausted.

Adam began reversing.

'Wait,' I said.

'What's up?'

'There's a car coming for me in a minute. I need to send it back.'

'Where are you going?'

'After the feast last night I got invited for that job interview at the new hotel, remember? I just called to cancel but nobody picked up. Do you mind if we wait for the car and then I can send it away?'

A heaviness had crept over me. My eyes felt gritty with exhaustion. The few hours of sleep in the hospital hadn't been enough.

'Why would you cancel?' Mikkel asked.

'I'm shattered, that's why.'

'I think you should go,' he said.

'What?'

'You have a tendency to get nervous. But with the fire, you have not had a chance to think about it. Go. You will be great.'

'I can't go to an interview now.'

'The cabins suffered, not us.'

'Mikki, back off. Let Maya choose what she wants to do,' Adam said.

'What do you think?' I asked him.

His eyes met mine in the rearview mirror.

'Why not go? They might not be able to reschedule. Get it out the way so you can relax tonight. Mikkel's right – you'll only worry about it until it happens.'

My stomach was already churning at the thought. Even if I was feeling one hundred per cent, my skills would pale in comparison with the other men (because it was always men) who would be interviewing for the position. They'd probably have years of experience running kitchens and refining their cooking techniques.

'Maya?' Adam said.

'See – she has started to worry already,' Mikkel said. 'You should just go. Because if you do badly you can blame it on the fire. Tomorrow, you will have no excuse.'

'I guess. But everyone else is going to be so much more qualified.'

'I wouldn't be so sure,' Mikkel told me. 'This place is so remote that only people like us want to live here.'

People like us.

I wondered what he meant by that. People tough enough to brave the cold? Who could deal with four months of darkness? Who didn't mind being alone? Six months ago I'd never have thought for a second that I would be one of those people.

At that moment, a sleek black Jeep with large snow tyres came bouncing up the track.

'Crunch time,' Adam said.

I felt my anxiety spike. As usual, it hit me in two sharp stabs of pain, one in the guts and the other smack in the chest.

'I can't. I don't feel well.'

'You must go and tell the driver,' Mikkel said.

'Alright,' I replied, surprised to have gotten off that easily.

Big mistake.

As soon as I got out, I heard a clicking sound. Mikkel had locked all the doors.

'That's not funny!' I yelled, tugging at the handle.

'We are not going to let you back in.'

'So I'll get a snowmobile and drive to the hotel.'

'The snowmobiles blew up.'

'Come on guys!' I shouted as I pounded the window with my fists. Mikkel raised his eyebrows at me, but didn't budge.

'Excuse me.'

I turned to see that the driver of the other Jeep had turned round and pulled up alongside us. He looked very confused.

'I must have the wrong place. End of the Road Cabins, I'm looking for.'

'This is it,' I said, gesturing at the post-apocalyptic scene around me.

The driver cleared his throat.

'I am supposed to be picking someone up for an interview at Ice Hotel.'

'That's me,' I said.

'You still want to go?'

I paused. There were still sharp, stabbing pains in my chest. I could feel myself begin to dissociate from the situation, feel the painful pounding of my heart, the fogging round the edges of my vision . . .

Sometimes, I repeat facts in my head to calm down.

There are more polar bears than people living on Svalbard.

There are more polar bears than people living on Svalbard.

There are more polar bears than people living on Svalbard

. . . and I'd even met one. I'd scared him out of my kitchen.

The tightness around my chest began to ease off slightly. I had faced off against a polar bear. Learned how to shoot. Survived a break-up. If I could do that, then surely . . .

'Yes, I'm coming,' I said.

Mikkel wound down the window, smiling in triumph. 'Good luck.'

I was going to need it.

The two of them accelerated away before I could change my mind.

I got into the passenger seat and we drove slowly down the track to the main road, the charred remains of End of the Road Cabins quickly disappearing from sight. I'd only been there for a few months, but even so, I was assaulted with a wave of melancholy. As soon as it had started to feel like home, it had disappeared. It was time to move on, seek out somewhere new, whether I wanted to or not.

Finally, I stopped looking behind me and faced forwards, tracing the dark curves of the road. I wondered what test awaited me at the hotel. I had no recipe to follow, and nothing but a glass jar of masala to flavour my food. Nothing to rely on. Well, nothing apart from myself.

I took a deep breath. For the first time today, I noticed the crisp shapes of the mountains in the distance. Wisps of cloud hung in a faded cornflower-blue sky, stippling the snow with an intricate network of light and shadow. This was only the second day that the sun had risen and showed me the place I had been living in for the past six months. My breath caught in my throat at the beauty of it.

The cabins may have been burned to the ground, but the Arctic was still here. It had been conquered, and mined, and was slowly melting as the world's temperatures rose, but when I looked out of the window I saw a wild, untouchable landscape, waiting to be explored. There were Russian ghost towns I hadn't visited, abandoned trappers' cabins I'd never seen. Fjords I'd never sailed down, hills I'd never climbed. For the first time since I'd arrived, I understood its appeal. It was a place that nobody could claim, so anybody was welcome to call it home. Even me.

Epilogue

6 Months Later

I stood with my hands on my hips and surveyed the restaurant. *My* restaurant, I thought with a thrill. It still felt hard to believe. Call it luck. Call it winning by default. I'd done both, since Hiro's first choice for head chef had turned down the opportunity. But Edo said that it wasn't how you come by an opportunity that matters, it was what you did with it that counted. I intended to prove him right.

The Third Pole, the restaurant was called. It would be serving an Indo-Nordic fusion menu and I'd worked hard at getting the décor perfect. There were several Kashmiri manuscript paintings on the walls, their gilded edges shining even brighter against the pale grey walls. The dining furniture had been made by a contemporary Scandinavian designer, as had the navy and dove grey sofas by the fire. Across the bare wooden floorboards was a handwoven rug I'd had commissioned from a women's artisan group in Kashmir. Hopefully the food would be as attractive as the interiors.

I felt a jolt of nervousness, but pushed the thought down. It was still a week until opening night. Still time to refine the dishes and get to know my team. Hiro had even allowed a pre-launch event so we could practise service.

Right on cue, my phone rang. I sighed in exasperation. This must be the fifth time today.

'Yes, Mikkel,' I said.

'I had a thought. About the tables. That if you are serving reindeer curry for our main course then maybe we could have some decoration on the table that is thematically relevant. Like reindeer horns, with small hollows for candles. Do you have something like this?'

'No, Mikkel. I don't,' I said through gritted teeth.

'And the music? You've got the playlist?'

'Yes.'

'I might need to add some songs. And take some songs away. And come in this afternoon to make sure that nobody has gone into the function room and changed the décors. And—'

'Mikkel. Listen. It's under control.'

There was a pause.

'Am I being a . . . bridezilla?' said a small voice, stumbling over the unfamiliar word. 'Adam says I am.'

'You are a little bit.'

'Sorry. I am just excited. And scared too. I am worried Adam will tell me this is a big joke and then run away from the altar.'

'He won't do that. Trust me. He loves you.'

'Well, at least he won't get very far in the Arctic.'

I couldn't help but laugh. 'Don't be mean.'

'Rita arrived an hour ago. She wants to know if you have time to come to the hotel and see us later?'

'If you stop giving me things to do. How's she looking?'

'Much better than when we last saw her.'

'That's great. I should be with you around nine. But right now, I should get back to it.'

I hung up, thinking how much I was looking forward to seeing Rita – Mikkel had pulled a few strings to get written permission from the governor for her to attend his wedding.

We'd kept in contact since she'd returned to America. She'd managed to find a free detox programme in New York, and was talking about enrolling for a degree in social work. Despite her worries, it sounded like she'd landed on her feet.

A guest I was less excited about seeing was Astrid. But, much to my surprise, it'd turned out her plus one wasn't Ryan. It was a friend of Mikkel's; a man in his forties who, by the sound of things, was as keen to commit as Ryan had been to avoid it.

My thoughts drifted to Jobin. We'd hung out together when I'd gone back to India for a few months and – gradually – he'd come round to the idea of us being friends. And the more time we spent together, the more I realised that fitted us best. We'd confused romantic feelings with the rush of sentiment that comes from reuniting with an old friend. Jobin might not agree right now, but whatever he thought, the Arctic and India were way too far apart to pursue a relationship.

The relationship I had with India had also improved. Bangalore had become more than just an assault on the senses. I'd started to find restaurants I liked, shady parks to walk in, and although I hadn't remembered much more about my childhood, I'd begun to make new memories there instead, including helping Dad and Uma choose a bungalow to buy. The one they'd finally selected was in a bad state of disrepair; broken windows, dodgy plumbing, weeds straggling up the brickwork. But the garden was a wild green oasis and the high walls shut out the noise of the city beyond the gates. They'd be able to fix it up beyond recognition.

I headed back to the kitchen, pausing at the door to take it all in before everything got too busy. The room was a hive of activity. Knives flashed as vegetables were chopped. Pots bubbled on stoves. My sous chef, Anjana, was showing one of the hulking Scandinavian commis chefs how to make her family's dal recipe. I'd met her when I was travelling in North India – she was a divorced housewife keeping herself afloat by running cooking courses. When she'd heard what I was doing, she'd all but thrown herself at me. I'd been happy to recruit her. So what if she'd never been abroad or worked in a professional kitchen before? Armed just with her spice box she made some of the best food I'd ever tasted. And it was obvious she was having a whale of a time.

'Chef?'

I looked in the direction of the voice to see my pastry chef beckoning to me frantically.

'Did I put too much saffron in this apple?'

I felt myself freeze. Every time someone asked me a question I wanted to turn tail and run out of the kitchen, screaming 'I'm not qualified to answer this!' at the top of my voice. But as I looked down at the bowl of lurid yellow mush, I realised that in this case the answer was apparent.

'A little too much. You only need to soak a few strands in a tablespoon of hot water.'

He hung his head.

'I used most of the pot.'

Most head chefs would have completely bawled him out. But I wasn't most head chefs.

'Just don't do it next time. Saffron's bloody expensive – you'll put us out of business,' I said instead.

'Yes, chef,' he said meekly.

'It's alright. You'll have to start again, though.'

I left him to it and went over to my station. I was working on a new recipe for the restaurant and one of my chefs had made me lobster bisque so I could try out some Indian spicing combinations with it. I put a cupful into a small saucepan and began my experiments. The usual mixture of turmeric-chilli-coriander-cumin didn't work. Neither did a mixture of whole spices. Ground coriander seeds and fennel? Mangalore masala contained both. I pulled out my cookbook and flicked to the relevant page to find the list of spices, written in my own handwriting on fresh white paper.

It had been Uma's idea. When I'd gone back to visit her and Dad in Bangalore, she'd been making parathas according to Mum's old recipe.

'I know it by heart,' she'd explained.

'Will you write it down for me?' I asked.

A few days later, she'd presented me with a slim, black leather-bound book. The first few pages had been filled up with all Mum's recipes that she remembered. The North Indian classics: palak paneer; chole batura; butter chicken.

'What about the recipes she learned from you?' I'd asked.

So Uma had written those down too. Recipes for breakfast idli and coriander chutney. Masala dosa and rasam. A tamarind aubergine curry her gran had cooked, which Mum had loved and I'd never gotten round to trying. Then Dad had come in and told me he still remembered the British dishes he'd explained to Mum, and the weird and wonderful ways she'd reinterpreted them.

Throughout my stay in Bangalore, the recipe collection

kept growing. Theresa added the Malayali recipes she'd taught Mum, and Jobin vividly recalled the halwa she'd made us. When nobody was around, I wrote down the recipe for paneer croquettes. It felt somehow wrong to exclude it.

I took the book travelling with me. Used it to write down the recipes I learned from the home cooks and professional chefs I met while I was there. By the time I left India, there were still plenty of pages remaining. Pages I'd fill in over the upcoming months with the recipes I created for the Third Pole. The things we think we've lost don't always disappear – they change.

In the bright, chaotic kitchen, I looked down at the book and felt time slow down a little. I opened it to an empty page.

'Lobster Bisque', I wrote neatly at the top.

I wasn't sure exactly what would go next, but it was important to make a start.

Acknowledgements

This novel came about as the result of two very different periods in my life – my PhD work on Arctic islands, and two years spent living in India, an experience that was at times overwhelming, but ultimately led to *The Arctic Curry Club* being written.

I'd like to thank my PhD supervisors at UEA, Henry Sutton and Karen Schaller, for their endless generosity during the years that inspired this book. Henry was the reason why I was accepted into UEA's MA programme and then the PhD; his endless cheerleading gave me confidence in myself when I had none.

Thank you to Hiteshi Mehta and Amulya Shruti, for being friendly faces in an unfamiliar country. To Amulya, for answering my questions about India. To my father-in-law CK Sharma, for helping me settle in, and my mother-in-law, Updesh Kaur, for the culinary education. Many of her recipes in this book, such as the aloo parathas, were passed to me from her.

Heartfelt thanks to Kelsey Camacho, a real life Arctic

374

explorer and writer living in Longyearbyen, for answering my endless questions about firewood and the cost of peppers.

Thank you to the people in the book world who took a chance on an unknown debut novelist. For my agent Ella Kahn, whose incisive editorial eye helped improve *The Arctic Curry Club* immeasurably, and whose unflagging dedication led to it finding a home. Thank you to the team at Avon for providing it with that home and especially to my editor Katie Loughnane, for understanding and believing in my vision.

To my first readers – thank you for wading through *The Arctic Curry Club* when it was still clumsy and unformed. Rowan Hisayo Buchanan, Molly Morris, Bikram Sharma, John Boyne and Amulya Shruti all provided sensitive, illuminating feedback that has been invaluable in shaping this novel.

Thank you to Imogen Hermes Gowar, Sharlene Teo and Sarah Young, for being there on my writing journey; for supporting me through the bumps in the road (and there have been many). To my creative writing group, Rowan Whiteside, Molly Morris and Abby Erwin, whose friendship has remained certain through uncertain times.

Thank you to the best parents in the world. The first people to supply me with books, to encourage my creativity, to believe in me from the very beginning. To my siblings Natalie, Chris and Michael, and my nephew Jude – I love you all. To my oldest friend, Mary Richardson, for a lifetime of friendship and for never laughing at my literary aspirations (even when we were eight).

Thank you to Christopher Potts, my A-level English teacher. My first writing mentor, who believed that my teenage self had what it took to become a novelist long before I did.

Finally, to Bikram: husband; best friend; soulmate. Thank you for sticking with me through the panic attacks, the meltdowns, the tears. Thank you for showing me that in what looks like weakness there is in fact strength. Thank you for the sacrifices you have made so we can be together. And thank you for the good bits – there have been so many.